Praise for *The Ghosts Between Us*

"This is one hell of a book, and through the tears cried, I enjoyed every minute."

—Becca, Goodreads

"I doubt I will forget this story anytime soon."

—Susan65, Goodreads

"This was a highly satisfying read, and Elliot has made my top shelf of favorite characters."

—Kaye Hallows, Goodreads

"An emotional roller coaster ride with characters you really want to root for."

—Prairieknitwit, Goodreads

"Prepare yourself for a beautifully written and heartfelt journey through grief and a rebirth"

—Angela S. Goodrich, Amazon

"Heartbreaking, beautifully written, and raw. Perfect tearjerker."

—R Keebler, Amazon

The
Ghosts Between Us

by
Brigham Vaughn

©Brigham Vaughn
ISBN: 9781099272820

Cover design by Brigham Vaughn
Book design and production by Brigham Vaughn
Editing by Sally Hopkinson
Cover Images: ©xy/AdobeStock
©David Gn/Adobe Stock
©Rawpixel.com/AdobeStock
©starsstudio/Adobe Stock
©oneinchpunch/Adobe Stock
©JackAnstey/rawpixel

Printed in the United States of America

First Printing, 2019

Published by Two Peninsulas Press

TWO PENINSULAS PRESS

Acknowledgements

The Ghosts Between Us is a project I've been working on (on and off) for the better part of five years. From the beginning, I knew it would be a challenging story to tell. I knew I needed to grow into it as an author and as a human being before I could do it justice.

It was the kind of story that pushed me to my limits and forced me to grow.

It's also a story that required a lot of help from others to come to fruition. I want to thank Ty Primeau for her willingness to discuss palliative care, hospice, and her favorite topic: death.

I want to thank Hospice House of Mid-Michigan and their staff for allowing me to take a tour of the facility and patiently answering my questions.

Thank you to Walt Nickles for his invaluable help with the research on organ donation.

I especially want to thank my beta readers: Ty Primeau, Kaye P. Hallows, A.J. Rose, Joanna Sooper, and Allison Hickman for their hard work picking apart my words and making them better. It was a good story before they got their hands on it. It became a great story because of their hard work. I am truly appreciative.

I also want to say thank you to Sally Hopkinson, who has the exhausting job of wrangling my rogue commas. I am so grateful to have you on this journey with me.

And to my proofreaders: Bree O'Malley and Angela Middaugh. Thank you for helping me put out the best possible version of this story.

To K. Evan Coles for letting me bounce ideas off you at all hours of the day and night and for offering feedback on covers and blurb for stories you didn't even write. You are the best co-author a writer could ask for.

Thanks to Rachel Maybury for her help with the blog tour. Thanks to the bloggers who helped spread the word. And to all of my eager ARC reviewers who were eager to get their hands on this story.

Thanks to my parents for allowing me to live with you while I pursue this crazy dream of being a full-time author.

And my readers and fans. I couldn't do this without your support.

Table of Contents

Chapter One

The wind whipped his hair across his face, and he lifted a bare hand to brush it away. The same damp, late-January wind snaked under the scarf I wore, chilling the sliver of skin between the collar of my shirt and my hairline. I shuddered and huddled into my scarf, jamming my hands into the pockets of my overcoat. Heavy wool or not, it wasn't doing a damn thing to keep me warm. The man I'd been watching didn't seem affected by the temperature at all.

A muffled sob from my mother made me glance away from him. She leaned in to my father, resting her head against his shoulder as his arm tightened around her. I looked away, and the aching hole in my chest widened into a chasm at the sight of the casket in front of us.

Because God has chosen to call our brother, Calvin James Allen, *from this life to Himself,*
we commit his body to the earth,
for we are dust and unto dust we shall return …

The priest's voice droned on as tears clogged in my throat. *Why, Cal? Why the hell did you have to die? You were only twenty-eight!*

We were supposed to grow old together.

Unable to stand the sight of his casket for another second, I looked out over the crowd and across the wind-tossed landscape. Mt. Calvary Cemetery was perched in the West Hills of Portland with views of the Columbia River and the Cascades and coast range of mountains. If Cal had to be buried anywhere, at least it was a beautiful place. I choked on the thought, unable to comprehend that we were burying my baby brother.

The most vibrant, fun-loving man I'd ever known was dead.

My gaze swept across the bevy of female mourners across the casket from me. There was no rhyme or reason to them, no unifying thread. A crunchy granola hippie chick stood between two women who could have been supermodels. It was so *Cal.* He charmed everyone, and he'd happily slept with any woman who caught his interest and returned it. Hell, one of them was clearly the Mrs. Robinson type, and at least twenty years Cal's senior. Cal didn't really have the attention span for long-term relationships, so most were probably one night stands or short, casual relationships, and yet, they'd braved the drizzly January winds and looked devastated by his death. He inspired that in people.

Cal's male friends were easy to spot as well, all sporty, adventure-seeking types like Cal had been, and those friends were grieving hard. But one man stood out, and I found my gaze repeatedly returning to him. He was tall, lean to the point of being lanky, with tangled black hair and sharp, high cheekbones. He was young—early twenties at most—and almost androgynous looking. Dressed less formally than most of the mourners, he stood out in his black beanie and black peacoat layered over a gray hoodie. But it wasn't so much his dress as his expression that struck me. He looked gutted, his eyes hollow and distant as he stared at the casket.

He looked the way I felt.

My mother let out a quiet, choking sob as the priest asked any family member who wished to do so to place a flower on the casket. As a unit, my father and mother moved forward to grab white roses from the basket sitting beside the casket and place the pale blooms on the dark, gleaming surface. When they stepped back, I slipped off a single leather glove and stretched forward to lay my own flower on the casket. Briefly, I pressed my palm against the wood and closed my eyes. *God, I'm gonna miss you. How in the hell am I going to make it without you, brother?* But there was no reply. Nothing but the feel of the cold, hard surface against my palm and the muffled sounds of people sniffling and crying.

Goodbye, Cal.

After I stepped back, the priest directed the remaining guests to add flowers. The grief-stricken stranger moved forward, and as the crowd parted to let him through, I saw him more clearly. The tip of his nose and the rims of his eyes were red, and there was a tear track down his cheek. He looked utterly bewildered as he laid a rose on the casket—no, not a rose. I frowned when I realized it wasn't a white rose like the rest but a red tulip. A lone spot of brightness in the otherwise dim and dreary scene. It occurred to me that he must have brought it himself because all the ones from the florist were uniformly white.

I stared at him, perplexed, as I wracked my brain, trying to place him. I felt sure I knew all of Cal's friends, but I'd never seen this guy before. Cal and I were close. How could someone I'd never met be so distraught over Cal's death? Dave Wegman, Cal's best friend since childhood, was grieving hard, and yet he seemed less visibly torn up than this stranger.

Who in the hell are you?

As the priest continued, I tried to force myself to pay attention to the remainder of the funeral, but Cal's sudden death had yet to sink in, and I struggled to comprehend that it was actually happening. I'd been walking around in a daze since I got the news, and I couldn't shake the sense that at some point I'd wake up and realize it had all been a terrible dream. But the casket in front of me reminded me this was no dream, no matter how desperately I wanted it to be.

My mother touched my arm. With a start, I realized the service had concluded, and people were beginning to leave. I turned as they approached us. Some offered condolences, and I shook their hands and responded, but for the life of me, I couldn't focus on any of their faces. The words we exchanged jumbled together and meant nothing.

"You're shivering, Sarah," my father murmured quietly to my mother as the crowds dwindled. "Come to the car so you can warm up."

I exchanged worried glances with my father when she barely responded. Despite the carefully applied makeup attempting to conceal it, I could see the paleness in her cheeks and the gaunt and sunken look to her eyes and cheeks. Grief had taken its toll on my vibrant, fun-loving mother. My father looked equally drawn and exhausted, and when I'd stared at myself in the mirror this morning, I'd looked no better.

"I'll be right behind you."

My father nodded and ushered my mother away from the grave.
I lingered, unable to tear myself away yet. I stared dully at the casket, wondering when the grief would finally hit me, but I couldn't seem to feel *anything*.

4

The stranger had stayed as well, and for a while, the two of us stood across the grave from each other in silence. I wondered who the hell he was and how he'd known my brother. I wracked my brain but continued to come up blank.

I recognized that I was focused on him in a desperate attempt to distract myself. Trying to place him was easier to think about than dwelling on the fact that my brother was dead. I'd never see Cal smile, never hear him laugh again. After I walked away, the discreet and efficient cemetery staff would lower his casket into the ground and cover him over with dirt. The image was like a blow to the chest every time I let my mind wander to it. I suddenly remembered the time Cal and I had been rollerblading, and we'd fallen in a tangle of adolescent limbs with Cal sprawled on top of my chest. I had felt like I'd never breathe again, and the more I let myself think about Cal being gone, the more that feeling grew.

Speculating about the man in the pea coat was easier than giving in to the pain.

"C.J.?" my father called, and I turned to look at him. "We're heading back to the house. Are you coming?"

"Be there in a moment," I choked out.

I took one final glance at the casket, and my gaze locked on the man standing across from me. I couldn't look away, pinned in place by the raw grief and anger in his gaze. The pain matched my own, but the icy hatred chilled me to the bone.

I shivered, tucked my hands into my coat, and turned away. I might never know who he was or what Cal had meant to him, but my family needed me, and that was all I could worry about now.

The luncheon following the burial was held at my parents' house. It was catered, and my mother's sister, my Aunt Eva, had put herself in charge of organizing it, so there was little for my parents and myself to do besides mingle.

Dozens of people hugged me and held my hand, their cheeks damp as they murmured, "I'm so sorry for your loss," or some variation thereof. They blurred together until I couldn't distinguish one from the other. I found myself wandering through the house, staring blankly at the familiar sights and wondering why it felt so alien now.

I'd grown up in the brick three-story house in the West Hills of Portland. Other than spending a few summers at home during my undergrad education, I'd moved out at eighteen. My mother had done some redecorating during the subsequent sixteen years, but the bones of the house were essentially unchanged. It was still sprawling, with gleaming hardwood floors, classical details, and tasteful decor. The scuffs on the walls from two boys were gone now, along with the scrapes gouged in the stairs from Cal attempting to surf down them. Cal had been wild, no question about it, and I had always been the sober, mature one. The consummate older brother, the one telling Cal to slow down, to think through his actions for one goddamn minute. The one following after him and cleaning up his messes.

The one living with his mistakes.

I'd been thirteen when the bike accident happened. Cal had been seven and enthralled by everything to do with BMX bikes. He loved jumps and trick riding, and my parents had pleaded with me to keep an eye on him and make sure he wore a helmet when we were out playing with friends. I'd liked riding my bike too, and although Cal was a good deal younger, we hung out a lot, so I didn't mind.

One afternoon, when we were riding at the end of the cul-de-sac, I helped our friend Dave build and set up a jump. Cal kept himself occupied, tinkering with our bikes. Cal was the first one over the jump, then Dave, then me. I had a vague memory of flying over it—exhilarated—and then not being able to stop. I'd landed hard, the bar of the bike frame an unyielding surface for my spread legs to land on. I'd passed out from the pain and woken up to Cal frantically shaking me.

Sick to my stomach and barely able to stand, I'd reassured him I'd be okay. He'd pleaded with me to not tell our parents in return for him doing all my chores for a month. Dazed and aching, I'd agreed, unable to resist my brother's tear-filled eyes and desperate apologies.

But when the pain lingered, I eventually had to confess to our parents what happened. There were numerous doctor's visits and discussions about damage to the vas deferens and surrounding area. In the end, it was discovered that the severe trauma—gone untreated—had left me sterile.

Cal had been grounded of course. At seven, he hadn't really grasped how seriously he'd impacted my future, but he'd understood enough to feel guilty and voluntarily spend the rest of the summer doing my chores. It had slowed some of his wild exploits down for a while too.

But eventually, like most kids, he forgot about it after a while. He moved on and went back to exploring the world at top speed with little thought for the repercussions while I was left to deal with the consequences.

Still, I'd forgiven my brother. He'd been so young at the time, and what he'd done had been an accident. I'd loved him too much to be angry, even when I reached adulthood and began to think about having a family of my own someday. And now Cal never would.

Grief rose, choking my throat, and a sudden desperate need to get away from the press of bodies and kind but banal expressions of sympathy overwhelmed me.

Unfortunately, a quick escape was out of the question. The house was packed to the brim with mourners talking in hushed voices as they discussed Cal and his death. I could barely make my way through the press of the crowd, and every time I tried, there was someone stopping me to tell me they'd loved my brother and how much they'd miss him. I forced myself to hold it together. I shook their hand and hugged them, told them how much I appreciated their kind words and presence, but inside, I felt dull and empty. I operated on auto-pilot and wondered why no one noticed that I was only half-there.

I choked down part of a sandwich Aunt Eva pressed into my hand, but it seemed dry and tasteless, crumbling in my mouth like sawdust. I abandoned the sandwich and plate on the nearest table after a few bites. There was a bar set up in the dining room, with black shirted servers pouring small glasses of wine. The crowd was a sea of dark fabric, men in suits, women in dresses or suits, all starched and pressed and polished. Cal would have *hated* it. I briefly contemplated the wine but decided against it. What I really wanted was a bottle of something stronger and a quiet room to lock myself in.

When I finally fled the crowds, I climbed the stairs to his third-floor bedroom. The door was ajar, and when I peeked in, I saw my mother sitting on Cal's bed, clutching a shirt of his.

8

"Mom?" I said quietly, and she lifted her head, staring blankly at me for a moment before she managed a tortured-looking smile. As I took a seat on the bed beside her, she let out a shuddering sigh.

"Oh, C.J."

"How are you doing?" I asked, rubbing her shoulder. She shrugged listlessly. Although she was only in her early sixties, and typically looked a good five to ten years younger, she seemed ancient right now. Lines etched her face, and her skin was bleached and sickly. I hardly recognized her as my beautiful, always-laughing mother. Planning the funeral had given my parents something to do, but I knew it would be even worse once the mourners went home and the day-to-day routine resumed. I dreaded it too.

"I miss him so much," she said with a sudden, gasping sob, turning so she could bury her head against my chest.

"Oh, Mama," I whispered, though I hadn't called her that since I was a little boy. I held her tight, completely and utterly helpless against her grief. I was a psychiatrist, damn it. I worked in a hospice with terminally ill patients. I should have been able to help her. Yet all my training fell apart in the face of my own family's tragedy. The anguish I felt threatened to crush me. I could only imagine how much worse hers was. She'd adored Cal. We all had, but they had been especially close. He'd gotten his zeal for life and his sense of humor from her. I'd never doubted her love for me for a moment, but Cal was her baby.

And now he was gone.

She cried for a long time, sobbing against my suit jacket while all I could do was murmur wordless sounds, helplessly trying to soothe her.

Eventually, she pulled away and stood. "I'm sorry, I keep promising I'll hold myself together, but …"

She pressed her palms to her face briefly before she shook her head and disappeared into the bathroom, presumably to wipe her eyes and pull herself together. Maybe more than anything else, it was hard to see her lose control. We were so much alike in that way, liking our lives tidy and well-ordered. We didn't do messes or disorganization. That was Cal and our father's territory. Cal took it to an extreme that went well above what my father tolerated, however. Christopher Allen Sr. had a messy desk in his study and a penchant for leaving items in his wake; Cal had a messy life.

I wandered around his bedroom while I waited for my mother to come out again, staring at the cluttered walls of the room. Photos— nearly all taken by Cal—covered almost every square inch. He'd never liked to commit to jobs or hobbies, bouncing from one to the other with the enthusiasm he tackled everything, but photography had stuck. He'd refused to make photography his career, although he was more than talented enough. Nature shots mingled with portraits, and it wasn't until I'd made a slow circuit of the room that I realized I was looking for something specific—or, more accurately—some*one* specific. But the mysterious man from the funeral was nowhere in sight. I saw plenty of Cal's friends and lovers in the photos, but the man with the long dark hair was conspicuously absent. *Odd.*

"He was so talented."

I nodded my agreement. I'd been so lost in my thoughts I hadn't heard my mother come back in the room. I looked at one of the photos that I presumed someone else had taken of Cal. He was standing on the beach, surfboard planted in the sand in front of him as the setting sun gave its last gleam around the cliff wall behind him. His face was in profile as he looked toward the water. The wetsuit was peeled down to his waist, his thumbs still hooked in it, baring a sliver of hip. Something about the photo was intimate, as if taken in an unguarded moment by someone he trusted. Cal was rarely without a smile, but in this photo, he had a serious expression of concentration on his face. It was a version of my brother I hardly recognized.

"Yes, he was." I wondered what the photo meant.

My mother hooked her arm in mine and let out a little sigh. "Come on, let's go back downstairs and face all those people who came to pay their respect. Or at least eat all our food." Her cheer sounded forced.

I snorted. "Mother!" In sense of humor, my mother and Cal were the ones who were alike, and I was never prepared for their jokes.

She offered me a wan smile. "You know I appreciate our close friends and family, but I swear, some of the other people just showed up to gawp and consume all the food and liquor." We left Cal's room and descended the stairs. "They didn't even *know* Cal."

"You have a good point," I admitted. "I saw the neighbors who haven't spoken to us since Cal colored their Koi pond green for St. Patrick's Day in high school." A small, genuine smile—the first I'd seen in a week—crossed her lips.

"I know most of them really do mean well, but Cal would have hated this, wouldn't he?" She paused on the landing and looked up at me. "We should have held a bonfire on the beach. I don't know why I let the funeral director and Eva pressure me into such a formal event."

I smiled sadly and nodded. "Yeah, we probably should have. Well, maybe we can do a smaller memorial someday. Just close friends and family."

"You're such a good boy, C.J. Your father and I are so grateful for everything you've done for us since Cal …" She trailed off as if unable to say the words.

"Of course," I reassured her. "Promise me if there's anything you need, you'll let me know."

"I will." She began moving again, and I followed.

"I know it's been a while since I've been up here, but Cal's room seems strangely clean," I commented. "Did Marissa tidy up yesterday?"

She shook her head. "No, Cal hadn't been home much. He hardly ever slept here anymore. Truthfully, I thought maybe he'd met someone, although he never brought the girl to dinner or anything." He'd done that in the past, showed up with a girl he'd been dating for a few weeks. Every time, my mother got her hopes up that one day someone would convince Cal to settle down. But it never stuck.

"Hmm." That was odd. Cal had preferred the chaos in his room to stay exactly the way he'd left it, so he'd rarely had my parents' housekeeper clean up after him, but I was shocked to hear that the order in there was of his own doing. Strange that he hadn't mentioned he was dating anyone to me either. He often told me

THE GHOSTS BETWEEN US

about his relationships when he didn't tell our mother. After all, I wasn't going to harass him about settling down and starting a family. I *did* privately agree with my mother's prediction that someday he'd meet someone who would knock him off his feet and change his whole world however.

People immediately surrounded us as we reached the foot of the stairs, a good many of whom had been looking for us. I got lost in the crowd again, the large group of friends and acquaintances blurring together until I could hardly remember who I'd already spoken to. I lasted an hour before the need to flee hit again. With some persistence, I worked my way through the crowd to the kitchen where the catering staff was working. They barely spared me a glance as they scurried to do their work.

Weary and mentally drained, I escaped out the back door, needing a few minutes to breathe. I ended up on the deck off the kitchen, lingering in the doorway as I stared out at the yard. Even in January, the grass still had patches of green, and it had started to rain—a cold drizzle that would force me back inside before long. A soft sound caught my attention, and when I turned my head, I spotted the dark-haired man from the funeral, leaning against the back of the house, sheltered from the rain by the deep eaves. His eyes widened when he spotted me. I parted my lips, but nothing came out. I had never expected to see him here, and I had no idea what to say.

"Hey," I managed after an awkwardly long pause.

His only response was a laconic nod of his head. I leaned against the closed door, huddling in on myself. Unfortunately, I'd come outside without my overcoat on over my suit so I knew I couldn't stay there long. I was desperate to know who the man was, however, so I'd have to think fast.

"Did you know Cal well?" I blurted out when nothing else came to me.

He took a long drag on his cigarette and tilted his head back to blow the smoke at the sky. "Yeah, you could say that." His voice was husky, but I couldn't tell if it was from smoking, suppressed tears, or was naturally that way.

"Skydiving buddies?" I asked, my tone joking. "Pottery lessons? The Peace Corps?" With my brother, all were possible.

"Lovers." The silence that followed his statement stretched between us as I gaped at him in shock. The man snickered, but there was nothing remotely amused about his tone. "Yeah. Together more or less exclusively for six fucking months. I was his dirty little secret."

"I—I'm sorry. I didn't know Cal was seeing anyone. I didn't even know he was … bi, I guess. Christ, I'm so sorry." The fatigue and grief had already numbed my brain, and this news left me struggling to string together words.

"Yeah, he didn't want to tell your parents. Said it was because of you."

"Me? I—I don't understand." I blinked stupidly at him. "I'm gay, and our parents were plenty supportive. Why would Cal be worried about coming out to the family?"

"I don't know, maybe because your parents desperately wanted someone to carry on the Allen name and genes," he replied bitterly.

"Oh, shit." That rang true, my parents had been eager for grandchildren, and although they would happily welcome any child I

THE GHOSTS BETWEEN US

brought into the family, I could no longer have a biological child. That had led to a certain amount of pressure over the years for Cal. We both knew they were grateful that Cal would presumably marry a woman and pass on the genes and the family name someday. Dating a man would make it that much more complicated.

"Yeah, oh shit." His tone was snide.

"I am so sorry; I had no idea. God, if I'd known …" My knees sagged, and I was suddenly grateful for the side of the house to lean against. It was the only thing keeping me upright.

He scowled at me. "You'd have done what? Waved a magic wand and fixed it all? It doesn't work that way."

"Of course not! I just wish I'd known," I whispered. "I would have supported him. Helped him tell our parents. I … I suddenly feel like I didn't even know my own brother."

The smile he gave me was melancholy. "I'm not sure anyone really did. Cal was larger than life. Too much for any one person to grasp. Maybe I was crazy for thinking I could ever keep him as mine."

"You had him for six months. That's longer than most," I pointed out.

He was silent for a long moment before he dropped the cigarette and ground it under his heel. "You were brothers for twenty-eight years. Was that enough?" He turned and walked down the steps into the side yard.

I opened my mouth but there was no good response. The answer was no. Of course. No amount of time with Cal would have ever been enough if you knew him. And this man had loved Cal, I was sure of it.

"Hey, what's your name?" I managed to choke out.

"Elliot. Elliot Rawlings," he threw back over his shoulder as he disappeared around the corner of the house.

"Nice to meet you, Elliot Rawlings," I whispered.

Chapter Two

I stood on the deck, staring out at the rain-soaked back yard as I contemplated Elliot's words. It wasn't until a shiver wracked my body that I realized I'd been so lost in my thoughts I hadn't noticed how chilled I'd become. Shivering, I rubbed my upper arms to warm myself before going inside.

The house was still crowded with mourners. It was stifling hot, but even as my skin lost its chill, I felt like I might never warm up inside.

Elliot's revelation rattled me. I didn't doubt that he was telling the truth; his grief was too real, too raw to be faked. But it upended everything I thought I knew about my brother. And worse, it made me question why he hadn't been willing or able to tell me. Despite the six-year age gap and massive difference in temperament, we'd always been close. Or, at least, I'd believed we'd been. Clearly, I was wrong.

When the last relative finally left, I collapsed on the couch in the living room, staring blankly at the fire someone had thought to build. I must have appeared normal enough to the people I interacted with, but now, I had no recollection about anything I'd said or done since my encounter with Elliot.

Someone cleared their throat, and I jerked my head up to see my father sitting in a chair by the fireplace. "How are you doing, son?" he asked, his voice rough.

"I'm … I don't know," I said. "Exhausted, I guess."

He nodded, then fell silent again. He looked haggard, his skin almost as gray as his hair, and the lines around his mouth were particularly pronounced. "Do you want to talk about it? About Cal, I mean?"

I shook my head. If not for the revelations from Elliot, I might have wanted to, but I didn't trust myself now. The last thing my parents needed was to learn that their son had kept a secret from them for the past six months. It would crush them while they were at their most vulnerable. Maybe someday I'd tell them—if I thought it would be helpful—but for now, keeping Cal's secret was for the best.

"I think I need to go home and crash."

"You can stay here," my mother offered. I glanced up as she entered the room.

"I appreciate it, but no. I'd like to sleep in my own bed tonight." Since we'd gotten the call from the police about Cal, I'd been sleeping at my parents' house, only running home long enough to grab clothes. As ready to drop as I was, I probably could have slept anywhere, but I wanted my own familiar bed tonight.

And I needed some space to process what Elliot had told me.

I stood with a weary groan, feeling every bit of my thirty-four years. I felt fifty-four, at least. With a concerted effort, I made it up the stairs and to the guest room where I gathered my belongings, then returned to the ground floor where I met my parents at the door.

The hug my mother gave me was painful, not because of her strength, but the lack of it. She suddenly felt frail in my arms, old. It was a reminder that at some point, I'd lose both her and my father. It sent a sharp pang through me, and I kissed the top of her head as if that would somehow make the truth go away. I'd always assumed I'd have Cal by my side when our parents died, but I was struck by the sudden, painful realization that once they were gone, I'd be completely alone.

My mother held onto me for a long time before finally pulling away and wiping at her eyes. "You've been so good to us, C.J. I don't know how we would have made it through this week without you."

My throat was so clogged with tears all I could manage was a nod. The hug and thank you from my father were no less heartfelt, and I knew if I didn't leave soon, I'd break down in tears. I hadn't cried since we left the hospital, and I was afraid if I started again now, I'd never stop.

My mother twisted her hands together as she stared at me. "I wish you had someone you were going home to."

I nodded. "It would be nice right now."

"You haven't met anyone since ..." Her voice trailed off.

"No. I needed a break, I think. I'll get back out there when I'm ready."

"I know you will."

"I'm not holding my breath on finding anyone though," I warned her.

She sighed. "You're such a pessimist."

"Sometimes, it's easier to assume the worst, and then if it doesn't go well, I won't be disappointed."

"Oh, honey." Her voice was soft.

"But, hey, if it does go well then I'll be pleasantly surprised." I tried to inject some humor in my voice.

"Well, don't let your previous relationships get you down about dating. I know you'll find someone wonderful, I can feel it. Someone we'll all absolutely love."

My mother, the hopeless romantic. Her tone was so determined that if it were possible for a person to single-handedly will it to happen, she would.

"I hope you're right."

I left before she could convince me to stay the night again. Simply getting into my car felt like a major ordeal, and I sat in the driveway for several minutes, too bone-weary to move. But, eventually, I started the car and drove across Portland to my home.

The air in the apartment felt stale after days of being shut up, and despite the cold outside, I cracked a window open. I wanted to shower before I crawled into bed, but I was running on fumes as I staggered into the bedroom. I shrugged out of my suit jacket and took off my belt and tie, but after I sat on the bed to toe off my shoes, I could barely move another muscle. I lay back, scooting far enough up the bed that my feet weren't hanging over the edge, managed to wrap myself in a blanket, and passed out.

I awoke sometime later, groggy and disoriented. I blinked the sleep from my eyes and stretched. It finally registered that my phone was ringing, and I stumbled out of bed, fumbling for the device on the dresser where I usually left it before realizing it was in my suit jacket pocket. The phone had stopped ringing by the time I finally found it. I staggered back to the bed and blearily tried to read the screen. Dave Wegman—affectionately dubbed *The Wingman* by Cal—had called. My phone beeped with an incoming voicemail, but rather than answer, I hit send to call him back.

"Hey. How are you doing?" he asked.

"Uh, hey, Dave. I'm okay." My voice was scratchy and hoarse.

"Did I wake you?" he asked, sounding concerned.

"Yeah, I kind of crashed when I got back from my parents' house. It's no big deal though." I scrubbed at my face, trying to clear the lingering fog.

"Sorry, man. You did seem pretty out of it after the funeral."

"It's fine," I reassured him. "If you hadn't called, I probably would have woken up in the middle of the night unable to get back to sleep. What's up?"

"Oh. Uh, some of us are getting together at *The Tap* to drink to Cal. I would have brought it up at the house, but I didn't want to bug you then. If you're too wiped out, we'll totally understand, but I thought you might want to come tonight."

"No, it's okay. Really." I scrubbed a hand over my face again. "It would be nice to celebrate Cal the way he'd want us to."

21

"By getting shitfaced," Dave said drily.

For the first time in over a week, I laughed. "Yeah, by getting shitfaced. Text me the details, and I'll be there. I'm going to go grab a shower."

"Will do. Glad you're coming," Dave said. His tone was warm, and it slipped over me like a hug.

"Thanks for the invite."

The shower helped clear the mental cobwebs, and by the time I was dressed and ready, I had a text with all the information from Dave, including a reminder to use Lyft rather than drive there. I groaned, knowing that the following morning was going to be brutal. Older than the bulk of the guys I'd be drinking with tonight, and, a lightweight by comparison, they'd always been able to drink me under the table.

Maybe they'll take it easy on me. I laughed internally at the idea. *Nah, not a chance; Cal wouldn't want them to.*

The Lyft ride was relatively short, and the bar where we were meeting was familiar. I didn't go out drinking with Cal and his buddies terribly often, but a few times a year I'd tag along. If I were honest with myself, some of the draw was Dave. David Wegman had grown up next door, three grades below me, which put him between my age and Cal's. He was a friend to both of us, although once I graduated high school, we drifted apart while he and Cal remained close.

I'd had a stupid little crush on Dave for years. Nothing had ever come of it—he was straight—but he'd never seemed at all uncomfortable with me being gay. I fleetingly wondered if he'd known about Cal and Elliot, but I didn't think tonight at the bar was the time or the place to ask.

T*he Tap* was a low-key place. Nothing trendy about it at all. Hipsters weren't welcome, and the food was mostly an afterthought, but they had an incredibly well-stocked bar. If you wanted a game of pool or darts, that was always an option, and various sporting events played on the televisions scattered around the room. It wasn't a place to be seen or to try to find a date— although I suspected there had been plenty of drunken hook-ups over the years. It was a place to kick back with friends and drink, and that was what Cal had loved about it.

I pushed the door open and scanned the room, but I couldn't see anyone I recognized. It was Dave's boisterous laugh that led me to the long table where everyone sat. They'd taken over the back wall of the place. It was lined with banquette seating on one side of the table and chairs on the other. Dave looked up from his seat at the far end, his grin widening when he spotted me.

"Hey there, C.J." He stood and engulfed me in a massive hug. Christopher John Allen Junior had been a mouthful to a kid, so I'd gone by C.J. to separate me from my father. It got too confusing otherwise. Once I got older, I wanted to be called Chris, but within the family, I tended to still get called C.J. Dave hadn't called me that in years, but I guess we were all a bit nostalgic today.

Dave's hug felt altogether too good, especially after a long, stressful day, and he didn't complain when I sagged against him and buried my head against his shoulder. It wasn't a polite hug, but one of shared grief and brotherhood, and I allowed myself to sink into it. He squeezed tightly before he let go and kept his arm around my shoulder as we turned to face the table of guys. Cooper and John had graduated high school with Cal, but the rest were more recent friends I vaguely knew. Elliot was nowhere to be seen.

A jock in high school, Cooper Haynes was a tall, beefy guy with dirty blond hair who had turned a passion for fitness into a career as a personal trainer and was now the owner of a gym. John was rather non-descript to look at, but his impressively deep voice had led to a career as a radio DJ. Rob, Shaun, and Jimmy were the other guys, although for the life of me I couldn't remember what any of them did for a living, or how they'd met Cal. I'd had drinks with them a few times, and I knew they'd been at the funeral today, but that was the best my still-sapped brain could muster. I greeted them with a nod, and a few people shifted down so I could slide in. Dave followed.

Before I could think twice, a pint of beer was thrust into my hands, and I took a grateful sip. Deschutes Brewery's Mirror Pond. Cal's favorite.

"Thanks for coming today," I said to the guys gathered, feeling out of place without Cal's boisterous presence at the table.

"Anything for Cal," Cooper said quietly, and everyone at the table repeated the sentiment, raising their glasses before taking a long drink.

For the umpteenth time that day, the press of tears threatened, but Dave settled a hand on my knee. Even through the grief, a flutter of warmth worked its way through my chest and was enough to stop me from crying. I looked over and shot him a grateful smile, and he squeezed once more before he let go. I had to duck my head and take a sip of beer to compose myself.

Dave was far too attractive for my sanity. Clean-cut, he had dark blond hair that was just long enough to tell it had a little bit of curl to it. His eyes were a rich, warm brown, and with darker brows and lashes that contrasted with his golden skin, his coloring was striking. With high cheekbones and impossibly full, pouty lips, he was a gay man's wet dream. Or at least, my wet dream. The body, honed from years of surfing, skateboarding, and snowboarding was nothing to scoff at either. With a height well over six feet, he ticked off everything on my checklist—or maybe he was the reason I had a thing for tall, fit guys who were clean-cut with high cheekbones; I didn't know anymore. Sadly, he was too straight, and too much Cal's friend, for me to ever consider making a move on him. *Damn it.*

I pushed thoughts of Dave out of my head and focused on the conversation around the table. The guys had been telling stories about Cal when I arrived, and apparently, they'd resumed. I let the conversation wash over me, sipping the glass of beer that never seemed to empty, as they told stories about my brother. Other people joined us, male and female, pulling up tables and chairs to expand ours. At first, I just chuckled along with the rest of the crowd, content to listen to the funny anecdotes, but after a while, I joined in.

I had just finished a story about Cal's first day of kindergarten when he'd glued another kid's hand to a desk when Allie Carmichael piped up. She was a short-term girlfriend from Cal's days at Portland State. They'd parted on good terms after graduation when he went off to the Peace Corps and had remained friends after his return.

"So, the first time I met Cal, he was naked," she said, pouring herself another pint of beer from the pitcher the waitresses kept refilling. I grimaced at my own drink, wondering just how many I'd had already. Cooper was in charge of the pitcher at our end of the table, and every time I looked away, he filled my glass. Everyone at the table laughed, and Allie continued. "The fire alarm in the dorms went off, and my roommate and I went to leave. I opened the door and there was Cal, naked as could be, streaking down the hall yelling 'Free Willy!' I honestly don't know if he was advertising or on his save the whales kick."

The table laughed uproariously, and I snorted, coughing a little as I nearly inhaled a mouthful of beer into my lungs. Dave nudged me with his elbow and leaned in to speak in my ear. He was so close I could feel every brush of his lips against my skin. "Pretty sure he was just trying to get in Allie's pants. She was a marine biology major he had the hots for. You do the math." I laughed, liking the warm rub of his shoulder against mine and the fact that for at least a short while, I wasn't totally alone. "Who can blame him, right? Any guy would go for Allie." I raised an eyebrow at him, and he chuckled. "Well, any guy with an interest in women."

"Yeah, that makes a difference."

He gave me a long, searching look. The rest of the room seemed to fade, the babble of voices and laughter around us muting as I focused on the man next to me. "What about you? Are you seeing anyone?" Dave asked.

I snorted. "No. My last relationship left me a little gun-shy."

Dave nodded, absently scratching his arm, which lifted the sleeve of his T-shirt to show off the tattoo on his bicep. I took a sip of beer rather than get caught drooling. "Yeah, Cal told me about Dickface."

This time, I did inhale my drink, and it took several hard thumps on the back before I could breathe again. "Dickface?" I said between coughs.

"Cal's term of endearment for whatever the hell the douche's name was. I know I met him a handful of times, but apparently, he didn't make much of an impression."

I chuckled and leaned back in my seat, shuddering when I realized Dave had his arm up on the back of the booth. The skin of his forearm felt hot against the back of my neck. "Alec Walters. But Dickface works." The stinging pain of the end of my last relationship was softened by another man's leg pressed against my own, and the warm concern in his eyes. It didn't matter that Dave was never going to return my feelings, right now, his presence was enough.

"Down with Dickface!" Dave shouted, and I laughed as everyone around the table chimed in, even though they had no idea what we were talking about. *God, Cal has great friends.*

Had, I corrected myself.

Conversations about Cal resumed as people told stories about him, regaling the table with bits and pieces of my brother's life that I had never been privy to, or had only heard from him. It reminded me of Elliot, and I had a fleeting thought, wondering if he'd shown up at the bar since I arrived. I craned my neck to look down the length of the table, but there were too many people blocking my view to be sure. I sat back, unsure if I was relieved or disappointed that I hadn't spotted him. I was curious about him, but at the same time, I had no idea what I would say if we did meet again.

"We should do a round of shots," John called out, pulling out his wallet and slapping a credit card on the table. "I'm buying,"
Everyone around the table cheered, but I let my head fall onto the table with a whimper. "This isn't going to end well," I muttered.

I felt more than heard Dave's hearty laugh. His hand landed on my back, rubbing between my shoulder blades. "Buck up, Buttercup."

It was a familiar statement, one both Dave and Cal had used for years, and I flipped him off without even lifting my head.

He leaned in and his breath was hot against my cheek. "In. Your. Dreams."

I elbowed him and sat up, rolling my eyes and taking a sip of beer rather than respond to his too-apt statement. Dave—much like Cal—was a flirt, and over the years, I'd grown used to the fact that he liked to tease. I knew he had no intention of following through, and I was pretty sure he either had no idea that I thought of him as anything but a friend or was secure enough in his sexuality to be flattered rather than unnerved. I also knew my drunken ass was going to be jerking off to thoughts of Dave once I got home tonight. Assuming I didn't just pass out and sleep it off under the table here, of course.

John coaxed the waitress into bringing over shots for the whole table, and I grimaced when I saw it was tequila. Mixing beer and any kind of liquor was a bad idea, but tequila? It didn't get much worse than that. Cal had loved it though, and if I wanted to celebrate my brother tonight, I might as well go big. *Go big or go home* is—was—

definitely Cal's motto.

"I want to make a toast to our friend, and brother" —John nodded at me— "Cal. I know right now he's lifting the skirts on every beautiful angel in heaven. So, let's drink to Cal because he's the best motherfucker we'll ever know."

In the shouted chaos of my brother's name, I almost missed the thud of the chair clattering to the ground, but I couldn't miss the sight of Elliot as he stood. Apparently, he'd been sitting at the far end of the long table from where Cooper and John and I were. Over the raised shot glasses, I saw the stricken look on his face and the way his black hair flew as he spun and made a beeline away from the table. *How did I miss him arriving earlier?*

I downed my shot and twisted in my seat, intending to follow him, but a hand on my arm stopped me in my tracks. I looked over to see Cooper reaching across the table.

"Hey, Chris," he shouted over the noise of the bar, most of which seemed to be caused by our group. "Are you leaving?"

"Just for a minute," I explained.

"Well, before I forget, I just want to tell you that I hope we won't lose contact. I know we started off as Cal's friends, but we all like you a lot, man. It would be good to have you around more often."

"I'd like that, thanks," I replied, absurdly grateful for the invitation. I'd never inspired the kind of loyalty in people that Cal had, and I'd come to terms with that long ago, but it was nice to think that Cal's group of friends liked me as well. Maintaining the connection to my brother was important to me.

"Cal was the best of us," John muttered, his eyes shiny with tears. He pounded once on the table with his fist, then drained the rest of his beer. I glanced around, looking to see if I could spot Elliot, but he was nowhere in sight. *Damn it.* I sighed as I settled back in my seat, frustrated that he was gone. But what had compelled me to go after him anyway? What could I really do to help? I didn't know the guy, and although I felt bad for him, I wasn't sure what I could do to make things better even if I did track him down.

Once again, I tuned into the conversation around the table, listening to some of Cal's exploits in the Peace Corps. A few more rounds of shots went around the table, and I was midway through telling a story about the time Cal had broken my leg while we were skateboarding when I realized I was drunk. "… and then I went flying off the board, grabbed Cal, and somehow pulled him down on top of me. He landed right on top of my left thigh and bam" —I smacked the table with my hand— "it broke in three places."

Everyone snorted with laughter, and when I shifted in my seat, I realized my bladder was overly full. The table was too crowded for me to get out, and I gently shoved at Dave's shoulder. "Hey, I've gotta get up. Let me out."

He frowned at me, covering my hand with his. "You leaving?"

"Just gotta piss."

Dave slid out from behind the table and I followed. I swayed a little as I stood, and I grabbed his shoulder to steady myself. "Need any help?" he asked, frowning.

I raised an eyebrow at him. "Uhh, I've been managing that on my own for a while now. Now, there's another reason a man might offer to help another man out in the bathroom, but I didn't think you swung that way ..." I teased.

Dave snorted and slapped my thigh. "Yeah, I just meant helping you walk to the bathroom. You're weaving a bit there, buddy."

"I'll be fine."

I tried not to let my body brush against his too much as I moved past him. I staggered a bit as I went to the bathroom, and it took me an inordinately long amount of time to make it over to the urinal and get my pants unzipped. Relieving the pressure felt amazing, and by the time my fumbling fingers managed to do up my pants again, I felt a thousand times better. I stared blearily at myself in the mirror as I washed my hands, noticing I had to squint to focus. *Well shit.*

As I made my way back to the table, I belatedly realized that I should have eaten something to sop up the alcohol I'd guzzled. A few bites of a sandwich at the memorial luncheon were all I'd had that afternoon, and I wracked my brain trying to recollect if I'd had anything for breakfast before the funeral. A hastily choked down granola bar early in the morning was the only thing I could clearly remember. *I am so fucked.*

I made a detour to the bar to grab some water and order some food, and when I returned to the table, Dave stood to let me in. I slid into the spot I'd vacated earlier without paying attention but quickly realized that people had rearranged their seating as others had cleared out. Now, Elliot Rawlings was next to me. *I thought he'd left.* From his alarmed gaze, he clearly hadn't expected me to be there either.

"Hey." Rattled by his presence, I set down the glass of water before

I spilled it.

"Hey," he responded, but it was like he looked right through me. He glanced away and let his hair fall forward, blocking me completely so I couldn't see his face at all. I could smell him though. Cigarette smoke mingled with a scent that reminded me of Earl Grey tea and vanilla. I hated smoking, always had, but something about the way it smelled on his skin was appealing. He was dressed like he'd been at the funeral, with dark jeans and a gray hoodie, although the coat and hat were gone now. I could feel the chill coming off his body—he must've come in from smoking outside—and in his attitude.

By the time my food arrived, the crowd had thinned, and the mood had turned somber. The loud, boisterous stories told to the whole table had become quieter reminiscing among pairs or small clusters of people. I ducked my head, choking down bites of fried food dunked in fat and growing more depressed as the day began to catch up with me. Mental and physical exhaustion combined with the dizzying effects of too much beer and tequila weighed me down. On top of the unsettling presence of my brother's lover, I felt my mood plummet.

"You all right?" Dave asked, laying a hand on the back of my neck. I shuddered at the heat and the pressure, my skin prickling with sensation.

"Yeah, it's just hitting me all of a sudden," I said with a heavy sigh. "Christ, I miss him so much."

"We all do," Dave replied roughly. He rubbed soft circles against the back of my neck with his thumb, and it made my head spin. I shifted in my seat, aware of my growing arousal. My thigh brushed Elliot's, and he glanced at me out of the corner of his eye as he pushed his hair back. His fingers were long and slender, like the rest of him, and his movements were graceful.

"How did you meet Cal?" I asked quietly, the words slipping from my lips before I could stop them.

Elliot's glance was wary, and he chewed at his lip for a moment before he answered. "He modeled for me."

I frowned. "You're a photographer?"

"Artist. Ink and charcoal mostly. Some pastels." I stared at him expectantly, wanting to know more, and he sighed, finally sitting back in the booth, staring blankly across the table like he couldn't bear to look me in the face. He played with the tips of his hair, wrapping it around his index finger. "Put up an ad for male, nude models. Cal showed up. Turns out he was a natural at it."

"Hmm." I drained the rest of my water and shook my head when Cooper mimed re-filling my beer. My head was already swimming, and I needed to lay off for a while or I was going to get sick. Dave was still touching me. His arm was draped along the top of the bench, his fingers accidentally brushing my back every so often as either of us shifted. I wanted him so bad I ached for it.

Having Elliot on my other side wasn't helping either. My muddled head kept mixing up the signals, turning my attraction to Dave into an interest in Elliot. There was nothing about him that was my type. Too young, too slender, too … surly. Not to mention too much my brother's lover. But his cheekbones were stunning, and the eyes underneath the dark lashes were a stormy shade of gray. I didn't want to notice those things, but I did. I couldn't stop.

The press of his slim thigh against mine, the way his fingers toyed with the strands of his hair, they both drove me crazy. They made me *want*. I wanted to feel someone else's skin against mine. To lose myself in the heated press of another man's body and for one fucking night not be alone.

"You know, Cal would have given you the shirt off his back," Jimmy slurred.

"He literally *did* give me the shirt off his back once," Shaun said with a laugh. "I totally burned the shit out of myself boarding one day, and he gave me so much crap for doing it. He slapped sunscreen on me and gave me his tee. He always took care of me, but he never let me forget I was a dumbass when I screwed up." Shaun wiped at his eyes and the guys all nodded into their beers.

That was my brother in a nutshell. He had been wild, living right on the edge of life, but with an innate goodness that more than made up for the stress he put people through.

We continued for a while, quietly swapping stories about Cal. Not about his wild exploits, but the quieter moments. The times he'd helped his friends and even strangers. It was hard not to let my thoughts drift to the way he'd died. Even thinking about it made me choke up, but there was some comfort in it too. Knowing it hadn't entirely been in vain. His death had saved lives.

After a while, the people at the table dwindled down to the core few, and we abandoned the extra tables and all huddled together. It wedged me between Dave and Elliot, and as the alcohol worked its way through my system, my thoughts bounced back and forth between the men on either side of me.

"He was my brother and my best friend." My eyes burned. "It's like ... it's like there's this hole now and I can't ..." I let out a strangled sound, unable to finish.

There was this horrible pain in my chest, and I felt aching cold bloom through me. *Maybe I should just go to a gay bar after this to pick someone up.* It wasn't something I liked to do, but with the world crashing down around me and the arousal that had been simmering in me for hours, I needed *something*. Hell, the idea of calling my ex had even crossed my mind, but thankfully, that impulse was quashed by the memory of Dave's voice calling out, "Down with Dickface." I wasn't quite that desperate; I hoped.

Arms on either side of me pressed close, but it wasn't enough; I needed more. I needed to feel something. *Anything.* My tongue suddenly felt thick in my mouth, and I realized my elbow was sliding on the scarred wooden table, unable to hold me up any longer. "Guys," I slurred. "I think I'm officially drunk."

I felt a hand on my thigh, softly stroking, and I ached for the touch and connection so badly that I didn't even stop to consider which side it was coming from.

Chapter Three

Reality returned in pieces, fragments of remembered images swirling alongside snippets of my current reality. *A hand on my thigh.* The sheets tangled around my legs. *Two bodies holding me up as I staggered across the bar.* The soft snoring of someone beside me. *The tight grip of hands on my hips and the fierce but oh so welcome ache as he took me.* The final piece that merged the two realities filtered through my mind as I slid back into sleep.

Earl Grey and vanilla with a hint of smoke.

The situation was simultaneously clearer and more confusing when I awoke the second time. The bed was empty, and I was sprawled on my stomach. Naked. Without opening my eyes, I knew I was in an unfamiliar bed in an unfamiliar room. My body hurt everywhere— from the pounding in my head to the twinge of discomfort in my ass. My eyes flew open, but I quickly slammed them shut at the sudden stabbing headache. *Bad idea.*

Some of the feelings were good though. It had been a very long time since I'd woken with the well-used feeling of having been fucked. And *very* thoroughly. My hips, thighs, and stomach muscles were sore too, and my lower lip felt tender, like I'd bit down on it. Or someone else had. I couldn't remember the night before clearly, just hazy images of being held down and fucked, the pace brutal and punishing, almost angry. I had wanted it though, so much. Had *begged* for more.

36

What I was studiously avoiding thinking about was *who* that man had been. I knew of course, but I wanted to keep my eyes closed, believe that I'd woken up in Dave's bed. That he'd had a sudden fit of bi-curiousness and been the one to fuck me until I passed out. But it wasn't. I knew it wasn't, and the truth, as much as the alcohol, was what made my stomach churn.

How had this *happened?* My throbbing head and muddled brain struggled to grasp what had taken place the night before. I remembered drinking at the bar and both Dave and Elliot—Christ, *Elliot*—helping me into a car. Dave had asked Elliot to make sure I got home safe, then something about needing to pay the tab. The Lyft ride had been quiet except for Elliot speaking to the driver. There had been no hint of anything happening with Elliot then, no flirting, barely even touching. But suddenly, his lips had been on mine in a hard, desperate kiss. And when the car reached his place and he'd tugged me to follow, I hadn't hesitated.

I'd been drunk—we both had been—and I had no doubt Elliot was hurting and as lonely as I was, but none of those reasons were good excuses for what we'd done. The day we buried my brother, I'd slept with his lover. My stomach roiled, and I clapped my hand over my mouth as I scrambled to get out bed.

"Bathroom's behind the wall there," a dispassionate voice informed me. My head throbbed as I frantically searched the large, open space and finally located the wall. I made a dash for it, shoving open the door to the bathroom and dropping to my knees in front of the toilet just in time. The contents of my stomach came up immediately, and I heaved for a long time even after there was nothing more to bring up. Every gut-wrenching moment felt like punishment I richly deserved. Punishment for betraying my brother.

I sat on the floor for a long time after my stomach had settled somewhat, my head resting on my forearm as I tried to will away the truth.

Eventually, I forced myself to get off the floor. I cleaned up, making sure I hadn't made a mess of the bathroom, then splashed my face with cold water, refusing to look at myself in the mirror. Thankfully, there was mouthwash on the counter that I took full advantage of, but after that, I couldn't delay anymore. I would have to face what I'd done. And the man I'd done it with.

My temples felt like they might shatter from the pounding in my head as I pushed open the bathroom door. I hurried over to the bed to where my clothes lay strewn on the floor. I tugged them on as quickly as I could. It was bad enough that I'd bolted out of bed to puke, but the fact that I'd done it naked was so much worse. I felt like I was on display.

I had no memory of Elliot's place from the night before, so now that I was semi-coherent, I took a good look around. He lived in a large, L-shaped space that looked like it was situated at the corner of the building. It was blank and industrial looking, obviously an old warehouse that had been turned into loft apartments.

Off to one side sat a low platform bed, a small nightstand, and a single dresser. The foot of the bed faced the simple kitchen. The room held a couch, but no television, and most of the area was taken up by an art studio. Directly in front of a large expanse of windows stood several huge easels, a stool, and a table filled with art supplies. The bathroom, along with what I assumed was a closet, was the only enclosed area.

The starkness struck me then. Everything about it was gray or black, without a single hint of color to liven the space. Devoid of personal items, except the art. It didn't look deliberately minimalist or ultra-modern. It was simply a studio and a place to sleep, not a home.

Unable to put it off any longer, I looked over at Elliot. He leaned against the concrete kitchen counter, dressed in nothing but a pair of a gray sleep pants. He stared at me impassively over the rim of his mug as if waiting for my response to a question he had silently asked.

I cleared my throat. "Uhm. Morning," I managed, rubbing at my throbbing temples.

"Morning."

"Do you—do you want to talk about what happened last night?"

"Why? Do you?" Elliot's voice was cool and dry. Emotionless.

"I guess. Well, I mean, maybe we should."

He sighed heavily and set the mug on the counter next to him. "Fine," he said flatly. "Go ahead."

"I'm sorry, first of all. I—it shouldn't have happened. Obviously." I let out an awkward laugh. "We were both drunk and ..." My voice trailed off.

"Yes, drunk and depressed. We made a mistake. It won't happen again."

"Do you not feel guilty about this at all?" I snapped. "I thought you were the one in love with my brother?"

"Don't you *dare* question how I felt about him." His tone was clipped and terse, and his face hardened as he spoke. "Yes, I feel fucking awful. But it doesn't change what happened. We fucked, and whatever our reasons were at the time, in the light of day, they're pretty flimsy. So, let's just go our separate ways and agree that we won't ever see each other again."

The guilt and the throbbing in my head made it incredibly tempting to just walk out the door and do exactly that, but some part of me felt reluctant. "Are you sure that's such a good idea?"

"Were you expecting me to make you a gourmet breakfast, and then we'd fall in love and live happily ever after?" he asked, the sarcasm nearly dripping from his lips.

"Jesus Christ. *No*. That's not what I meant at all," I protested. Although, that was basically the way my last relationship had started. At least Alec—*Dickface*—and I had gone on a few dates before we'd hopped into bed. A niggling little voice in the back of my head reminded me that I had never been as well fucked by my ex. But between the pain in my head, the uneasiness of my stomach, and the overwhelming guilt, I could hardly think straight. "Look, I just meant that we're obviously both having a hard time dealing with Cal's death."

To my surprise, Elliot flinched. Was it at my brother's name being spoken aloud or at the mention of his death? Elliot quickly looked away and reached for his mug of tea again. "And?" There was that wintry note in his tone again.

"And I think maybe having someone to talk about it with might be good for both of us. I guess I'd like to know more about Cal from you … I—I feel like I didn't know my brother very well. That's all. I wasn't suggesting anything else."

"I have no interest in any contact with you."

"Fine." I ground my teeth together. "Look, at least let me leave you my number in case you change your mind."

Elliot sighed heavily as he put his mug down again. It landed with a heavy thud, tea splashing over the edge and filling the air with its aroma. Earl Grey, of course. I'd probably never smell the damn scent again without thinking of the man. He pushed a sketchbook across the counter toward me. "Fine."

A pencil rested on top of the paper. I reached to pick it up and froze when I noticed what was on the page below. Elliot had drawn a sketch of a nude man lying in bed. He was curled up half on his stomach with an arm shoved under the pillow and the tangled sheets lying across his thighs. The face was hidden, but the body and short dark hair were familiar. An odd shadowy mark in the small of his back seemed out of place, however. I tried to brush it away with my thumb, but it only smudged it further.

The scene could have been tender, but the rough, heavy marks from his sketching spoke of something else. Anger, maybe. Frustration. Certainly passion.

The intimacy there unnerved me. Not that I thought the night before had meant anything more to Elliot than it had to me, but still, after a night like that, there *was* a certain level of intimacy between us. As I stared at the sketch, memories came trickling back. I knew what the spot along his hipbone tasted like. I'd buried my teeth in his neck, slept with my head against the tea-scented tangles of his hair. My hands knew the feel of his pale, smooth skin, and my body burned with the memory of his touch.

I swallowed hard as I neatly wrote my number in the corner of the page, along with my name. The scratching of the rough drawing pencil against the paper was audible in the otherwise silent room. When I was done, I set the pencil on the counter and looked up, staring at Elliot. Now, he was as somber and composed as ever, but I couldn't forget that I'd seen—and felt—him lose control. Right now, his face was blank and cold, his gaze distant. I could see the red marks my stubble had left on the almost translucent skin of his cheeks and jaw and bite marks on his neck. They were reminders that, although I ached from the rough fucking, he wouldn't be walking away unscathed either. It was a strangely satisfying thought, but it unsettled me as well.

I turned, collected my jacket from where it hung on a rack beside the door, and left his apartment without another word.

When the door to his place closed behind me with a heavy thud, I breathed a little easier, grateful to be free of the choking tension that had settled like a cloud around us.

I found my way out of Elliot's building with no problem, but the sharp, biting wind forced me to huddle in the doorway as I waited for a Lyft car, too proud to go back inside. Thank God for Google maps and GPS because I had no idea where in Portland I was. Doing the walk of shame was a rather new and humiliating experience for me. I'd realized I was gay in my early teens and come out to my parents in high school. I'd dated a little then, and by and large, my experiences with men didn't include one-night stands. I preferred dating and relationships and, in fact, had thought I was headed down the road toward marriage until my ex—*Dickface*, I automatically corrected myself—had ripped that future away from me.

The reminder of Cal and his nickname for my ex made me feel ill all over again. Thankfully, I managed not to puke on the sidewalk, but it was only through sheer willpower. My phone pinged with a text from Dave, asking if I'd made it home safe the night before. *Sorry I couldn't help you get home. I had to wrap things up at the bar. Elliot seemed a little less drunk than you, so I figured he'd keep an eye on you if you got sick or something on the way home. Hope you're feeling okay today.*

My head's a wreck, but I'll survive, I replied. I couldn't tell him the truth. Dave had been looking out for me last night when he put Elliot and I into the Lyft together. He'd had no way of knowing that Elliot and I would betray Cal's memory that way.

I closed my eyes and rested my head back against the rough brick of the building, sick at what I'd done. *You slept with your brother's lover the same day you put his body in the ground, you asshole.* I had to keep repeating the fact to myself because it seemed impossible. It wasn't like me. Not at all. I'd betrayed my brother, and I had no way to ask for his forgiveness.

I knew I'd never be able to forgive myself.

The ride home was blessedly quiet. The driver had no interest in making small-talk so we were both silent. I stared out at the streets of Portland instead. It was relatively deserted, the biting January weather keeping the foot traffic to a minimum. Everything was as gray and grim as Elliot's apartment. Thoughts of him made my stomach lurch, and I must have let out a sound or done something to alert the driver I wasn't well because he glanced back at me in the mirror. "If you're gonna be sick, I gotta pull over. You can't puke in my car, buddy."

I swallowed hard and fought back the nausea. "I'm fine." He gave me a skeptical look, but I urged him to continue. "Really, I'm fine. I swear. I won't get sick."

Neither of us spoke again after that. I forced my mind to go blank, to not let the crowding thoughts work their way into my brain. Not yet. I could freak out when I got home, but for now, I needed to hold it together.

The first thing I noticed when I pushed open the door of my apartment was the cold. I cursed when I realized I'd left the kitchen window open all night. I hastily shut it and tried not to shiver as I shrugged out of my jacket and kicked off my shoes. Shivering hurt. Hell, standing and sitting hurt. *Existing* hurt. The hangover and rough acrobatic sex had done a number on me. I couldn't deny that I had enjoyed the sex though. Responded willingly, even eagerly.

Disgusted, I hurried into the bathroom to shower. I needed to cleanse myself physically and psychologically.

The scalding hot shower warmed me, but it didn't wash away the guilt or the regret. My fingertips grazed a slightly raised area on the skin of my throat as I shaved. I wiped at the small mirror hanging on the wall of the shower, then craned my neck so I could see it better. Jesus Christ, Elliot had left quite the mark. I rubbed at it absently, wondering what the hell we'd been thinking the night before.

It had been months since I'd been touched by anyone, and even before Cal's death, I'd been struggling with loneliness. The death of my brother had gutted me, and I certainly was drunk the night before, but none of those were good excuses. I should have had the presence of mind to tell Elliot no, to walk away. If I'd wanted to, I could have gone to a gay bar or club and found some random guy to go home with.

If it had been with anyone but Elliot, I would have been okay with what happened, but the fact that I'd let myself get involved with Cal's lover was unforgivable.

My brother, the boy I held just hours after he was born, was dead. We'd played together and fought in equal measure, Cal's adventurous, devil-may-care attitude urging him to explore everything, consequences be damned. He was fierce, forging forward while I held back, and at times, I'd envied him. I was prudent, steady, and cautious. I thought things through and weighed my options while Cal hurtled ahead, somehow managing to scrape by, making it work out to his advantage even when he made a colossal mistake.

Maybe it was odd, looking up to my younger brother, but I'd always wanted to be just a bit more like Cal. I wondered if he knew how much I admired him. I felt a sharp pang of regret as I realized I'd never actually said that to him in so many words.

I broke.

It began as a quiet sob that I tried to choke back, but the sudden onslaught of emotions was too much. Guilt and grief mingled, and another sob escaped me. Behind my tightly clenched eyelids, the stinging press of tears threatened to spill down my cheeks. Since Cal's death, I'd been holding myself together, pushing myself to get through the next day without breaking down, but the emotions finally spilled over, unable to be contained any longer. I slid to the floor, muffling my harsh sobs with my hands. Even in the hot shower, the tears felt scalding, and my chest tightened as I struggled to draw in a breath.

"I'm sorry, Cal," I murmured. "I'm so fucking sorry."

I didn't even know what I was sorry for. For his much too early death, maybe. For not telling him how much I admired and cared about him. For not knowing that he was bisexual and that he'd been dating someone for six months. For fucking his boyfriend in a drunken, grief-stricken state.

I let out another sob and let my head fall back against the tiled wall of the shower with a thud. The dull pain almost felt good. I certainly deserved it for what I'd done. Long after the water had run cold and goosebumps rose on my skin, I sat there, drowning in grief, wishing I was the one who had died instead of my brother.

Chapter Four

I'd taken some time off work after Cal's death, but it left me at loose ends. The funeral was on a Thursday, and by Saturday, I was stir-crazy. I tried to keep myself busy, taking care of all the chores around the apartment that had been neglected in the past week, and going to the gym to work out, but those tasks weren't enough to keep me occupied, and they left me with too much time to think.

Saturday afternoon, I looked around my apartment and felt loathing wash over me. I *hated* the place. I'd never been crazy about it, and it finally struck me that it wasn't a home. After Alec and I broke up, all I'd cared about was finding a place to sleep at night that was a convenient distance from my work.

A framed photo of the West Hills of Portland on the wall opposite me made my thoughts drift to Alec Walters and how we'd met. I'd been at a dinner party hosted by a mutual friend. I'd caught a glimpse of a man from across the room and been stunned by his good looks. He'd smiled widely when he caught me staring. He'd quickly wrapped up the conversation he'd been in the middle of and came over to introduce himself. He'd seemed warm and open as we spoke, and I'd been a little overwhelmed by the attention of such a handsome, successful man. We'd hardly paid any attention to the people around us that evening.

Unlike a lot of the gay men my age I met, Alec seemed more

interested in building a relationship than hooking up with as many guys as possible. We had mutual interests and seemed to be on the same page about what we were looking for. We went on a few dates before we hopped into bed together, and by the time he made me brunch the following morning, I was a goner.

We often went to dinners, art galleries, and charity events around Portland so Alec could network for his job. He was proud of my career as a doctor, and he made me feel special every time he introduced me as his boyfriend and glowingly praised my work.

He was an up-and-coming architect, and it was easy to get wrapped up in his dreams of being a power couple.

I ignored the fact that he was more concerned about going out and being seen than spending time with *me*. Everything was about furthering his image, not doing things we both enjoyed. I got so caught up in the idea of what we *could* be that I ignored what we were.

And he was good at deflecting my concerns. Every time I got frustrated with him, he bought me a gift or took me out to dinner or to do something I loved. He was slick and charming and said all the right things to make sure I overlooked the negative aspects to our relationship.

He talked of marriage, of having kids in a few years, of building a life together. So, I didn't hesitate to move in with him.

We'd found a swanky place in the Pearl District to live in. I'd liked the area itself well enough. It was tucked into the West Hills and offered great views of the city and a multitude of things to do. We'd both liked the art galleries, culture, and interesting businesses it offered. The building we'd lived in was impressive enough to raise eyebrows when Alec bragged about it—something he loved to do—and it was close to the architectural firm he worked for. My commute was terrible, however. It put me on the opposite side of the river from where I worked on the east campus and I spent far more of my day battling traffic than I wanted.

But by the time those things irritated me so much I could hardly stand it, I'd signed a lease, and I was invested in the relationship too much to back out. Things seemed to change after we lived together as well. Alec grew emotionally distant, and our sex life petered out. He worked longer hours, and when he was off work, he went out with his friends more often. There was no way I could stay out that late and be functional at work the next day, so I stayed home.

Plenty of nights, I wandered our stylish, spacious apartment, wondering why I felt more alone in a relationship than before I'd met Alec. And why I fell asleep alone more nights than in the arms of my boyfriend.

When I questioned him on it, he assured me it was just temporary. He was working so hard to get a promotion, and he was just going out so much to take advantage of networking opportunities. He didn't want to be away from me, but he had no choice. In the end, I felt terrible for not being more supportive of him and his career. Still, doubts and questions nagged at me whenever we were apart.

The answer came about a year into living together when I walked in on him fucking a college student.

That day, I'd had a violent headache that had come out of nowhere. They were rare for me, but a combination of allergies, a storm rolling in, and some major stress at work had combined to make me miserable. Dr. Edward Washburn, my boss, had been kind enough to cover for me, so I'd gone home, planning to crawl into bed and sleep it off.

Instead, I'd found my boyfriend in bed with someone else.

I unlocked the front door and pushed it open, intent on getting horizontal as soon as possible. The sound of voices made me pause in the hallway.

Is that moaning? *I shook my head in annoyance—making another wave of pain wash over me—and wondered if Alec had left porn playing that morning or come home during lunch to watch it and jerk off.*

"Alec?" I called out as I pushed open the bedroom door, fully expecting to see an empty room or my boyfriend naked in bed.

I was right on the latter part, but he certainly wasn't alone. At first, all I could see was two people in profile.

"Yeah, you like that, do you?" Alec growled. A hot flush rose in my body as the sight in front of me assaulted my brain. Alec's strong hands gripped a strange man's hips and a look of intense concentration hardened his face. His abs contracted and expanded as his hips slapped against the round ass of someone. Someone who definitely wasn't me.

I let out a strangled sound of disbelief. They both turned to look at me. For some reason, I focused on the stranger rather than Alec. Maybe it was curiosity. Or maybe I just couldn't bear to look at my boyfriend. They both froze as I catalogued everything. The guy Alec was fucking was young. Young enough that I had a flash of concern but a tattoo on his bicep made me hopeful he was at least eighteen. He was blond and handsome. Muscular.

And then he smiled at me. "Hey, I didn't know we were having company, Alec. Fuck, I'd love to get spit-roasted." The world around me swam as my vision went white with rage.

"Get. Out," I said hoarsely.

"Who the fuck are you?"

"I live here," I snarled. "I don't know who you are, and frankly, I don't care. But my name is on the lease, and I don't want you here. Get out or I will call the police."

He gave me a disgruntled look and uncoupled from Alec, who still hadn't moved. The stranger dressed in silence while Alec and I stared at each other, but he left with a parting, "Call me, Alec!" that made my blood boil.

"I guess I know why you've lost interest in sex with me," I sneered at Alec once the apartment door closed. Either the sound or my words seemed to snap Alec out of the daze he'd been in.

"Come on, Chris, you're overreacting," Alec said, holding placating hands up at me.

"Overreacting?" My voice rose. "Are you fucking kidding me? I swear to God, if you weren't wearing a condom I will ..." I didn't know what I'd do, but the thought enraged me. If he'd cheated on me and put my health in jeopardy, I was going to lose my shit.

Alec tore a used condom off and held it up before he tossed it in the trash beside the bed with a wet splat. "I used a goddamn condom. I'm not an idiot."

"Really?" I laughed hollowly. "Because you're fucking someone other than me, in our bed, in the middle of the day. Not the brightest move you've ever made."

Alec scowled as he got off the bed. "You're never home in the middle of the day. What are you doing here, anyway?"

"Don't turn this around on me!" I wasn't about to justify why I'd come home, although the throbbing headache that had sent me home had only increased with my anger. "What the fuck were you doing with that guy?" I spat.

Alec rolled his eyes. "Come on, Chris. Our relationship has gotten pretty stale. I was just looking to spice things up a bit."

"And you didn't bother to mention this to me?" I shook my head in disbelief. "No, fuck that. Spicing things up is buying a vibrating cock ring or giving each other blowjobs in a public place."

Alec's eyes lit up. "I didn't know you were into public stuff."

"I'm not! And I sure as hell am not going to be after this! And fuck you, Alec. Cheating on me isn't spicing things up. It's just cheating. How long has this been going on?"

"With this guy?"

"I don't know. With anyone? How many random guys have you been nailing behind my back?"

When Alec paused like he was trying to remember, I felt my stomach drop. Jesus Christ. One of my first priorities was a full-panel STI screening. Because clearly, it had been more than the one guy. Alec and I had stopped using condoms the year before, and who knew if Alec had been using condoms every time during these affairs. It was a small consolation that he and I had hardly had sex in months.

"Don't answer that. I don't want to know." A wave of fatigue washed over me

as I walked over to the closet to grab an overnight bag.

"What are you doing?" Alec caught my arm, and I realized he was still naked. Clearly, he didn't feel an ounce of shame.

"Leaving, Alec," I said simply. "I'm done."

"We're the perfect couple, Chris. We have the perfect life. This means nothing to me."

Alec had pleaded and cajoled, then tried flattering me, but I'd finally seen through the charming veneer and realized how little was underneath.

I'd packed enough for a few days, gone to my parents' house, and crashed. After sleeping for the better part of a day, I dragged myself out of bed and called Cal and Dave. They went with me to the apartment to get my personal belongings. I'd wanted the buffer, but Alec hadn't even been there. It left me strangely disappointed. A good portion of me wanted to see Cal punch him in the face.

I left most of the furniture there. I hadn't wanted to bring any more baggage with me than was strictly necessary. I stayed at my parents' place for a few weeks while I searched for a new apartment, and I argued on the phone with Alec until he finally agreed to let me get out of the lease for the Pearl District place. I found an apartment that was generic but close to the hospital, furnished it with the basics, and threw myself into work.

I looked around the room now. The carpet was neutral, the couch was comfortable but nothing exciting to look at, and the end tables and coffee tables were a dime a dozen. The walls would have been empty if not for Cal staging an intervention and bringing over some framed photos he'd taken of the city we lived in and the places we'd visited together. I looked at them now, realizing that apart from them and a couple of potted plants my mother had given me, it was completely and utterly soulless.

It looked less personal than a model unit. I hated it. I hated everything about what my life had become after the breakup with Alec.

I had few friends and almost no social life. I'd poured all my time and energy into my career and staying healthy and fit. They were important to me, but they left me feeling a bit hollow.

I hadn't dated at all. I'd been so starved for touch and connection that'd I'd fucked a guy I didn't know or like.

I could practically see my brother shaking his head at me. *"Pretty pathetic, man," he'd tease me.*

"I know, Cal. I know," I whispered aloud.

I checked on my parents later that day. They tried to be cheerful when we spoke, but I could hear the helpless weariness in their voices. Talking with them was especially difficult because of the secrets I carried now. In addition to the guilt over what I'd done with Elliot, I felt like I had to censor myself, watch everything I said very carefully. It made me dread talking to them, but on Sunday morning, when I returned from running errands, I forced myself to call my mother. I felt guilty that it was a chore when it was something I typically looked forward to.

After we made small-talk for a while, she asked me if I would come to dinner that evening. "Unless you have other plans, we'd love to have you there." I could hear her struggling to keep her voice light and cheerful.

I stifled a sigh. Of course, I wanted to be there for them, and normally, I looked forward to the traditional Sunday dinners, but I knew it would be difficult this time. I didn't have the energy to call up friends and be social, so the only other alternative was sitting at home alone, which didn't appeal either.

"Sure, Mom." I tried to force some cheer into my own voice. "I'll be there."

When I arrived the following day, my mother greeted me with a hug, and my father offered me a drink as soon as we were in the living room. "Scotch, C.J.?"

"No thanks," I said quietly. I hadn't had a drink since the night of Cal's funeral. The thought of it made me vaguely sick. I wasn't sure if it was because of how much I'd drunk that night or what I'd done after.

He topped off his own glass, and I saw my mother's lips tighten. The only time I'd really seen them fight was after my grandfather's death when my father started drinking too much.

Our parents had always been honest with Cal and me about Dad's alcoholism. They'd sat down and had frank discussions with us numerous times, especially once we each reached high school and started going out with friends. They hadn't gone into major detail, but they'd never sugarcoated what a toll it had taken on them or their relationship. Cal had little to no direct memories of my father's heavy drinking at all. But I had been old enough to remember pieces of it. And it had left its emotional scars.

Looking back, I could see little cracks in my parents' marriage that his excessive drinking had caused. But over the years, it seemed like they mended and healed. They seemed close again, loving. I'd often catch them kissing in the hallway and laughing quietly as they curled up by the fireplace or watched a movie. They seemed to be a happy, loving couple. The kind I wanted to emulate.

As far as I knew, other than Edward Washburn—a family friend and my boss—no one outside of the family ever knew about my father's alcoholism.

For years, my father told people he'd cut back on drinking because of his heath. As a physician and someone who exercised religiously, it was plausible. No one appeared to question it. So, when Cal was out of high school, and our father started drinking socially again, no one seemed concerned.

I'd occasionally catch my mother or Ed watching him out of the corner of their eyes. But his drinking didn't become problematic. Eventually, even they seemed to relax, convinced he had a handle on himself. He seemed to have no trouble limiting himself to a glass of wine with dinner or a drink while out with friends. We'd all deluded ourselves into believing he had it under control.

The sick, sinking of my stomach made me wonder if we'd all been wrong. Was it all happening again? Had my father crossed a line from casual use to dependency trying to cope with Cal's death?

I had no idea how to broach the subject with him or my mother, or if I even should.

"Rain's really coming down out there," my father said, peering out the window at the sodden yard. Holding the cut-crystal glass filled with expensive Scotch and wearing a tailored cashmere sweater, he looked every inch the successful doctor he was. But I'd never seen him look so haunted and haggard.

"How was the traffic?" my mother asked me from where she sat on the ivory-hued sofa. Her color was better than the last time I'd seen her, but she still looked drained.

"Oh, the usual. There was an accident on the 217 so I had to detour around it." I turned my back to the fireplace. They had a fire lit, and the heat of the flames felt good. The rain had left my clothes a bit damp, and I was grateful for the fire that chased away some of the cold in my bones. Too bad it couldn't as easily chase away the emotional fatigue I felt.

"I just read an article saying that Portland ranks up there with D.C. and Chicago in terms of traffic congestion," my father said. He took a seat in the chair near me.

"Really? I'm surprised. I would have thought the MAX train and the number of people who bicycle to work would help."

He shook his head. "No, it's the reverse commuters who are living in Portland but working in Hillsborough and Washington counties who are the problem."

"Huh." I knew we were all trying to put on a brave face as we talked about inconsequential things: the weather, how terrible traffic had been, anything but the topic that loomed over everything else.

The sound of a timer beeping drew our attention. "Oh, I should get that," my mother said as she stood. "Dinner will be on the table in about ten minutes."

She disappeared through the doorway, and my father and I followed her more slowly.

"Have you been in to work yet?" I asked him.

He nodded. "Your mom and I went in for a few hours yesterday and took care of a few urgent issues demanding our attention, but thankfully, Ellen and Jonathon have everything else running smoothly."

"Good."

My mother had begun her career as a pediatric nurse. For most of my life, she had worked as a nurse at my father's practice, eventually running it. A few years ago, they'd hired an office manager named Ellen. My mom had gradually handed over more responsibility to her in the past few years as she transitioned to a part-time position in order to volunteer at a low-income clinic downtown.

Dr. Jonathon Weiss had come to the practice as my father's junior partner when I decided not to join his pediatric clinic staff. I'd felt guilty about not following in my father's footsteps for a long time. But knowing how well Dr. Weiss fit in was a relief.

"I'll be glad to work next week," he said with a sigh. "It'll be a good distraction. There's only so much sitting at home and grieving I can do."

I glanced at the tumbler of Scotch, now half-full. *Grieving or drinking?* I wondered, but I couldn't form the words. Cal's secrets weighed heavily on my tongue, and I felt like an enormous fraud. What right did I have to judge the way he was coping? *I got plastered and slept with Cal's boyfriend,* I thought viciously.

I was a monster and a hypocrite.

I paused when I reached the dining room. It still held a large, gleaming wood table with upholstered chairs. Two antique sideboards that had been passed down through the generations were situated on opposite sides of the table.

My gaze drifted to the empty chair where Cal always sat. When I noticed it had no place setting in front of it, pain gripped my heart like a vice. My breathing went shallow as I struggled to hold back the flood of emotions.

My father stepped up behind me and put his hand on my shoulder. "That's going to take some getting used to, isn't it?" he said quietly.

"Yes," I choked out. It wasn't like Cal made it to dinner every week. When he traveled, we'd go weeks or months without seeing him, but knowing he was never coming back was a bitter pill to swallow.

My father squeezed my shoulder and sighed. "Your mother broke down in tears when she went to set the table, and I felt so helpless. I can't make this any easier for her, or any of us for that matter. I don't know what to do to help."

"I know. I don't either."

"Christopher, will you come grab the platter?" my mother called from the kitchen.

"Yes," we both answered out of habit, and she replied, "No, no, not you, C.J. Your dad."

He chuckled as he turned to go into the kitchen, and I managed a half-hearted smile. Growing up, sometimes I'd wished they'd named me something totally different like Adam or Patrick. Anything but Christopher John Allen Junior. But it was part of the family legacy my father hoped to build.

I walked to the sideboard and poured myself red wine from the bottle my mother had already opened. It didn't appeal, but since I customarily had a glass with dinner, it would seem more unusual if I didn't today. The last thing I wanted was more questions.

I avoided the framed photos on one sideboard. At least half of them were of Cal, and I couldn't bear to look him in the eye—even in a photo—knowing what I'd done. When my parents came in the room, I hurried to take one of the dishes from my mother's hands, grateful to be of use.

"Dinner looks great," I told her, and she gave me a wan smile. It was one of Cal's favorite meals—roast pork loin, mashed potatoes, and homemade rolls—but I chose not to comment. What would it have done but hurt us all more?

In silence, the three of us took our seats at the table and began eating. We tried to carry on like it was any other dinner, but we were all quiet and a little listless, conscious of the empty chair on one side of the table as we passed the bowl of green beans and asked for the butter.

As often as we were able, Cal and I had gone to these family dinners. Sometimes, it was just one or the other of us, but by and large, we did our best to be there. For a long while, Alec had come on a regular basis, and even Cal had brought a few girls home over the years. I suddenly pictured Elliot sitting across the table and grimaced. I stared at Cal's empty chair, trying to picture the two of them together, holding hands, being affectionate like Alec—*Dickface*, I reminded myself—and I had been. I couldn't imagine it, couldn't quite see them in such a domestic situation, and I wondered if it was the idea of Cal being settled down or Elliot as his partner that threw me.

Or was it that, for the briefest second, I had pictured *myself* with Elliot rather than my brother? The thought sent an uncomfortable shiver down my spine and made guilt and shame burn within me. When my mother called me by my name, I jerked my head up, startled. "What?"

"How are you doing, sweetheart?"

"Fine," I lied. Her gaze searched my face, and a little furrow appeared on her forehead. It was clear she didn't believe me, but she didn't push it. We were all hanging on by a thread.

"Everyone at the office has been so nice," she said with a tremulous smile. "So many of them showed up for the funeral, and they sent flowers and a note. You should see the pile of cards we've received from patients."

My father just nodded, pushing at an uneaten slice of pork on his plate. I forced a smile onto my face and responded, "That is nice." Everyone there knew Cal and me, and I wasn't surprised that they had rallied around my parents.

"When do you go back to work, C.J.?" my mother asked.

"Tomorrow."

"Are you sure that's not too soon?" she asked with a worried frown.

"No, I need to get back. I'm going stir-crazy, to be honest. It'll be better if I can keep myself occupied."

"You've always been so dedicated to your work. So focused." She set down her fork and stared at me, her eyes brimming with tears. "Sometimes, I don't think we told you enough how proud we are of you. I know everyone was drawn to Cal, and he got a lot of attention, but I hope you know how proud of you we are."

"Of course," I choked out.

My thoughts were bleak. *You wouldn't be if you knew what I'd done.*

Chapter Five

I'd never been so grateful to return to work as I was on Monday. I knew getting back into a routine was the only thing that would keep me from thinking too much and letting myself stew in the grief and guilt I carried with me now.

I pulled my car into the parking structure at the east campus of Portland Medical Center and waved at Bob, the white-haired security guard on duty. He'd been working at the hospital for thirty-plus years, and it was a relief to see a friendly face. When the gate arm lifted, I eased forward, following the winding route to the top of the structure. I let out a sigh of a relief as I pulled into the spot marked with my name. The familiarity loosened a fraction of the tension within me.

My ID badge let me into the staff-only stairwell, and I jogged down the stairs to the first floor. The sliding glass doors opened with a hiss. I strode forward but as soon as I crossed the threshold, I felt the strangest sense of vertigo. Suddenly light-headed, I blinked and rubbed my head, trying to clear it. I closed my eyes and leaned against the wall in the corridor to steady myself. For a moment, I heard the whoosh of the heart-lung machine and saw my brother's face, bruised and cut, against the stark white sheets.

I blew out the breath I'd been holding in a harsh rush of air and straightened, forcing my suddenly leaden feet to move forward. Despite the myth that hospitals smelled like sickness and death, to me, Portland Medical Center's halls always smelled faintly of citrus-scented floor cleaner and coffee. I found it comforting.

Now, the scent made me flinch as I fought back the onslaught of memories of Cal's brief hospital stay. Cal hadn't even been at the east campus, but at the main campus near downtown. It was ridiculous that I was reacting so strongly to a *scent*.

Get it together, Chris, I sternly lectured myself.

But my limbs felt heavy and uncooperative as I moved down the hall toward my office. I nodded and smiled at the familiar faces I passed, but I moved on autopilot.

"Welcome back, Dr. Allen," Sherri said as I walked through the doors of the hospice facility. Sherri had been working as a receptionist at the hospital for more years than I'd been alive. She was a round, motherly sort of lady, with brassy reddish blonde hair that was no more natural than the startlingly red nails she always sported. Her brisk efficiency was legendary among the hospital staff, however, and the patients always appreciated her warm demeanor.

"Thanks, Sherri." I pasted another fake smile on my face as I walked past her desk.

"Oh, wait, Doctor. The staff signed a card and got this plant for you."

Lost in my thoughts, it took time for her words to register, and I stopped in my tracks. "Hmm?"

She handed me an envelope and a potted fern, and I took them automatically, fumbling to form words of thanks. "Tell—tell everyone I said thank you. That was … very kind."

Why is this so difficult? I had been looking forward to getting back to work, and now, the hospital was the last place I wanted to be. I'd thought it would distract me from thinking about Cal, but instead, it was bringing back memories I'd sooner forget.

I veered right down the hall that led to the staff offices, then unlocked the door to mine. I flipped on the light and closed the door behind with me with a sigh. I felt a terrible sense of guilt as I carried the fern into my office and set it on the window ledge behind my desk. I knew many people from the hospital had been at the funeral home visitation or at the funeral itself, but now I couldn't recollect who they were. I absently set my leather messenger bag down and took a seat at my desk.

I turned my attention to the card in my hand. It was like most sympathy cards, full of platitudes and overly sentimental, but I deeply appreciated the intent behind it. I leaned back in my chair as I read through the handwritten messages that colleagues had left. I knew some of them well, others less so, but the heartfelt condolences were moving. I knew how difficult it was to offer condolences to someone who'd lost a family member; no words could ever adequately convey true feelings. Compared to most of them, I was relatively new to the team, and the fact that my co-workers and colleagues cared enough to reach out touched me.

I swiveled in my chair to face the window behind the desk and propped the card on the windowsill beside the fern. I ran my fingertips across the soft green fronds and stared out the window. It was cold today, sleeting, and the view out my window was dismal under the best of circumstances. My office overlooked the corner of the building and an industrial-size air conditioning unit. The bit of greenery would be nice to get me through the rest of the winter. The clouds and rain had been heavy this winter, even for Portland.

As I swiveled back to face my desk, I caught a glimpse of a framed picture of my family and paused. I reached out to pick it up. A few years back, Cal, my parents, and I had all gone to Seattle for a cousin's wedding. During a whale watching tour, my mother had asked another passenger on the trip to take a photo of the four of us.

"Get in here close," my mother urged over the sound of the boat's engine and wind as we lined up against the railing. "Come on, Christopher, you too."

My father grumbled a little under his breath, but he scooted in, kissing my mom on the cheek when she shot him a fondly exasperated look.

He turned it into a kiss on the lips, and she giggled, quickly kissed him back, then faced the camera. Her face was already pink from the salty breeze, but I thought it became a little brighter after that. They'd been married for more than thirty-five years and yet they sometimes acted like newlyweds. "Sorry about that," she said with a laugh. "Got a little distracted."

I stood on her other side, and she wrapped an arm around my waist, pulling me in closer. "Come on, C.J. You too, Cal."

"I'm here. I'm here," Cal said. He flung an arm around my shoulder, splattering water droplets everywhere. I was glad I had the hood of my rain slicker up. It had been a miserably dreary and rainy day, but everyone else was in high spirits. All of us loved being out on the water. Usually, I would have been every bit as happy to spend the day on the boat—shitty weather or not— but my parents' affection reminded me that I was on vacation without my partner. I shouldn't have been. Alec had been invited, but he'd turned it down. He claimed it was work, but I wasn't entirely convinced. He had been working

a lot of hours lately—hardly unusual for an up-and-coming architect—but I had a growing suspicion that it had more to do with not wanting to come home to me. Unfortunately, we seemed to be growing further and further apart, and I had no idea how to fix that.

"Are you still alive in there, C.J.?" Cal yelled in my ear. "I can't believe you missed the whale!"

I snapped out of the trance I'd been in and craned my neck around, but I saw nothing but the choppy steel gray waves and frothy whitecaps. "Whale? Where?" My mother let out an exasperated laugh. "There was no whale. Damn it, Cal, stop teasing your brother. Sometimes, I would swear you were still children, not grown men."

"You asshole," I said with a laugh as I grabbed my brother around the waist and hauled him closer. "You know how much I wanted to see one."

The woman holding Cal's camera waved at us. "Would you still like a picture?"

"Yes, yes, I'm so sorry about that!" my mother said. "Everyone, put your hoods down so we'll be able to see your beautiful faces. And at least try *to focus, please!"*

"Say whale!" Cal yelled after we followed her instructions. I grinned at the camera, simultaneously annoyed at my brother for his childish teasing and relieved that he'd pulled me out of the melancholy path my mind had been wandering down.

He had always known when I was getting lost in my thoughts and was quickly able to snap me out of it. *What would I ever do without him?*

But here I was, without Cal now. And somehow, I was going to have to figure out how to cope. I looked down at the photo again, and I was struck by how alike my brother and I looked in it. I was an inch or so shorter, my hair neater and darker than Cal's sun-streaked medium brown. We both had hazel eyes; mine had tended toward brown while his often appeared greener. But despite the differences in our build and my more angular face, our features clearly marked us as brothers. Over the years, people had often commented on the similarities, and I knew that, at first glance, it was easy to confuse us.

My stomach tightened, wondering if that had been part of what drew Elliot to me. Had he been drunk enough to confuse me with Cal on some level? I couldn't decide if that made it better or worse. And what was *my* excuse? Sickened by my actions, I stared down at the photo of our family, guilt twisting my stomach.

I was still staring at the photo when I heard a quiet knock on my door. "Come in," I called out as I set the frame down. I turned and was unsurprised when I saw my mentor poke his head in the door.

Dr. Edward Washburn had been a friend and mentor to me and, in many ways, was another father figure. He was one of the primary reasons I'd chosen to go into psychiatry with a subspecialty in hospice and palliative medicine. He was one of the pioneers in the field, and he'd inspired me to join him.

Ed smiled warmly, blue eyes crinkling at the corners as he looked me over with an assessing glance. "How are you doing, Chris?"

I shrugged and gestured for him to come in. "Hanging in there, I suppose." That was my pat answer these days. I didn't know what else to say.

Ed was in his sixties, with nearly snow-white hair. He was still fit and trim from a lifetime of swimming and golf, and his attractive features were enhanced by his warm, caring manner. He had the kind of demeanor patients trusted and was one of the most dedicated doctors I'd ever met. Right now, he was looking at me like he looked at his dying patients. He closed the door, crossing the room as I slipped out from behind the desk to greet him with a hug. He pulled back and frowned. "Don't bullshit me, Chris. We've known each other too long for you to do that."

I sighed heavily. "Under the circumstances, I'm doing the best I can."

He patted my shoulder before squeezing gently. "You seemed pretty out of it at the funeral and after."

I looked at him, startled. "You were there? I mean, of course you must have been, but why don't I remember seeing you?"

"Yes, I was there. Your father is my best friend, and you and Cal are my godsons." Ed shook his head and sank into a chair while I followed suit. "I wanted to be there for all of you."

"Jesus, I'm sorry. Did I at least acknowledge you?"

"You did." His smile was reassuring. "Dissociating to a certain extent during a stressful event is normal, Chris. I was like that at my mother's funeral. I showed up, I did what I was supposed to, and after, I couldn't remember half of it. It's a coping technique. You know that."

"I *do* know that, I just ..." I shook my head slowly. "I guess I didn't realize how out of it I really was."

"Have you had any problem with dissociation since?"

I thought about it for a moment. As much as I'd like to find excuses for my behavior with Elliot, it wasn't the case. No matter how much grief had made the funeral a blur, I couldn't blame it for what I'd chosen to do after. At the time, I'd wanted Elliot, and no amount of grief or alcohol would excuse it. "No."

Ed smiled reassuringly. "Then I wouldn't worry about it, son."

"It's just all so overwhelming. I don't know how to cope." I pointed to the overflowing bookshelf across the room. "How many books about death and grieving have I read to learn how to help our patients? How many lectures have I attended on the subject? And when it comes to my own life, none of it applies."

Ed settled back into his chair. "Chris, I know you want to tackle this like you do your work, but you can't. Grieving your brother's death will take time. You can't manage your pain; you must let yourself experience it as it comes to you. You'll have days where it's easier and days where it hurts so much you won't want to get out of bed. That's normal." I swallowed hard, knowing he was right. I'd told patients and their loved ones the same. "Lean on your friends, your family, all of the people who care about you, Chris. That's the best way to deal with it."

"Thank you, Ed."

"There are some wonderful grief counselors I can put you in contact with if you'd like—I can even recommend someone outside of Portland Medical Center if you'd prefer."

"I think I'll see how I do on my own for a while."

"Of course. And you can come to me if you need to talk. Any time, son. I hope you know that."

"I do, and I appreciate it." I looked down at my hands, blinking back tears. "You have no idea how much."

Ed gave me time to compose myself, then cleared his throat. "Now, are you up to doing some work today? There's no shame if you need a little more time off."

"I want to work," I said firmly.

He smiled at me. "Then I think I better get you up to speed on your patients."

Ed and I went through them one by one, discussing progress and approach until I was sure I knew where everyone stood.

Ed left my office with a hug and a stern reminder to call him if I ever needed it. I agreed that I would. As I turned to sit in my chair again, I caught another glimpse of the family picture on the windowsill, and my throat closed. For a short while, I'd thought about something other than Cal, but the grief and regret returned with a vengeance. Ed had been whole-heartedly sincere in his offer to let me open up about Cal's death to him, but I'd be hard-pressed to do that.

When I'd chosen Ed's specialty over my father's, it had been like stepping into the protective circle of an uncle. He'd made no bones about our connection when I put in for the fellowship position here at PMC and then been hired into a full-time staff position. His support had carried major influence. I'd earned my place here through grueling years of work and a resume that spoke for itself, but Ed's influence had helped sway the decision. He was too close to the family for me to open up to about the secrets I carried. I'd have to carry the burden alone. And maybe after what I'd done, I deserved it.

With a heavy sigh, I took a seat at my desk and logged into my computer.

Thankfully, as soon as I got to work, the rest of the world disappeared. I worked through lunch, using the single-minded determination that had gotten me through med school and my psychiatric residency to focus. There were patients to attend to and an email inbox that would take hours to clear out. I had never been more grateful.

I had just made it home from work when I got a call from Dave. I greeted him with some trepidation, wondering how much he remembered from the night at *The Tap*, and if he'd realized that Elliot and I had done more than share a ride on the way home. I'd been hesitant to call Dave for that reason.

"How are you doing, Chris?" he asked. I was relieved to hear nothing but warm concern in his tone.

I sighed, unknotted my tie, and dropped it on the bed. "Hanging in there, I guess. It's been rough. You?"

"About the same." His voice was hoarse and choked. He cleared his throat. "Sorry I didn't call sooner. Things have been out of control at work."

Dave worked as a junior editor for the Associated Press in investigative reporting at the Portland office. When big stories hit, he ran himself ragged.

"Don't worry about it," I reassured him as I worked the top two buttons loose on my shirt. I was embarrassed by the way I'd let Dave get to me that night. I needed his friendship, not to get wrapped up in some stupid attraction that would never be returned. How lonely was I that I had let myself get caught up in his spell that night? "I know your job gets crazy."

"Yeah, you know the drill, huge story broke and I was up to my eyeballs in fact checking." He sounded completely spent. "In this case, it was nice; took my mind off things."

"I bet. I was glad to go back to work today," I admitted, wandering into the kitchen to figure out what I wanted for dinner.

"So how bad was your hangover on Friday?" he asked.

I let out a pained sound. "I don't want to talk about it."

Dave chuckled. "Me either. I am glad you came though."

I deeply regretted what happened with Elliot, but I was glad I'd gone to the bar that night. The camaraderie and love for Cal was something I wouldn't have wanted to miss. "Yeah, I am too," I finally said.

"So, you ... you know about Cal and Elliot right?" Dave asked, sounding apprehensive. Surprise made me lose my grip, and I dropped the bag of rice in my hand. It landed on the counter with a thud. I placed it back on the shelf carefully and stepped away.

"Know that they were a couple? Yeah. I saw Elliot at the funeral, and then he was there at my parents' house. He told me then." My heart hammered too fast in my chest as I struggled not to panic. Just thinking about Elliot sent me into a tailspin.

"I'm so fucking sorry, Chris. I wanted to tell you about what was going on. Hell, I argued with Cal about keeping it a secret, especially from you."

I sighed heavily as I leaned back against the counter. "It's been pretty rough. The fact that he didn't feel like he could be open with me …"

"I know." Dave's tone was understanding. "He only told me a few months ago, and he mentioned how conflicted he was about not telling you."

"I'm just trying to understand it all."

"If you want to get together some time soon, I'm happy to tell you what I know. I loved Cal, but I'm not going to keep secrets from you now that he's dead." Dave's voice hitched at the end, as if saying Cal was dead aloud was still hard for him. I couldn't blame him. It was for me too.

"Thank you. I'd like that." I hesitated before asking the other question that had been lingering in my mind. "How well do you know Elliot?"

"Not very well," Dave admitted. "I knew him through Cal, and only for a few months. I think I met him in October—no, maybe November. He was hard to get to know. Quiet, reserved. Very intense. It always seemed like there was a lot going on in his head that he didn't speak aloud. I think he was good for Cal though. He settled Cal a little bit at least."

"Well, anyone who managed to get Cal into a relationship obviously settled him," I pointed out.

"Yeah, true." Dave's laugh was rueful. "I was convinced it was a sign of the pending apocalypse."

"Yeah. That sounds about right." I let out a chuckle, but quickly sobered. "I just wish Cal had trusted me. I know our parents wanted grandkids, but even if they were miffed for a while, I have to believe they would have supported Cal. No matter *who* he dated. Hell, my mom probably would have thrown a party just to celebrate Cal being committed to anyone for more than a month."

"I agree." Dave hesitated. "You know, I think his secrecy was about a lot more than just his relationship with Elliot. Cal was going through a bit of a crisis, trying to figure out who he was and what he wanted to do with his life, if that helps at all."

I mulled that thought over, then sighed. "It gives me a clearer picture of Cal I guess, but no, it doesn't really help. It's eating me alive that he didn't discuss any of this with me."

"I know." Dave blew out a breath. "I'm sorry I'm making this worse."

"No, I appreciate the insight into Cal. No matter how painful this is, I need to know who my brother really was." A thought occurred to me, something I'd been wondering about for a while. "How old is Elliot? He looks younger than us, but I wasn't quite sure."

"Twenty-three or twenty-four, I think," Dave said. "He seems pretty mature for his age. Honestly, I'd say Cal was the more immature of the two. Obviously, meeting Elliot had a huge impact on Cal's life."

"Yeah, I'm starting to see that," I said thickly.

"I wish I could say something to make this easier," Dave replied.

I let out a regretful laugh. "Yeah, me too."

We talked for a while longer and made tentative plans to get together for dinner sometime in the next few weeks. I simultaneously felt better and worse after I hung up the phone. Talking to Dave was good, and it was nice having another view of Cal and Elliot's relationship, but the fact that Cal had told his friend and hadn't told me hurt deeply.

The conversation made me lose my appetite, and I left the kitchen after I hung up with Dave. I changed into comfortable clothes and spent the evening screwing around on my computer and watching TV, but I felt listless and bored.

I went to bed early and tossed and turned, the sheets sweaty and tangled by the time I awoke, dreams of Cal and my childhood so real in my mind that I awoke believing my brother was still alive.

Chapter Six

The following morning, I fixed my usual bowl of yogurt. I ate it while I scrolled news articles on my phone, but when it chimed with a text, I jerked in surprise, sending granola and a blueberry flying across the table. I nearly dropped my phone when I read the message, my heart slamming in my chest as I realized who the unknown number belonged to.

Can we meet? -Elliot

My mouth was dry and my hands trembled a little as I responded with, *Why? I thought you didn't want any contact with me.*

No response came for a long time. *There's something of your brother's you need to see.*

I stared at the message in astonishment for a few minutes, then shook my head at its cryptic nature. I knew I should respond, but I couldn't quite bring myself to do so. Instead, I dumped out the remainder of my food, washed the dishes, and dressed.

Elliot's message lingered in the back of my mind and vied for attention as I met with patients. But that afternoon, a new patient quickly took precedence. Ed had already briefed me on her condition, but I read through her case files more thoroughly. It was rare for us to get pediatric patients, but it happened occasionally. Hazel Buchanan was seventeen and had been battling acute lymphoblastic leukemia for almost three years. This was a recurrence. She'd originally been diagnosed when she was just five. Chemotherapy was the treatment of choice for this particular cancer. After the first time she was diagnosed, her cancer went into remission, but this second time, the treatment had failed to work. A bone marrow transplant was her last option. Her entire family had been tested and an older cousin was an excellent match.

After her bone marrow had been killed off with radiation, the transplant had taken place. The donor stem cells had been introduced, and the procedure itself had gone through without a hitch, but in the days that followed, her symptoms showed that she had experienced graft failure. The transplanted cells hadn't begun producing new cells as planned.

It was a devastating blow to her and her family. It happened in fewer than 5% of patients. Unfortunately, Hazel was one of the unlucky ones. Sometimes, a second transplant could be done, but in this case, Hazel's body was too weak to handle it. An infection, on top of blood loss, had ruled her out as a candidate.

The oncology team had broken the news that Hazel had run out of options, and that it was time for her to transition to hospice. She'd been transported straight from the oncology floor of the main hospital downtown to the hospice facility here at the east campus.

Now it was my job to help her prepare for her death.

It was clear that Hazel was a fighter, no doubt about it, but when I walked into her room, my heart nearly broke. Chronologically, she was nearly an adult, but she looked closer to twelve or thirteen. Her dark eyes were too large in her narrow face, and her thin arms were bruised from repeated IV drips and blood draws. She had a nasal cannula for oxygen and wore a brightly colored scarf to cover her bald head. She had been clutching a stuffed animal, which she furtively tucked out of the way as I used some hand sanitizer from the dispenser by the door.

I smiled warmly at her as I approached her bed, though she couldn't see my mouth behind the mask I wore to protect her from further infection. In hospice, everyone on staff still used sterile procedures. Not only to protect themselves from patients with infectious diseases, but to give our patients the best quality of life possible, however short it was.

"Hi, Hazel," I said softly. "I'm Dr. Christopher Allen. If you'd like, you can call me Chris."

She nodded and managed a weak smile.

Hazel's parents stood as I greeted them. They were both relatively young, in their late-thirties at the most. Her father, Ryan, reached out to shake my hand. Strain and exhaustion made his handsome face look haggard, and his blond hair stood on end like he'd been running his hands through it. Lissa looked equally sorrowful, but I could see that Hazel would probably have looked just like Lissa if given the chance to grow up.

I gave her parents a reassuring smile as well. "I know the nurse probably told you'd I'd be stopping by today, but I'm a psychiatrist here at the hospice center. I came here to introduce myself and see if there's anything I can do to help you. If you need to vent or you have questions, that's what I'm here for. We can talk about anything you'd like. I won't be here for very long today, but I'd like a chance to get to know you, Hazel, if you're willing to share a little about yourself with me."

Hazel shot me a wary glance but nodded. "Okay."

I looked at her parents. "If you and Hazel are all comfortable with it, I'd like to speak to her alone for a few minutes."

They glanced at each other, then their daughter, seeming to speak to each other without words.

"It's fine," Hazel said. "Go get coffee or a slice of cake or something." She got a melancholy look on her face. "The double chocolate fudge cake here is pretty good."

"Do you want me to bring you some?" Lissa asked eagerly. When Hazel shook her head with a sad smile, Lissa's hopeful expression fell.

"Not hungry, Mom."

"Okay, sweetie." Lissa smoothed a hand over Hazel's scarf-covered head. "We'll be back in a little bit. You let the doctor know if you need anything."

"I will."

When they left, I gestured to the seat beside the bed. "May I sit?"

"Sure." Her gaze, while not hostile, was slightly wary.

"So, double chocolate fudge cake, huh?" I asked. "I don't think I've tried that one."

"Yeah. It used to be my favorite. I remember it being really good, but I can't taste anything anymore."

"You have ageusia? Loss—"

"—of taste? Yeah," she answered. "It sucks."

"Yeah, it does. It's a really crappy side effect of the chemo. It's not always permanent though. It may improve."

She shrugged one thin shoulder. "Does it matter anymore? Even if it comes back, I won't be around for long. I'm not going to get a second transplant. And without it, I'm not going to get better," she said flatly.

It was a crushing realization for a seventeen-year-old to come to. "I know."

"It's not *fair*," she burst out. "You know?"

"No, it isn't."

"There's just so much I wanted to do."

"Can you tell me a little about that?"

"About what I wanted to do?"

I nodded.

"Hand me that purple journal." She pointed at a stack of books on the nightstand. Hospice encouraged patients to decorate their rooms like they were at home, and Hazel's was cheerfully strewn with Mylar balloons and what looked like a travel collage poster on one wall. It looked more like a teenage girl's bedroom rather than a hospital room. "Um, please," she tacked on with a small, sheepish smile.

I retrieved it, but when I went to hand it to her, she shook her head. "You can look."

I flipped the cover open to see brightly colored lettering stating: "Hazel's Bucket List."

I flipped to the next page to see a neatly written list, and I scanned the first few items.

Swim with turtles
Cliff diving
Stand on the equator
Kiss a boy
Have a picnic in Central Park
Find the love of my life
Become a marine biologist

I felt a sharp jab of familiar pain. Cal had made something similar. He'd been about Hazel's age when he compiled a list of all the things he wanted to do in his life, although he'd been perfectly healthy at the time. He'd done it just for the fun of it because he thrived on travel and new experiences. The world had so much to offer, and he didn't want to miss out on any of it. He'd done more than most other twenty-eight-year-olds, but he hadn't even come close to completing his list.

I glanced at the stuffed turtle beside her. She hadn't managed to tuck it away completely out of sight. "You like turtles, huh?"

Hazel nodded, her expression shy as she plucked it from its hiding spot. "Um, yeah. Sea turtles are kinda my thing. I really wanted to be a marine biologist."

"That sounds like it would have been a very rewarding career."

"Yeah." She looked away. "I called her Shelly when my dad gave her to me. So lame, right?"

I grinned. "I like puns."

Hazel rolled her eyes. "It's dumb. But I was little, so I didn't know any better. My dad bought her for me when I got sick. The first time. And she's always been my good luck charm. My reminder that, you know, I could *beat* this. But it didn't work this time."

Tears welled in her eyes, and she scrubbed her forearm across them to angrily rub them away. "It didn't work, and it's not going to work, and everything on that list is just a sad joke."

I nodded. "I wish I could tell you I had a solution. Or a way to make this easier, but you were right earlier when you said this was unfair. It is. It's horribly, horribly unfair."

"You're not going to tell me something like 'this is all part of God's plan' or some dumb shit like that, are you?"

"No, I'm not." I clasped my hands together and leaned forward. "Are you religious, Hazel?" Her chart had indicated she wasn't, but I liked to hear patients explain their belief systems themselves.

She shook her head. "Not really. I mean, maybe there's something out there, but I don't know. I have a hard time believing in anything right now."

"It's helpful to some people, but not to everyone," I admitted. "It hasn't helped me after my brother's death."

Hazel turned inquiring eyes on me. "Your brother?"

I nodded. Telling her about Cal was a risk. Most training dictated that maintaining a personal distance from a patient was critical. But Ed had admitted to me that he didn't always strictly adhere to that rule. At times, it was necessary, of course, but he said he'd sometimes found that the distance could be as much of a hindrance as anything. And that, in certain circumstances, it was more beneficial to the patient to let them see the human behind the lab coat.

"Yes," I said aloud. "My brother Cal died recently. He was older than you—twenty-eight—but still much too young. It's been very hard on all of us."

"What did he die of?"

"A car accident. Well, he was hit by a car. He stopped to help a woman change a tire. An oncoming car lost control and hit him. Just a terrible, freak accident."

Hazel's eyes looked wide. "That's awful."

"Yes, it was."

"Did he donate his organs?"

I looked at her in surprise. "He did, actually. It was a small consolation to our family that he could help other people that way. Why do you ask?"

"I asked if I could, but they told me no," Hazel said bitterly. "I've been too sick and with all of the chemo and everything ..."

"I know. I'm sorry about that."

"You actually sound like you mean it when you say that."

I smiled faintly. "I do mean it. And I'm sorry you're not going to get to cross all those things off your bucket list. My brother had one too, and I'm very angry and sad that he won't be able to either."

"He had a list too?"

"Yes. He did some amazing things on it."

"Like what?"

"Like joining the Peace Corps. And skydiving and learning pottery and running with the bulls. Although he hated that one because he felt sorry for the bulls. He really loved animals and—oh! He swam with sea turtles once."

"That's so awesome."

"It *was* pretty awesome. I went with him, actually. We had a great time. Would you like to see a few pictures of it? I know it's not the same as being able to do it yourself, but ..."

"Yeah, that would be cool, actually." Excitement made Hazel's sallow cheeks turn faintly pink. "I mean, if you don't mind."

"Give me a minute." I pulled out my phone and brought up a browser, navigating to the website Cal had set up for all his adventures. It took a little while, but I finally found pictures from our trip to La Jolla, California.

I shifted so Hazel could see the photos on the screen. "Oh, wow!" she exclaimed. "Did you go just to see the turtles?"

"No. We swam and surfed and did all sorts of cool things on that trip. We saw the turtles when we went snorkeling in a cove off San Diego. There's some amazing cliffs and the La Jolla marine park there." I scrolled through the photos slowly, narrating what we'd seen. "We saw seals, spiny lobsters, and moray eels. Oh, and that bright orange fish is a Garibaldi. Did you know they're the state fish of California?"

"No. I had no idea."

I grinned at her. "Cal, my brother, was always making fun of me because I'd do a ton of research about whatever place we were going. He was always happy to show up and see whatever was out there, but I liked to know what we might encounter."

"Are there sharks there?"

"A few, but they're the small, harmless kind. Sevengills and Topes, mostly." I scrolled forward and pointed to a photo where Cal and I were swimming on either side of a small shark. "That's a Tope. And my brother's the doofus throwing the hang ten sign."

"How did he get the picture?"

"Selfie stick with an underwater camera. I always wound up lugging around his extra gear." I smiled at Hazel. "But I have to admit, he got some amazing shots, so it was worth it."

I scrolled through a few more pictures of the rocky reef, red kelp, and other plant life. "There. I found the ones with the turtles! Let me disinfect my phone before I hand it over." I gave it a quick but thorough cleaning with a disinfecting wipe from a nearby canister. "You can go through the pictures at your own pace now."

I handed the phone to Hazel, watching her face as she slowly went through the images, her eyes shining. "They look huge!"

"Yeah, you don't really realize it until you see humans next to them. A small one followed us around, but most were big, in the 150 to 200-pound range."

"Did you know they can get up to 400 pounds at their biggest?"

"I don't think we saw any *that* big."

"What were they like?"

"Hmm, very chill. You know the scene in *Finding Nemo* with the turtles?"

She nodded.

"They really are just totally laid back. They never seem like they're in a huge hurry. Definitely not afraid of humans. They poked their heads up from their hiding spots when we swam by. And if they're in open water, they'll let you swim right up to them." I pointed at the photo she'd stopped on. "You're really not supposed to pet them, but Cal couldn't resist."

"I'm *so* jealous." But rather than despondent, Hazel sounded excited. "That would be totally awesome."

"It was an incredible experience. We always talked about going back, but we didn't make it."

Sad understanding crossed her face as she handed my phone back to me. "Thanks for showing me, Dr. Chris."

I smiled at her. A lot of my patients called me that. Young and old. "You're welcome. Would you like me to come back and talk with you again?"

She nodded. "Yeah, you're pretty cool for a doctor."

I grinned at her. "I'm probably the least cool person I know outside of the hospital, but compared to a lot of the docs around here, maybe I am."

She managed a small giggle. "Could I see more pictures when you come back?"

"Sure. I'll even bring my laptop so you can see them on a bigger screen."

"Neat." Hazel stifled a small yawn. Clearly, even that bit of excitement had worn her out.

"I'm going to let you rest now unless there's something you'd like to talk about?"

She shook her head and yawned, widely this time. "I'm pretty tired."

"It was good to meet you, Hazel," I said.

"You too," Hazel mumbled. By the time I reached the door and turned back to look at her, she was asleep. My heart ached at the sight of her. Pediatric patients were always the hardest. Since Cal's death, they hadn't gotten any easier.

As I passed the seating area just down the hall, I saw Ryan and Lissa. They looked as exhausted as their daughter, but they sat close together, holding hands. Clearly, they were a tough family, but years of fighting had fatigued them. With my brother's death so fresh and raw, my heart went out to her parents. No doubt they were nearly at the end of their rope.

Although the death of a child was particularly cruel, there was one part of the grieving process that would be especially hard—relief when it was finally over. Hazel had been suffering, and that took its toll on her family.

I couldn't prevent her death. What I could do is help make it as good of a death as possible for her and her family. If I could bring any of them an ounce of peace, I would have done my job.

They smiled wanly at me as I approached. I gestured to the chair opposite them, and Ryan nodded for me to sit.

"How's she doing?"

"Hazel's asleep. We talked for a little while. More of an introduction than anything, but I hope she'll open up to me more as we get to know each other."

Lissa frowned. "She's been rather stand-offish with most of the doctors. No offense, they've all been great, but she's just so fed up with dealing with them. She wants to go home and be a normal kid."

"I understand." I gave her a sympathetic smile. "It seems like she relaxed a little around me, so I'm hopeful we can develop a good rapport."

Ryan frowned. "She seems so angry right now."

"It's a part of the grieving process. She's been robbed of her future and—" Lissa let out a quiet sob and buried her head against her husband's shoulder. He reached out and stroked her hair, soothing her.

I gentled my tone and leaned forward a little. "It seems like all three of you are a bit overwhelmed right now. I'd be more than happy to schedule some time to meet with the two of you as well, either together or individually."

"Us?" Lissa lifted her head and wiped at her eyes. "Shouldn't we all be focusing on Hazel?"

"Well, we believe in taking a holistic approach. Supporting patients *and* their loved ones. Truly, it benefits everyone."

Lissa and Ryan glanced at each other. Again, they seemed to share a wordless conversation before he nodded at me. "That might be good. Thank you, Doctor."

After we agreed on a date and time to meet, I shook both of their hands and took my leave.

Thoughts of the Buchanan family occupied my mind for the remainder of my workday. But for the first time in my career, I began to wonder if I really had what it took to take care of my patients. If I couldn't deal with my own brother's death, how could I begin to help them?

Chapter Seven

A fter the day was over, I went to the gym, thinking maybe with enough physical exertion, I could quiet my mind.

I knew I should contact Elliot; after all, *I* was the one who wanted to know more about Cal's secrets. But I'd assumed I'd never hear from Elliot again, and now that I had, I felt rattled and off-kilter. How could I look him in the eye after what we'd done?

Unfortunately, after forty-five minutes on the treadmill, I was no closer to the goal of quieting my mind than I had been when I started. The burn from lifting weights didn't help either, and even after I was sweating and spent, my muscles shaky with fatigue, my stomach still churned with doubt.

I wiped off the sweat and guzzled water, trying to decide if lifting more weights might help. I felt a slap on my shoulder. I glanced over to see Jason, the trainer I'd worked with a few times when I initially joined the gym. It was the place Cooper owned, although with as busy as he was running this location and trying to set up a second, I rarely saw him there.

"Hey, what's up, Chris?" Jason asked with a grin. He was handsome, if you liked the blond muscle-bound jock type.

"Not much," I replied, draining my water bottle.

"You looked like you were pushing yourself pretty hard out there. Everything okay?"

I sighed and looked down at the towel in my hand. "Just trying to work through some stuff in my head." He had no idea about Cal—we'd never discussed anything personal—and I was grateful I could get away with being vague. The last thing I wanted to do right now was talk about my brother's death.

Jason frowned at me. "Be careful, okay? If you're distracted, you're more likely to pull a muscle or hurt yourself in some other way."

"Yeah. I'll be more careful," I promised.

"Good." Jason tilted his head and stared at me. "Actually, if you're up for it, let me show you something that might be good for you. Have you ever boxed? I think hitting a punching bag would be great for you right now."

I shook my head. "No, never tried it, but I'd be up for learning."

"Follow me then. I'll show you the basics today, and we can work more on it the next time you come in."

"Sounds good."

The moves were easy enough and although my muscles burned with exertion, the solid thwacks as I hit the bag felt good. I had plenty of built-up frustration in me, and by the time I finally stopped, I was shaking.

My lungs heaving, my muscles aching, and my body drenched in sweat, I bent over, gasping for breath. "Holy shit."

"Holy shit is right," Jason said, sounding impressed. "You have some pent-up rage there, dude."

"It's been a rough couple of weeks," I admitted, panting.

"Well, looks like this is a great outlet for you then."

"I'll definitely be doing this again." I straightened with a grunt. "Thanks."

"Any time."

I staggered off to the locker room to shower, struggling to put one foot in front of the other. Jesus Christ, I hurt everywhere. For a short while, I'd forgotten about Elliot and his cryptic message however, so at least I had accomplished something.

I struggled with how to reply to him as I showered and dressed. I gave Jason a distracted wave goodnight as I headed out. In my car, I stared at my phone, typing out and erasing message after message. I finally settled on something simple and forced myself to send it to Elliot. *When and where?*

The response was surprisingly quick. *Tonight, if you can. Springwood Apartments, Building B.*

I frowned, wondering why the hell Elliot wanted to meet at an apartment that wasn't his. I doubted he'd answer even if I asked, so I replied that I'd be there in an hour. Springwood Apartments was quite a distance, but as I followed the GPS, I realized that it wasn't that far from Elliot's place. It was in a somewhat gentrified part of town, although the apartment complex was a modest one. The type graduate students tended to flock to, and, in fact, it wasn't far from campus.

Each building had multiple units, and I followed the signs until I got to building B. I had arrived well before the hour mark, but I was grateful for the time to collect myself. What did Elliot want from me? My mind whirled with possible scenarios as I sat in front of the building, drumming my fingers on the steering wheel.

A few minutes before we were supposed to meet, a small silver car pulled up, and Elliot got out. Even in the dim light, I recognized the long, slim lines of his body. I took a deep breath and swung open my door, nerves making my heart beat too fast. He glanced over and nodded at me before slipping a cigarette between his lips and ducking his head to light it. With the streetlight behind him, his face was in shadow until the flame from the lighter and the bright flare of the cigarette illuminated it. It emphasized the hollows of his cheeks and the circles under his eyes. Dressed in a variation of what I'd seen him in at the bar, he blended into the shadows, black and gray against the inky night, the glow of his pale skin standing out starkly.

"What am I doing here?" I asked, my voice coming out more clipped than I intended.

He blew a plume of smoke out to the side, then licked his lips. "Cal lived here."

I stared at him in shock as he took another drag on the cigarette. "He *what?*"

Elliot emphasized each word, like he was speaking to someone especially slow. "Cal. Lived. Here."

"Christ. Did I know anything about my brother?" I rubbed at my head, and a sudden thought occurred to me. "Fuck, I wish you'd told me before. The hospital gave my parents his key ring. I assume the one for the apartment is on there."

Elliot clamped the cigarette between his lips as he dug in his pocket. "I have one," he muttered around the cigarette.

I swore under my breath and took the key from him when he offered it, trying not to flinch when our fingers touched. It was a small graze of our skin together, but it was enough to make my breath hitch. Enough to make me remember his lips on mine, the smoky taste of him, and his hands on my skin as he drove into me.

He frowned and yanked his hand away. I shoved my own hands in my pockets. The bite of the key against my palm helped center me, remind me why we were here.

"I'll take you up there once I finish my cigarette," Elliot said and turned away. He was silhouetted, the light behind him showing his profile in stark relief. I stared at him, wondering what was going on in his head. I crossed my arms over my chest, ignoring the aching muscles that grew progressively sorer the longer we stood in the cold air. I wanted to snap at him to hurry up, but I had a feeling that the more impatient I was, the slower he'd go.

He wasn't quick, unfortunately, and my gaze drifted to his lips while he leisurely smoked the cigarette. His lips were full, in contrast with his narrow face, and I felt a warm flush creep down the back of my neck as a flash of memory assaulted me. I remembered him sucking my cock, and every purse of his lips was all too reminiscent of that.

I cleared my throat, guilt warring with the sudden sharp stab of desire that had my dick stirring. What was *wrong* with me? Being attracted to Elliot when I was drunk was one thing, but now I was sober and clear-headed. No matter how good the sex had been, how could I possibly justify still wanting the man standing in front of me? Just as I started to turn away, unable to look at him a moment longer, he finished his cigarette and dropped the butt on the ground, grinding it out under his heel. I scowled; smoking was bad enough, but smokers who littered drove me nuts.

"This way." Elliot gestured toward the building, and I followed, falling into step behind him. Neither of us spoke on the way into the building or up the stairs to Cal's apartment. It was a generic, average place, clean and well-maintained but otherwise unremarkable.

Elliot's body was strung tight with tension as we reached the top of the stairs. He gestured to the door marked 242B with a short, jerky motion. I twisted the key in the lock, apprehensive about what I'd find as I swung open the door.

But I shouldn't have been. Cal's apartment was bright and colorful, furnished with a hodge-podge of things, thrift store furniture living side by side with a few nicer pieces. It looked very much like his room at our parents' home and was littered with his possessions. I glanced around and saw belongings of his I hadn't even realized were missing from the room in our parents' house. His surfboard leaned against the living room wall, and I saw his camera on the coffee table. My shoulders sagged with relief.

"Thank you," I whispered, my voice husky with suppressed emotion, intensely grateful that Elliot had let me know about the place.

I glanced behind me when no response came. Elliot still hovered in the hall just outside the door. His face was bleached stark white, and even from several feet away, I could see him trembling. "I can't," he choked out. "I thought I could, but I can't do this right now."

I stepped into the hall and closed the distance between us, worry overriding every other reaction I had to him. I grabbed Elliot's arm, but he shrugged me off, his gaze pleading with me to not push. I had a thousand questions for him, but I wouldn't force him to be there if it were that painful. "You don't have to stay," I reassured him as I heard the apartment door close behind me. He nodded jerkily and turned away.

"Wait! Your key." I held it out as he slowly turned back to face me.

"Don't you want it?" His voice was hoarse.

"I can get Cal's. I think you should keep this one." I didn't know why, but it seemed important that Elliot still have some link to Cal, still be able to come to this apartment if he needed to. I had no idea why Cal had been living there, but it was clearly a place Elliot was familiar with. I pressed the key into the palm of Elliot's hand and folded his fingers around it. We stood that way for a long moment, my hand clasped around his as we stared at each other. His fingers were cool, trembling a little in my grasp. He finally let out a deep, shuddering sigh and nodded, his look one of relief and gratitude.

His hand slipped from mine as he turned away. He jammed his closed fist in his pocket and clattered down the stairs. Long after the slam of the door at the foot of the stairwell had stopped reverberating in the air, I stared after him, bewildered and worried.

I buried myself in work and going to the gym for the rest of the week, unwilling to let myself think more about Elliot. Cal's death was a raw wound that lived at the edge of my consciousness. Sometimes I could go about my day and not think about it for short stretches, but every time something reminded me of him, it rose to the surface. I was moody and distant with co-workers, I struggled to act normal around my patients, and the whole time I felt on edge.

Although curious about Cal's apartment, I was reluctant to approach my parents to ask them for Cal's keys. Part of my apprehension was fear about having to come up with a plausible explanation about why I needed them, but the other part was fear of going back to Cal's place. My brother had been living a double life, and I had no idea what else I might discover about him. What other secrets lurked in that apartment?

After a tense Sunday dinner where my father drank too much and my mother stared miserably down at her plate, I couldn't convince myself to stall any longer.

When I put on my coat, my mother pressed a bag full of food into my hands despite the fact I'd been living away from home for more than a decade and was plenty competent in the kitchen. If she wanted to feed me, I wouldn't argue. We were all lost now. I would do anything to make her feel better. I stood by the door, ready to leave, and finally summoned up enough courage to say the words that had been lingering on my tongue the entire night. "Mom, could I have Cal's key ring?"

She blinked at me in surprise, her brown eyes puzzled as they scrutinized me, but then her expression cleared and she nodded. "Sure, honey. The keychains would be something nice to remember him by. Let me go grab them; they're in my dresser drawer."

She disappeared up the stairs, and my father let out a heavy sigh. "I'm worried about her."

I turned to look at him, raising one eyebrow. "What makes you say that?"

"She's working incredibly hard at the office, and once she gets home, she's on the computer or her phone all the time with some online support group. I know it's how she's coping, but I'm afraid she's not really letting herself mourn Cal."

I cleared my throat. "Are any of us?"

My father gave me a tired smile and ran his hand through his salt-and-pepper hair. His color was a little better than the last few times I'd seen him, but he still looked exhausted, and the lines around his mouth seemed like they'd multiplied in the last few weeks. "You have a point."

"I'm not sure it's really sunk in," I admitted. "Some days, I think it has, and then other times—like tonight—I expect to see him walk through the door."

"You have no idea how many times I've almost said, 'let me call Cal and ask him'," my father replied. "About the most inconsequential things."

"I know. Me, too."

We fell silent until my mother joined us a few minutes later, carrying Cal's keys and wallet in her hand. "I thought maybe you'd want both."

"Sure," I agreed as she pressed them into my hands, the guilt over the secrets I held multiplying until it nearly choked me.

She glanced at my father and then looked back at me. "And if you wanted his car, I'm sure Cal wouldn't—"

I cut her off with a shake of my head. "I can't. Not yet. Maybe someday, but right now, I can't even think about driving his car."

She subsided. I knew after Cal had been taken to the hospital, his car had been brought back to my parents' house. It was currently stowed safely in their three-car garage, but I doubted any of us were in any hurry to do anything with it.

I glanced down at the keys, seeing the familiar key to the 1967 Mustang Fastback that he'd restored during his car-obsessed phase in his late teens. Cal had taken a beater and brought it back to its former glory through a hell of a lot of hard work. He'd driven it ever since. Several key chains hung from the ring, one from when he was in the Peace Corps. It was handmade, crafted from red, yellow, and green embroidery thread and beads to represent the colors of Ghana's flag. Another key chain was from a trip the two of us had taken to Yosemite the summer after he'd graduated high school. It had been just the two of us, and I could remember it so clearly. Cal, still slightly awkward and gawky, burning with enthusiasm to explore every inch of the park, taking picture after picture, bursting with life and happiness at the world in front of him.

"I can see why you'd want to keep that," my mom said, and I nodded, grateful not to have to speak the lie aloud but guilty for letting her assume that was the only reason I wanted the keys.

"It was a good trip," I finally managed. I reached out for her and pulled her into a tight hug. What was I supposed to do? Keeping Cal's secrets felt like an ever-increasing weight dragging me down.

Once home, I searched through the photos on my computer, trying to find all of them that included Cal, especially from the Yosemite trip. He and my mother had sent me hundreds of pictures over the years, and I'd saved them in a folder, but they were all jumbled together. Somehow, organizing them into subfolders—as best I could anyway—seemed to make the pressure in my chest lessen, as if tidying the files would somehow tidy Cal's life. Make it less chaotic and more sensible.

The sight of his easy grin and constant mugging for the camera made me miss him acutely. It wasn't any one particular photo that triggered it, but about halfway through, the frustration built to a boiling point.

"Goddamn it, Cal! Why?" I cried out, slamming my hand down on the desk. My palm smarted from the blow, and it took everything in me to keep from putting my fist through the computer monitor. Pain was easier than confusion and less complicated than wondering why my brother hadn't trusted me with his secrets.

Pain was simple. Understanding was not.

Chapter Eight

"Mr. Wu?" I tapped my knuckles gently on the door to his room. "It's Dr. Allen. May I come in?"

A woman called out, "Come in" in answer.

I opened the door to see the frail, elderly man who'd been my patient for over six weeks and his daughter. He was dying of COPD—chronic obstructive pulmonary disease. When I'd first gone into palliative care, I'd assumed that most of my patients would be dying of cancer. I'd been surprised to discover that more of them had non-cancerous lung conditions than anything else. I thought of Elliot's smoking and winced.

Emily, my patient's daughter, gave me a concerned look. "Is everything all right, Dr. Allen?" She spoke quietly, and I glanced over to see that her father was sleeping.

"Yes, just a stray thought that crossed my mind. I'm sorry. How are you doing?" I wiped Elliot from my mind and shot her a reassuring smile.

"Oh, I'm all right." She stood and approached me, holding up a book. "I've been reading to Dad, but he dropped off for a bit. The nurse said he didn't sleep much last night."

I frowned down at my tablet, which contained Mr. Wu's chart. I hadn't seen any indication of sleep issues in it. "Has that been happening a lot?"

"No, I don't think so," Emily said.

"Not often," Mr. Wu rasped from the bed.

I walked toward him and took a seat in the chair on the opposite side of the bed from his daughter. I looked my patient in the eye. "Well, if it continues, I'd like you to tell someone. We can give you something to help."

He nodded.

"Would you like me to stay, Doctor?" Emily asked.

"Only if you'd prefer to."

She shook her head. "I think I'll grab some tea." The hospice floor contained a small lounge for family members. It was stocked with coffee, tea, and a few snacks. It was a quiet, relaxing place that offered them a place to take a break.

After she excused herself, I looked at my patient again. "Is there a reason you couldn't sleep? Something specific on your mind?"

Mr. Wu shook his head. "I don't think so." Though born in China, he had come to the United States as a very young child, and his voice held only the faintest trace of an accent. He closed his eyes briefly, then opened them to look me in the eye. "Lately, I've had the feeling that some night when I close them, I won't open them again."

I nodded. Truthfully, based on his declining health, it could be any day now. "That is possible," I acknowledged. "It was my understanding from the last time we spoke that you had come to terms with that."

"I did. I thought I did, anyway."

"Has something changed?"

"I saw a picture of my granddaughter yesterday. She is going to be in a play. I won't be able to see it." Sorrow crossed his face.

"I'm sorry; I understand how difficult that must be."

"There is never enough time, is there?"

I thought briefly of my brother's death and of Elliot's words. *You had him for twenty-eight years. Was that enough?*

"No," I replied aloud, answering both. "No, there isn't."

"I thought I was ready." His voice broke on the last word, which triggered a coughing fit. I helped him sit upright and handed him a tissue, gently patting his back until it subsided.

There was little else I, or anyone else, could physically do for him at this point other than try to keep him comfortable. He was literally drowning from the inside out, and it would only get worse as it progressed. His skin was damp and clammy by the time I helped ease him down onto the pillows again. He lay fairly propped up anyway to help him breathe. But I knew it would grow more and more strained as the days passed.

When he'd had time to gather his strength, I looked him in the eye. They were turning cloudy from cataracts, but his gaze itself was still sharp. His body was deteriorating, but his mind was still strong. Losing Cal so young and unexpectedly had been a tremendous blow to our family, but at least, there had been no slow decline or lingering death. Cal had simply been there one day and gone the next.

"What is it you wish you had more time for?" I asked Mr. Wu.

He clasped his hands together over his stomach and was silent. "To watch my grandchildren grow," he said eventually. "I will miss so much of their lives. I won't see them graduate, or get married, or have children. I worry they won't even remember me."

"How old are they again?"

"Ten, thirteen, and fifteen."

"Well," I smiled reassuringly at him. "The thirteen and fifteen-year-old will certainly remember you. And I have every reason to believe the ten-year-old will as well. That's Sarah, the one in the play, right?"

"You remembered her name." His voice was full of wonder.

"It's the same as my mother's." I smiled at him as I sat back in my chair. "But I have no doubt Sarah will remember you. My grandfather died when I was nine, and I remember him very clearly. I'm sure Emily and James and their spouses will do everything they can to help their children remember. Showing them photos, talking about you, reminiscing, all these things will help. I'll talk to Emily about it. I'm sure she'll understand why that's important to you and to your grandchildren."

"Thank you," he rasped. He coughed again, and I stood to help him sit forward, but the fit subsided more quickly this time. It still seemed to take a lot out of him, and he was pallid and trembling by the time it was over.

"Have you considered having your grandchildren come here to see you?" I asked when he'd had a chance to recover. Though his two children came regularly, I didn't think his grandchildren had been in.

"I don't want them to see me like this."

"I understand that," I said, my tone filled with compassion. "But it might be beneficial. Many families find that it helps with the grieving process."

He nodded, but I could see his eyelids growing heavy, so I excused myself. I found Emily in the family lounge, and she gave me a tired smile when I approached her.

"How is he?"

"Fatigued. He had several coughing fits in the short time I was there."

The lines around her mouth deepened. "It won't be long now, will it?"

"I'm afraid not." I gestured to the chair near her. "May I?"

"Of course."

"After speaking with your father, I think one of the things weighing on him is a fear that your daughter won't remember him." She gave me a puzzled look. "He seems concerned about that with all three grandkids, but particularly Sarah because she's the youngest and it's been a while since he's seen her."

I set my tablet on the table beside me and leaned forward. "I know it's difficult. But I visited my grandfather in hospice as a child. I won't lie. It *was* jarring to see him so ill. But in the end, we had more time together, and it gave me an opportunity to make a few very good, lasting memories with him. I believe it would be helpful for all of you."

"I've considered it. I just didn't want to make this harder on either my father or daughter than necessary."

I offered her an understanding smile. "I understand. But I do believe, in the long run, this will help your daughter. And it will give your father some peace of mind."

"I want that." She hesitated. "Maybe a part of me has been holding out because I was afraid once he said goodbye to her, he'd lose the will to live."

"His illness is progressing," I said as kindly as possible. "No matter how strong-willed he is, there is a point at which his heart will give out. I know you aren't ready to lose him, but the time is quickly approaching where the choice to bring them in will be taken away from you. My advice is to make the best of what little time is left. Letting your father go will be hard, but if you can give him this closure, it will make it easier. I truly believe that."

We spoke for a few more minutes before I excused myself to go see my next patient. But the situation had brought forth memories of what it had been like to lose my own grandfather, and they lingered as I went about my day. While I ate my lunch in my office, my mind conjured memories of my grandfather's death.

I balked at the door and gripped Dr. Washburn's hand tightly. My own palms were sweaty, though I'd wiped them on my jeans just a few minutes before. At the age of nine, I rarely wanted to hold anyone's hand, but right now, I was too scared to pretend to be grown up.

"Are you frightened, C.J.?" Mr. Washburn asked. His voice was kind.

"A little bit," I admitted.

He smiled reassuringly down at me. "That's understandable. This is a new experience, isn't it? Sometimes those are scary."

"Yeah."

"What are you scared of?"

"I don't know what it'll be like," I admitted. "I mean, what if Grandpa ... isn't really like I remember."

Mr. Washburn crouched down. "He probably will be a little different. Being sick takes its toll on you. He's tired, and he might be in some pain or discomfort, although we're doing our best to take care of that. But he might look or act a little differently. He might even smell different if he's not using the same shampoo or shaving cream. But he's still your grandfather. He still loves you like he always has. And he'll still be very glad to see you."

"Okay."

"Are you ready to see him?"

"Yes." I let go of Mr. Washburn's hand and opened the heavy hospital room door myself. Mom and Dad were already inside.

Wanting to be brave, I looked straight at my grandpa. Mr. Washburn was right. Grandpa did look different. His hair seemed thinner on top, and his skin looked very pale. But his face lit up when he spotted me.

"There's my little man. Come say hi."

I looked at my dad for reassurance, and when he gave me an encouraging smile, I walked over to him. I perched on Dad's knee as I looked at Grandpa. "Hi," I said, a little shyly. This was the man I'd tossed a ball around with, the one who had read to me, the man who was teaching me how to sail. But I was still nervous about what to do. What if I did something wrong?

He reached out a hand, and I took it. His fingers were cool against mine as he looked me in the eye. "Did your mom and dad tell you I'm very sick?"

I nodded.

"And that I'm not going to get better?"

I nodded again.

"I know it's not easy coming here and seeing me like this, and I don't want you wasting your whole summer in the hospital with a sick old man, but I hope you'll come by and see me some while I'm here." He frowned. "I'm not going to be up to teaching you to sail anymore, I'm afraid."

"It's okay, Grandpa," I gave him a small smile. "I'll come visit you here. Maybe we could read or play board games instead."

"I'd like that."

My father hugged me tighter and kissed the side of my head, and the fears I'd had went away as I talked to my grandpa.

I saw my grandfather several times a week that summer. We read to each other and played board games until he was too ill to focus. After that, I read aloud to him and, eventually, sat by his bedside reading quietly to myself when he was sleeping. Late one night, at the end of the summer, my father gently woke me.

He crouched down by the bed, and I squinted up at him. The light he'd turned on next to the bed seemed very bright. "Christopher" —he never called me that— "do you remember how we talked about the fact that Grandpa is getting worse?"

"Yeah."

"Kathy—Grandpa's nurse—called. He's going to be gone very soon. I'm going to go to the hospital, and Mrs. Moody is going to come over and stay with Cal." My little brother was only three, so he didn't go to the hospital to see Grandpa like I did. "But it's up to you if you want to come with your mom and me. You don't have to. Or, if you want, you can say goodbye to Grandpa, and then Mom can bring you home. You don't have to sit with him until he dies."

I thought about it for a minute. "No, I want to stay with Grandpa. I think he'll like having me there."

He kissed the top of my head. "You are such a sweet boy. Your grandpa might not be awake enough to know you're there, unfortunately. He certainly won't be able to talk to you."

"It's okay," I said. "I want to be there anyway." We'd talked about death a lot. What it was like. What to expect. I was ready.

"Get dressed then and brush your teeth real quick. We're going to be leaving as

soon as Mrs. Moody gets here."

Mrs. Moody gave my father a disapproving look when she saw me. "Are you sure that's wise? He's so young. He doesn't need to see that."

My father squeezed my shoulder. "Dying is a perfectly natural process, Teresa. We appreciate you taking care of Cal tonight, but C.J. wishes to be there, and that is something my wife and I support." It was the same stern voice he used when he was lecturing Cal and me, and she didn't argue back anymore than we did.

Mr. Washburn was at the hospital when we got there. My dad hugged him hard. "It's the middle of the night, Ed. You didn't have to come in."

"I told the staff to notify me. I've known your father since you and I roomed together in college. I wanted to be here for him and for you."

I got a hug from Mr. Washburn too before my parents and I went in my grandpa's room. I was nervous, not sure what to expect, but Grandpa was just sleeping. His chest made a weird rattle-y noise every time he breathed in and out. My father crouched beside the bed and looked me in the eye.

"If you want, you can talk to Grandpa a little, tell him you're here and you love him and you're going to miss him, but you understand he has to go. Or whatever else you want to say to him. This is probably going to be your last chance, you understand?"

My eyes were wet, and my chest hurt, but I nodded. Grandpa didn't move when I held his hand and told him all the things I wanted to. I kissed him on the forehead and sat back. I didn't know if he could hear me or not, but I hoped so. My mom said goodbye to Grandpa too, and then she took my hand. "Why don't we give your dad a few minutes alone with Grandpa?"

We went back out in the hallway for a while until my dad called us back in. We sat in Grandpa's room as the sun started to come up. I tried not to fidget, but I was kind of bored with nothing to read or do. I didn't realize it was going to take so long. I didn't want him to go, but my parents had explained that he was hurting, and I knew I didn't want that to last too long.

I was falling asleep in the chair when Grandpa made a little noise. It wasn't loud or anything, kinda like a big sigh, but my father sat upright and took his hand. "I'm here, Dad. We all are. Sarah and C.J. Cal's at home sleeping, but he loves you too. We're going to stay with you until you're ready to go."

Grandpa breathed hard for a few minutes, and then the room went quiet except for the machines. My mother held his wrist, and I knew she was taking his pulse. She did that to me whenever I was really sick. "He's gone," she said quietly, and I looked over at my dad to see tears sliding down his face. He pulled me close, and my mother came around the bed to hug us both. We stood for a long time like that, all of us crying quietly.

After a while, we pulled apart and both of my parents kissed my grandpa goodbye. I expected it to be scary. I'd heard dead bodies were creepy things, but when I pressed my lips to the cool skin of his cheek, it wasn't scary at all. He was still my grandpa, even if he was strange and still and different *somehow. But mostly, he seemed peaceful, and I was glad for that.*

My grandfather's death stuck with me for a long time. As I grew up and realized how rare it was for anyone to see death take place, I understood what a privilege it was to be there for him during his last moments. And as I studied medicine and spent more time talking to Ed as an adult, I realized what Ed did was incredibly valuable.

Along with a whole host of other health professionals, he gave people their best possible death. He brought them peace and comfort and guided them to accepting the inevitable and facing it with grace rather than fighting it. I wanted to do the same.

My job could be utterly gut-wrenching, but in the end, knowing I could help my patients and their families find peace with their mortality rather than fear it made every second of heartache worthwhile.

Chapter Nine

Thoughts of my grandfather's death still lingered in my mind as I went to the gym after work, then threw some chicken and vegetables in the oven to cook.

While I showered, the memories of my father's struggles after the death rose to the forefront.

I'd only been nine, so I hadn't noticed anything much at first. Both of my parents regularly enjoyed a glass of wine with Sunday dinner or a bit more if they had friends over. I knew my dad had a bottle of Scotch in his study and that Cal and I were never allowed to touch it. Our parents seemed exactly like our friends' parents. I'd never seen either of them drink to excess, and I had memories of my father ranting about how irresponsible drunk drivers were.

So, at first, I didn't notice anything strange after my grandfather died. Maybe I noticed that my father went to bed a little earlier than usual. That he was quiet and a little haggard in the mornings. Loud noises bothered him more, and he didn't play with Cal and me as much on the weekends. He was usually in his study. Working, he said, although I sometimes saw him just sitting in the chair at his desk, staring blankly at the wall.

But he'd just lost his father. All those things were perfectly reasonable.

I remembered Cal throwing a tantrum one day after Dad wouldn't come out and play with him, and my mother, frazzled-looking, sat me down at the kitchen table to talk. She'd told me she understood how hard it was for Cal and me to see Dad acting differently. She'd explained it by saying that he was having a hard time after Grandpa's death. She asked me to help keep Cal from pestering Dad so much. I liked to be a helper and feel-grown up. Cal was always pestering me, and if Dad was sad and tired, I knew he probably didn't like that anymore than I did, so I agreed.

I tried very hard to keep Cal out of the way after that. But he was loud and excited, and I couldn't always stop him. And he didn't understand why Dad didn't want to read him his bedtime story anymore or give him a bath.

It went on for months. The holidays were strange and quiet. Rather than go pick out a Christmas tree as a family, Mom ordered one and had it delivered. Mom, Cal, and I decorated without Dad. On Christmas Eve, she tried to be cheerful as she helped us make gingerbread cookies and read us *The Night Before Christmas*. But reading that story had always been Dad's job, and it felt strange to have him missing from our celebration. We didn't go to midnight mass like usual. And on Christmas Day, Dad opened gifts with us— looking haggard and flinching every time Cal shouted with excitement—and he fell asleep on the couch in his study before dinner. Mom told us not to wake him. Aunt Eva and my cousins didn't come celebrate with us that year. It was just the three of us around the big dining room table, which seemed empty without Dad at the head of it. Mom tried to be cheerful, but Cal threw a tantrum halfway through. I finished my food alone while Mom put him to bed early.

I knew something was different about my family all of a sudden, but

I didn't really understand what it was. My father shouted at my mother sometimes and snapped at Cal and me occasionally, though he never got violent. But, for the most part, he wasn't even around enough to yell. Most of the time he was simply … no longer there. He was in another world, and none of us could reach him.

My mother tried to hide the conflict from us, but occasionally, I heard hushed, tense arguments between my parents. I heard her plead with him to get help. And I heard him deny that he had a problem. Over and over again.

Until the day came that he could no longer deny it.

It was almost Valentine's Day, and I sat at the table, carefully writing my name on the Batman Valentines for my classmates. Cal was playing on the floor with some toys while Mom washed the lunch dishes. Dad was in his study. We'd hardly seen him at all that day.

When she was done with the dishes, Mom crouched down beside me. "Do you remember Mrs. Acosta who lives a couple streets over?"

"Yep." I carefully attached a sticker to the envelope for my friend Ryan. I'd given Ryan the best card and the best sticker. I wanted Ryan to like me as much as I liked him.

"Can you look at me please, C.J.?"

I glanced up at my mom.

"Mrs. Acosta fell last week and got hurt. She was in the hospital for a while, but she's home now, and her daughter is here taking care of her. I'm going to run over there with a lasagna and see if there's anything I can do to help. I'm not going to be gone very long though, so I'm going to leave you and Cal here. You

are not to leave the house while I'm gone."

"Okay."

"Your Dad is home, and I've told him where I'm going. I want you to keep an eye on Cal though and don't bug your Dad except if there's an emergency. Do you understand what I'm saying, C.J.?"

"I have to keep an eye on Cal and not bug Dad unless there's an emergency," I repeated. We'd talked lots of times about what to do if there was a fire or a bad earthquake.

"I won't be gone long. I promise. You take care of your brother, okay? You two can watch TV if you want. Just remember to be patient with him and be on your best behavior."

"We'll be good," I promised. She kissed the top of my head and left.

But long after I finished my Valentine's Day cards, Mom still wasn't back. Cal had been fussing for a while. I tried to distract him with toys, and I read to him for a while. Watching TV helped, but after a while, he started complaining he was hungry. I looked around for snacks, but Mom had put the snack basket up because it was almost dinnertime. I could drag a step stool over to get it, but I was afraid of getting in trouble. I glanced out the window. It was getting dark out, and I wondered when Mom was coming home.

Cal started wailing, and I didn't know what else to do. I walked slowly down the hall to the study. I knew I wasn't supposed to bother Dad if it wasn't an emergency, but Cal really needed him. My stomach felt funny as I knocked on the door. "Dad?" I called out. My voice sounded very small as it echoed around the house. I listened closely but I couldn't hear any sounds from inside. I knocked louder and tried to make my voice bigger. "Dad!"

118

But he still didn't answer. Why was he ignoring me? I tested the doorknob. It was unlocked, and I opened the door enough that I could peek inside. "Dad? Cal's hungry. He won't stop whining."

I could see him on the couch, lying on his back. There was an empty bottle tipped onto its side on the floor nearby. I fixed it and patted the rug, wondering if any had spilled out. But the rug was dry. Dad was snoring, and when I shook his shoulder, he didn't wake up. He let out a snorting noise and rolled onto his side away from me. I stood there staring at his back for a long time. I didn't know what to do. Mom was gone, and Dad was here, but he wouldn't wake up. I could still hear Cal crying on the other side of the house. I closed the study door behind me as I went back to the kitchen.

Cal's face was red from crying and covered in tears and snot. I ripped off a piece of paper towel and tried to wipe his face, but he just cried harder. I hugged him. I didn't know what else to do. "Mom will be home soon, Cal," I promised him, but I wasn't sure. Why wasn't she back yet? It was totally dark now, and I was hungry too.

"I'll get you something to eat, Cal," I promised him. I left him crying on the floor and pulled open the door to the refrigerator.

Cal was picky. There were a lot of foods that I liked that Cal wouldn't eat right now. I saw cheese and bread though. Cal's favorite food was grilled cheese. Mom wouldn't be mad if I made that for both of us, right? I'd helped her make it before, so I knew how.

Mom had told me to take care of Cal, and she wasn't here, so that's what I had to do, right?

"Stop crying, Cal," I begged. "I'm going to make you food," I said. He didn't stop crying though.

So, I got out what I needed, then dragged the step stool over to the stove, like when I helped Mom cook. I did exactly what I had seen her do. I turned the knob until the fire shot up, and I put a pan over it. I knew I wasn't allowed to use the sharp knives but the butter knives didn't cut the cheese very well, so I ended up with big chunks. I didn't think Cal would mind extra cheese. I never did.

The butter was hard, and when I tried to spread it on the bread, it tore. The sandwich looked very sad, but I put it in the pan anyway. It sizzled like it was supposed to, so I felt very proud of myself as I got the plastic thingy out of the drawer to turn it over. I was being a good brother and taking care of Cal like I was supposed to. I didn't know how long to let it cook, but when I saw smoke, I grabbed the turner and flipped it. Half of the bread stuck to the pan and some of the cheese came out. Worse, the bread was black in the parts that hadn't ripped off.

I wrinkled my nose. The grilled cheese didn't look at all like the ones Mom and I had made together. I was tired and mad that this was so hard. I wanted to give up, but Cal was still crying, and I wanted to take care of Cal like Mom had asked. I did better with the other side, although the cheese wasn't very melty when I put it on a plate. We had just enough bread that I could make two sandwiches. I knew Cal wouldn't eat the burned one, but I could eat it when it was done. I concentrated very hard as I made the second grilled cheese, and it was even a little melted as I carefully put it on a plate. I felt very pleased with myself as I carried it over to the table. "C'mon, Cal," I said. "I made grilled cheese."

He stopped crying a little and rubbed at his eyes.

"You have to sit at the table to eat," I coaxed him. That was one of the rules at dinner.

Cal crawled up into the chair, and I helped push it in like Mom did every night. I got my plate and sat at my spot next to him. Cal was hiccupping a little as he gnawed on the sandwich, but at least, he'd stopped crying. I took a bite of mine. It wasn't very good. It was cold, and it tasted kinda burned, but I was still proud of myself. I'd taken care of Cal like I'd promised my mom.

But as we ate, I started to smell something funny. A weird burned smell and something else that was gross and didn't smell like food at all. I looked over at the stove and saw the plastic turner hanging over the edge of pan. The flame was still on and the turner had melted. I ran over and turned it off, but the pan was too hot to touch. I tried to grab the plastic, but it was hot too, and I yelped when it burned my fingers.

I threw it in the sink with a clatter, trying not to cry. I didn't know what to tell Mom. I knew I'd messed up, and I was afraid she'd be mad at me. I walked over to Cal, who was still eating his grilled cheese. Now I felt like Cal. I didn't feel grown up at all. I wanted to cry and beg for Mom, but she wasn't there.

I sat there for a long time, my fingers hurting, until I heard the sound of the door opening.

"C.J.? Cal? I'm home! I'm sorry I took so long, I …" I heard the sound of running feet, and Mom burst into the kitchen. "No, no! Oh, God, please …"

She took one look at me and Cal and burst into tears. She grabbed us both in a big hug. "Are you okay? What happened? I never meant to be gone so long. Oh, God, if something had happened to either of you, I never would have been able to forgive myself."

She pulled back, tears streaming down her face as she let go of me and picked up Cal. "What happened? You know you're never supposed to use the stove when there isn't an adult helping." But she didn't sound mad at me. She just sounded sad and scared.

I looked at the floor. "Cal was hungry. I knew we weren't supposed to eat

121

snacks so close to dinner. I thought it would be okay if I made Cal and me food. I tried to make grilled cheese like you taught me, but I burned it. And I didn't mean to melt the ..." I couldn't think of the word for the plastic turner.

She wiped tears from her eyes. "The spatula?"

"Yeah. I left the burner on, and it melted ..." I looked down again. "I'm sorry. I tried to clean it up, but it was really hot." I held out my fingers. "I got burned."

She kissed them gently. "Is it still hurting?"

"Only a little."

"Let's go run your hand under cool water then. It'll help."

After it felt better, I looked at her. "Why were you gone so long?"

"I'm sorry about that. I shouldn't have been. The Acostas needed more help than I expected. The daughter went to the pharmacy to pick up her mom's prescription, but it took a lot longer than either of us expected. I shouldn't have left you here though." She shook her head and sighed. "I should have just taken you over there with me. I would have come back to get you when I realized how long I'd be, but I couldn't leave Mrs. Acosta alone."

"I'm sorry. I didn't mean to burn things."

She kissed the top of my head. "I know. I'm not mad at you, sweetheart. I know you were trying to take care of your brother, and you did the best you could. Why didn't you ask your dad for help with dinner?"

"I tried, but he was asleep on the couch. He was snoring, and he didn't wake up when I shook him ..."

She went very still, and she set Cal on the floor next to me.

"C.J., I want you to go up to your room. Now. And take Cal with you. Please shut the door behind you. I need to wake up your Dad and have a discussion with him." Confused, I dragged an unhappy Cal up to the playroom. I tried to distract him with toys, but he wouldn't stop whining about wanting Mom.

After a while, I couldn't take any more. I quietly opened the door and tip-toed down the hallway. I could hear Mom yelling, and I slowly crept down the stairs. I stopped on the landing, hiding behind the wall. I could peek around it through the railing and see into the living room. I could see my mom, but not my dad.

"I've reached the end of my rope, Christopher!" she shouted. "This is the last straw. I covered for you at work last week when you prescribed penicillin to Tommy Wise, and you missed all the alerts in his chart about him being allergic to it. If I hadn't been there to catch it, you could have killed one of your patients."

My father said something, but his voice was lower, more rumbly, and harder to hear from where I sat.

"No!" she yelled back. "No, it wasn't just a slip-up that could have happened to anyone. You have a drinking problem, Christopher. I wanted to give you time to pull yourself together. The drink or two every night when you got home was one thing, but I've seen the number of bottles you try to slip into the recycling. You are well beyond any sort of reasonable alcohol usage. You are an alcoholic."

I didn't know what an alcoholic was or what exactly they were arguing about. Drinking? Drinking what? I didn't know. But I could tell that Mom was angry.

"I told you I was going to be gone and begged you to stay sober enough to keep an eye on our children, and you couldn't even do that. C.J. said he came to you

and couldn't wake you up. I shouldn't have trusted them with you, but you're their father. Risking our boys' safety is the last straw. I can't do this anymore!

"You are neglecting your job, your wife, and your children. What is it going to take to get you to stop?"

Dad shouted something I couldn't understand, and Mom disappeared. I could still hear her though. "If you don't get help, I will take the boys and leave. And report you to the Oregon Medical Board. I understand you're struggling. I love you, and I want to help. But this is where I draw the line. I won't allow you to risk our patients or our children. So, tell me, Christopher, what is it going to be? Your career and family or the booze?"

There was silence for a long time, and then I heard Dad say something. There was the sound of Mom crying, then her saying, "Will you let me call Ed, at least? We can start from there."

Dad was gone for several weeks. As I got older, I found out he hadn't gone to rehab. He and Ed had gone to Ed's vacation cabin in the Cascades while he detoxed. How my father quit drinking cold-turkey, and stuck to it without the structure of AA, I never quite knew. But he was adamant that he could do it, and apparently, it worked.

He threw himself into work and exercise after that. At the time, I didn't connect those things with him no longer drinking, but as I became an adult, I realized they were how he dealt with his disease. I could think of worse coping methods. It was certainly far better than the alcohol.

In the months that followed, Cal and I slowly got our father back. He slept less during the day, made us pancakes on weekend mornings, and played with us again. Our family returned to normal.

It was almost like those awful months never happened. Sometimes, I felt like I was holding my breath though, and it wasn't until I was an adult that I realized I had been waiting for him to relapse. And now, I was concerned that my fears had come true.

Cal and I had discussed our own risks before. As the sons of an alcoholic father, we knew we had an increased risk of alcoholism ourselves. One night when I was in my first year of med school, Cal called me, drunk. He was seventeen.

Cal sounded a little rambling and incoherent on the phone, but I gathered that he and some friends had been at a party that had been broken up by the police. Cal had fled—on foot—and was waiting for me at a nearby gas station.

"You could have called Mom and Dad to come get you, you know?" I snapped as Cal got in my car. I had been up late studying and was irritated at being woken up. But he was my brother. It's not like I'd leave him there. As much as I was tempted.

"Yeah, I know."

I was glad he hadn't driven anywhere in the state he was in. Apparently, his car was parked a few streets over, but there was no way in hell I was going to take him to get it until he sobered up.

"But there would have been a family discussion."

I snorted. He wasn't wrong. Our parents loved us unconditionally, but their love also came with a lecture if we'd done something they disapproved of. Needless to say, excessive underage drinking was one of those things. I hadn't drunk much in high school. And not a ton in undergrad either, but it wasn't like I'd never made a mistake. And it was my job to look out for my brother. So, I took him back to my crappy little apartment and let him sleep it off on the couch. In the morning, I woke him up bright and early, handed him a mug of strong coffee, and told him we needed to talk.

He squinted at me with one eye half-closed as he accepted the mug. He was wrapped in one of the blankets I'd tossed at him last night, and his hair stuck up on one side. He wore the pukka shell necklace he'd bought in Hawaii on a family vacation a few years ago and a pair of boxer shorts that had frogs on them. "You're evil for waking me up this early," Cal muttered.

"I came and got your drunk ass at two-thirty in the morning, and *I'm not ratting you out to Mom and Dad. If I were you, I wouldn't be complaining."*

"Ugh. That's fair, I guess." He took a sip of the coffee and made a face. "Gross. Don't you have any cream?"

"I'm out. I've been doing nothing but studying lately, and I haven't had time to go to the store. You'll survive." I took a seat on the couch next to him. "I have an exam in a couple of days, so I have a lot of work to do today. I'm going to have to run you back to your car soon so I can get enough done before I go to class. But I want to talk first."

Cal groaned and let his head fall back on the couch cushion. "Oh, my God, I should have just called Mom and Dad. I'm going to get a lecture either way, apparently. At least, they would have let me sleep in."

I glared at him. "I'm not lecturing you. I just want to be sure you're going to be okay."

Cal lifted his head and glared at me. "I called you, didn't I? I didn't drink and drive."

"I know. But that's not what I'm talking about." I hesitated. "Look, we have

to be a little more careful than most people about drinking."

"Why? Because Mom and Dad expect us to 'live up to our potential'?"

"No. Because Dad's an alcoholic."
"Oh, come on," Cal argued. "Dad's been fine for what ... almost fifteen years?
Do you really think he's an alcoholic? Or did he just have a drinking problem
when Grandpa died?"

"I'm not going to argue diagnoses with you, Cal. Whatever you want to call it,
Dad had a serious problem. I know you don't really remember it, but it was
bad. You know what he's told us about it, and I can remember being really
fucking scared that Mom and Dad were going to split up."

Cal pulled his feet up onto the couch and hugged his knees. "I know."

"So, I'm not telling you not to drink. I just want you to know that all those
times Mom and Dad warned us about our risk factors ... well, they were right.
Dad had a problem with alcohol and whatever you want to call it; we're more
likely to have that same problem too. So ... just be careful, okay? I don't want
to see you fuck up your future or anyone else's."

At the time, Cal had merely nodded, seeming to blow me off. But he
did appear more careful after that. He still went to parties, but as far
as I knew, he didn't really get drunk again in high school. Even in
college, he was more responsible about it than a lot of his friends.
Occasionally, he drank heavily while he was out celebrating
something, but I had never caught a whiff of a problem. I was no
teetotaler either, so I could hardly judge.

Cal was reckless sometimes, but he wasn't stupid. And privately, I'd
thought Cal was right. I'd been convinced Dad had everything under
control and that he was going to be just fine.

But I couldn't forget that every time I'd seen him lately, he'd had a glass of Scotch in his hand.

Chapter Ten

The following day after work, the route I took home brought me by Cal's apartment. It wasn't a conscious decision to go there, but as I turned off the main road and into the complex, I acknowledged that clearly my subconscious felt I needed to be there. When I pulled up in front of Building B, I couldn't bring myself to get out of my car. I played with my phone instead, staring at Elliot's name and trying to decide if I should let him know I was there. I felt terrible even mentioning Cal's place, considering the reaction he'd had the last time we were at the apartment, but it seemed odd to be there without him. I felt like I didn't really belong there alone.

I forced myself to send the text, but my phone remained silent.

After twenty minutes of waiting for a reply, I scrubbed a hand over my face and got out of my car. There was no point in waiting any longer, and I'd done what I could. As I approached the door, I jiggled Cal's keys in my hand. My chest was tight as I sifted through the key ring, finding one that looked like it might belong to an apartment doorknob. It didn't fit in the lock, and I was puzzled until I realized it was probably one for Elliot's place.

I had no way of knowing for sure if my theory was right, but I stared down at it for a moment, wondering if I was. The idea of my brother being serious enough about *anyone* to exchange keys was mind-boggling to me. It made sense though; if he'd given Elliot a key, why wouldn't Elliot have given him one?

The second key I tried fit perfectly. I sucked in a deep breath as I swung the door open. I paused for a moment, hand on the doorknob, then forced my leaden feet to move inside. I'd seen the place before, but I was still treating it like a bomb about to explode because I was afraid of what other secrets of Cal's I might discover.

I moved slowly through the apartment, taking in the sights of my brother's life.

I began in the dining room, which was sparsely furnished with a folding card table and two mismatched chairs. A messy pile of papers was strewn across it, along with various items it looked like he appeared to have tossed there and left: a charger for some electronic device, playing cards, a pack of gum, and a handful of change. Nothing of much consequence, but the familiar clutter made me smile wistfully.

I cringed as I walked into the kitchen, expecting spoiled food, but it was mostly empty of perishables. The fridge held condiments and an assortment of beverages. The freezer had a nearly empty box of frozen waffles and some ice cube trays. The cabinets held a predictable assortment of dishes and dry goods. I smiled at the stash of candy bars I ran across. Despite Cal's athleticism, he had never been a particularly healthy eater, preferring convenience over nutrition, and he had an endless sweet tooth. Our mom had been forced to keep our candy separate so Cal wouldn't eat all of mine, but he'd stolen mine anyway when she wasn't looking. I'd never snitched on him. The candy made him happy, and I never liked it that much, so it was our little secret.

The thought of secrets made me continue my tour, where I

discovered two bedrooms and one bath. One bedroom was clearly the one he slept in, with an unmade bed and a pile of clothes that had been dumped on the floor by the closet like he would return at any moment. I blinked back tears.

But when I opened the door to the second room, surprise caused me to blink. The room was set up as a studio, with a white backdrop stretched along one wall and lighting equipment scattered around. A desk held a laptop and some camera gear but was otherwise relatively empty. I stood in there a long time, trying to put together the pieces of the puzzle that had been Cal's life. None of them seemed to fit together into a picture I could recognize.

Eventually, I ended up back in the living room, looking around the space. It was the most furnished, and the most lived in. There was a slouchy, comfortable-looking couch in a dark blue fabric, brightened by the multi-colored pillows and striped blanket he'd bought when he was hiking in the Andes. He had a decent-sized TV—he'd always liked watching movies and sports—but books were scattered across the coffee table as well. A semi-folded stack of what looked like clean clothes sat in a laundry basket, and I saw a collection of discarded shoes and papers on the floor. His snowboard and camera were still in the spots I'd seen them before, and if Elliot had been back since last week, he hadn't touched anything I could see.

I was grateful to Elliot for allowing me a glimpse into a portion of my brother's life I'd known nothing about. I spotted an untidy stack of photos on the coffee table and walked over to study them. I sank onto the couch, leaning forward to look through the messy pile of prints. They were all portraits of couples, artistically angled and abstract enough that it took me a moment to realize that every single one was of a same-sex couple. They were beautiful, done in a gritty black and white reminiscent of old film, and leaps and bounds above the quality of what Cal had ever shot before. He'd always been talented. These were truly stunning.

"Oh, Cal," I whispered, letting the photos fall back onto the table. "What did I do so wrong that you couldn't trust me?"

I wiped at my eyes, fighting down the rising urge to give in to tears. The sound of someone clearing their throat made me lift my head in shock. Elliot sat with his back against the wall, one arm propped on his updrawn knee as he fiddled with his lighter.

"Jesus Christ," I muttered, my heart rate skyrocketing at the unexpected sight.

"Sorry." His face looked pinched, his body tense, but he seemed less panicked than the time before. "You texted me so …"

"No, I'm glad you came. I just wasn't paying attention, I guess."

"You seemed pretty engrossed."

I nodded, and we both grew silent, the moment stretching and growing uncomfortable as we avoided making eye contact. I had no idea how to approach him, and I knew he probably felt just as uncomfortable. Even without the uneasiness from the night of angry, desperate sex we were both avoiding discussing, the situation was difficult and awkward at best. I finally cleared my throat. "I was surprised you texted me to tell me about the apartment last week."

Elliot crossed his legs and leaned forward. The movement was so fluid and graceful I found my gaze lingering on his long limbs. "I almost didn't. I thought about packing up his things and keeping them"—he swallowed, his Adam's apple bobbing in his throat—

"but that didn't seem fair to exclude you from his life."

"You have no idea how much I appreciate that," I said, glancing over at him. As our gazes met and held, I remembered him looming over me, his skin glowing in the dim light. I could see his dark hair falling over his face as he gripped my calf and drove into me. I'd tangled my fingers in the soft strands and forced him to look me in the eye as he'd fucked me. At the time, with grief and alcohol coursing through my veins, it had felt unreal. Now that my body no longer ached, it was easy to believe what happened had been a dream. But my skin prickled with remembered sensation. I shuddered and looked away, loathing myself for responding to him in any way.

"I don't know if you want to tell your family about this place—if you haven't already that is."

I shook my head, as much to clear the images from it as to answer his question. "No, I haven't told them anything. I don't know if I should or not. I don't want to keep secrets, but I don't want to hurt them either."

"It's your choice."

I nodded. Never one to shy away from responsibility in the past, I dreaded having to make that decision now. *Why did you leave everything such a mess, Cal? It's too much for me to handle.*

"Have you decided what you want to do with his stuff?" Elliot asked softly.

"To be honest, finding out he had this place was such a shock I hadn't thought about it." Practical matters began to crowd my brain.

If he had a lease, it would have to be broken. My mom was the executor of Cal's estate, so I'd have to tell her about Cal's secret apartment. Which would lead to questions about Cal's secret life.

"I guess I'll have to tell my family, won't I?" I said aloud. "To deal with the lease and everything."

"Not necessarily. The lease isn't in Cal's name."

"Oh. Is it in yours?"

"No. Joanne—someone I knew from art school—lived here. Her girlfriend got an amazing job offer in Italy and Joanne wanted to go with her. She was looking for someone to sublet it around the same time Cal was looking for a place to work on his photography." I glanced down at the photos on the table in front of me. "I put them in contact. It's not even a legal sublet—the leasing company didn't know Cal was living here—but as long as she paid the rent on time, they weren't likely to notice."

Somehow, it didn't surprise me that Cal hadn't gone the legal route of filling out an application and getting the leasing company's approval, but in a way, it made this easier. Legally, at least, there was no reason my parents needed to know about it.

"So how much time is left on the lease?"

"A few months. It ends in April. Cal swore he was going to move in with me when it was up but—" Elliot's lips became a thin line, and I wondered if that had been a point of contention between them.

"I'll pay your friend for the remainder of the time on the lease. Just let me know how much."

"After Cal died, I let Joanne know and paid her for the remainder of the lease. I wanted some time to decide what to do about his belongings."

"I'd be happy to pay you back."

"That's unnecessary." Although tempted to argue, his tone didn't invite me to press any further, so I nodded.

Elliot and I were both silent for a long time before I finally sighed and stood. "I guess I should head out."

Elliot frowned and looked around the apartment. "Why did you want me to come here tonight? I thought you needed something specific."

"No." I gave him a perplexed look. "I just wanted to let you know I was here so you wouldn't be surprised if you came by." In a way, I'd wanted his permission to be there.

He tilted his head and studied me for a moment before nodding. "I must have misunderstood."

Did I want Elliot to show up? Did some part of me hope to see him here? I didn't think my text had been that ambiguous, but maybe I was wrong. "I would like to sit down with you some time and talk—if you're willing. I just"—my voice cracked— "I just want to know more about my brother. You're the only person who can help me."

A look of discomfort crossed his face. Maybe he was struggling as much as he had the last time we were here in Cal's apartment and was simply hiding it better this time. He took a deep breath and nodded, tucking his hair behind his ear, his lips thinning. "Just give me a little time?"

"Thank you. Take whatever time you need."

Elliot stood and walked toward the door. Halfway there, he paused to glance back at me. "I'm not sure what you're planning to do with this place, but a few of my things are here."

"Of course," I replied. "I didn't even think about that. And if there's anything of Cal's you want just let me know."

"Thanks."

"It's the least I can do, and I'm not in any hurry to pack this place up." A sudden wave of grief hit me. Packing up and giving away Cal's belongings was going to make his death so final. Was I ready for that? I scrubbed a hand over my face, feeling the rasp of whiskers on my jaw. Damn, it had been a long day.

"Okay." Elliot jammed his hands in his pockets. We were both silent, neither of us making a move to leave.

"Did you want to get your belongings now?" I asked eventually.

"No, it's nothing major. Clothes, art supplies, that sort of thing. I can do it another time."

"Just come by whenever it works for you then."

"Gee, thanks."

His sarcasm made me flush. "That didn't come out right. I know you didn't have to tell me about this place at all. You could have kept it a secret and run off with his belongings. But I'm grateful, and if Cal trusted you, so do I."

He nodded slowly. "I ... I appreciate that."

"He was the man you loved, the last thing I want to do was take that away from you." I let out a heavy sigh.

He leaned back against the door and closed his eyes for a moment before opening them, his gray gaze intent on mine, sad and resigned. "I'll text you. Give me a couple of weeks to deal with some things first."

"Of course." He turned away and reached for the doorknob. "Sorry I dragged you over here for nothing. I didn't mean to."

Elliot nodded, but he didn't turn around, just pulled open the door and stepped through it without another word. He didn't say goodbye either, but it didn't surprise me. I lingered there by the door, breathing in the remnants of his smoky tea scent, hoping desperately I'd hear from him like he promised.

But a dark part of me wondered if it was his link to my brother I was so desperate for, or something else.

While I waited to hear back from Elliot, I threw myself into work.

A week passed before I remembered I hadn't called Dave to find some time to get together with him, so one night after work, I dialed his number.

"Hey, stranger," he greeted me. "I'm glad you called."

"Are you available for dinner tomorrow night?" I asked.

"I am actually." He sounded vaguely surprised. "It's been nuts lately, but I'm finally getting a bit of a break. I'd love to do dinner."

We figured out the when and where, and I went to bed in a surprisingly good mood, really looking forward to seeing him.

After work the next day, I headed straight to the restaurant. I took off my tie and loosened a few buttons at the top of my shirt. I looked beat, but there was nothing to be done about that.

A glance at the clock on my dashboard told me I was a few minutes early, but I figured I'd go in and snag us a table. The hostess showed me to a booth immediately, and I texted Dave to let him know I'd arrived.

Almost there was his prompt response. I examined the drink selections until Dave arrived. I hadn't touched liquor since the day of Cal's funeral, but beer seemed doable.

As always, he gave me a huge hug. It wasn't quite as long or as intimate as the one at the bar, but it still felt damn good. Not in a sexual way, but the brotherly affection was nice. When I pulled back, I paused, my hands still on Dave's shoulders. "You look like shit."

He snorted. "You ever think maybe *this* is why you're single? There's this thing called tact."

"Yeah, well, ask me out on a date, and you'll see a whole different side of me," I teased, letting my hands drop. "You're a friend; I'm supposed to be blunt with you."

Dave laughed and reached up to pat me on the shoulder.

"I'll give you that one," he teased as he slid into the booth. I followed suit.

He did look utterly exhausted. Circles ringed his eyes, and I wondered when he'd last slept. He was still gorgeous of course, nothing could take away from the natural good looks he had, but there was no doubt he was struggling.

"So, you said work has been busy?"

Dave looked up from the menu. "Yeah, we've had some pretty big stories lately with the bridge collapse and the ensuing scandal."

"Oh, right. I almost forgot about it," I said. The bridge had collapsed the same day Cal had died, and I'd had too much on my plate since to think about it.

"I still feel guilty," Dave said. "I hate that I couldn't make it there in time to say goodbye to him."

"I know." I reached out and touched Dave's hand. He smiled sadly at me.

"I would have liked to have been there." He swallowed, his eyes haunted.

"You know there was nothing you could have done," I pointed out gently.

"Yeah. I know." Dave's shoulders heaved as he exhaled heavily. His pain was palpable.

I understood why Dave wished he'd been there to say goodbye however. It had been difficult seeing Cal lying there on life support and knowing that he was already gone. But at least, I'd been able to say goodbye to him in person. Even if there was no chance he'd heard me. Not unless the afterlife neither Cal nor I believed in actually existed. I knew Cal had been dead from the moment he'd arrived at the emergency room. Machines had kept his heart and lungs going, but his consciousness had been gone. He hadn't known our family was by his side. Or that Dave wasn't there. Still, I knew it had to be eating Dave alive that he hadn't had that opportunity to stay goodbye. For his own sake, if not for Cal's.

"Please don't blame yourself."

Our entire family had discussed organ donations plenty of times over the years, and it was indicated on all our driver's licenses, so the choice to do so for Cal had been without question. It had been giving up hope that he could recover that was gut-wrenching. But there had been a patient in desperate need of a heart in Seattle, and we hadn't wanted to delay it any longer. At least, it was a comfort to know he'd helped so many people in his death.

"I'm trying not to. It's just been so difficult to even believe he's gone." Dave leaned forward. "I almost sent him a text the other day without even thinking."

"I've been fighting the same instincts," I reassured him.

"It's ..." Dave's voice trailed off as the waitress approached.

"Hello. I'm Nadia. What can I get for you boys?" the waitress asked cheerily.

"Alesong White, please," I said, forcing a smile onto my face. "And for you?" she gave Dave an interested look.

"Hmm. I think I'm in the mood for something sweet. I'm guessing you aren't on the menu" —Dave winked— "so maybe the Alesong Plum in Love."

The waitress giggled, and this time my smile was genuine. The man never turned off the charm. It's why I'd never taken any of his flirtation with me seriously. The waitress was his type; I wasn't.

No doubt Cal would have flirted with her too. For a moment, I considered Elliot, wondering if Cal had still flirted with women while they were together. If he did, it must have driven Elliot crazy. He didn't strike me as the type to share.

For a short while, we were busy looking at the menu and ordering food, but once we had our burgers in front of us, Dave leaned forward. "How are *you* holding up?"

"Fuck, I don't know. I'm hanging in there, I guess. Trying to keep busy going to work and to the gym. Keeping an eye on my parents. Sunday dinners are hard."

Dave gave me a sympathetic smile. "Yeah, I bet."

"My mom's been spending a lot of time on the computer— according to Dad—and I'm not sure how he's doing. I think he's drinking, so he's not really coping. Hell, I know it's going to take time, for all of us, but I wish I could do more."

"Honestly, it's just going to take time." Dave sighed. "It did when I lost my mom."

"I'm sure."

I had nearly forgotten that Dave's mother had died of breast cancer when he was still in college. I'd been in med school at the time, and Dave and I hadn't been as close then. I'd gone to the funeral, but because I didn't see him on a regular basis, I wasn't around to see the impact.

As we ate, we talked about other things, mostly Dave's job and my new interest in boxing.

"Can I ask you something?" I asked a while later, leaning forward to push away my mostly empty plate.

Dave frowned. "You can ask me anything, Chris, you know that."

"Did you know Cal was subletting an apartment?"

His look of astonishment was the only answer I needed. "What? No. I thought he was still living with your parents."

I smacked the table with my palm, which made the dishes rattle. "God damn it! What was going on with him, Dave? He wasn't honest with our parents, with me, or with his best friend. I don't fucking get it."

"I don't know," Dave replied with a worried frown.

"Why was Cal so fucking secretive? It doesn't seem like him at all."

"It doesn't," Dave admitted. "He's always been so open about everything. I'm every bit as perplexed as you are. I wish I had more answers for you, man."

Dave and I lingered at the table with another beer each, talking through what we knew about Cal's life after he met Elliot. There was little Dave knew that I didn't or that he hadn't already told me though, and I grew frustrated.

"Why don't you talk to Elliot?" he suggested, draining the last of his beer and sitting back in the booth.

I tried to hide the jolt his suggestion sent through me. "I have. A little. He's the one who told me about Cal's place," I replied tightly. The whole topic of Elliot was one I wanted to avoid. I couldn't face Cal's best friend and tell him I'd slept with my brother's boyfriend.

A look of surprise crossed his face, but he just nodded. "So, what's the problem?"

"Well, I don't know Elliot at all, and I think he wants as little to do with me as possible." Although maybe that wasn't entirely accurate; he had reached out to me about Cal's apartment.

"He's not exactly keeping in contact with me either," Dave said.

"Hmm." That was odd that he'd decided to stay in contact with me and not Dave.

"Yeah. I was the one who let him know about the funeral and the trip to the bar that night, but I haven't heard from him since. You say you've talked to him?"

"Just—just a few times," I stammered, afraid Dave would see the truth I skirted. "He told me about Cal's apartment. I've asked him if he'll tell me more about Cal, but he said he needs more time. I hope he'll open up to me eventually but I'm not sure if it'll happen." I sighed and looked down, realizing I'd been shredding the napkin on the table in front of me. "And who would blame him? I'm part of the reason Cal stayed closeted; Elliot should fucking hate me."

Then again, maybe he does. Maybe the night together had been nothing but revenge, a way to punish me for contributing to Cal keeping their relationship a secret. A way to get back at his lover's family. But I would swear there had been more to it; an electric need that wasn't only fueled by hate and anger. A thread of something else, something more powerful and desperate.

Or maybe I was trying to justify something that was inexcusable.

"I'm sure he doesn't hate you," Dave said gently, resting his hand on mine and forcing me to stop shredding the napkins. "He's probably just grieving in his own way. Give him time."

I shrugged, weariness suddenly settling over me. "What else can I do?"

The topic turned away from my brother and his lover, and Dave and I eventually wrapped up dinner. Dave stopped me on the sidewalk in front. "Would you like to come watch the Winterhawks' game with me and the guys some time?"

"Yeah, that would be great." I needed to get out more, and hanging out with Dave and his friends would be good for me. "You weren't planning to invite Elliot, were you?"

Dave raised an eyebrow at me and put his hand on my arm to shift our bodies to the side when people brushed past us. "Do you *want* me to?"

"No, no, of course not. I was just wondering."

Dave gave me a slightly skeptical look. "Okay."

"Just wondering if he knew the other guys well," I lied, unsure if I was relieved or disappointed by the news Elliot wouldn't be there. "I'm trying to put together all of the pieces."

"He'd met them a few times," Dave said, his expression smoothing out as if my answer had put his questions to rest. "They didn't know he and Cal were seeing each other, and I don't think he felt particularly comfortable with them."

"Yeah, well, they don't seem like they'd have that much in common. Then again, he and Cal don't really either." I chuckled. "I could see *you* with Cal more than Elliot."

Dave shrugged. "You know what they say: opposites attract. Maybe that's why Cal and Elliot worked."

"Yeah, maybe." A sudden gust of cold air made me shiver. "Did Cal seem different to you in the time he was with Elliot?"

Dave hummed thoughtfully. "Not that I noticed then. Looking back, yeah, I can see that. He was quieter, a little distant, like he had a lot on his mind."

"If only he'd kept a journal or something. Or, you know, fucking talked to me. I wish I knew what was going on in his head."

"Cal was obviously going through something major, but we may never have the answers." Dave's voice was gentle. "We might just have to learn to live with that."

"What if I can't?"

Dave shrugged. "For your own sanity, you may have to. It looks like it's tearing you apart."

"It is," I admitted. "But it's something I have to do. I can't live with all these unanswered questions."

"Please don't let it consume your whole life, Chris," he said. "I know it's easier said than done, but grieve for your brother, then move forward. You're too good of a guy to let this eat you up. Cal's dead, and it hurts like hell, but you and me, we're still alive, and we can't forget that."

I considered Dave's words as he hugged me goodbye. His arms around me felt good, but more for what they represented than the fact that they belonged to him specifically. He understood what I was going through.

But after, as I trudged to my car, I felt lonelier than ever. Going home to sleep alone made me depressed.

It had been a low-key ache since this breakup with Alec, but it didn't usually bother me that much. Now, since Cal's death, it had become acutely painful. And every time I thought about not being alone, it was Elliot's face that popped in my head.

Chapter Eleven

Another week passed with no word from Elliot. Although he'd taken care of Cal's rent for the next few months, there were still practical matters to consider. Packing Cal's belongings would take time and felt so final. If I ignored it, I could almost believe the funeral was a bad dream and Cal was just on an extended vacation or another stint in the Peace Corps. Sorting through his belongings and deciding what to do with them would make it all too real.

At least, Elliot had bought me some time to sort through his possessions at my own pace. Items that didn't hold any sentimental value to me, or that Elliot didn't want to keep, I'd donate to charity. Cal would have approved, and I certainly didn't want to sell them. If they helped some broke college student or struggling family, so much the better. At least, they'd be used and appreciated rather than gathering dust in the back of my closet as a sad memorial to my brother's life.

On Saturday morning, a text startled me from a deep sleep. I rolled over, groggily reaching for my phone on the nightstand and saw a text from Elliot that jolted me wide awake. *Cal's apartment. 10 am, if you want to talk.*

It was just a few minutes after nine, and I fumbled to type a response. *I'll be there.*

After I showered and dressed, I swung by a coffee shop. I ordered a latte and a bagel for myself, and then hesitated. "Actually, can you add an Earl Grey tea and another bagel, please?"

The barista agreed with a cheerful smile and rang up my order, but I immediately felt idiotic. Was it weird for me to buy breakfast for Elliot? It was something I'd do for any of my friends, but Elliot and I weren't friends. I didn't have a clue *what* we were, but certainly not friends.

I couldn't stop second-guessing myself for buying it. I nearly dumped the food in the trash before I even left the coffee shop, and then again just outside Cal's apartment building, but I felt too guilty about wasting it. I juggled the containers as I opened the apartment door and stepped inside. Elliot was there already, sitting cross-legged on the couch with his sketchbook on his knees. His hair was pulled back at the nape of his neck, and he had a pencil between his teeth while he sketched with another. I cleared my throat, and he looked up, eyes wide and unguarded. He pulled the pencil out of his mouth and gave me a tight nod as his expression closed off. He flipped the sketchbook shut before I could get a glimpse of what he'd been drawing, laying it, and the pencils, on the table.

"I brought you tea and a bagel," I blurted out, nervous and flustered. Elliot responded with a single, raised eyebrow. "I was getting something for myself anyway."

I set his tea and bagel on the coffee table, then took a seat on the floor nearby. I set my cup of coffee on the floor and scowled down at my bagel as I smeared it with cream cheese. *I should have trusted my instincts.* But after a moment, Elliot reached for the tea, cupping it in his hands. He closed his eyes and inhaled. He looked so young and so vulnerable in his skinny jeans and oversized sweater that a lump rose in my throat. Despite the strength I knew lurked in his limbs, they were narrow, like he barely ate enough to fill them out. He wasn't gaunt, but his hands seemed over-large compared to his narrow wrists where they peeked out from the black sleeves. I could see the veins on the back of his hands, a faint hint of blue underneath the pale skin.

His vulnerability tugged at me, made me want to take care of him. The smudged shadows under his gray eyes and his narrow, hunched shoulders made me want to bundle him up and take him home.

Christ, I'm turning into my mother. I scowled down at my coffee cup.

We ate and drank in silence. Elliot seemed distracted, staring off into space as he neatly tore off pieces of bagel and chewed them thoroughly. I didn't push him. After we were done eating, the silence grew awkward, and I finally cleared my throat. "What now?"

"I don't know; this is your show," Elliot said, sounding irritable. "I didn't want to do this in the first place."

I closed my eyes for a second, a headache beginning to form. When I opened them, I looked straight at Elliot. "I understand that. I know this is difficult for you. I'm sorry. I want to help, but I don't know how to make this any easier."

His lips tightened. "Let's just get it over with. What do you want from me?"

I sighed and leaned forward, bracing my elbows on my knees. "I'm at a disadvantage here, Elliot. I want a chance to get to know who Cal was, and you're apparently the only person who actually knew this side of him. It kills me that he had this whole other life with you that I didn't have a clue about." Just thinking about Cal made me emotional, and I had to fight back the tears.

Elliot seemed to relax slightly, and his smile was melancholy as he shoved his hand in his pocket, pulling out a lighter. I opened my mouth to tell him he shouldn't smoke in the apartment, but he didn't reach for cigarettes. Instead, he began to toy with the silver lighter. "I think he *wanted* to tell you."

"Nothing hurts worse than knowing he didn't feel like he could."

"Maybe I shouldn't have told you about my relationship with your brother." Elliot looked down, staring at his fingers as he flipped the lighter over and over with the deftness of a magician with a coin. "Maybe I should have stayed away. Not gone to the funeral. Not told you about Cal and me."

"No!" I protested, and he looked up at my vehement outburst. "No, I'm glad you were there to say goodbye, and I'm glad you told me. It hurts, but I'd rather know. I just don't understand it."

"I think he was planning to tell you about it at some point. He was working up to it."

"But *why* was it so difficult for him? I came out to my parents at fifteen. Cal was nine. He was old enough to see that they were supportive. We had the kind of family gay men dream about." A dark look passed over Elliot's face, but he just nodded. I was tempted to ask him about his own family, but I suspected it would be delving into territory that was far too personal. "Even if he were worried about telling our parents because of the issue of children— which I can understand—why not tell *me*?" My throat felt raw from suppressed tears.

"I think he hated the idea of forcing you to keep his secret. It's one thing to be in the closet, it's another to ask someone else to do it for you." His voice held an edge of resentment.

"What about the two of you? Were you out together?"

Elliot sighed. "It was … complicated. We argued about it a lot, but by the end, yeah, we were out in public. I think he figured Portland was big enough that he wasn't likely to run into family or anything. Obviously, Dave knew, although I don't think any of the other guys did. We hung out with them a few times, but Cal was careful about not touching me. I don't think they had any idea we were a … couple."

I nodded. I'd dated a few closeted guys over the years. It wasn't fun. "So, not hiding, but not telling everyone either."

"Basically. A few people from art school knew about Cal, but I've always been open with them."

People. Not friends. "What about your family?" I asked.

He just shook his head, his lips thinning as he frowned. He bounced his leg on the sofa, suddenly jittery and anxious. "They haven't been a part of my life for years."

Not wanting to pry further, I changed the subject. "Can you tell me about Cal's photography?"

Elliot's shoulders lowered and his pinched expression eased. "After Cal posed for me, we discussed art and sexuality a lot. He saw some of the portraits of gay couples I did, and I think it intrigued him. He wanted to capture that with his camera. So, several times, we worked together. We hired models, and I'd sketch while he took photos. It progressed from there. It became kind of an obsession for him, even after I was ready to move on to other subjects."

"Was ... was it difficult for him to realize he was bisexual?"

Elliot sighed and leaned back, a distant look settling over his features. "At first, it was just ... attraction, and he was fine with that. Surprised because he hadn't seen it coming, but I'm sure you know better than anyone how he was. He just went with it, said he'd try anything once. Or twice. Just to be sure."

I nodded, a small smile turning up the corner of my lips. "Yeah, that sounds like Cal."

"Cal was so fucking charming; it was no surprise that I fell for him, but I don't think he ever expected to return the feelings. It didn't take long for us to figure out it wasn't just sex. There was something more there, and he didn't know how to handle it. I mean, he didn't do relationships with women really, so one with me was even harder for him to grasp. Sex was easy for him, but anything more freaked him out."

"I can imagine." Cal had always been a free spirit, and he'd never felt the need to be pinned down by a relationship. At twenty-eight, I couldn't really blame him for not being in a hurry to settle down. Throwing in a sudden and unexpected attraction to a man, along with my parents' desire for biological grandchildren, would have been an enormous amount to deal with. I'd begun to grasp why my brother hadn't told anyone what he was struggling with.

"At one point, he talked me into having a fucking threesome with him and a woman he knew." Elliot scowled. "He thought it would

152

help him be sure about his feelings. It was a disaster. I'm not interested in women at all—never have been—and I told him that, but he reassured me it would be fine. I didn't have to touch her, and he swore it was exactly what we needed. I should have trusted my instincts."

I grimaced. It sounded like a recipe for disaster to me. Elliot nodded. "Yeah, it went exactly as well as you'd anticipate," he said viciously. "I was uncomfortable and jealous, she was uncomfortable and felt left out, and Cal was confused and frustrated. We nearly broke up then. Or called it off, I guess, since we weren't technically together at that point. Loving your brother was easy, but being with him wasn't. Most of the time, it was worth it, but sometimes, I wondered if I was crazy for even trying."

It didn't surprise me to find that Elliot and Cal's relationship hadn't been smooth sailing. I loved my brother, and in a way, I idolized him, but I knew that he wasn't perfect either. I was surprised by Elliot's frankness, however.

"How long did you know him?" I asked.

Elliot stuffed the lighter back in his pocket. "Nine—no—ten months; we met last March. He posed for me, and things went from there." He looked down, this time playing with the frayed seam of his jeans as he let out a small, rueful laugh. "I don't typically sleep with my models, but Cal ..."

"Yeah, I understand." I really did. Everyone who met Cal fell for him in one way or another. "He got to people."

Elliot flinched. "He did. Sometimes he was oblivious though. He didn't realize how much he hurt people. Not intentionally, of course, but ... sometimes he just didn't understand that it *hurt* to love him when he wasn't ready to love back." I watched Elliot visibly shrink, drawing in on himself, his gaze suddenly troubled. His voice was very soft. "Or maybe he wasn't willing."

My heart hurt for Elliot. "I can imagine how difficult that would be."

Ducking his head, Elliot pulled the elastic out of his hair and let it fall; hiding his face from my view, but not before I saw the pain written on it. The abrupt change in demeanor told me everything he wasn't saying. We'd ventured into something intensely difficult and painful, and I needed to back off. I saw his shoulders jerk, and a soft, nearly soundless whimper escaped him. He pulled his hands back into his sleeves and brought them to his face, blocking the small glimpse of his face I could see through the heavy, dark waves of his hair.

The conversation was over, but truthfully, I was shocked that Elliot had been so open with me at all. I stood and picked up our trash, sure he would want some privacy. I had to fight every instinct in me telling me to reach out and comfort him. I disappeared into the kitchen and tossed the remnants of breakfast in the trash bin; I'd take it out to the dumpster when I left so it didn't stink up the place. I braced my arms on the counter and closed my eyes, trying to process everything Elliot had shared. It was helping; I felt like I was getting a broader picture of what Cal's life had been like and starting to understand why he hadn't told me what was going on. But was I hurting Elliot in the process?

Is what I learn worth Elliot's pain?

I let out a shaky sigh and forced myself to stay busy, pulling things out of the cupboards and stacking them into neat piles instead of going to Elliot like I wanted to.

He came in the kitchen a while later, eyes red-rimmed, his gaze blank and distant, the sketchpad clutched in his hand.

"Are you headed out?" I asked, keeping my voice casual, like nothing had happened. He responded with a quick, tight jerk of his head, but didn't speak. "I will too then."

I grabbed the trash and followed him out of the apartment and down the stairs.

He walked with me to the dumpster, but once we were back on the sidewalk in front of our vehicles, he lit a cigarette. He let out a sigh and some of the tension leached from his body. I still hated his smoking, but at the moment, he deserved anything that would comfort him. I fumbled with how to tell him how much I appreciated him opening up to me.

"I want to thank you, Elliot. I know it wasn't easy," I said sympathetically. Not easy was an understatement.

Elliot exhaled, blowing the smoke away from me.

"Are you willing to help me sort through Cal's things?"

"I guess. I don't know why you need *me* to do it," he replied roughly. I'd grown to realize his voice was always a little raspy, but it became more so when he was emotional.

"I've been thinking about what to do with Cal's belongings." He nodded jerkily. "I'd like to keep a few things, but I'm sure there are a few you'd like as well. Whatever else we don't want can be donated to charity. I think Cal would have liked that."

"Yeah."

"I don't want to risk getting rid of something you'd like to keep; I thought if we worked on it together it would kill two birds with one stone. You could tell me about Cal's life since you met him while we sort through his belongings."

His lips thinned, becoming tight, hard lines, making his already angular face look pinched and fatigued. "Fine." Elliot took a final drag on the cigarette and stamped it out on the ground. "You've got my number; just shoot me a text when you want to do this shit."

"I will," I promised, and he turned to leave. I called out after him, "Thanks again, Elliot."

He gave me a distracted wave without turning, climbed in his car, and drove away.

I drove straight to the gym. A workout seemed like the best way to release the tension coiled inside me.

Thankfully, Jason was available for a private boxing session, and after a quick warm up, I threw myself into it.

"Damn, you are really getting into this," Jason said in an admiring tone when I finished a round with the punching bag. My thighs were cramped and aching, and I bent over, my lungs straining to draw in a breath. "Are you interested in some actual sparring? You might like having a live opponent."

I straightened and shook my head. "No. I saw a few too many head injuries during my ER rotation. I get why people might enjoy it but I can't really stomach the idea of rattling someone's brain around in their skull."

Jason grinned. "I get that. No problem, just wanted to suggest it."

"Of course."

I left the gym, a bit more settled than when I'd come in.

I kept myself busy the rest of that day, but when I lay down in bed, I grew restless again. The image of Elliot's thin, hunched body on the sofa, crying silently to himself haunted me.

How alone *was* he? It didn't sound like he had any family he kept in contact with, and although he mentioned people from art school, I had no idea how close they were. The fact that he hadn't referred to them as friends wasn't exactly a great sign. Was he by himself in the large, cold loft of his? Did he sleep alone in his bed, aching for Cal?

It had been difficult after my breakup with Alec to return to sleeping alone. We'd lived together for the better part of a year, and no matter how angry I still was with him, I missed the companionship. The bed had seemed too large, the sheets cold. Did Elliot feel the same?

Over the past few weeks, vague memories of the night I'd spent in bed with Elliot had returned. I could remember sleeping beside Elliot, my nose buried in the tangles of his hair. I could still faintly feel his skin, hot under my palm, his narrow ribcage rising and falling with his deep, even breaths. It had felt so right, so perfectly natural for our bodies to be tangled together. For the first time in more than a year, I hadn't felt alone.

Why was it that now, sober and clear-headed, I wanted that again? I rolled over onto my stomach, annoyed by the interested stirrings of my body at thoughts of Elliot. He confused me, put me on edge, but a part of me still wanted him. No matter that he was grieving the loss of my brother and probably didn't want to be anywhere near me, I still wanted him.

Chapter Twelve

I exchanged a few texts with Elliot the next day, and we finally agreed to meet on Saturday morning to sort through and pack Cal's belongings. Having a plan made my life easier.

Work consumed me that week. Mr. Wu died peacefully in his sleep. I met with his family, but it seemed they were all coping as best they could. His grandchildren had come to see him before his death, so they'd all been able to say goodbye to him.

I had several new patients come in, and I met with a handful more who were in palliative care. It varied from week to week, but at the moment, I had an unusually high number of patients who had recently been diagnosed with severe, chronic conditions. I felt frayed at the seams as I met with them and struggled to help them cope.

Hazel's health continued to decline, and she was struggling to come to terms with the fact that she didn't have much time left. Her health was growing worse, and her bucket list would go unfulfilled. Understandably, she was angry. Her father was too.

"She's getting a lot worse, isn't she, Doc?" Ryan asked me grimly almost as soon as he took a seat in my office on Thursday morning. I'd had several sessions with him and Lissa over the past few weeks, but he was alone today. Lissa hadn't wanted to leave Hazel's side. "The nurse said she had a really rough night. She was up coughing a lot."

"Yes, the pneumonia is weakening her." She'd been prescribed an antibiotic to fight the infection, but I had little hope it would do much for her.

Infection and hemorrhage were the leading causes of death in leukemia patients. Infection was the slower one. Was that better or worse for her family? I wasn't sure. Alleviating suffering, reducing symptoms, and maximizing the quality of life were always the goal in hospice, but I had my doubts that treating the pneumonia was for the best. Was it actually better for Hazel to linger and give her family more time to say goodbye? Or was it kinder for her to go quickly? These were the questions I wrestled with on a day-to-day basis.

Cal's sudden death had made me less sure I knew the answers.

The suddenness of his death had driven home how truly unprepared most of us were for death. Even I, who had spent the better part of fifteen years thinking about it, was floundering. I would have given almost anything to have Cal around for longer. But what if the trade-off was knowing he would suffer for longer? What a wretched choice families had to make for their loved ones.

"It's so unfair." Ryan's voice broke. "Why can't I trade places with her?" He looked up at me, anguished. "Why can't I take this on for her? Why not me instead? I hate feeling so *helpless* to do anything. And I'm just so angry all the time."

My anger was there too, bubbling under the surface as I thought about how grossly unfair it was that Cal would never grow old. All the plans we'd made were destroyed now, and there was no fixing any of it.

"I snap at Lissa sometimes, and God, I even snapped at Hazel the other day when she was refusing to eat. My child is dying, and I'm angry with her …" He buried his head in his hands. I could tell he was struggling to hold it together, and I let him be. He needed time to process it. To sit with the words. When he looked up, his eyes were dry, but I could see the strain on his face as he tried to compose himself. "I know she can't just will this away, but a part of me blames her for giving up. For not getting better. I'm a *monster*."

I spoke quietly, reassuring him that he wasn't a monster, that his feelings were normal and part of the grieving process. I threw out every platitude and soothing phrase I could dredge up from my training. I tried as hard as I possibly could to help him come to grips with it. And yet, as he trudged from my office, looking worse for wear than when he'd walked in, I felt a sharp stab of despair. Was I losing my edge?

Cal's death crowded my mind and kept me from being as objective as I had been before. The words I spoke seemed meaningless. A child was dying. A family was grieving.

And I could do nothing to help them.

That night, I showed up at Dave's house with a six pack of Rogue Ales beer, a bag of chips, and a fake smile plastered on my face in time for the Winterhawks' game against the Silvertips.

Thankfully, Dave's warm, easy grin helped push a few of the burdens from my shoulders, and as always, I welcomed the hug he gave me. Cooper and Shaun were already there, and Rob and John were on their way.

BRIGHAM VAUGHN

"It's great to see you!" Cooper greeted me cheerfully.

"Hey, good to see you too," I responded.

"How are you doing, man?" Cooper's expression turned serious.

"Just taking it one day at a time."

"Yeah, that's all you can do." Shaun slapped me on the shoulder.

I shoved work and Cal out of my head and forced myself to take part in the banter and comradery as we watched the game. It worked—more or less—and I welcomed the distraction. Sitting between Dave and Rob was comforting. I wasn't so alone.

Long after the rest of the guys left, Dave and I hung out on his couch, watching a movie. I'd stopped drinking after a single beer since I needed to drive home, but Dave continued. By the time the credits rolled, he seemed loose and relaxed.

"I should go," I said, stretching. But I was reluctant. My apartment was so empty, and I had no desire to go back there.

Dave shrugged. "You could always spend the night, if you want to."

"Nah, I'm sober, and I think I'm a little tall for this couch," I pointed out.

"Who said anything about the couch?" Dave asked with a grin.

"Offering to share your bed?" I raised an eyebrow at him. It was a one-bedroom place. "I didn't bring my pajamas."

Dave snorted. "That never stopped your brother. I saw his naked ass more times than the asses of any of my girlfriends, I swear. Which is unfortunate. I've dated some women with *spectacular* asses."

"Yeah, Cal was never too particular about who he flashed." Alec had been horrified when Cal crashed at our apartment and didn't bother to take a change of clothes into the bathroom when he showered. There was no getting Cal to do anything he didn't want to do, and making a big deal about it only made him more likely to do it again.

"I swear he got off on it. Not flashing me, but people in general."

I let out a quiet snort and shrugged. "I never spent a lot of time thinking about what got my brother off, but yeah, probably."

"Everything got your brother off."

I made a face. "I'm not sure I needed to know that. Or want to know how *you* know that."

"Yeah, well, what happens in the dorms at PSU stays in the dorms at PSU." Dave smirked at me. "And it was only the one time."

I raised an eyebrow at Dave. "Wait, *what* was only the one time?"

"Finding out what gets Cal off. I learned a hell of a lot more about your brother than I intended to one very, very fucked-up night." Dave snickered.

"What happened? Did you walk in on him and a girl doing something kinky or something? That wouldn't surprise me."

For the first time, Dave looked apprehensive. "No, it was just Cal and me that night …"

I stared blankly at him as I struggled to put the pieces together. I blinked when they finally clicked into place. "Wait, *you and Cal* fooled around?"

Dave shrugged. "We got high, and I dunno, I guess he was bored or curious or something. We traded blowjobs, then woke up in the morning and agreed we'd never talk about it again."

"So you're bi too?" My mind reeled.

"Nah, call it heteroflexible." Dave gave me a crooked grin. "I don't mind the occasional blowjob from a guy, but it doesn't go beyond that. I don't need a dick up my ass, and I can't see being in a relationship with a man."

"So you and Cal never considered dating or anything?"

Dave snorted. "No. It wasn't like that with Cal. That night was … whatever, but mostly, Cal was like a brother to me. You know that."

Anger rose in me, fast and sharp, and I was on my feet before I realized what I was doing. "Well, he was my brother, and I *thought* you were a good friend," I snapped. Had everyone in my life lied to me? "But apparently, I had no idea what was going on with either of you! Why the fuck did neither of you talk about this shit with me?"

"Dude, calm down, Chris." Dave stood slowly and held up his palms. "It wasn't like either of us were going to have some big coming out because we sucked each other off once. Christ, you would have made such a big fucking deal about it; it wasn't worth the hassle."

"Fuck you!" I snarled, shoving at his chest. "Fuck you and fuck Cal. You both *lied* to me!"

He staggered back, struggling to retain his balance. When he did, he squared off, anger making the lines of his face hard and unrecognizable. "It's not all about you, Chris. Jesus, sometimes Cal and I just wanted to do our own thing without you in the middle of shit. Whine and cry all you want about the fact that we didn't immediately come running to tell you about it, but we didn't need your input on what it meant that our dicks got hard around guys occasionally. Fuck! Not everything fits into the neat little boxes you put things in. You're gay. Great. But Cal and I were … I don't know. Not gay, not straight, and I don't know what the fuck it means, but you're turning it into this huge *thing* like you always do."

I sputtered as I tried to formulate a response, but Dave cut me off. "Besides, I knew about the little crush you had on me then, and I didn't want you to get your hopes up. I was never gonna be the guy for you, and I didn't want you to think that would change."

"You couldn't have just fucking told me that?" Hurt and anger made my voice sharp.

"No, I couldn't. God, you should see yourself when you're upset. It's like kicking a puppy. I didn't want to be cruel."

"Did you just call me a puppy?" I stared at him incredulously.

"No, damn it! I just mean … you're such a nice guy, Chris, but everything is so fucking black and white for you. Cal *worshiped* you, and he didn't know how to tell you that he didn't know what the fuck he wanted, and I didn't want to tell you that maybe I'm not quite as straight as I appear. I get that you guys were close, but hell, you don't even have any friends outside of Cal's friends."

I stared at him, reeling from the verbal blow. "So, *our* friendship is nothing, then? I was just Cal's annoying brother hanging around because I didn't have any friends of my own?" I spat. "It would have been nice to know that we weren't actually friends before now, you asshole."

I turned to go, vomit rising in the back of my throat as I considered how little I knew about the two men I'd considered my friend and my brother. Had no one been honest with me? I strode out of the living room, toward the front door, my stomach roiling.

"No! Wait, Chris." Dave jogged after me. "I didn't mean that. Shit. It … it didn't come out right, I swear. Let me explain."

"Fuck you," I said savagely. I wrestled the door open, clumsy and uncoordinated. "I've heard enough from you to last a goddamn lifetime."

I slammed the door behind me with enough force to rattle it in the frame.

Chapter Thirteen

I slept like shit that night, sleepwalked through my Friday, then tossed and turned a second night. When I went to meet Elliot at the apartment on Saturday morning, I felt bleary and run-down. He raised an eyebrow at me when he walked in the door and saw me staring blankly into space, but he didn't ask questions, and I'd never been more grateful for Elliot's general stand-offishness.

We started in the living room, and for the most part, we worked in silence, only speaking when we had a question about what to do with an item. It turned out some of the furniture belonged to Joanne, but she wasn't planning to come back for it, so we'd have to deal with it too. The rest was Cal's. It seemed impossible that Cal had accumulated that much stuff in such a short time, especially since he wasn't living there full-time, but he was a bit like a magpie. As a kid, he'd always come home with pockets full of rocks and leaves, discarded bolts, and other odds and ends he collected throughout his day. He'd never really outgrown it and spent more time exploring thrift stores and flea markets than anyone else I'd ever met.

Although he'd never settled into a career, he was never hurting for money. He had a trust fund from our grandparents and worked hard at odd jobs. He wrote freelance travel pieces and sold some of his photography to stock photo sites. The lack of financial stability and planning would have driven me crazy, but without fail, things always worked out for Cal. And in the end, he hadn't needed a 401k or an investment portfolio. His life had been short, and he'd done what had made him happy. I was prepared for a future but miserable now. By the time I was buried, which of us would have lived a fuller life?

Twenty-eight was too young to die under any circumstances, but it reminded me I needed to take a long, hard look at my life and figure out what I needed to change.

I folded in the flaps of the box I'd been filling with items to donate, then sat back on my heels with a sigh. Exhausted from the fight with Dave and hours of packing, I tilted my head side to side, cracking my neck as I stretched. The bulk of the boxes were going to be donated to charity, but a fair number were items either I wanted to keep, or I knew my mother would want.

I offered his camera to Elliot, but he waved me off. "Nah, I have one," he explained. "You keep Cal's." I had no idea what to do with the surfboard I'd decided to hold onto—I already had one of my own, which I hadn't used in a while—but I'd figure it out eventually. Maybe I'd hang it on my wall.

The belongings for my mom would be a lot more difficult to manage however. I sat back and surveyed the room.

"Fuck," I muttered under my breath. "How the hell am I going to get these home without my mother knowing?"

Elliot looked up from the pile of photos he was attempting to sort. I'd left that task to him since he knew far more about both art and Cal's particular project than I did. "You decided not to tell her?" He sounded relieved.

"Honestly, I haven't really decided anything," I admitted as I leaned against the wall. "I go back and forth. It'll be difficult for both of them, but my mother especially. She'll be hurt Cal wasn't honest. I think she had a pretty good idea he was dating someone, but of course, she assumed it was a woman."

Elliot nodded. "How do you think she would have responded if he'd told her the truth?"

I blew out a heavy breath and shrugged. "Honestly, I don't know. She would have been shocked, no doubt about that. If I tell her now … she'll be hurt."

Elliot winced, and I hastened to reassure him. "It won't hurt them that he was with you—with a man—but they will be disappointed that they never got to know you. And that Cal didn't feel like he could be honest. Our mom … she would have loved nothing more than to have had her boys settled down. I understand why Cal was concerned that our parents would be upset about it being even more difficult for him to have biological children. I'm sterile—and it was Cal's fault—so that put a lot of pressure on him. If he were the only hope for biological grandkids *and* dating a man, that means having a surrogate and getting fertility specialists involved. But I think once they got past that … they would have come around. They would have wanted to get to know you, and they would have been thrilled that Cal found someone he cared about."

My voice came out rough, imagining how it might have played out and realizing it was never going to happen. Cal would never have a chance to be with anyone again, to fall in love, and have children. I would never hold my nieces and nephews and tell them stories from our own childhood. All the times I'd threatened to tell Cal's future kids about what a wild man their father had been would never happen. I felt my breath hitch as I struggled to compose myself.

Elliot looked away, deftly sorting photos while he gave me a moment.

When I pulled myself together again, I continued. "My parents treated my ex like a future son-in-law"—my laugh was rueful—"well, until we found out what a jackass he was." I looked over at Elliot. "Like I've said, they'd have done the same for you."

Elliot gave me a skeptical look. "I don't think I'm really son-in-law material. It's probably just as well it never happened."

"Why do you say that?"

"I doubt Cal and I would have lasted. I might have met your parents, then dropped out of his life anyway."

"I meant why don't you think you're son-in-law material. But I suppose I'm curious about both. Why do you think you and Cal would have split up?"

"I'm just not sure that we could have worked. That Cal could really commit to something that long-term."

"Well, you said you were more or less exclusive for six months. That's a hell of a lot longer than he committed to anyone else," I pointed out.

"He was getting restless toward the end."

"You think he was struggling to stay committed then?" I asked, realizing he'd never answered my question about being son-in-law material, but I let it slide.

Elliot shrugged. "It felt like it. He wasn't sleeping well when we were together, staying out later, and making excuses to not spend the night with me."

"Were you guys living together? I mean, obviously on paper you had separate places but ..."

Elliot shrugged. "Yeah, sort of. Not officially living together, but a lot of the time he was at my place or I was here." He gestured around the apartment. "You know how it goes."

"You said he got the apartment to work on his photography, right? But it looks like he spent a lot of time here."

"I offered him space in my loft, but he didn't want it." Elliot scowled. "I think he wanted his own place while he was figuring things out. He loved what he was doing with his art, but he seemed really reluctant to share it with anyone."

I leaned over, reaching for the photos Elliot had spread out on the floor between us and picking one up. It was a particularly erotic image of two men. Their faces weren't visible, and all I could see was a portion of their bodies, from chest to thigh. One man was behind the other, hips pressed tightly to the other's ass. It was difficult to tell but the pose suggested the one man was fucking the other. It sent a shiver down my spine and made my mouth go dry with lust. I set down the photo and returned my focus to Elliot. "Because of the subject matter?"

"Yeah."

"I'm struggling to understand why the fact that he was getting more serious about his photography was such a secret. Maybe gay erotic photography wasn't the career my parents envisioned for him, but they wanted him to be happy more than anything else in the world."

Elliot spread his hands wide. "I don't have all of the answers for you, Chris."

With a jolt, I realized it was the first time I'd heard Elliot say my name. "I'm just trying to understand."

"I know." The look he gave me was filled with understanding. "I struggled to understand Cal, too. It's odd, he seemed so straight-forward, but I think there was a lot under the surface that people didn't see. That he never let them see. Not me and not even you."

"I just wish I had him here to ask those questions to, you know?"

"Yeah, I know." The pain in Elliot's voice echoed my own.

We both grew silent again, each of us retreating into our own thoughts for a while as we sorted through my brother's life, searching vainly for answers to questions we were barely ready to ask.

"I have an idea I want to run by you." The apprehension in Elliot's voice made me lift my head from the pile of papers I'd been rifling through. Had my brother kept *every* piece of paper he'd ever been given?

"Okay?"

"What do you think about arranging a gallery show for Cal's work?"

I blinked. "A show?"

"Yeah. Cal was *good*. More than good enough to be showcased."

I set down the envelope in my hand. "Did he *want* to do one? You said he didn't want anyone to see his work."

Elliot hesitated. "Yes and no."

"You're going to have to elaborate," I said when he didn't continue.

"Cal was proud of his work. He was insecure about other people viewing it though."

"My brother? Insecure?" It was baffling. He was the most confident person I'd ever met.

"I know. It seems out of character. But this was different. With anything else, he didn't care if he failed," Elliot continued. "He'd just move on to the next thing. But this ... this mattered more to him than anything else ever had."

"I understand that." It was odd, hearing someone else explain my own brother to me. And yet, it made perfect sense. I could reconcile what Elliot was describing with the man I had known. "I wonder if that was partly why he didn't tell me or my parents about it."

"I think so."

"But you think he would have wanted a show eventually?"

"I do. We talked about it a few times. I offered to give him an introduction at the Holloway Gallery where I show."

"You're with the *Holloway* Gallery?" I was dumbfounded.

"You're familiar with them?"

"Yes." They were, by far, the most prestigious gallery in the city. It was near where Alec and I had lived in the Pearl District, and we had gone to a couple of openings there. Alex loved events with the opportunity to rub elbows with Portland's elite. If Elliot had regular shows there, that was impressive as hell. "That's quite an accomplishment."

"Thanks." He cleared his throat as if embarrassed. "Anyway, Cal didn't believe me when I said his work was something they'd be interested in. I showed one of his shots to the owner, who was blown away. He said Cal was welcome to submit his work to them any time."

"Damn. That's a hell of a gesture."

Elliot gave me a wry smile. "Cal was pissed. He acted like I'd betrayed him. I'd just wanted to prove to him how talented he was, but I should have realized how personal it was to him. I overstepped."

"He must have appreciated the gesture at least, even if he didn't appreciate the way you went about it."

"No. He held a grudge for a long time. And he made me swear I'd stop bugging him about it."

"So what makes you think he would have ever wanted to show his work?"

"Because of this." Elliot tossed a notebook on the floor between us.

I flipped through the pages and found sketches of a gallery layout he'd made. Which works he'd want to show and some ideas for how he wanted to display them. Plus, a neat list of numbers that presumably corresponded with photos, along with titles, and some scribbled notes about lighting and framing. Elliot was right. The information put a completely different spin on Cal's feelings about displaying his work.

"He wanted to show it then," I said slowly. "He just wasn't ready yet."

"Yes."

"What should I do?"

Elliot shrugged. "It's up to you. It's not my call to decide what kind of legacy your brother leaves. I just thought ... It seems like a waste for an artist to create something *this* stunning and not have anyone see it. Cal was extraordinarily talented. He saw things other people didn't see, and he captured the emotions between people in a way that was raw yet nuanced. It's a rare gift."

"It never would have occurred to me to show Cal's work in a gallery," I admitted. "I'll have to think about it."

"It's just an idea. You don't need to make a decision now."

I nodded. Thoughts were whirling through my head though, and for the first time since Cal's death, I felt a real spark of excitement. "I do like the idea," I admitted. "Cal's life ended so abruptly, right as he'd found something he was passionate about. I like the thought of there being a concrete legacy left behind. Something to remember him by. I am glad he was able to donate his organs, but this would go beyond that. It would keep his memory alive in another way."

"I thought so too."

"Ever since I got the call about Cal's accident ..." I remembered the frantic terror as I raced through the hospital to the emergency room, and I saw the answering distress on Elliot's face. "God, nothing feels real anymore. I need something tangible to hold on to."

"I was so angry," Elliot said after a long pause, his voice raw. "Dave called me as soon as he heard, and he was the one who told me Cal was dead. I resented that I couldn't be there by his side. That I hadn't been the person who was called first."

My heart dropped into the pit of my stomach at the realization of what had happened. For some reason, I'd never even considered the fact that Elliot hadn't been there to say goodbye to Cal. I had been so focused on my grief I hadn't considered Elliot's situation. The thought of what he'd gone through left me gutted. "I'm sorry. God, I am so sorry, Elliot. I would never have wanted to keep you from him. If we'd known ..."

He let out a heavy, resigned sigh. "Yeah, I know. It's not your fault." Elliot scowled. "For a while, I was angry with you, at your whole family, for keeping me from Cal, but I realized it was him. He was the reason I wasn't there." I hardly knew how to respond, but Elliot continued, his voice barely above a whisper. "Some days, I think I love and hate Cal equally."

"I'm sure it was complicated, under the circumstances," I offered.

Elliot let out a bitter chuckle. "*Cal* was complicated."

"I wish I could do something to make this easier on you."

"You can't." His words were blunt, and his tone had gone flat. "I appreciate the offer, but there's not a damn thing you can do, Chris. I have to deal with my feelings for Cal." He looked down, toying with his hair. "I shouldn't have taken it out on you. I was angry with him, and I thought I was angry with you that night."

I didn't have to ask which night he was referring to. "I guess we both needed an outlet. I didn't want to be alone." I laughed, but there was no humor to it. "It was either you, or Dave—who's obviously not an option—or my cheating asshole of an ex-boyfriend."

"I wouldn't be so sure about that."

"Which part?"

"Dave not being an option," he said flatly.

"Cal told you about the time they fooled around in college?" Elliot nodded. "I only found out from Dave a few days ago. Anyway, at the time, I didn't know Dave was even remotely 'heteroflexible'—or whatever he wants to call it—and he certainly made it clear he doesn't want to fuck me. Much as I used to wish otherwise." The biting note in my voice surprised me.

"Hmm." Elliot changed the subject. "Well, I guess it's good to hear I was better than a mostly straight guy and an asshole ex-boyfriend."

I chuckled. *Better? Yeah, Elliot had been a lot better than my ex.* But that wasn't what Elliot had been referring to. Still, it was good we were finally discussing it, getting everything out in the open.

"After that night, I was so angry with myself and guilty about what we'd done." I had to swallow hard before I could continue. "It was what I needed that night, as fucked up as that sounds."

For the first time, I saw Elliot look apprehensive and truly concerned. "I didn't—didn't hurt you, did I?"

"No. No more than I wanted to be anyway," I reassured him.

"You like the pain?"

"Not usually, but that night, yes." I looked away, glancing out the window. I could see little more than a glimpse of the sky and the waving branches of a bare treetop. It felt strange having this conversation here in the living room with the lights on and no sense of closeness with the man I'd had sex with. We weren't touching or holding each other, there was no intimacy beyond the need that coursed through me every time I looked at him. "Sex or working out help me clear my head and focus. That night, everything felt like it was spinning out of control," I admitted. "I've been single for a while, so I've been working out until I'm ready to drop. But it only does so much. You being rough that night kept me focused, and it was the distraction I needed, I guess."

"I've been feeling so guilty too," he admitted, his voice going whisper-quiet. "Not just for the fact it seemed like an insult to Cal's memory, but I felt like I'd taken advantage of you." Elliot stood, beginning to pace, his hands shoved in his pockets and his shoulders bowed. "You were so drunk."

"You *didn't* take advantage of me. It was what I wanted and needed, even if in hindsight it obviously wasn't the best decision. And you were drunk too."

"Not as drunk as you. If you'd been anything less than enthusiastic, I would have just let you sleep it off in my bed, but I— Anyway, I just wanted to be sure."

"I'm sure," I said firmly. "I wanted it. Hell, if it weren't for—" I cut myself off. "Never mind. I just mean you shouldn't beat yourself up on my account."

He turned slowly to face me, and something about the way he looked at me compelled me to stand so we faced each other. "What were you going to say?"

I licked my lips, nerves spiking within me. "If it weren't for— weren't for your history with Cal, I'd want it to happen again."

Elliot went still, his eyes wide. "You would?"

I nodded. My fingers trembling, I reached out, helpless against the urge to touch him when he was so close. For once, he wasn't snarling and pushing me away in anger or hiding from me. His hair was still gathered at the nape of his neck, and I had a rare glimpse of his entire face. I skimmed my index finger along his jaw, so lightly I was hardly even grazing the skin. He let out a soft, shuddering breath, his lashes half-closing as his lips parted.

"I want it now," I continued. "I shouldn't. Oh, God, I shouldn't want you, but I do."

Up close, I could smell him, the familiar, maddening scent of tea and smoke. I could see his pulse beating in his neck—so fast—and mine was equally rapid. My finger trailed down his neck to where it fluttered. He shivered in response. Goosebumps broke out on his arms, and his nipples tightened under the thin T-shirt he wore. I wanted to lick and bite them, make him cry out.

"I shouldn't want it either," he said faintly.

I felt frozen, pinned in place as we stared at each other for the longest time. Everything about him was beautiful, and I finally understood the allure of the forbidden fruit. Temptation lingered in every interaction between us despite my gut screaming that this was a terrible decision. I couldn't help myself. I stepped forward until my chest lightly brushed Elliot's. My eyes closed as I leaned in, my forehead resting against his, the air from our mouths mingling, our lips nearly close enough to touch.

"We shouldn't," he whispered.

"I know."

I closed my eyes, fighting the warring instincts within me. Thoughts of Cal finally drove me away from Elliot and yet it took every ounce of control I had to step back and not give in to the urge to kiss Elliot. Conflicting emotions flickered through his eyes, but I wasn't sure if it was relief or disappointment.

"I should get back to this," I said inanely, turning away before I could change my mind.

We both resumed working, but I couldn't stop thinking about Elliot. My hands shook from the need to reach for him, and my heart pounded in my chest every time I remembered our bodies pressed together.

Elliot was beautiful. His face was all angles and planes. There was nothing soft about it except maybe his lips, which contributed to the intriguing androgynous nature to his features. The long hair added to that, but even without it, I suspected he'd still skirt the line between masculine and feminine. Was that some of the appeal he'd held for Cal?

Androgyny had never been something I'd been drawn to before; I'd always dated more stereotypically masculine-looking guys. Yet, despite the guilt and regret, there was no denying that a big part of me still responded to Elliot. And the more common ground Elliot and I found, the more difficult to ignore the attraction I felt for him. Nothing about him was my type—he couldn't have been more different from Dave or Alec—and yet something about him drew me in. It must have been the same for Cal.

On a mundane, domestic level, I struggled to picture Elliot and Cal together. Elliot's quiet intensity seemed so different from Cal's exuberance. Maybe Dave was right that the differences were what drew them together. It sounded like there had been a lot of problems in their relationship though. Based on what Elliot had said today, it was clear Elliot and Cal's relationship was far more complicated than I'd realized at first. Elliot had seemed to think the relationship was ending, and he'd implied that Cal might be cheating on him.

It seemed unlikely. As far as I knew, Cal had always just checked out of any relationship when he felt the urge to move on. But his relationship with Elliot had proven that I knew less about my brother than I'd thought.

181

Was Elliot right? If Cal hadn't died, would their relationship have ended, and would they have gone their separate ways? Would Cal have lived his whole life never telling his family about the man he'd loved?

And was it my responsibility to keep Cal's secret, or tell my family the truth?

Elliot and I worked silently for hours after that. I had too much going on in my head to bother with idle conversation, and Elliot seemed to need the space.

What I found the most interesting was that despite Elliot's moodiness and the pull I felt toward him, being around him was less stressful than when I was with anyone else. Elliot was mired in his own grief, and he already knew the worst thing about me: I was so selfish I'd betrayed my brother's memory to assuage my loneliness.

It was a relief to know no secrets hung over me when I was with him.

Chapter Fourteen

"After dinner, could you help me with something, C.J.?" my mom asked as she offered me a second slice of the lemon tart she'd made.

I smiled at her but waved off the second helping of dessert. "Of course. What do you need?"

"I've been trying to sort through Cal's room, and I need you to take a look at a few things of his."

I froze, then tried to cover my hesitation by clearing my throat and reaching for my water. "Uhh, sure," I said when I'd set it down again. "I didn't realize you were tackling that yet."

She gave me a sad smile. "I didn't mean to. But was missing him, and I started to look through his things and ..." She laughed weakly.

My father's low grunt didn't go unnoticed. "You spend more time in there than you do with me."

She glanced at him and pinched her lips into a narrow frown. "Well, what do you want me to do, Christopher? Forget about our son?"

"Of course not!" He brought his fist down on the table, and my mother and I both flinched. "But I'm damn tired of waking up and finding my wife in our dead son's bedroom instead of in our own."

I stared in shock. I hardly recognized this side of my father. Growing up, he'd rarely raised his voice to any of us. It was only when Cal did something stupid that nearly got him killed that he yelled.

And a few times right after my Grandpa Allen had died.

"Well, maybe if you paid a moment of attention to me, I'd want to be there," my mother snapped, anger making two bright spots appear on her cheeks. "All you do is work, drink, and sleep off your hangovers in your study."

I stared back and forth between them, suddenly feeling like a child. Even now, as an adult, I had no idea how to respond.

Discussions and disagreements I'd seen between them over the years were always levelheaded and respectful. I knew my parents occasionally lost their tempers and argued, of course, they were human after all. I vaguely remembered them going in their room and fighting behind closed doors a few times, but never in front of Cal and me, and never like this. Of course, that wasn't entirely true, was it? They *had* fought like this when Dad was drinking before.

"Maybe there's a reason all I do is work and drink." My father's chair scraped on the floor as he pushed back from the table. For a moment, he weaved where he stood. I glanced at the highball glass next to his barely touched plate. It was nearly empty and had been refilled twice.

My stomach dropped to my toes, and I felt suddenly queasy.

God, what is happening to us?

184

With Cal gone, our family was crumbling around me, and I had no idea what to do or how to save it.

My father continued. "Maybe if I felt like you wanted to talk to me instead of that fucking support group, I'd want to spend some time with you." Mutely, I watched him pick up his tumbler of half-melted ice and the dregs of his Scotch. "I'll be in my study. If anyone cares."

As my father disappeared from the dining room, my mother clenched her hands on the edge of the table and clamped her eyes closed. Tears leaked out from the corners, and I felt like my heart would splinter into a thousand little pieces at the way she hunched in on herself. I wanted to reach for her, but I had no idea what to say. Instead, I sat there immobile, fear and worry tumbling inside me until I didn't know which way was up.

"Mom?" I finally croaked.

She pressed her hands to her face for a moment, and when she lowered them, her eyes were mostly dry, and her smile was forced. "Sorry you had to see that, C.J. Why don't you run up to Cal's room? I'll be behind you as soon as I clean up a little."

"I can help with the dishes," I offered lamely, unsure what else to say.

She shook her head and gave me another tight smile. "It'll only take a few minutes to load the dishwasher. You go on up."

"Okay," I agreed a little reluctantly.

I carried plates into the kitchen, then trudged up the two flights of stairs. I hesitated when I reached the door to Cal's room and, after a few moments of indecision, pushed it open. The room seemed empty and lifeless without the collage of photos covering the walls. Or maybe it was just that Cal was gone.

The only thing that hadn't been touched was the bed. One of Cal's shirts lay on the pillow, and I wondered how often she went in the room to breathe in his scent. My brother's hugs had always smelled of sunshine and warmth, and I missed them acutely.

I took a seat on the chair by the desk. Although I saw a few boxes in the room, I wasn't sure exactly what my mother wanted help with. Instead of rummaging through them, I slipped my phone from my pocket and tried to kill time on it.

A quick tour of the various social media apps was more depressing than distracting. I rarely spent time on them, and when I did, it was to wish other people congratulations or condolences on the big events in their lives. Unlike Cal, who'd had thousands of friends, I had a few dozen. People I'd graduated high school with and never spoke to, friends from college I rarely interacted with any longer, a few colleagues.

I paused when I remembered Dave's comment on Friday night about not having my own friends. He was right. As much as it stung to hear, I was pretty damn alone with Cal gone. Most of the mutual friends Alec and I had during our relationship had sided with him after the breakup. I had no idea *why* since he'd been the one at fault, not me, but if anyone could spin a story to make himself look like the injured party, it was my ex-boyfriend.

Dave's words had been cruel but accurate. Who did I have in my life right now? *Elliot?*

Jesus. My family was disintegrating, and the closest thing to a friend I had was my dead brother's boyfriend.

I stood and began pacing the room as I waited for my mother. The sight of a skateboarding trophy peeking out from a box made me pause in my tracks, and I slid it out from under some random junk.

I turned it over in my hands and looked at the date. I had been swamped with school at the time, but I'd come home one Saturday to see Cal compete. Father's Day was the next day, so we'd celebrated Cal's win and the holiday together over dinner. Unfortunately, I'd managed to ruin the entire evening.

"*Your mother and I have discussed it, and we're going to have the office redecorated soon," my father said as he placed a slice of chicken on my plate. "I'd like you to have some input. Especially in the room that will be your office. I know it'll be a while before you join the practice, but—"*

"I'm not joining the practice," I blurted out. The words had been hovering on the tip of my tongue for weeks, and I knew I couldn't delay telling my father any longer.

He froze, carving knife and fork poised in the air. "What did you say? We've been talking about this for years, C.J."

"I know. I just … my gut is telling me I want to do something else with my life." I took a deep breath. I hated disappointing him this way, but it was unavoidable. I'd wrestled with this for months, and I knew it was the right decision. "I'm sorry, Dad. I know for a long time it was your dream to have me join your pediatric practice. And it was my dream too. Or at least, I thought it was until I did my psychiatric rotation. Pediatrics was great, but it didn't click

for me the same way psychiatry did. The more I talk to Ed—"

My father scowled and set the utensils on the table beside the plate with a clatter. "Ed poached my own son? I don't believe it."

I caught a glimpse of my mother, who sat with her hand pressed over her mouth, and Cal, who was staring slack-jawed at my father and me. The two of us arguing was a rarity.

I rolled my eyes. "Come on, Dad. It wasn't like that, and you know it. I just found my calling somewhere different than either of us expected. I want to specialize in psychiatry and do a subspecialty in hospice and palliative medicine. This is where I belong. I'm sure of it."

"You know I think highly of Ed and what he does," my father said stiffly. "But it certainly seems like he was recruiting you."

"He wasn't recruiting me!" I said, exasperated. "It's just that I believe in what Ed is doing, and I want to be a part of it."

"I never thought you'd choose someone else over your own family like this."

"What?" I sputtered. "How on earth is this choosing someone else over our family? Ed has been a part of our family for years. He's my godfather, for Christ's sake. I'm going into medicine like both of you. Explain this to me, Dad, because I really don't understand what you're so upset about."

"Your plan has always been to get your medical degree, settle down, and have a family. Just like your grandfather and I did. Your sterility means that your family may be a bit different. Thanks to your brother, he's the only hope we have for carrying on the Allen genes. And if he isn't more careful, he's going to get himself killed, so I don't think we can count on that."

"I'm sitting right here!"

"He was seven when the bike accident happened! You can hardly blame him for a childish mistake. I don't! And what do you expect from him now? He's still a teenager."

"I expect my sons to make smart decisions about their lives! But I'm very disappointed in you *right now."*

My mother spoke up, "Christopher, I think you're overreacting a little and pushing—"

"How am I overreacting or pushing? C.J.'s wanted to be a pediatrician since he was a child! Don't you remember him coming into the practice with me on weekends when I caught up on paperwork? He brought in his stuffed animals and gave them checkups. He's the one who told me—in middle school—that he was going to grow up and be just like me. He begged for a lab coat with 'Dr. Allen' on it for his twelfth birthday. The plan has always been for him to go into pediatrics, join me at my practice, then take over when I retired. Based on what he said he wanted. I never pushed him into medicine. All I did was encourage him to pursue these dreams."

I scrubbed my hands over my face. "I'm sorry, Dad. I know you're disappointed. And I know you never pushed me into medicine. Besides, it's what I still want to do; I just discovered I want to go in a slightly different direction with it than either of us expected. You can understand that, can't you?"

He scowled down at me. Since he was still standing while I sat, he loomed over me, and it made me feel like a small child again rather than a grown man.

"You've spent years preparing to go into pediatrics. You've tailored your studies toward it; to suddenly go off in a different direction is reckless and irresponsible. You are throwing away a perfectly good future with no thought of how this will

impact anyone but yourself."

My parents had never coddled me, and they'd always had high expectations, but they'd always supported my choices as well. And Jesus, it wasn't like I planned to drop out of school to join a cult. I was still going to be a doctor. Albeit not a pediatrician like my father had envisioned. "Look, I'm sorry I'm messing up the plans we had. I hate to do this to you, but palliative care and hospice is where my heart is," I argued. "After everything that happened with Grandpa—"

"Leave my father out of this."

For a moment, all I could do was stare at him. "I'm just saying that watching Grandpa Allen die changed my view of what doctors do and what a huge part death plays in all of this. I want to help people have the best possible death. It's not like I plan on completely abandoning medicine!" I pushed my chair back from the table to stand. "Sure, I'll have to backtrack on a few specialized courses, but it's not like I'm giving it up completely to become a ... poet or something. Your money hasn't gone to waste on classes I'll never use."

"It's not the money, and you know it," he snapped. "Your mother and I have been working toward this goal at the practice for years. The timing works out perfectly. Once you had your medical license and board certification, you'd come work for me—"

"I thought I would be working with you, not for you?" I crossed my arms over my chest.

"Yes. Of course." He waved it off like that comment meant nothing. "But that's not my point. The point is that we have been planning on this happening, and now we're going to have to re-work all of it!"

"Oh, I'm sorry." I glared at him. "Did me finding my calling inconvenience you?"

"It's more than a damn inconvenience! I need to find someone to fill your place. And no one I find will ever replace my son. It's certainly not like Cal is going to step in."

"Thanks, Dad." I glanced over to see Cal scowling at both of us. "Glad you think so highly of my potential."

"You know I didn't mean it like that. But you've shown no interest in medicine whatsoever, nor do you seem to have the discipline for it! You flit from hobby to hobby and—"

"Oh, for fuck's sake," Cal yelled. "How did this become about me and my failings?"

"Stop swearing!" my mother scolded.

"Would you butt out of this, Cal? It isn't—"

"Damn it, Cal, this is between Dad and me—"

"I dunno, for once it was nice to have it be about C.J. and—"

We spoke at once, our words overlapping each other. My mother stood. "Would everyone please be quiet right now before you say something to each other you'll truly regret?" She hardly raised her voice, but the stern delivery cut through the babble of noise, and we all fell silent.

My father scowled. "I'm done with this conversation anyway. Perhaps you'll come to your senses, C.J., and we can move forward like we planned." He walked out of the room before I could retort that following in his footsteps wouldn't be coming to my senses.

My mother approached me and laid a hand on my arm. "I'm sorry your father didn't take this well, C.J. He shouldn't have said some of what he did, and I know he'll regret it once he has time to cool down. You two so rarely fight, and I know it's hard on both of you. He's just disappointed."

"I know he is, but—"

"You've done nothing wrong. And he will come around once he's had time to digest the idea that our plans for the future have radically shifted."

I sighed. "I am sorry about that. I know it's going to be a pain to find someone you both trust to take over the practice."

She squeezed my arm. "We'll deal with that. Mostly, your father is hurt because he's spent years building this practice with the hope that he could leave it to one of his children as his legacy. And maybe someday, you could do the same with one of your children."

"I know that, Mom."

"I know you do, but you're not a parent yet. You don't know what it's like to raise a human and put your hopes and dreams into them. Sometimes, we go too far. It isn't fair if we don't allow them to find their own hopes and dreams. But your father will adjust, and you two will work through this. I know it."

"I never meant to be a disappointment," I said thickly.

She reached up to cup my cheek in her hand. "You're never a disappointment. Your father is disappointed. Surely, you can see the difference."

I nodded, but at the moment, it was hard to see the distinction. I had worked my whole life to please them. To earn their praise. Disappointing them wasn't in my vocabulary.

My mother sighed. "I'm going to go have a talk with your father. You two eat. Don't let this dinner go to waste." She walked out of the room, and I was left staring at a dining room table heaped with food that I had no appetite for.

Cal reached for the mashed sweet potatoes and piled them on his plate. He saw me looking at him and shrugged. "What? It's nice to not be the family disappointment for once. I'm going to enjoy this while it lasts."

It had taken weeks for my father's disappointment to subside. And even then, he was a bit cool toward Ed for a while. But eventually, when he saw I wasn't wavering, he softened. And when I finished my residency, he was as proud as anyone. Still slightly disappointed in my choice but proud and supportive.

Clearly, disagreements like that made Cal hesitant to open up to us—especially our dad—about his sexuality and choice of career. I always assumed Cal didn't worry too much about what any of us thought about the way he lived his life, but maybe he cared a lot more than he ever let on. And maybe he wanted to be sure the things he was exploring—like his art and his relationship with Elliot—stuck before he made a huge announcement that led to a massive upheaval in the family. I could certainly understand that. It was still disappointing as hell that he hadn't come to me at least, but I understood the why a little better now.

The sound of my mother's quiet steps outside the door forced me to shake off the thought, and I stood as she walked into the room. "Okay, tell me what you need." I slipped my phone into my pocket and plastered a smile on my face.

"In a hurry to leave?" she asked. Her tone was light, but I could see the hurt lurking at the edge of her words.

"Of course not. I just want to help any way I can." I hesitated. "Mom?"

"Yes?"
"Can we talk about what happened at the dinner table?"

She twisted her hands together. "I'm not sure that's such a good idea, C.J."

"We can't just ignore the fact that dad's drinking too much."

"*Christopher* ..." Her eyes closed and her mouth tightened briefly before she looked at me. "How much do you remember about when Grandpa Allen died?"

"Quite a bit. Dad started drinking too much then." It was the only stain in my otherwise nearly perfect childhood.

"And he was able to stop."

"But what if he can't this time?" I asked quietly. She looked down but didn't reply. "And I worry about you too, Mom."

"We're all struggling."

"I know." Hell, I knew that better than anyone. "But why are you making it harder on yourself? You don't have to pack up Cal's bedroom yet."

Maybe I shouldn't talk since I was packing his apartment, but I had a deadline.

"I just need to do *something*. I can't sit here and feel sorry for myself."

"I understand." In that way, my mother and I were very much alike. "What was that Dad said about the support group?" I asked.

"I joined an online support group for parents who've lost children." She turned away and straightened something on the desk. "I asked your father to go to in-person group meetings, but he wasn't willing, so I'm doing it myself online. And I've met a lot of very supportive people on there. They really know what I'm going through. It helps."

"That's good," I said encouragingly.

I decided to drop the issue of Dad's drinking and the cracks in their marriage for now. Maybe they just needed a little time to deal with things separately.

She turned back to face me and squeezed my arm. "Thank you." She pointed to a box on the desk. "That's what I want you to look through. I think there are some things you may want to keep."

"Okay."

I smiled when I opened the box. Most were souvenirs from trips Cal and I had taken together. None were of any real monetary value. Cal favored roadside attractions—the kitschier the better—and even the ones from the national parks we'd visited were mostly cheap plastic keychains and snow globes. But, oh, the memories they brought back.

It occurred to me then that all the trips we'd taken together had been Cal's idea. I'd liked travelling, though not nearly as much as he did, and I preferred a different style of vacation. But I'd done what my brother wanted because I'd loved to see the excitement on his face and hear his delighted laugh at the world's biggest ball of twine on a road trip that took us through Kansas. Everything we'd done on those trips had been to make him happy, not me. I'd enjoyed it too, but in the end, everything we did was about what Cal wanted.

A sick, sinking sensation grew in the pit of my stomach.

My friends had been Cal's friends. My vacations had been Cal's vacations. My lover—the most recent one anyway—had been Cal's boyfriend. Except for my career, did I do anything for myself, ever? Or was it all because I wanted to be more like *Cal*? I'd always thought of him as larger than life, but had I pushed my own desires aside because I'd felt overshadowed by him? Had I *let him* overshadow me? Had I lost a sense of who I was to become a pale imitation of my brother? It made me ill.

"C.J.?"

I blinked as my mother's voice pulled me from my reverie. "Yeah?" I asked hoarsely, hoping she wouldn't ask what I was thinking. I couldn't bear to share my feelings with her now, although we'd always been honest with each other.

"Everything okay?"

Well, maybe not always honest. A pang of remorse went through me as I considered the lies I'd told to hide Cal's secret life. Cal's death had changed everything. I wanted to tell her so bad I could taste the words on my lips. I wanted to rid myself of this awful burden and set myself free, but it would crush her in the process. I looked at her worried brown eyes and unfamiliar pinched expression and knew I couldn't do it.

"Yeah, just got lost in thought."

What was one more little white lie on top of all the others?

Soon, I'd drown in them.

Chapter Fifteen

I took several boxes of Cal's belongings home with me from my parents' house. Over the next few days, I sifted through them slowly. In part because I was afraid of another emotional time bomb. And my fears were justified when I discovered a flash drive containing photos of the whale watching trip we'd taken. As I scrolled through them on my laptop, I found a picture another passenger had taken—the one I kept in a frame in my office at work—but also ones Cal had taken of the white-capped ocean and rocky shoreline. Some of my parents. And a particularly good one of me. I'd modeled for my brother from time to time when he wanted someone to practice on, though I'd felt ridiculous doing it. But this one was a candid. I looked young, even though it had only been taken a few years ago. The breakup with Alec had aged me considerably. And Cal's death had taken an even bigger toll. I wouldn't be surprised if I started seeing gray hairs soon.

In this particular photo, I looked young and pensive. Not unhappy, exactly, but contemplative. Had I been thinking about my relationship with Alec? Or was it something else? Cal must have snapped the photo just before he'd come over to hang out with me at the railing.

"I don't see any whales!" I shouted over the roar of the engine and the wind.

"We just got out here! Be patient," Cal chastised as he leaned against the metal bar. The roll of the sea made both of us grab for the metal handrail to anchor

ourselves.

"You are the least patient person I know. How are you so chill about this?"

"You can't control sea creatures." His tone was philosophical. "And it's useless to try."

"I'm just hoping to see some puffins!" my mother said as she slipped in between Cal and me at the railing. She tucked her hands into the crooks of our elbows and hung on.

"What is it with you and puffins?" Cal sounded bewildered.

"Every family vacation we've been on where we're supposed to see them, we never do! I'm determined that this time will be different."

"Our mother, the eternal optimist," I joked, looking over the top of her rain slicker hood at my brother.

He snorted. "Better this than her usual. If she's looking for puffins maybe she'll stop trying to set me up with every eligible girl she runs across."

She laughed. "I've had even less luck with that! At least I know puffins exist. I'm starting to doubt you'll ever find a woman to settle down with."

"Yeah well, we can't all be C.J. and fall head-over-heels."

"Alec is definitely not a woman," I reminded him.

"Clearly. But you are moving in with him in a couple of weeks." Cal rolled his eyes. "Ugh. Monogamy. How tedious."

Our mother let out a little snort. "Fine, settle down with two women, see if I care. I just want my boys to be happy." She leaned her head against Cal's rain slicker.

"You just want grandkids," Cal said drily.

"Aren't they the same?"

"Not for everyone," Cal said as he exchanged another glance with me over our mother's head.

"Are you three even watching for whales?" our father said from behind us.

Cal glanced over at him. "No, Dad, Mom is pestering us about grandkids."

"So, the usual then?" he joked as he squeezed in between Cal and Mom.

"Pretty much." I didn't mind though. I did want a partner and kids and a nice little house to raise them in. I had the partner at least. I thought of Alec. Successful, driven Alec who had stayed home to work this weekend rather than come on the family vacation with us. He'd just gotten a promotion at the architectural firm and really needed to show them he'd earned it. I understood.

Still, I missed him. And a niggling worry kept popping in my head that we were growing further apart by the day, not closer. He'd been distracted lately. Ignoring my texts during the day. Working late. And when we both had free time, he was out with his friends rather than making plans with me. I couldn't remember the last time we'd had sex either.

My stomach took a swooping dip that had nothing to do with the pitch and yaw of the boat. Shit. A pattern was starting to come together. Was Alec growing bored with me? Or, was he just overwhelmed with work and apprehensive about moving in together? God, I hoped it was the latter.

"Oh, look!" my mother suddenly yelled. "A puffin!"

"Hey, maybe there's a chance of Cal finding a woman to settle down with after all," I teased.

Cal flipped the middle finger at me.

"I saw that!" she warned us.

"We're adults, Mom."

But she only laughed. "You'll always be my babies."

None of that day had seemed significant at the time. It had just been an ordinary, silly time our family spent together. And yet, now I could see all the pieces. The growing disconnect between Alec and myself. My loneliness. My mother pushing Cal about settling down and having kids. Cal trying to push back and remind us all he didn't fit into the little molds we kept trying to put him in.

I turned my attention back to the laptop. The first group of photos were of the rest of that day and that trip. The puffins my mother saw. Her delighted face as she watched them. A small pod of whales we spotted. Then photos of our cousin's wedding. A hike we went on together.

The photos became random after that. From other trips and ordinary days. I ran across some photos and a video of Cal and Dave. A strange feeling swept over me as I stared at the picture of them mugging for the camera together. In light of what Dave had told me, I couldn't help but analyze their closeness. Was that a little more than friendship showing in the way Dave had his arm draped over Cal's shoulder, or Cal's fingers dug into Dave's ribs? Did they stand closer than most straight men? Was it close friendship or something else in their eyes as they looked at each other? There was a short video of the two of them goofing around together, and I watched it over and over, searching for clues. But all it did was make me more confused. They didn't seem any different than they ever had to me.

And in the end, did it matter?

Did it change *anything* to know that one night, Dave and Cal had let one thing lead to another? I already knew about Cal and Elliot. Did one single act with Dave really make any difference?

Dave and Cal had been close. And that closeness had turned sexual one time. In the scheme of things, what did it matter? Lots of people—of every gender and orientation—hooked up with friends when they got a little drunk or high or lonely. People had sex for all sorts of reasons. Maybe Dave was right. Maybe I *was* too black and white about people's sexuality. Did it matter if people occasionally stepped outside of what they were usually into to explore something new?

Cal and Dave hadn't done anything wrong. And neither of them had been obligated to tell me about any of it. Sure, it hurt to be left out of Cal's life, and our family dynamic had meant that we'd always been close and in each other's business. But it wasn't fair of me to lash out at Dave. My reaction had been way out of proportion. I was angry, but it had more to do with my feelings about Cal's secrets and my hurt at hearing Dave say he wasn't attracted to me than anything.

Maybe it was time I learned to mind my own fucking business.

Because, frankly, I was tired of thinking about my brother's sex life for any reason.

The next evening, after beating the shit out of a punching bag and eating dinner, I worked up the nerve to call Dave.

"Hey there," he answered after a few rings. He sounded subdued.

"Hey. Uh, look, I want to apologize," I said before he could get anything else out.

"No, *I'm* sorry." He sighed. "I'd been drinking, and while that's a terrible excuse for anything, it didn't exactly help."

"I know." I took a deep breath. Jesus, if anyone understood alcohol leading to bad decisions lately, it was me. "But I also know I overreacted and took my feelings out on you when I shouldn't have."

"Water under the bridge, man."

"No, hear me out. Please. I've been pretty damn hurt that Cal kept his bisexuality a secret from me," I admitted. "Hearing that you knew and that you hadn't told me about your attraction to men, however minor, kinda brought it all to the surface."

"Fair enough. But I said a lot of shit I shouldn't have. I didn't mean what I said about you not having friends. You *are* my friend. I hope you know that."

"I know. But you had a good point, actually." I shifted on the couch.

"What do you mean?"

"I mean, over the years, I let Cal overshadow me." I swallowed uncomfortably. "I let myself play second string to him, and I kinda lost who I was. I mean, I've got my career, but ... that's about it. When Alec and I broke up, I shut down. I stopped dating, and all of our mutual friends sided with him so ..."

"They were pretty shitty friends to begin with if they dropped *you* after Alec cheated on you."

"True." I sighed. "God, I'm fucking pathetic."

"Hey! Don't say that," Dave said. "You're a great guy, Chris. You just need to make a few changes in your life. Join Grindr or something and get your dick sucked."

I snorted. "Not my scene, Dave."

"Well, how do you usually meet guys?"

"Uhh, well, I met Alec through a mutual friend at a dinner party."

"There's a guy at work I could set you up with," Dave offered.

The earnestness in his voice made me laugh. "Oh, God, just because the guy is gay doesn't mean we'll hit it off."

"I know *that*. But seriously, Brendon's tall, blond, and has a great sense of humor. He's been single for a few months, and I really think you guys would get along."

I groaned. "No thanks. But if I get that desperate, I promise I'll let you know."

"Oh, fine." He fell silent. "I'm glad you called," he finally said. "I felt like shit about the way things ended between us the other night."
"Yeah, me too. Friends?" I offered.

"Definitely." Dave sounded like he was smiling. "And I don't want you to think it's only because of Cal."

"That means a lot," I admitted.

"Look, I hate to run off, but I actually have a date tonight," Dave admitted. "The waitress from when we out to dinner the last time."

I shook my head. "I didn't even see you ask for her number."

"She left it on the check."

"You are smooth, man." I smiled wryly. What I wouldn't give for half of his game.

"What can I say? It's a gift."

I snorted. "First date or second date?"

"Second. We grabbed drinks last week and had a nice time, so I asked her out again."

"Good. Good. I'm really glad."

"I'm not looking for anything serious, but she seems to be on board with that." There was silence for a beat. "Are you sure you don't want Brendon's number?"

"Oh, my God, give it a rest," I said with a laugh. "I don't need your help, Dave. I swear."

"Fine, fine. Just promise you'll let me know if you change your mind. You seem lonely, Chris. I'm worried about you."

I rolled my eyes but thanked him anyway. "I appreciate the concern. For now, I think I've got plenty on my plate to deal with."

"Okay."

"Have fun tonight."

"Will do. Later, man."

"Later," I echoed before I ended the call. I absently played with my phone while I considered the conversation. Was getting involved with anyone something I really wanted right now? With my head a mess and my family imploding around me, trying to meet someone seemed impossible and unwise.

And why was it that my mind kept returning to Elliot?

The next Saturday, I arrived at Cal's apartment a little earlier than I intended. I'd finished my workout and grabbed something to eat, but Elliot hadn't arrived yet. I set another Earl Grey and bagel with cream cheese on the coffee table for him.

Maybe I *had* turned into my mother, but he seemed to enjoy them. It felt like the least I could do to thank him for everything he was doing for me. I knew he was struggling to share details of his life with Cal, and he was only doing it to help me. A few meals here and there were paltry, but I could do so little to repay him otherwise.

As I waited for Elliot to arrive, I wandered aimlessly around the apartment, trying to decide what area to tackle next. I opened a closet in the hallway and peered inside, smiling when I saw Cal's guitar. Our father had bought it for Cal when he was twelve, and he'd played for about six months before he got bored with it. I wondered if he had decided to take it up again. I reached for the guitar and carried it into the living room. I strummed it lightly, pleased to hear it was more or less in tune. The smooth, glossy wood felt familiar under my hands. After Cal grew bored with it, I'd picked it up and taught myself how to play. I'd given it back to Cal during my residency when I barely had time to eat or sleep, much less dabble in music.

I miss it though. I idly plucked at the strings. Nearly forgotten tunes swirled in my head, and I closed my eyes, my fingers remembering the notes, even if my conscious mind didn't.

The sound of the door opening pulled me away from my playing, and my fingers stilled, apprehension washing through me as I looked up to see Elliot come through the doorway.

To my surprise, he looked relaxed and his gaze was soft. "You're good."

I shook my head and glanced down at the guitar. "I barely remember how to play. It's been years since I last held this guitar."

"It was yours?"

"Only for a while. After Cal was through with it." A look passed between us, and I felt a funny lurch in my stomach as I remembered my earlier conversation with Dave. More proof that I'd been living in my brother's shadow. Was Elliot nothing more than another of Cal's discarded playthings?

I didn't want to believe that. It was clear Cal had cared for Elliot, and whatever the strange pull I felt toward him, it had nothing to do with my brother. I didn't want him *because* he'd been my brother's boyfriend, right? I hastily changed the subject. "Did Cal play it?"

"Not that I ever saw. I didn't even know he had it here."

"It was in the hall closet," I pointed toward it. "I guess we should get to work," I added after an awkward silence.

"I could sort through some things, if you wanted to play more," Elliot offered, his voice quiet, his gaze not meeting mine.

"Uhh, sure." We'd left off working on the living room closet the time before, so I stayed on the couch and settled the guitar on my lap again. Elliot shrugged out of his jacket and draped it over the armchair. He settled gracefully onto the floor, crossing his legs to get comfortable as he pulled a half-filled box closer to him. He picked up the tea and held it up for a second as if waiting for confirmation that it was for him. I nodded, and he gave me a small, fleeting smile that transformed his face from its typical solemnity to something warm and open.

I strummed the Gibson gently, watching as he worked, alternating bites of food and sips of tea with contemplative frowns at the array of Cal's belongings spread around him.

Neither of us spoke. If he had a question about an item, he'd lift it up to show me. I'd nod if I wanted to keep it or shake my head if it should get donated.

After he was done eating, he neatly stacked the trash out of the way, then shifted so he was facing away from me. He dug something out of his pocket. I couldn't tear my gaze away as he collected his hair at the nape of his neck and twisted an elastic around it, gathering it into a low bun that left a few soft curls loose. I wanted to feel them against my fingertips.

My gaze traced along the tight muscle of his biceps and the length of his body. I stared at the curve of his spine, the pattern of bumps and ridges appearing as he leaned forward to reach for something and his snug T-shirt stretched tight. The fabric was so thin I could see every movement his muscles made, and I remembered the touch of them under my palms, his skin smooth over top. My breathing grew shallow, remembering the jut of his hips against my own and his heated breath against my neck.

Desire thickened my cock, and I felt it nudge against the fly of my jeans, insistent need for the man across the room clawing at me with a sudden fierceness that took my breath away. I flubbed the song and my fingers stilled. Elliot glanced over his shoulder at me. "You okay?"

"Sure," I said hoarsely. "I mean, yeah, I'm fine. Just out of practice."

The look he gave me was probing and unconvinced, but after a minute, he turned back and reached for another pile.

He hunched over them and, in a few minutes, seemed completely absorbed in the task. I resumed playing. I played until my fingers cramped and ached, the music slowly coming back even though it had been years. I hadn't realized how much I'd missed it.

Elliot paused in his sorting and stretched, lifting his clasped hands over his head. I heard the soft pop of his spine as he straightened. He pushed a springy curl of hair behind his ear, and I felt a sudden sharp longing to kneel behind him and touch my lips to the back of his neck. Instead, I looked down at the guitar as he swung around to face me. I couldn't meet his gaze when I was sure my need for him was written all over my face.

"Hopefully, I didn't make your ears bleed with my playing," I joked, trying to dispel the weird tension in the room.

A faint, wry smile crossed his lips as I glanced up again, lightening the serious set of his face. Two smiles in one day. It was a new record. "No, not at all. I found it really relaxing actually."

"Would you—would you mind if I kept this?" I asked, holding the guitar up by its neck.

He shook his head. "I don't play, and it doesn't have any sentimental value to me. You should have it."

"Thank you." I set the guitar aside, and our gazes met and held for a long moment before I forced myself to look away. The rumble of his stomach broke the silence. I lifted my head, and he had an abashed expression on his face as his palm flattened against his midsection.

"Guess I'm hungry," he muttered. "I should get out of here."

"Or I could order pizza," I blurted out, not entirely sure why I said it but unwilling to let him go. It was the first non-combative interaction we'd had that lasted any length of time, and I wasn't eager to see it end. "I planned to stick around since I haven't actually done any work yet today. Unless—do you have somewhere else to be?"

He shook his head and propped his elbows on his crossed knees. "I got a lot of work done last week." He didn't mention plans with friends, and once again, I wondered how isolated he was.

I leaned back and dug in my pocket for my phone. "You're a full-time artist, right?"

"Yeah." His finger traced through the carpet in front of him, making patterns using the nap of the fabric. "Got lucky in art school. Peter Holloway was a friend of the department head, and he saw my work and approached me. I've been with the Holloway Gallery ever since." His finger swirled and then tapped the carpet for emphasis. His voice sounded almost dreamy. "Getting a scholarship to The Art Institute of Portland was the first bit of luck I'd had in years and getting discovered was the second."

"That's amazing." I liked the glimpse into the very private life of the enigmatic man in front of me. He nodded absently but didn't continue, so I cleared my throat. "What do you like on your pizza?"

"Whatever." He shrugged. "Seriously, order whatever you want. I don't care."

"Even if I want anchovies?" I teased.

He lifted one shoulder in a shrug. "Sure."

I smiled. "I was kidding. I'm not a fan of them."

"When you've been as broke as I was, you learn to not be picky," he said shortly and stood, his normally graceful movements jerky and rough. He turned away from me to move the boxes that were going to be donated. I watched him, frowning at the tension in his body as he trekked the distance between the living room closet and the door. I itched to ask him more about his past, but I was afraid it would make him clam up.

Instead, I searched on my phone for a pizza place nearby, dialed the number, and placed my order. Elliot and I worked side by side as we sorted through the remainder of the items in the closet while we waited for the food delivery. The earlier ease between us was gone, and the ringing of the doorbell was a relief.

"Moving in?" the delivery guy asked with a smile when I opened the door. He nodded toward the pile of boxes near the door.

"Out," I replied. It was close enough to the truth, and I had absolutely no desire to go into the details.

The delivery guy went to hand me the receipt to sign but I still had the pizza in one hand. "Elliot, can you grab this?" I asked.

Our forearms brushed as he took the food from me, and up close, I could see the darker ring around the pupil of his eyes and the faint darker specks that mingled with the light gray. Entranced, I stared at him for a few heartbeats. He didn't look away either, and it took the delivery guy clearing his throat before Elliot stepped back. My breathing was light and rapid as I took the receipt and pen, added a generous tip, and signed.

Elliot wouldn't look me in the eye after I closed the door. He placed the food on the coffee table and took a seat on the floor.

"Help yourself."

He silently flipped open the lid of the pizza box and dug in. I took the salad I'd ordered and transferred it to a paper plate I'd dug out of Cal's cupboard. Elliot had inhaled half the meat lovers' pizza by the time I finished my salad. It gave me a surge of pleasure to see him enjoying something.

As Elliot wiped his hands on a napkin, I noticed the strength of his fingers. Despite their delicacy, it was clear he was someone who worked with his hands. I noticed the smudge of ink on his index finger and remembered the pencil sketch he'd done the morning after our drunken sex. I wished I could see more of his work.

"Thank you," he said softly. "I can chip in for my half."

I waved off his suggestion. "Nah, it's fine. Glad you enjoyed it."

"I don't always remember to eat." He laughed uncomfortably. "I start drawing and lose track of time."

I nodded in understanding. "I was like that in med school. I'd start studying and five hours later, I'd realize I had a pounding headache from skipping meals."

Elliot leaned back on his hands and looked up at me. "You're a shrink, right?"

"A psychiatrist, yes. I work with patients who have chronic or terminal illnesses."

"Like hospice?"

"Yes. Not all my patients are dying, but many of them are. So, I help them either cope with living with illness or coming to terms with the fact that their illness will eventually lead to their death."

"How do you handle that? It seems difficult."

"Some days it is. Some days it's the most amazing thing in the world. I have the opportunity to give people comfort and share the end of their lives with them. It's never easy to help the terminally ill accept that they're dying, but I've had the privilege of meeting some extraordinary people through my work, which makes it worthwhile."

"Cal said you loved your job. That you'd found your calling."

I tilted my head to look at Elliot more closely. "He told you that?"

"He talked about you all the time," Elliot said with a soft, huffing laugh.

"Really?"

"Yes. I heard about C.J. over and over. Confused the hell out of me at first since you both have those initials."

"Yeah, Christopher Junior and Calvin James." I laughed ruefully. "Our parents weren't altogether that clever, I guess."

"Once I figured out he didn't have multiple personalities and was talking about his brother, I realized how much he looked up to you."

I laughed aloud at Elliot's rare bit of humor, and I sat back on the couch, relaxing a fraction. He seemed to be letting go of some of the hostility he had toward me. If I ignored the mistake we'd made the night of the funeral, I could almost believe we were simply two people grieving Cal's death and leaning on each other for support. It was nice.

"Yes, well, the feeling was mutual. I usually wished I was as outgoing as Cal."

Elliot shrugged. "He admired the way you had your life all figured out."

My sigh was tinged with bitterness. "I don't know that I'd go that far."

"I'm sure you know Cal was … scattered. He didn't know how to focus. He envied you for your ability to do that."

"I guess we all admire the traits in another person that we lack," I mused. "Cal made me feel old and boring."

Elliot scoffed. "He made me feel the same way, and I was younger than he was."

"You're what, in your mid-twenties, right?"

"Twenty-four."

"You do seem more mature than that. Twenty-four seems like a long time ago to me. A lot more than ten years."

"At thirty-four you're so old?"

I shrugged. "No. Now, I feel ancient, but that has nothing to do

with my age. I'm just … exhausted. Mentally, physically, emotionally
…"

Elliot's laugh was hollow. "I know. I wonder when I'll feel normal
again."

My answering laugh came out more bitter than I intended. "Will we
ever?"

Elliot's gaze met mine, and for the first time, there was no hostility,
no distrust, not even the lurking attraction that usually seemed to
simmer there. Just sympathy.

"I hope so."

Chapter Sixteen

A knock on the door pulled me out of my review of patient charts. "Come in."

Ed stuck his head inside. "Do you have a minute, Chris?"

I smiled at him. "Sure, what is it, Ed?"

He came in, shut the door, and took a seat across from my desk. His furrowed brow and uncharacteristically somber appearance made me uneasy. "I ran into Ryan Buchanan in the hall as I was making my rounds."

"Okay." My heart beat a little too hard in my chest. Based on Ed's demeanor, this wasn't going to be a pleasant conversation with my mentor.

"He said you were arranging something with the local aquarium for our patient?"

I sighed. "I'm exploring an idea. I ran the idea by Hazel's parents before I did any research. She's struggling with the fact that she'll never get to accomplish anything on her bucket list. She wanted to become a marine biologist, and I wondered if we could give her an opportunity to taste that. One of Cal's ex-girlfriends works for the Oregon Coast Aquarium, so I planned to run it by her to get some ideas."

"Hazel's in no condition to leave the hospital, Chris, you know that."

"I do. I hoped Allie could help me figure out something we could bring to her."

Ed sighed heavily and sat back in his chair. "I'm not convinced this is a good idea."

"Oh, come on, Ed," I implored him. "We've gone well above and beyond for our patients before. We arranged a fucking wedding last year."

"We did."

It had been an incredibly touching situation. The couple was young. They'd been engaged and had a date set for the wedding when the bride was admitted to the hospital in kidney failure. She was extremely low on the organ transplant list, and when it became clear that her condition was deteriorating rapidly, she'd been moved to hospice. The couple had expressed their wishes that they get married before she died, so with the help of her sister, we'd arranged for a small wedding with their immediate family.

One of the hospital chaplains had officiated, and the cafeteria had even provided a small wedding cake.

"Large gestures aren't completely unprecedented," I argued.

"They're not, Chris, but I am a bit taken aback that you didn't come to me about it first. We have a protocol for these situations. You should have called the team together and discussed it with everyone first. This seems very hasty and ill thought-out for you. I have real

concerns that you've lost any sense of objectivity about this patient."
I scowled at him. "Are you telling me I *can't* look into this?"

"No. I'm telling you I have concerns, and I want you to be sure you
follow our standard protocol before you move forward with it."

"Duly noted." I straightened some of the papers on my desk. "Is
there anything else?"

Ed sighed, shook his head, and stood. "Just be mindful that you're
in a vulnerable position right now. While things are still raw from
Cal's death, you may have more trouble than usual maintaining
objectivity and separating your personal life from your work."

I nodded tightly. "I'll take that under advisement."

"Have you thought more about speaking to a professional?"

"What can they tell me that I don't already know? I can recite
Elisabeth Kübler-Ross's five stages of grief or discuss the dual
process model developed by Stroebe and Schut in my sleep."

"Seeing a therapist who is wholly outside of the situation can give
you perspective you aren't capable of on your own. You *know* this,
Chris."

"I know that right now you're keeping me from helping my patient
cope with her impending death," I snapped.

"And you are dangerously close to crossing the line right now. I'm
not stopping you from trying to arrange something for Hazel, but I
am asking you to follow standard protocol. I don't want to pull
rank, but I will remind you that, whatever our relationship outside

of the hospital is, when we're here, I am your boss. If I feel your lack of objectivity is getting in the way of taking care of your patients, I *will* step in."

Ed let himself out of my office without another word. I rubbed at my temples as I considered his words. *Am I losing my objectivity?*

I thought about it all day as I met with patients. Most were palliative care patients—ones who were coping with recent diagnoses of lifelong chronic illnesses—as opposed to the terminally ill ones. It was still tough, but right now, a bit easier to cope with. As I let them speak and I took notes on their fears and concerns about what the rest of their lives would bring, my mind kept drifting back to Hazel and my brother. Sure, in some ways Hazel reminded me of Cal. The zeal for life was palpably similar. I wasn't doing anything for her that I wouldn't have done for any patient. Was I?

Ed was wrong. He had to be.

I t was raining hard when I left work, and signs of spring were slowly beginning to emerge. The grass looked lusher and greener, and it was already March. A month and a half since Cal had died.

I automatically pointed my car in the direction of the gym, but working out suddenly didn't appeal anymore. I didn't want to go home either. There was nothing there for me.

Dave and I had tentatively patched up the damage our argument had caused, but I wasn't sure we were quite ready to hang out without it being a little awkward. And I didn't have the energy to deal with that right now.

So, what did I have?

My thoughts turned to Elliot, but I brushed them away. That was ridiculous. I couldn't call him up just because I was lonely and having a shitty day. I could say I wanted to talk to him more about the idea of an exhibition of Cal's work—and that was true—but it felt flimsy and desperate.

I contemplated my options as I navigated the roads. What if I checked out the Holloway gallery? I hadn't been there in a year or so, and I was suddenly curious to see what it was like these days. Plus, it would help me decide about showing Cal's work there.

Winding through the heavy traffic to get to the Pearl District was tedious and occupied most of my mental attention, but I found parking relatively easily. The gallery itself was quite empty when I walked inside, and I realized most people had probably just gotten off work and were heading home for dinner. To their families.

I shook off the feeling of melancholy that swept over me and turned my attention to the art on the walls.

"Good evening." An attractive young woman approached me. "Is there anything I can help you with, sir?"

"Not at the moment," I said with a smile. "I haven't been here in a while, so I wanted to check it out."

"Are you just browsing or are you in the market for something specific?"

"Maybe a little of both. My place could use something to breathe a little life into it, so if a piece catches my eye, I might buy it." My words pleased her and startled me. Well, they were true enough. I'd come here to check out their work, and I *did* need to add some sense of home to my apartment. I had bought some pieces by local artists for the place Alec and I'd had together. I'd left it all there though. I loved having Cal's art on my walls, but it couldn't hurt to find a few things I picked out on my own as well.

"Well, I'll let you browse. My name is Joy. If you have any questions, don't hesitate to find me."

"Thank you, Joy." I smiled at her again, then turned back to the art on the wall. I slowly made a circuit of the room, but nothing particularly grabbed my attention. I was no art expert, but I knew what I liked. And while I could see that they had many beautiful works by painters and sculptors, I wasn't compelled to bring any of them home with me.

After I perused everything in the front room, I approached the desk where Joy sat. "Excuse me. Do you have anything by an artist by the name of Elliot Rawlings?"

Her eyes lit up. "Oh, yes, we do. Follow me and I'll show you where it is. He's been with us for several years. Peter Holloway discovered his work himself, right out of art school. Elliot is one of our youngest and most talented artists."

That information meshed with what Elliot had told me, and I felt a surprising sense of relief. I hadn't consciously realized I had some doubts about his story, but it was good to get confirmation that he'd been honest with me. And, maybe, given all the secrets of the people around me, it was no surprise I was a little hesitant to trust anyone right now.

Joy stopped in front of a wall that held a series of large black and white pieces. "Let me know if you have any questions."

I thanked her and heard the tap-tap-tap of her heels retreating as I studied the first piece. It was beautiful. Based on the rough sketch he'd done of me the morning after we slept together, I wasn't surprised. This was equally simple, and I could easily identify it as his work. It had a sense of originality to it that even my untrained eye could spot.

It was a charcoal portrait of a nude man with his face partially obscured. Even if I hadn't recognized the tangle of dark hair and high cheekbones, the title of *Self-portrait, XI* told me what I suspected. I eyed it critically. Elliot seemed strong and vibrant in the drawing. Less thin. I realized with a jolt what a toll Cal's death must have taken on him.

Grief could easily have caused him to drop twenty pounds, and even in the portrait, his frame was relatively spare. It felt uncomfortably voyeuristic to stare at him this way though, and I moved on to the next. It was of a woman. The sight of a nude woman did little for me, and based on what he'd said, Elliot felt the same, yet there was a raw sensuality to the piece that made me want to reach out and touch.

I slowly looked through his work, coming across several more self-portraits. I didn't linger as long on those as I did the others, but I still hadn't seen all his work yet when I heard the tap-tap-tap of high heels on the polished concrete floors again.

"I'm sorry, sir." Joy sounded apologetic. "Monday nights are our early night. We will be closing shortly."

I smiled to reassure her. "That's not a problem. I don't think I'll be buying anything today, but I will be back again."

"Of course." Any disappointment over the lack of a sale didn't show as she guided me toward the exit. "I hope you have a pleasant rest of your evening, and we look forward to seeing you again soon."

"Thank you. You as well," I murmured as I exited the gallery onto the rain-soaked street. I flipped the collar of my coat up as I hurried toward my car. Once in it, I reached for my phone. Without thinking twice, I selected Elliot's number and hit send.

"Chris?" Elliot sounded bewildered when he answered a couple of rings in. I could hardly blame him. We'd texted, but never spoken on the phone before. "Is everything okay?"

"I want to do the gallery show of Cal's work," I said.

He was silent for a second. "Any particular reason you decided that now?"

"I went to the Holloway Gallery after I left the hospital tonight. I saw a lot of incredible art there, including yours."

"Oh." He cleared his throat. "Thank you."

I'd also seen the prices listed. Not only did his art speak to me, it clearly sold well if they could demand that much. Based on that and Joy's reaction to his name, he was highly respected. If he said Cal's work was good, I trusted him.

"I like the idea of showing Cal's work," I said slowly. "It seems like a waste to let his work get dusty and unseen. I'd rather someone buy it and enjoy it."

"I would too." Elliot's tone was heartfelt. "This call isn't mine to make, obviously, but what do you think about donating the profits to a charity? Making money off his work seems wrong."

"That sounds perfect to me," I said immediately. That had been one of my reasons for hesitating. "We can explore some options about what charity to donate to, but I love the idea of Cal's work helping people. I certainly don't need the money and neither do my parents."

"Neither do I."

I could believe it. Especially because he seemed to live very simply. I let out a sigh. "I'll have to discuss it all with my parents first. My mom is the executor of his estate. If Cal's work is being sold, they'll need to sign off on it."

"Of course. Are you ready to tell them?"

I leaned my head against the headrest and caught a glimpse of myself in the rearview mirror. Faint lines creased the skin around my haggard brown eyes and a furrow etched my forehead. I let out a heavy sigh. "About Cal's work? Yes. About the rest? I don't know."

"Sometimes, I regret telling you about any of it," Elliot said. "I didn't mean to burden you with all of it."

"Why should you carry that burden alone?" I responded.

"I'm used to it."

His words made me ache.

"Mom?"

I stared at the alarm clock groggily, wondering why she was calling at one in the morning. A sudden wave of panic made me bolt upright, and my heart pounded in my chest as all the awful possibilities crossed my mind. "Wait, are you okay? Is Dad okay?"

"We're fine, honey. I just needed to ask you some questions."

"In the middle of the night? You scared the *shit* out of me," I admitted.

"I'm sorry." She sounded so contrite. "I didn't realize what time it was. You go back to bed."

I leaned against the headboard and scrubbed a hand over my face. "No, I'm awake now. What did you need?"

"Well, do you have Cal's camera? Or does Dave? Because I can't find it anywhere. When I didn't find it in his room, I assumed it was in his car. I went out to look for it, but I can't find it." She sounded nearly in tears.

"Hey, hey, it's okay, Mom," I said soothingly. "*I* have Cal's camera."

Her sigh of relief was audible. "Oh. Well, good. I am glad. Did you take it from his room then?"

I cleared my throat. "Uhh, no. It was with …" I hesitated and took a deep breath as I tried to pull together my thoughts. "Look, Mom, Cal was seeing someone, and I just found out about it recently."

"Oh! I wondered. He was gone so much, and he just seemed … different, lately. Was she nice? Do you think she was good for Cal?" She sounded so eager and curious, and I couldn't stand the idea of breaking her heart.

Fuck. How did I answer that without giving away Cal's secret and potentially hurting my mother more? God, I wasn't awake enough for any of this. I spoke carefully. "Well, from what I can tell, Cal was pretty serious about the person he was dating. I think he was happy."

She sniffled. "That poor girl; she must be missing him so much. Do you think I should reach out to her?"

"No!" Alarmed, I sat upright again, all traces of sleepiness gone now. "I mean, no. I'm sure dealing with his death was hard enough, but meeting Cal's family now that he's gone would just make it worse."

"You're probably right." She sighed wistfully. "I just wish I'd met her."

"I know, Mom. Look, I think you need to try to hold on to the fact that Cal was happy and had finally met someone he cared about. That's really all you can do at this point." It was the best I could offer her.

"I *am* glad. I just can't help but think about how much he could have done with his life. I can't stop picturing him with a family. I want that for both of you."

I felt a lump in my throat. "I know, Mom. And it's unfair that Cal will never have that."

The hitch in her breath made my chest ache. "I'm so lost without him, C.J."

"Me too, Mom. Me too."

I tossed and turned the rest of the night. That morning when I arrived at Cal's apartment, I found Elliot already there.

He sat cross-legged on the floor with a sketchpad in front of him and, for once, he didn't hide what he was working on. He glanced up at me with an almost shy, half-smile, and I stopped in my tracks at the way it lit up his face.

"Oh good, you didn't get food," he said, pushing his hair back from his face. I raised an eyebrow at him, and he gave me a sheepish look. "I, uh, brought some today."

I spotted food storage containers on the coffee table. "Oh, thanks. You didn't have to though."

He shrugged and pushed the sketchpad aside. "Neither did you the last couple of times."

I draped my coat across the nearby chair and took a seat on the floor near him. "But I did," I admitted.

"Why?" He pried the lid off a container.

"You're giving up your time to help me go through Cal's shit and telling me about your relationship with him. I know it's the last thing you wanted to do, and I'm grateful," I admitted.

He shrugged and glanced at me under his lashes. "I don't hate it."

The look and his words hit me like a one-two punch to the gut. "Really?"

He shoved the container at me. "Here. I made frittata."

I took it from him, slightly bewildered by the abrupt change in mood and conversation. But he'd reached out to me, and I didn't want to discourage him. "You *cook*?"

"Not often."

The frittata looked like they'd been made in a mini muffin tin, and I reached for one of the bite size rounds of egg and what looked like vegetables. "They look good." I took a bite. They were tender and flavorful, and when I finished one, I immediately reached for another. "They taste good too. Thanks."

"Thanks. When I bother to cook, it usually turns out decent."

"More than decent."

His smile was fleeting but sincere. "I make huge batches so I can grab something while I work."

"Yeah, I do that too."

"There's coffee there. I wasn't sure what you put in yours so there's cream and sugar in the bag."

"Thanks. Do you always drink tea?" I ate another frittata. There was bacon in this one. God, they were so good. This was a side of Elliot I'd never contemplated.

"Yeah. I drink it by the potful when I'm working. Which isn't very good when I want to sleep. It used to be coffee, but the acidity was bothering my stomach. The Earl Grey isn't much better for my sleep because it's still pretty high in caffeine, and I hate the decaf version, but I've pretty much given up on a normal schedule."

I smiled to myself. I wasn't used to this new, talkative Elliot, but I enjoyed it.

I ate another frittata. "Med school fucked up my sleep schedule, and I'm not sure it's ever recovered. Hence, the coffee addiction. I meant to pick some up today, but I ran late. I didn't want to leave you hanging."

"You're fine." He grabbed his sketchbook. "Wild night?"

I snorted. "*Rough* night, anyway."

"Hot date or one of your patients?" He resumed sketching.

"Neither. Family." I sighed and reached for the coffee and popped off the lid. It smelled heavenly, although I was inured to bad coffee after years of drinking whatever was available at the hospital. This was from the same local coffee shop I always went to. I wondered if we had the same taste or if he'd gone there because he knew I'd like it. "My mom called in the middle of the night and scared the shit out of me."

"Something wrong?"

My laugh was hollow as I ripped open a packet of sugar. "What isn't these days? She's a wreck, my dad is a wreck, and I don't know how to fucking help."

"That sucks."

"It really does. But, anyway, she called last night—panicking—that she couldn't find Cal's camera." I dumped in some cream and stirred it.

Elliot grimaced.

"I told her I had it, but then I had to explain where it had been. So, she ... sort of knows about you now."

He froze, his eyes wide and startled looking.

"Not that you're a guy," I hastily assured him. "Just that Cal was dating someone."

"Oh." He resumed sketching. "What did you tell her?"

"That Cal was seeing someone—someone he cared about a lot—and he'd been happy."

"How did you manage to keep gender out of it?"

I shrugged, "Hell if I know. Careful wording, I guess? She didn't push it."

"That's good."

"You really don't think I should just tell them?"

This time he shrugged. "What good is it going to do? Has knowing made *you* happier?"

"Happier? No." I smiled sadly. "But I'd still rather know. I'd rather have the honesty."

"Most people aren't like you. They don't want to know the truth about anything. They stay on the surface and pretend like it's all going to magically be okay." His words held a bitter undertone.

"You're right, of course, but I can't help but think my parents should know. But then I think about how much they're fighting now and how much my dad is drinking and ..."

Elliot tensed and shot me a troubled look. "Your dad drinks? Cal never mentioned that. He made your family sound like the fucking Cleavers or something."

Elliot wasn't far off. The Allen family had never been perfect, but compared to most families, we *were* practically the Cleavers. "That's the weird thing; we always have been. Sure, we argued occasionally, but we really got along. I don't know where this is coming from. He drank too much for a while after his father died, but he stopped without any problem, and he was rarely a nasty drunk. Just kinda quiet and withdrawn."

"Hmm." A hefty dose of skepticism colored Elliot's voice.

"But he *was* downright nasty to my mom the other night. I know he's hurting—we all are—but I don't know what to do or say. Or how to make it better."

"You can't fix everything for everybody, Chris," Elliot said gently. "No matter how much you want to."

"But that's who I am. That's what I've always done. I was the one who smoothed over the fights between my dad and Cal and ..." I felt a lump in my throat. "I don't know who I am without that. And I don't know who I am without my brother."

The confession fell from my lips before I could stop it. I stared down into my half-empty coffee cup. I couldn't look at Elliot, couldn't stand to see whatever expression he had on his face. But I felt his fingertips, warm and dry against the side of my hand as he gently took it and arranged it carefully on my thigh before letting go. I looked up at him in surprise, both at the unexpected touch and the odd gesture.

"What are you doing?" I asked quietly.

He didn't look up and his pencil flew over the page. "Don't move. I'm sketching your hand."

"My hand?" I stared blankly down at it.

"Yes."

"But *why*?"

"You have great hands." Our gazes met, and he quickly looked away. "Artistically speaking."

"Thanks?" I looked down at it again. I could see blunt fingers and veins crisscrossing the back, but they were nothing special.

"They have character," he clarified.

"Huh." I couldn't make sense of it, but artists were supposed to be weird and eccentric, I supposed. "Can I see what you're working on?"

"One sec." He added a few short, sharp strokes before setting down the pencil. He turned the paper to face me, and I looked curiously at the page. I saw a perfectly shaded sketch of me playing the guitar and a rougher one of my hands. He had captured the latter perfectly, down to the short, trimmed nails and the fine dusting of black hair on the back, but the drawing of my whole body was one I didn't recognize.

I could see that he'd captured my features—the heavy stubble, the dark brows, the slight furrow on my forehead—but I didn't recognize the intensity and sensuality of my features. The man on the page was rugged and handsome, sexy, yet vulnerable. Was that how Elliot saw me? I shot him a glance, but he was busy fiddling with his pencil and didn't meet my gaze.

I looked at the sketch again and noticed that he had also captured the pain in my eyes.

My gaze was raw and wounded, edged with worry. It was exactly how I felt.

I didn't know what to say or how to respond. Instead, I reached out and rested my fingertips on his denim-clad shin in silent thanks.

That was the odd thing about all of this. I hardly knew him, yet Elliot understood me better than anyone else in my life.

Chapter Seventeen

I was a mess of nerves on Sunday as I drove to my parents' house for dinner, and I could hardly sit still during the meal. My parents seemed too distracted to notice. Was I worried or relieved that they weren't paying any attention to my mood? It was difficult to be sure.

But when my mom pushed her chair back from the table to clear the dishes, I stopped her.

"Wait, Mom. There's something I need to tell you both."

They both frowned at me. "What is it, C.J.?" my mother asked as she sank back down into her seat.

"Well, I discovered that Cal was doing some photography."

She gave me a puzzled look. "That's hardly news, sweetheart. His bedroom was covered in pictures he'd taken. He's been selling stock photos for years."

"I know." I licked my lips. "It seems he was taking it more seriously lately. Exploring some different options. I think he might have been looking into making a real career of it."

"About damn time he figured something out," my father said. He'd been drinking steadily all evening, and I was suddenly grateful that Cal wasn't there to hear his comment. And then I felt a pang of guilt at my relief that Cal was gone, for any reason.

"Well, that's wonderful," my mother said, her tone a good deal softer than his had been. "What type of photography?"

"Portraits." I licked my lips. "Nudes. Of couples."

She blinked at me. "Was Cal doing *pornography?*" Her tone was hushed. "I mean, I have mixed feelings about it. On the one hand, I know some people find it empowering, but the treatment of women …"

I let out a startled laugh. "No. Mom, no, Cal wasn't doing porn. I swear. This was extremely artistic. Not graphic. Just the human body. Or two human bodies together. The subject was love."

"Oh." A perplexed expression crossed her face. "I'm not sure why you seem so hesitant to tell us this then, C.J."

I took a deep breath. "Because it wasn't of straight couples. It was homosexual couples."

"Oh." She looked even more perplexed. "Well, it's not like Cal was ever closed-minded about anything. Perhaps he just found a … niche. Did he tell you about this when he was alive?"

"No." I shook my head. "I found out after he died."

"How did you find out?"

"Talking to some of his friends. Going through some of his belongings." They were half-truths at best.

"I don't understand why he wouldn't have told us about this." She glanced over at my father. "We would have been pleased he'd found a career he enjoyed."

My father nodded.

"I know." I felt my heart clench. "And I think Cal would have too. I think he would have told us about it when he was ready. He just ran out of time."

A wave of sorrow passed over her face. "I wish I could tell him how happy I am that he found something he was passionate about. We were always proud of him, but I'd always hoped he'd find his calling."

"I know, Mom. I did too."

"I wonder how many other secrets he kept from us."

Guilt flushed my skin. "I suppose we'll never know." I took a deep breath. "I've been talking to a friend of his. He's an artist. We've been talking about Cal's work a lot lately, and we thought it might be nice to do a gallery show of it."

Surprise flickered across my father's face. "You think Cal's work was good enough to show at a gallery?"

"Yes," I said promptly. "And Elliot agrees." I told them a little about Elliot's own work and that he was with the Holloway Gallery. They both seemed suitably impressed.

"Well, it's clear he's talented, and I trust your judgement about him," my mother said. "So, if you trust him, so do I."

"If we all agree to it, Elliot suggested we could sell Cal's work and donate the proceeds to charity," I added. "I'm not sure which, but there are dozens of issues Cal was passionate about. I'm sure we could come up with something."

"Well, if you think the gallery would be interested, it seems worth exploring at least," she said slowly. "Don't you think so, Christopher?"

"I don't see why not."

I felt like a weight had been lifted off me. "I'll talk to Elliot, and we'll get things started then."

My mother smiled at me. It was tinged with sadness. "This is the most enthusiastic you've sounded about anything lately," she said. "It's nice. This Elliot person seems like he's been a good friend."

"He has." A part of me wanted to blurt out the truth then and tell her that he'd become a lifeline since Cal's death and that he'd been far more than just a friend to Cal. But I was too afraid of breaking the fragile stability in my family. My dad had been drinking heavily again tonight, but he seemed to be holding it together better, and my parents weren't arguing. I couldn't bear to disrupt that.

I texted Elliot to let him know the news and, that night, slept better than I had in a long while. In the morning, I went to work with a renewed sense of energy.

My phone rang while I was reviewing charts, and I answered with my usual spiel of my name and position at the hospital.

"Dr. Allen? This is Allie Carmichael with the Oregon Coast Aquarium. You left a message for me about a patient of yours. I'm sorry I haven't been able to get back to you sooner."

"That's okay. And please, call me Chris."

"You said you had a patient with a terminal illness who was interested in marine biology?"

"Yes." I gave her a more detailed rundown of Hazel's condition and her bucket list. "She wouldn't be able to go to the aquarium, unfortunately," I explained.

"Oh, that poor girl. Of course, I'd like to do whatever I can to help. We do have a traveling educational program for schools. Why don't I tell you a little more about what that entails and discuss how we could modify it for her?"

"That sounds perfect."

Once we'd thoroughly discussed logistics and concerns, the conversation shifted to more personal matters.

"How are you doing?" she asked, her tone turning more serious. I knew she was referring to my brother's death.

"It's been tough, but I'm doing my best."

"I hope you know how fondly I think of Cal. I know it's been what, seven years since we dated? But he is—was—such a wonderful person. The world is a much poorer place without him in it."

"That's a really nice thing to hear," I said. "I'll be sure to pass that along to my parents. I know they'll appreciate it too."

"I'm afraid I have to run. We have a sick sea otter I need to check on. But it was good talking to you, Chris. I'll run our ideas by my colleagues and see if they have any additional suggestions. Just call me as soon as you get the okay from your boss."

"I will. Thanks again, Allie. I'll talk to you soon."

I hung up the phone, feeling a renewed sense of optimism. All I had to do was convince Ed our plan was solid.

I had an hour before I needed to meet with any patients, so I neatly compiled the suggestions Allie and I had come up with, then took it to his office.

"I don't know, Chris. Do you really think it's worth putting her through the physical stress of that?" he said after he'd looked it over.

"It would be short," I promised. "Allie has some ideas for how to modify one of their traveling aquarium exhibits. They normally bring them to schools, but they could do a massively scaled down version for Hazel. Allie even offered to open it up to the other hospice patients if we're interested. If not, they'd just bring a small tide pool tank with anemone and sea stars and such to Hazel's room. There would be a little presentation, Hazel would get to touch them, and she'd get an official shirt and badge with her name and 'marine biologist' on it."

Ed sighed. "It sounds wonderful, but I'm not convinced it's the best choice."

I leaned forward and spoke earnestly, "This kid is dying, Ed. She has a dozen things listed on her bucket list and no chance of accomplishing any of them. I can't give her the rest of them, but I can make sure she gets this one thing. That's worth doing, isn't it? Giving her some joy before the end?"

"You know it is. And we've always done what we can to accommodate patients' wishes, but this is extravagant, Chris. It would have to be run by the infection control and security departments first, and you know damn well the hospital P.R. team will want to contact the press about it. It's going to take time to arrange, and frankly, I don't think she has it."

"Please," I insisted. "Just give me a chance to *try*."

Ed leveled a stern look at me. "Even if we are able to work through those issues, I still have concerns about your objectivity. Have you thought about what I said?"

"I have considered it, and you're probably right," I admitted. "I do see a lot of similarities to Cal in Hazel, and I'd be lying if I said otherwise." A lump rose in my throat. "There was nothing I could do for him at the end, and I still struggle with it. I have a chance now to help Hazel, and I want to take it. Maybe it *is* tied up in grieving my brother, but in the end, is that really so bad? I'll give a dying girl one last burst of happiness before the end. No matter how hard it will be to lose her, I will feel better for having been able to give my patient that joy."

Ed rubbed his hand across his face and sat back in his chair with what sounded like a resigned grumble. "Okay. Email me your proposal and I'll forward it to the appropriate people. I can't promise you anything, but we'll give it a try."

"Thank you," I said earnestly.

"Don't make me regret this."

I knew I couldn't tell Hazel what we were planning—she'd be crushed if it fell through—but I did visit her that afternoon and give her a hint. I'd cleared that with her parents, and they'd agreed something to look forward to might give her the strength to fight off the current infection. With the help of some heavy-hitting antibiotics, anyway.

"I might have a surprise for you," I said as I took a seat beside her bed.

Hazel smiled weakly at me through her oxygen mask. Her breaths were labored and wet sounding. I tried to hide my wince. Ed was right, she was rapidly declining. There wasn't much time left. *Shit.*

"Yeah?"

"I know you're really bummed about not being able to finish your bucket list, but I'm trying my hardest to help you check off something. We have to work out the details, so I'm not going to tell you what it is, but I want you to keep fighting this infection, okay?"

She nodded.

"Because if you can, you'll get to experience something really, really cool."

"One last cool thing before I die?" she asked, and the raw honesty tore at my heart.

I nodded, hoping she couldn't see the wetness in my eyes.

"Yes. One last cool thing before you die."

"I'd like that."

On Thursday night after work, I dropped off two boxes of Cal's belongings at Dave's place. "There you go. Everything of Cal's that you said you wanted should be in there."

"Thanks, man. I could have helped, you know," Dave chastised me.

"Nah, it's fine. Hauling boxes is a good workout, and I skipped the gym the other night." I closed the door behind me. I'd messaged him on the pretext of wanting to drop off Cal's belongings and because we hadn't had much time to hang out lately. Both were true, but I was there to tell him about the gallery show. Elliot and I had been texting back and forth about it, and he'd arranged a meeting between the gallery owner and my parents and me this coming weekend.

Dave squinted as he looked me up and down. "You look all right to me. Even if you did miss a workout. I don't think you've let yourself go too much."

"Thanks, asshole," I said with a laugh. "Nice of you."

He snorted. "Seriously. You look … better. More relaxed and less miserable."

"I'm trying," I admitted.

"Good." He clapped me on the shoulder. "That's what I like to hear. Anyway, want a drink?"

"Sure." I followed him toward the kitchen. Like the rest of his place, it was neat and well cared for.

"What do you want?" He opened the fridge and peered in. "Beer?"

"Actually, I'll take coffee, if you don't mind." Dave looked at me in surprise, and I explained, "Just cutting back a bit right now on the alcohol." My father's drinking problem loomed heavily, and it no longer held any appeal for me.

"Oh. Okay. Sure. I just brewed a pot a little bit ago actually." He brought out two mugs and poured the coffee into them. "I shouldn't drink it this late but ..."

Yeah, I knew how that went.

"What about you? How's work been?" I asked, leaning against the counter.

Dave shrugged. "Same 'ol, same 'ol. Too many hours. Too few dollars for the amount of shit I put up with. It's fine though. Hopefully in another year or two, I'll get an editorial position and be sitting a little more comfortably."

"I hope so." I stirred a little cream and sugar into my drink. "You seeing anyone?"

"I'm having fun with Nadia but that's it." I gave him a blank look, and he clarified, "The waitress who gave me her number when we went out. The one I mentioned I had a date with?"

"Ahh, yeah. I remember now. Well, that's good. She seemed great, and you said you're not looking for serious, right?"

Dave shook his head. "I most certainly am not."

"Perfect then."

"Yep." He took a sip of his coffee. "What about you? Have you given any thought to dating?"

I shrugged. "I've considered it."

"By which you mean you are failing utterly to do anything but too proud to admit you need my help?"

"Something like that."

He grinned, that shit-eating, crooked grin that used to make my stomach flip. Funny, it didn't have the same effect now. The argument we'd had a few weeks ago had done one thing for sure. It had completely ruled out me ever looking at Dave the same way again. I still cared about him as a friend, but he'd made it abundantly clear he had no interest in me, and that had completely cooled my ardor. I couldn't decide if I was relieved or disappointed. Unrequited longing wasn't fun, exactly, but there had been a thrill to it that I couldn't deny.

"Just give me the word and I'll set you up with Brendon," Dave continued.

I rolled my eyes. "Oh, my God, will you shut up about your co-worker? Just because Cal nicknamed you *The Wingman* doesn't mean you need to make it your job to badger me into a relationship. You're worse than my mother."

"Fuck you," Dave said, but it was without heat. "Honestly, I'm surprised to hear you haven't met someone. When you walked through the door, I thought you had the look of a man who had recently gotten laid and was *very* happy about it."

"You seem pretty concerned about my sex life there, Dave," I joked. "No, I haven't gotten laid lately." How long ago had Elliot and I fucked? A month and a half ago? That wasn't recent. And it had hardly made me *happy*.

"Well if you're not getting your knob polished, can you tell me what is making you so cheerful? I'm sure getting Cal's shit packed up has been rough."

"It has been." I shrugged. "I'm glad to have it nearly over with. It's been kinda cathartic, I guess."

"Well, that's something."

"But it'll be a relief not to have to go to that apartment every Saturday to sort through my brother's life."

"You got it done pretty fast, all things considered."

"Namely my brother being a packrat?" I joked.

"Yeah. That."

"Actually, it wasn't too bad. Cal seemed to be getting his shit together. It was a little messy, but nothing like I expected. And Elliot was a ton of help."

"Now that surprises me."

"Elliot helping?"

"Yeah, he doesn't seem like the helpful sort. Especially since he had such a fucking chip on his shoulder about Cal keeping him a secret."

"I guess we realized we could help each other," I hedged. "Plus, he got to keep some of Cal's stuff that was important to him."

"What did you do? Hold it over his head to keep him coming there?"

"What? No!"

Dave laughed. "It didn't sound like you at all, but grief makes people do strange things."

"You're telling me. But, no, I would have given Elliot anything he wanted. I just had no idea what those things were, you know? It wasn't that much anyway. Some books, several items from things they did together, that leather satchel he used for a camera bag, that sort of thing. Oh, that reminds me. There's something I need to talk to you about."

That was as good a segue as I'd get.

"Okay?"

"You knew about the photography Cal had been doing, right?"

"The gay and lesbian stuff? Yeah."

"Elliot suggested putting together a gallery show of the best of Cal's work."

Dave's eyebrows practically hit his hairline. "*What?*"

"I was surprised too when he mentioned it, but Cal's work does deserve to be seen. He was really fucking good, Dave."

"I know he was." Dave said. His tone was short. "But that's some pretty personal shit. Do you even know if Cal would want that? He certainly never said anything to me about that."

"He left a notebook with some plans for it, but to be honest, I can't know for sure. But he's dead, Dave. I can't exactly ask him, and I have to go with my own gut instinct and Elliot's opinion."

Dave narrowed his eyes. "I'm not sure I'd trust his opinion. How the fuck do you know he's not doing it for the money?"

"First of all, he was the one who suggested donating any proceeds to a charity in Cal's name, so I'm pretty sure money isn't the motivator. Second, my mom is the executor of Cal's estate, so none of the money could go to Elliot even if he wanted it. And third, what the fuck do you have against Elliot?" I asked, baffled. I'd thought they got along at least reasonably well.

"Why aren't *you* pissed at him?" Dave countered. "He helped keep your brother's secret."

"Well, he wasn't exactly thrilled about that," I argued. "He wanted Cal to come out. And what the fuck was he supposed to do? March up to my parents' house and bang on their door? Track me down at the hospital? Spill all of Cal's fucking secrets against his wishes? Even if he'd been tempted, he's hardly the type."

"Since when did you turn into Elliot Rawlings' biggest champion?"

"Since when did you start disliking him so much?" I asked, baffled. His anger felt out of proportion, and I wondered what the hell was wrong with him. I was also deflecting a question I really didn't want to answer.

"Why are we even arguing about this, Chris?"

"Maybe because I can't figure out why you're being such a dick," I said.

Dave dragged a hand through his hair. "What the fuck is going on with you, Chris? You have never been so damn combative before!"

"I'm sorry I'm not just rolling over and taking everything like I always have before," I snarled. "Maybe I'm finally starting to realize that some things matter to me enough that I want to fight for them."

Dave gave me a puzzled frown. "Things like what?"

"Like figuring out a way to build a concrete legacy for Cal. What's so wrong with that?"

"There's nothing wrong with that," he said slowly. "And maybe I am being too touchy about it, but I think you're rushing into this gallery show without really thinking it through."

"Nothing is set in stone yet," I said, "We're still exploring our options."

"I hope you know what you're doing here, Chris," Dave said, and I wondered if he meant more than the gallery show.

Because if I were being honest with myself, I *was* taking his criticism of Elliot more personally than I should, given the circumstances. But I couldn't exactly admit that aloud without bringing up even more questions I didn't want to answer.

O n Saturday, I met Elliot in front of the Holloway Gallery. My parents were meeting us there in twenty minutes, but I wanted some time to make sure our stories were straight.

Elliot stared at me. Dark shadowy marks under his eyes told me he hadn't been sleeping well, and I worried I was making that worse for him. "So, you want me to meet your parents now but not tell them about Cal and me?"

"That'll be easier," I assured him. I'd told myself that so many times I'd begun to believe it. "They'll get to know you first. They'll be able to form an unbiased impression of you without having all that baggage attached. And after they know and like you, we can"—the look on Elliot's face made me correct myself—"I can tell them about you and Cal."

"Chris, I'm not convinced this is a good idea. I'm afraid it's all going to blow up in our faces if we're not careful."

"It'll be fine," I assured him. The annoyed huff Elliot let out let me know he completely disagreed with me, but he didn't argue.

We made small talk while we waited, and he was pacing and smoking when they arrived. I didn't miss the quick look of disapproval in both my parents' eyes when they spotted it. And from the way he quickly stubbed the cigarette out, I suspected he didn't either. At least this time, he threw it in the nearby bin.

"Mom, Dad, this is Elliot Rawlings. Elliot, my parents: Christopher Sr. and Sarah Allen."

"It's lovely to meet you." My mother smiled warmly at Elliot and held out her hand.

"Nice to meet you, Elliot." My father gave Elliot's hand a shake, but his own trembled a little. I gave my mother a worried glance, and she looked away as if unable to meet my gaze.

"Tell me more about how you knew Cal," my mother said.

Elliot threw me a troubled look, and I tried to hide my reaction. Damn it, he was right. I should have told them. I'd put him in an awful position.

"I'm a full-time studio artist. I've been showing my work here at the Holloway Gallery for a few years. As for how I knew your son, I put up an ad for models and Cal answered it. We talked about art and photography a lot, and he was curious about my work."

"So, you're why Cal became interested in this subject?" My mother's voice held nothing but kind curiosity, but Elliot tensed.

"I suppose so. I asked him to pose for me, and we discussed my series on same-sex couples."

"I'd love to see your work sometime, Elliot."

"I …" He darted a glance at me, and I gave him an encouraging smile. "Thanks. I could show you some of my work here at the gallery. There are quite a few self-portraits though. Nudes. Uh, full-frontal."

"Oh." She gave him a small, kind smile. "Perhaps you could show me something else some other time, if that would be more comfortable for you."

I reached out to brush my hand across his back in reassurance and quickly drew back. *Shit, what the hell am I thinking?* I stuffed my hand in my jacket pocket instead, but the gesture didn't go unnoticed by my mother.

Her eyes gleamed, and I could see the gears turning in her head. Hoping to head her off, I looked at my watch. "It's about time to go into the gallery to meet with Mr. Holloway. You ready?"

Elliot reached for the door but not before I caught a glimpse of relief in his eyes.

"So, tell me more about your work, Elliot," my mother prompted when we were inside. "Did you always want to be an artist?"

As Elliot and my mom talked, I glanced over at my father. He had been unusually quiet so far, and I wondered if he was drunk or nursing a hangover. Or both.

I felt nothing but relief when Joy approached us. "Great to see you, Elliot. You're here for the meeting with Peter?"

"Yes." He gestured to all of us. "Along with the artist's family. Christopher and Sarah Allen, and Christopher Allen Jr." I had never seen Elliot interact with anyone before, especially not in such a professional setting, and I was surprised by how smooth and polished he came across. Then again, if he had regular gallery shows here, he'd be used to that.

"Lovely to meet you all," Joy said. She turned to me with a small smile. "I believe we already met, however. You were here last week?"

"Yes."

"It's nice to see you again. Why don't you all follow me back to Mr. Holloway's office. I know he's eager to meet with you."

The meeting went well. My father hardly spoke, my mother asked a few questions, and Elliot ran the show. I was grateful. I had no idea what to ask, and my Google searches the night before hadn't been particularly illuminating. By the time the meeting concluded, we'd settled on a tentative plan, and Peter Holloway had offered to draw up contracts for the lawyer of Cal's estate to look over.

As devil-may-care as my brother had been, I was glad he'd listened to my father's insistence that he have a will drawn up and updated regularly. It would have taken months in probate court to get it all straightened out otherwise.

I left the gallery optimistic that this show would be a good thing for all of us.

"We'd love to take you two out for brunch so we can get to know you better, Elliot. Are you available?" my mother asked when we reached the sidewalk again.

Elliot glanced over at me, alarm in his gaze.

I cleared my throat. "You know what, Mom, Elliot mentioned he had something going on this afternoon, and I have something planned too. I'm sure this won't be the last meeting we have. Maybe we can have brunch some other time?"

"Oh, all right," she said, clearly disappointed. She reached up and hugged me before pressing a kiss to my cheek. I could see Elliot and my father shaking hands. "It's good to see you, even if it wasn't for long."

She turned to Elliot and hesitated for a second, as if trying to figure out if a handshake or a hug was more appropriate. She was a hugger, but not everyone was. Elliot solved her dilemma by holding out a hand.

"It was nice to meet you, Mrs. Allen," he said as I hugged my dad goodbye.

"Sarah, please." She smiled warmly at him. "There's no need for formality. You were obviously a good friend to Cal and are becoming a good friend to Chris."

I saw a glimpse of something in Elliot's gaze. Sadness? Anger?

I wasn't sure which.

Chapter Eighteen

"I'm going to tackle Cal's office next."

I'd thought I'd lied to my mother when I told her Elliot had other plans after the gallery meeting, but after they left, he'd informed me he had a few errands to run before he went to Cal's apartment. I'd come straight here. A few minutes ago, I heard the rattle of keys in the lock and the door opening, so I wasn't surprised by Elliot's appearance in the bedroom doorway.

I looked up from the pile of clothes I was sorting through. Most—except a well-worn and well-loved leather jacket and his favorite wetsuit—were being donated. I'd nearly finished the bedroom, and I knew I'd been putting off sorting through the office for some reason, but apparently, Elliot was braver.

"Sounds good." I tucked another T-shirt into the trash bag.

"I figured since I've already been dealing with his photography ..." Elliot's voice trailed off, and I gave him a long, searching glance. He leaned a shoulder against the doorframe, and when I took in the dark smudges under his eyes, worry spiked in me.

"Is everything okay? You look ..."

"Like death warmed over?" Elliot's laugh was a scratchy bark. "Yeah, I stayed up all night working, and it's hitting me hard now."

I dropped the shirt I'd been folding, then walked over to him. "You could have taken a break today or gone home and slept for a while before you came over. I appreciate your help, but I don't expect you to wear yourself thin doing it."

Elliot shrugged. "I would have just tossed and turned anyway. I've been sleeping like shit lately."

"Is there anything I can do?" I asked tentatively. Elliot and I were getting along so much better now, but some things still made him snarly and remote.

"Hit me over the head so I can go to sleep and wake up in about two years? If ever." His laugh was a little bitter.

I blinked at him, unsure if he was punchy because he needed sleep or if it was a thinly veiled cry for help. "Uhh, well, I'm pretty sure inflicting head injuries on people violates my Hippocratic Oath. I could put you in contact with a doctor if you're having sleep issues though. Sometimes, sleep can be difficult during the grieving process. Seeing someone couldn't hurt."

He held up a hand to stop me. "I was kidding, Dr. Allen." He gave me a tired smile and pushed his hair off his face, gathering the dark strands at the back of his head and securing it with the ever-present elastic tie on his wrist. "I'm apparently out of practice at telling jokes, but I promise, that's what I was going for."

"I'm glad," I admitted, the worry I'd felt dissipating a little but not entirely.

He gave me a disarmingly soft smile and shook his head. "I'll be fine. I promise. I *am* really fucking exhausted, but it's only because I sketched all night. Don't worry about me so much." He yawned, then touched his fingertips to my forearm before he levered himself off the door jamb.

He left the scent of Earl Grey and confusion in his wake.

An hour later, the closet and dresser were empty of clothes, the bathroom was cleared out, and I stood looking around Cal's bedroom and wondering what the hell to do next.

"Chris?"

I turned to see Elliot standing in the doorway again. His voice had a funny note to it, and he held a laptop in his arms. Cal's laptop. I recognized the scratched surface and *Eat Sleep Surf* sticker that had come with the wetsuit I'd given him for Christmas a few years ago.

"What is it?"

"I think ... I think you need to see something."

Elliot looked dazed, like someone had punched him in the gut, and I wondered what the hell he'd found on that laptop.

"What is it?" I approached him slowly.

"I ... I broke into Cal's laptop. I wanted to see if the high-res photos from his shoots were on there. We shared a Netflix account, and I knew he was lazy about creating new passwords. I tried the one I knew and it worked." He looked miserable.

The lack of adequate security protection didn't surprise me. Cal had always used the same password for *everything*. I couldn't count the number of times I'd lectured him about it.

"That's fine," I reassured him. "But my brother's carelessness with passwords can't be what's bothering you. Did you not find the photos or something?"

"It's not that. They're all backed up on there like I hoped, but I also saw a Word file on his desktop. It says *C.J.* and I opened it." He looked away. "Sorry. I wasn't even thinking that it could be referring to you. I thought it had something to do with *him,* and I was curious."

"Okay," I said slowly, not really understanding what he was getting at.

He licked his lips. "It's … it's a letter from Cal. To you."

I blinked. That was the last thing I'd expected him to say. "What— what does it say?"

Elliot shook his head and thrust the laptop at me. I took it automatically. "I didn't read it. Not past the first couple lines. Once I realized it was an actual letter to you, I couldn't keep going."

"Oh." And now I felt like I'd been punched in the gut.

Elliot gave me a tremulous, sympathetic smile, and the part of my brain that wasn't wondering what the hell my brother could have had to say to me in a letter was thinking that no one else could possibly understand the slew of emotions coursing through me like Elliot did.

"I … I'll just …" I held the computer against my chest as I stumbled back and sat heavily on the edge of the mattress.

My gaze drifted down to the battered laptop in my arms, and when I glanced up again, Elliot was gone.

I drew in a shaky breath and settled so my back was against the wall. I ran my hands across the top of the laptop with the sense I was about to uncover another bombshell. The prospect of a letter from Cal unnerved me. When had he written it? Why? Was it filled with all things he hadn't been able to say to me aloud?

I thought of the secrets he'd kept and wondered if I'd finally get the answers to all the questions that had been swirling through my head since his funeral. Worse, I wondered if I'd be even more confused when it was over. The possibilities left me terrified.

My heart lodged in my throat as I shakily lifted the lid and dragged a finger across the touch pad. The screen came to life and the letter was already open.

At first, the words swam before my blurry eyes, but I sucked in a deep breath, and when I could focus again, I began to read.

I'm such a fraud these days. Chris, I have all this shit I want to tell you. Every time I see you, I want to blurt it out. I know you'll laugh and give me hell for waiting so long. You might be mad that I've kept this a secret, but you'll forgive me. I know you will. So why is it so hard for me to say it to you? Some nights I pick up the phone, wanting to call you, but I can't. We hang out and I spend the whole time with my tongue stuck to the roof of my mouth. I thought maybe it would be easier in an email or a letter or something.

My breath caught as I read, hearing Cal's voice in my head as clear as if he'd spoken the words aloud.

I've written and deleted this so many times. It's probably never going to get sent at this point. I'm too much of a motherfucking pussy. God, can't you just see Mom smacking me upside the head for using that phrase? The woman swears like a sailor but forget it if either of us say motherfucker or pussy.

Speaking of pussy ... or the lack thereof, that's my huge secret.

I'm in love. With a guy. I think. I mean, I know he's a guy, but the love part is confusing me. It's so weird to say, but I can't even tell you how he makes me feel. Elliot, that's his name. He's this insanely talented artist with a smile that makes me weak in the knees.

Fuck, I can't wait for you to meet him. Aside from the fact that, well, he's a dude, he's not the kind of person I expected to be with, but I think you'll like him. He's quiet. Serious. Really intense. That smile I mentioned? It's rare, but when he's happy ... fuck, he makes the whole world light up. I make him happy. Sometimes. Sometimes, I think I hurt him. Not intentionally, but I'm a fucking failure at being a boyfriend. Fuck, C.J., this is why I wish I could talk to you about this. I need your advice. You're the kind of guy I want to be like in a relationship. Dependable, supportive ... all that shit you've had figured out your whole life. At twelve, you were more mature than I am now. Especially when it comes to this kind of thing.

You know me. I flirt without thinking. It's like ... breathing to me, and it's never been a problem before, but now, it hurts him. We'll go out to dinner and I'll smile and wink at the waitress, and he just ... disappears. His face goes all blank and he pulls away, and I know I've fucked up, but I can't figure out how to fix it. I'm terrified of letting him down. Christ, he deserves better. I know he does. I want to be better for him, but I can't seem to get it right.

Not telling Mom and Dad and you hurts him too. He thinks he's my dirty little secret, but he's NOT. That's not it at all. I'm just a fucking pussy, and I don't know how to tell the whole world I'm bi. I know a lot of guys like me call themselves heteroflexible, but that's just equivocating when I'm in love with him. I'm so fucking confused though. I spent twenty-eight years as a straight man. With a gay big brother, of course, I thought *about it. I considered the idea that I might be into dudes too, but honestly, no guy ever really turned me on. Okay, that's a lie. There was one weird night with Dave that involved a lot of weed and blowjobs, but that doesn't really count. I mean, Dave's sort of ... whatever, I guess. Not that he isn't good looking, but he doesn't do it for me, you know?*

There's a lot of guys I'd look at and go, wow, he'd look amazing in front of my camera, but it was aesthetic appeal. I didn't want to bang them; I just wanted to photograph them. And even now, I still don't really find men that attractive, but Elliot ... he's just this incredible person, and he's so fucking beautiful. I can't get enough of him. I don't really know what it means. I just couldn't see giving up a chance to be with someone like him just because he has a dick, you know?

I love him, C.J., that's the really scary part. Me, who has never loved anyone but my family, and well, Dave, but other than that one weird night, he's basically been another brother. It's crazy. I've screwed around with how many amazing women? I've never fallen for them like this. I've never felt like not being with them would make me stop breathing. But Elliot? He just ... turns me inside out and makes me crazy. I've skydived and base-jumped and stood on the edge of volcanoes and, man, none of that has been as intense as loving him. Nothing has ever felt so reckless but right. That need I have to push myself harder, fly higher, do something wilder gets filled up by him. He told me once he was scared that the thrill would wear off, that I'd fall out of love with him once I came down from the high. Once it stopped being new and different.

You know what scares me? That he might be right. That I'm going to hurt him. I'm scared I'm too fucking stupid to treat him well, too afraid of commitment to give him what he needs. I'm scared I can't ever be the man he deserves. How do I fix this, Chris? I love Elliot, but I'm screwing this up. I know I'm screwing this up SO FUCKING BAD, and I don't know how to make it right.

Please don't be mad that I kept this a secret. At first, it was just … sex, you know? Nothing serious and it seemed stupid to make a whole big announcement. Why the hell did you and Mom and Dad need to know that all of a sudden I liked dick too? But then I got to know him better, and I fell for him so motherfucking hard. I should have told you all then, I know that, but I started to doubt myself. What if we didn't last? What if I couldn't make a relationship with Elliot work, and I made this whole big announcement and then went back to women? How dumb would that be?

Then I wondered if it would bother everyone if we did stay together. What if it worked out? What if I'd actually found the person I wanted to spend the rest of my life with? What if our parents had two queer sons? No guarantee of little Allen grandbabies and all that. I mean, I know gay guys can have kids, adopt or use a surrogate or whatever. So it's possible, but it's just that much more complicated than knocking your girlfriend up and deciding to make a go of it. Which, if I'm being honest here, is pretty much how I saw it happening for me. Shitty, I know. But I've never claimed to be anyone's idea of a role model. Realistically, I figured that's how kids would happen for me. I'd knock some girl up, then do the right thing. That's my destiny as a father. But being a father with another guy? Choosing to make it happen? That's fucking terrifying. I couldn't take that kind of leap.

And I fucked up your chances to ever have biological kids. God, have I ever told you how sorry I am about that? It haunts me, especially now. One stupid mistake of mine and it changed your life forever. I never meant to take that away from you. You say you've forgiven me, but how can you not be pissed about it? You're too damn nice for your own good.

Am I making too big of a deal of this? Maybe, but then I think how hurt Dad was when you went into psychiatry instead of being a pediatrician like him and I

THE GHOSTS BETWEEN US

wonder. I'm afraid I'll be letting Mom and Dad down. Or am I nuts to worry so much about this? I don't know. I just can't help it. Me, who never thinks anything through, overthinking this to death. Fucking ironic, isn't it?

And now I think maybe it'll hurt all of you that I kept silent for so long. Mom especially. It breaks my heart imagining her face. Although, I think she'd like Elliot. She'd want to fatten him up on good food and give him lots of hugs. He's never had a family like ours, C.J., but I think he needs it. We don't talk about his past much, he doesn't like to, but I think it was ugly.

So, I wait, trying to get the balls to tell you all the truth. I'm sorry, brother. I don't want to hurt anyone, least of all you. You've always been my best friend, and it's killing me to not be honest with you. Maybe one of these days, I'll get my shit together but until then—

The letter ended there. I sat for the longest time, staring at the screen with wet eyes, struggling to make sense of it. It sounded just like Cal, vibrant, a little rambling. Funny.

But the raw vulnerability was new. I wiped at my eyes, my heart aching at the confusion behind the words and how hard he'd been struggling to make things with Elliot work. And it hurt me more than I could possibly express to know that, although he'd wanted to, he hadn't felt able to tell me how much *he* was hurting at the time.

I felt a light touch on my arm, and I jerked in surprise. I looked up to see Elliot staring at me with a look of concern. I wondered how long I'd been sitting here, lost in my thoughts.

"Are you okay?" he asked quietly. He took a seat on the mattress next to me and gave me a searching glance.

"I—I think so. Maybe. I'm just trying to take it all in. Fuck, I don't ... Do you want to read it?"

Elliot chewed at his lip. "Should I?"

"Yeah. I think it would be good." I closed the lid and held the laptop out to Elliot. "It might not be easy to hear all of it, but I think in the long run ..."

He took the laptop from me without another word. He shifted so he sat with his legs crossed, the laptop balanced on them. Like me, he hesitated, and his fingertips skimmed across the top of it, pausing to worry the corner of the sticker where it had begun to peel. He blew out a breath before he lifted the lid.

A part of me wanted to watch his reactions to the letter, but it felt too personal and intrusive, so I stood. I walked around the room slowly. It was nearly empty now, except for the furniture and the bags of clothes to be donated. Eventually, I found myself standing in front of the wide window, staring out into the bare branches of a tree. It had been sunny when I left the house this morning, but the sky had darkened and clouds hung heavy in the sky.

I heard a small hitch in Elliot's breath and glanced over my shoulder at him. He was hunched over the laptop, his elbow next to the track pad and his thumbnail caught between his teeth. His hair—still up in the bun he'd put it in earlier—left his face bare, and I could see the tightness in his jaw and the furrow between his brows.

It seemed too intimate to see him this way and I looked away. Had I made a mistake suggesting that he read the letter? God, what if I'd totally fucked this up?

He looked up eventually, gaze stricken and vulnerable, before his expression closed off and he glanced away.

"Can you ..." The words came out choked, and I knew he was asking to be left alone.

"Elliot ..." I said weakly, but he just shook his head and set the laptop on the floor beside the mattress. He lay down and turned away from me.

I watched him for a few moments, but he was silent and still except for the slow rise and fall of his breathing. I struggled with myself, wanting to go to him, comfort him, but knowing he needed to be alone.

In the end, I walked out the door and closed it partway behind me, my heart aching.

But whether the pain was Elliot's or my own, I wasn't sure.

B efore I left the apartment, I placed a note on the coffee table telling Elliot to call me if he needed anything. For a while, I drove aimlessly through the streets of Portland. I had no destination in mind and only half an idea of where I was. I wove through industrial areas that transitioned to residential; the occasional glimpse of a familiar landmark or the Willamette River the only thing telling me where I was. If I got too turned around, I could always use the GPS on my phone, but a part of me enjoyed being lost.

Eventually, I found myself on a street I recognized, driving past an

Italian restaurant I used to eat at all the time during college. It was an old, hole-in-the-wall place that served the best spaghetti and meatballs I'd ever tasted. My mouth watered, remembering it, as I circled the block and parked in the lot behind the restaurant. The interior smelled of garlic and marinara, and the lobby was packed. As I waited in line to place my order, I composed a text to Elliot asking if he wanted me to grab dinner for us both. My fingers hesitated over the send message button, but eventually, I did. By the time I reached the front of the line, there was still no response, so I ordered two of my usual meals. Even if Elliot didn't want to eat, I could take the leftovers home.

Half an hour later, I left the restaurant with a takeout bag, but I still had no idea if Elliot was at Cal's apartment. My stomach was growling by the time I reached the complex.

"Here goes nothing," I muttered to myself as I unlocked the door to the apartment.

Elliot's car was still in the parking lot, but the living room was dark and silent when I pushed the door open. I thought it smelled faintly of Earl Grey, but I couldn't decide if it was my imagination or not. I couldn't see a light on anywhere. I frowned and set the bag of food on the coffee table. Lights from the parking lot streamed into the apartment, and I used them to navigate through the boxes and bags scattered throughout the living room and bedroom.

The lights were off there as well, although the blinds were open and another streetlamp lit the room with an amber glow. I jerked in surprise when I realized there was a figure lying on the bed, facedown, and my heart slammed in my chest at the unexpected sight. After a moment of panic, I recognized the tangle of dark hair and the narrow length of Elliot's body.

I scrutinized him, and a strange unease crept over me when I realized how still he was, how silent. He'd talked about how worn out he was, but what if something was wrong? What if something had happened to him? What if his joke about not wanting to wake up hadn't really been a joke?

He twitched, his body jerking in his sleep, and I let out a noisy exhalation of relief.

The sound must have woken him because he bolted upright, flying up into a kneeling position, his hands gathering his hair to shove it off his face. He stared at me, and even in the dim light, I could see his shocked, stricken expression.

"You ..." his voice trailed off and then his face fell. He sagged backward, drawing his knees up to his chest and wrapping his arms around them. His breathing was audible in the otherwise quiet room, ragged and strained, and I could see him shaking.

"Are you okay, Elliot?" I asked softly.

He shuddered and dropped his head to his knees without answering. I sank onto the bed beside him. He flinched when I touched his narrow back, but he didn't pull away.

"I'm sorry I startled you."

"I ... I thought you were Cal," he said roughly. He lifted his head, and even in the dim light, I could see that his cheeks were wet. "I think maybe I was dreaming about him, but I woke up and for a second, I would have sworn he was the one standing there." I rubbed soft circles on Elliot's back with my thumb as his gaze pleaded with me, but I didn't know what he needed. He didn't shy

269

away from my touch though.

"I'm not Cal," I told him, although why I felt the need to remind him of that, I wasn't sure. Maybe it was the way he was staring at me, his wide eyes so needy and hurting. Perhaps it was the way he unconsciously leaned into my touch as if seeking comfort. But mostly, I thought it was the way the air thickened around us and my skin ached to touch his.

The worry that had gripped me at the thought of him being hurt had dissipated, but in its place was desire that stripped me bare and left my nerves raw and exposed. His vulnerability ate at me.

When I leaned in, he did too. I moved my hands to his cheeks, brushing away the tears with my thumbs, and the raw ache inside me grew as I felt his skin against mine and smelled his scent. "Elliot …" I whispered, torn between knowing I should move away and wanting to touch him more.

It felt wrong, so, so wrong, yet I couldn't stop myself from brushing his hair away from his face. The strands were softer than I remembered, baby-fine and silky. He shuddered when my fingertips grazed the shell of his ear and he looked down, his lashes casting long shadows onto the sharp jut of his cheekbones.

"I'm not Cal."

"I know," he repeated, his voice throaty and hoarse as he leaned in. "I know who you are." His knees fell to the side as he moved toward me, bringing his hand up to grip the back of my neck. The pleasure when his lips touched mine was so sharp and intense it sent a shudder through me.

The kiss was less angry than the last time but just as desperate, and when I trailed my lips across his cheek, they came away wet and flavored with salt.

"What are we doing?" I whispered, brushing my lips against the corner of his eye.

"I don't know." Elliot feathered his lips against my jaw, and he fit himself closer to me, one hand still on the back of my neck, the other gripping my shirt. "I just know it doesn't hurt so much when I'm with you."

I shuddered at his words and the way they resonated within me. "Me too. I just wish I didn't feel so guilty," I hesitated. "I want you but ..."

He sat back on his heels and looked at me. My skin prickled, missing his touch, and I wanted to reach for him, but I couldn't bring myself to.

"Maybe this isn't such a good time," I admitted. "We both had pretty rough days."

"Yeah." Sorrow etched lines into his face, and he suddenly looked much older than he was. As ancient as I felt.

"Should we talk about it?"

He laughed humorlessly and shook his head. "You always want to talk."

I shrugged helplessly. "It beats ignoring things."

"Does it?" He looked away, out the window. The blinds painted stripes of light and shadow across his skin. I wasn't an artist like Elliot or a photographer like Cal had been, but I suddenly wanted to be. I knew I'd remember this moment for years to come, and yet I wanted to capture every last detail for eternity. We hung on a precipice and I had no idea what direction we were going. I could only feel the inevitable pull toward Elliot. It felt like gravity.

"I think so, yeah. Not talking about things is part of why this is all so fucked up," I said.

"Cal not talking about things, you mean?"

"Yes."

"So, what, if he'd told you about me before, we wouldn't be attracted to each other? I'd just be Cal's boyfriend and nothing else. Is that it?" His voice held a sharp edge that hadn't been there before.

"I don't know about that." I looked away. It seemed impossible to imagine not being attracted to Elliot. But I didn't know which had come first. My feelings for him were tangled up in my grief. I had no idea how to separate the two. They were as inexplicably linked as Cal, Elliot, and I all were. Did the cause and effect really matter? Nothing would change the fact that getting involved with Elliot would be a terrible idea. Nothing would change how much I wanted him despite that. I scrubbed my hands across my face. "God, this is fucked up."

"You think I don't know that?" Elliot shouted and scrambled off the bed. I jerked in surprise at his harsh tone. "Do you think I *want* to feel this way for you, Chris?" he asked savagely. "Do you think I want to look forward to spending every damn Saturday sorting through Cal's shit just to spend time with you? You *get* me, in a way no one else in my life does. And how *fucked up* is that?"

"I know," I admitted, simultaneously shocked and elated that he had admitted his feelings and that they echoed my own. "I feel the same way. I … I care about you, Elliot. I hate to see how much you're hurting. But it's damn complicated. And I hate that I wonder if you're just into me because you're trying to hold on to a piece of Cal."

He recoiled like I'd slapped him. "You really think that?"

"I don't know." I looked away. "I wonder."

"This isn't about Cal." His tone was harsh.

"Isn't it?" I met his gaze again. "We never would have met if not for Cal. We never would have slept together or gotten to know each other without him."

"True." He shoved his hands in his pockets. "But no matter how much I loved him, Cal's gone. I can only hold on to what we had for so long. And reading that letter … well, it turns out I was right all along. Cal definitely cared about me, but he had one foot out the door our entire relationship."

I couldn't deny what he'd said. "I'm sorry."

"Stop apologizing for your brother, Chris," Elliot whispered, his voice raw. "You're not Cal. You don't need to be. But I don't think you know that."

I laughed bitterly. I couldn't deny that either.

"Figure out what the fuck you want. Because whatever is happening between us isn't going away. I don't understand it, but I'm getting tired of fighting it. And I want to kiss you without feeling like I'm kissing your brother's ghost."

Chapter Nineteen

I spent the night following Elliot's surprising confession more confused than ever. His words played over and over in my mind, but they made no more sense to me than they had initially.

I ached to be with him. But was it the right choice? It felt too selfish to be. I tossed and turned, staring up at the dark ceiling, wondering why nothing made sense anymore. Every decision seemed destined to hurt someone I cared about.

If I moved forward with a relationship with Elliot, the truth would have to come out eventually, and that would hurt Dave and my family.

If I gave up Elliot—and my heart rebelled at the thought—it would mean hurting him.

Either way, I'd be causing people who were already in pain to suffer more. How could I make that decision?

I got out of bed; worried and aching, I paced the floors of my apartment, seeking relief from the crippling doubt in my head and my heart. But no solace came.

The next morning, I pulled up in front of Cal's apartment with anxiety churning in my stomach and so exhausted my bones ached. I didn't expect Elliot to be there, but I wanted to get some more work done there anyway. I had no idea how Elliot and I would address the awkwardness between us in the future, but I knew we'd have to eventually.

I found a note on the coffee table. It looked like it was from a page of sketch paper that had been torn out of a notebook. The words were written with a looping scrawl in heavy, dark pencil.

Chris,
Took the food you left on the coffee table. Hope you don't mind. Didn't want it to sit here and rot.
I won't be here next Saturday. Sorry I've left you to clean up the rest, but I can't do it anymore. I got everything I want from the apartment. The rest can go to the thrift store.
I'll help you plan the gallery show if you need it, but otherwise, please don't contact me unless you're ready for us to be together. You know where I live and how to contact me if you do.
-Elliot

"Damn it, Elliot." So much for talking about what had happened yesterday. But could I really blame him?

I stood in the living room with the letter clutched in my hand for the longest time. It hurt to realize that the Saturdays Elliot and I had spent here together were over now. The idea of not seeing him again except for planning the gallery show caused an ache in my chest. But he'd left me an opening.

If I wanted to see him again—for more than meetings at the

gallery—all I had to do was call or text or show up at his apartment and tell him how I felt. The question was could I really do it? Could I go through with it? It was one thing to spend time with Cal's ex because we had work we needed to do. But admitting that I wanted to see him because spending time with him made me happy was difficult. And telling him I was ready for more than friendship? Impossible.

The myriad of questions dogged me as I packed the last of the boxes. By the time I contacted the thrift store and arranged for someone to meet me at the apartment the following week to pick it up, I had convinced myself it was crazy to even consider anything with Elliot.

But as I made a final sweep through the apartment and turned out the lights to leave for the day, I knew I'd left something very important behind. And it had nothing to do with my brother.

On Monday morning, I was tempted to call in, but there was work that needed to be done to plan the aquarium visit for Hazel, and I couldn't let her down. Ed had emailed me the night before that he'd gotten approval from infection control and security, so we needed to get the final details hammered out as quickly as possible.

It was the only thing that forced me from my bed that morning.

When I reached the hospital, I headed straight for Ed's office. But to my surprise, he looked grim when he ushered me inside and closed the door behind us.

"Everything okay?" I asked. Unease stirred in me and made my stomach knot with worry.

Ed put a hand on my shoulder, his blue eyes filled with compassion. "I'm sorry, Chris. Hazel died."

I closed my eyes. "When?"

"Last night. She was unconscious most of yesterday and died sometime in the middle of the night."

"Were Lissa and Ryan there?"

"Yes."

I sighed, a sliver of relief working its way through the anguish. I hated the idea of her dying alone. Although all the staff here was incredible and they would have been there for her, it was a solace to know that she'd been with her family.

"It's for the best, Chris. She'd fought long enough."

"I know," I said, my throat almost too tight to speak. "Some patients are just so much harder to lose than others. And I wanted so desperately to make this aquarium visit happen before she died."

"I know. I'm sorry we weren't able to." He peered at me with a worried frown. "Do you want to talk about it?" All I could manage was a tight shake of my head. "Chris ... I'm concerned about you. Personally and professionally."

"That makes two of us."

"Are you *sure* you don't want to talk? If not to me, to someone else. Please consider it."

I let out a heavy sigh and looked into Ed's worried eyes. A part of me desperately wanted to say yes, but I didn't have the energy to try to make sense of the mess in my head well enough to explain it to anyone.

"Not today."

He frowned, but he didn't fight me on it. "Well, I don't think you're in any condition to meet with patients. I want you to take the rest of the day off." His tone was stern.

I opened my mouth to protest, then shut it. He was right, even though I hated it. "I hate to leave you in the lurch like that."

He shrugged. "Gets me out of the latest bullshit ribbon cutting ceremony admin wanted me to be at this afternoon. It's some new satellite lab or something. I'm all for giving patients better access to testing, but we don't have to make a huge fuss over every one we open in the city," he grumbled. This was not a new complaint on his part, by any means. "If they would just spend the money on the staff, we'd get better patient satisfaction scores."

"Well, if it'll help you out," I managed a feeble joke.

"Damn straight. Now, who will I be seeing?"

I tried to gather my thoughts. "The first patient I planned to see was Mrs. Benson. Advanced Hepatocellular Carcinoma."

"Ahh, yes. I believe she came in shortly after Cal's death. I spoke with her initially."

"That'll make it easier."

"You have nothing to worry about Chris; she'll be in good hands."

I managed a wan smile. "I had no doubt of that, Ed, but I want to pull my weight around here. You and the rest of the staff have been more than accommodating, but ..."

"But nothing. This is what a team does. We work together. And I don't want to hear any more arguments from you. Take the rest of the day, spend some time grieving Hazel, then come in tomorrow and focus on your patients."

"I will."

I left the hospital and went straight to my parents' house. My mother looked surprised when she answered the door.

"What are you doing here, C.J?" She held a dishtowel and she absently wiped her hands on it. "Not that I'm not glad to see you, of course, but you're usually at the hospital at this time."

"I lost a patient today," I admitted. "And it's hitting me hard. I stopped by to see if I could take Cal's car out for a spin to clear my head."

Her mouth widened into an 'O' of surprise, but she quickly covered it with a smile. "Of course, sweetheart. You certainly don't need to ask my permission. You know he'd want you to use it."

She was right of course; Cal was unfailingly generous.

But as I turned the key in the ignition and the car roared to life, it didn't ease the turmoil in my head. The rumble of the engine was familiar, as was the pine-scented air freshener dangling from the rearview mirror. I caught a whiff of cigarette smoke and wondered if it had been from Elliot. Cal had smoked in high school but quit in college, so I didn't think it had been his. But at this point, what did I know? There was so much I hadn't known about my brother. For all I knew, he'd taken up smoking again.

I eased the car out of the garage and onto the street. Although I hadn't had a specific destination in mind when I left, within a few minutes, I realized I was on a route that would lead me to Mt. Calvary Cemetery. I hadn't been there since the funeral, I realized with a guilty start.

I parked and walked slowly to Cal's gravesite, unsure what impulse had drawn me there. The cemetery was peaceful at that hour, and the spring grass was green and lush. Although my parents and I had picked out a simple headstone, it had yet to be completed. I took a seat on the damp ground as I stared at the space where it would go. Words felt thick in my throat as I trailed my fingers across the lush green grass.

We'd both been raised Catholic, but Cal and I had wandered away from our parents' religion in our teens. Cal had explored most of the major world religions before cheerfully declaring himself an atheist. My own journey had been less clear-cut. If pressed, I generally considered myself an agnostic. My medical training had made me inclined to view miracles with a hefty dose of skepticism, although at times like this, I could see the appeal of religion. It would be comforting to have faith that Cal had gone to heaven and was looking over us. I wanted to believe that with every fiber of my being, but I just couldn't blindly believe.

I sat there for a long time, wanting some sense of closeness, something to connect me to my brother, but there was just the wind whistling past and the chirp of birds in the distance. I lacked faith, and, in the end, it wasn't something that could be manufactured out of thin air.

"This was a mistake," I muttered to myself as I stood, attempting to brush the dampness from my trousers. "You're no more here than you are at your apartment, brother."

I started the car with a stomach that felt filled with lead and the deflated sense that I was worse off than I had been before.

"How was your drive? You were gone a long time," my mother asked as I pushed open the back door and stepped into the kitchen.

"It was okay." I smiled wanly at her. "I went to the cemetery."

"Did it help?" she asked quietly.

"Not really. I didn't find the answers I was looking for."

"Oh, sweetheart." She gave me a look of pity and pressed her fingertips to my cheek.

I reached for her hand and curled my own around it. "I'll be okay, Mom."

At this point, I wasn't sure if it was the truth or another lie.

I spent the evening looking through Cal's photos on his laptop. Not the ones he'd taken recently, but the ones from years ago. To my surprise, they were organized and neatly labeled with dates. There was even a Word file with a key, explaining what each folder held. It was an astonishing level of detail from a man who had once declared that organization was the death of creativity.

I clicked from photo to photo. I didn't know what I was searching for, exactly. It was like a timeline of Cal's life, a bright slideshow of a life fully lived but far too short.

I stopped when I reached the snorkeling trip where we'd seen the sea turtles. I paused on the one of us on either side of the largest turtle we'd seen. Even behind a mask and snorkel, Cal's eyes sparkled and his grin was wide.

I thought again of Hazel, with her own bright eyes and abruptly ended future, and something in me broke. I thought desperately of my own life and where it was going. I thought of the future I'd wanted and what mattered most to me.

One thought loomed crystal clear in my mind: Elliot.

I missed him. And despite the list of reasons why I was terrified to pursue anything with him, and there was no denying how long that list was, one truth was undeniable. My life felt incomplete without Elliot Rawlings in it.

I was on my feet before I made a conscious decision to go to him. I scooped up my wallet, keys, and phone. I thought of calling him and dismissed the idea, choosing instead to put on my shoes and walk out my door to go to him. I needed to see him. Touch him.

It had only been two days, and I missed him acutely

God, had that only been two days ago? That seemed impossible. I felt like I'd lived a thousand lifetimes since then.

The drive to Elliot's loft was a blur of purpose-filled determination to win him over. But as I eased the car into a guest spot in the parking lot behind Elliot's loft, my resolve wavered. My hands were shaking as I turned off the car.

I got out of my car and walked to the building, but the burst of energy that had convinced me to go to Elliot was fading, and the emotional turmoil of the day had sapped my strength more than I'd realized. A wave of exhaustion hit me as I walked up the stairs to Elliot's loft. I knocked on the door, but when no one answered, I couldn't decide if I was relieved or disappointed. I wanted him more than ever, but I was still terrified of the fallout. As I turned to leave, the door opened.

"Chris?" Elliot asked hoarsely. "What are you doing here?"

I turned back to face him, regretting the fact that I'd even come. From all appearances, Elliot had been asleep, and I wondered what time it was. I hadn't paid any attention to the clock.

His hair was a wild tangle around his face and his eyes looked dazed and half-closed. He had no shirt on, and my eyes trailed down to the top of his pants. They sat so low I could see the ridges of his hipbones. Every molecule in my body wanted him and fighting that urge made my hands shake. But I still couldn't seem to say it aloud.

My lips parted but nothing came out. I stared at Elliot, willing him to understand what I couldn't put into words. His gaze searched my face as if he was trying. But he said nothing either. Eventually, I shook my head. "Never mind, this was a bad idea. I just … go back to bed. Sorry I bothered you."

"Wait." He snagged my arm when I turned to walk away. "You came here for a reason."

"It doesn't matter. It really wasn't that important anyway," I lied.

Elliot could have yanked me toward him or told me to follow, and I would have protested and walked away. Instead, he stepped back, leaving the loft door open as he walked farther into the room like he didn't care one way or another. "I'm going back to bed," he groused. "Join me if you want."

I followed Elliot into the loft, closing the door behind me. The lights were out except one beside the bed. With his eyes half-closed, he unfastened his pants and pushed them down. He had nothing on underneath, and I stared at him while he slid under the covers and turned off the lamp, blinking as my eyes strained to see with the light suddenly gone. Left in the dark, my dick partially hard, I stood there debating what I should do. I hadn't come for sex; in fact, that had been the furthest thing from my mind, and I wasn't sure what Elliot expected.

"Get your clothes off and get in bed," Elliot said gruffly as I waffled. "I was up for almost fourteen hours sketching, and I'm exhausted. Get in bed or get out."

I undressed quickly, letting my clothes fall to the floor and crawled into bed still wearing briefs. I lay on my back beside Elliot, unsure what to do. We'd held each other after the drunken night together, but sober, would Elliot welcome it? Elliot muttered something

285

under his breath, rolled over onto his side, shoved at my shoulder to roll me onto my side as well, then curled up behind me. "Fucking *sleep*, Chris."

I closed my eyes, feeling the brush of his hair against my upper shoulders. The scent of the sheets and his arm around my waist settled me. I felt Elliot's breathing smooth out, becoming deep and even, and in moments, he was out cold. The clawing, tearing pain of losing Hazel began to recede a little.

Exhaustion took over, and I finally drifted off to sleep in his arms.

Chapter Twenty

Hours later, I awoke to lips on the back of my neck and the prod of a hard cock against my ass. It took me a minute to emerge from the thick cocoon of sleep and remember where I was. The vanilla tea scent on the pillow and the wiry body behind me quickly reminded me whose bed I was in.

Elliot's.

From the sound of his breathing, he was awake too. He didn't have his arm around me anymore, but our ankles were tangled together under the sheet, and we were pressed together head to toe. I unwound our bodies and turned to look at him. Light filtered in through the skylights, and I could see him staring at me, his gaze solemn.

He spoke first. "Why did you come here, Chris?"

"I needed you," I admitted, the dimness of the room giving me the courage to speak honestly. "I'm tired of fighting this too. I'm not going to pretend like things aren't still fucked up because of how we met, but I need you in my life." He nodded, and I knew there was one other thing he needed to hear. "And I'm not doing it because of Cal. I promise."

"Okay," he whispered.

I pretended like I didn't see his fingers trembling as he reached for me. When he kissed me, I closed my eyes and greedily kissed him back.

At some point, I'd have to deal with my conflicted emotions about how we met. I'd have to deal with my family crumbling around me and the death of Hazel hanging over my head. But for now, there was just Elliot's body against mine, the needy give and take of our lips, and the way he made everything else go away.

The room was lighter when I awoke again, but it wasn't quite morning. Elliot lay sprawled on his stomach, snoring lightly. My hands itched with the urge to touch him, and eventually, I gave in and ran my fingertips across his skin. He jerked in his sleep and flew upright, staring at me wide-eyed.

It was eerily reminiscent of the time he'd woken, mistaking me for Cal, and I held my breath.

"Sorry," I said quietly. "I wasn't trying to wake you."

"It's okay." His face softened and he settled back beside me. "Can't sleep?"

"I guess. I'm not sure what woke me."

Elliot slid a hand under the sheets and found my cock nearly hard. "I can guess."

As if we'd choreographed it, I reached for him as he pushed me onto my back and kissed me. He used his knees to nudge my thighs open and settled over me.

I gripped the muscles of his back as he slanted his mouth over mine, crying out when his hands roamed across my body. His hands were hot, scorching my skin as he gave me frenzied, frantic kisses I felt clear down to my toes. His hair fell around us, cutting us both off from the rest of the world. Where we were, there was just heat and need, wet, gliding tongues, and desperation.

His narrow, jutting hips hurt as he ground down against me, but I welcomed it, remembering the sharp bites of pain in my body from before. I ached for it again.

As slight as he was, he gripped me with so much strength. I remembered the ferocity of the way he took me before. I wanted him. In me, under me, surrounding me; I wanted to drown in Elliot.

"Please," I whispered. He reached up to grip my wrist, slamming it down onto the mattress. I could easily overpower him if I wanted to, but I didn't have any desire to. Letting Elliot take control made it so much easier for me to let go of the thoughts swirling through my head.

When he bit down on my lip, my hips jerked up to meet his. I could feel the hard length of him, the way his cock nestled into the groove alongside my hip, and I rocked against him. His strangled cry was enough of a reward that I did it again.

Sweat built between us, and I gasped when his bare, damp skin slid against mine. My back arched when his nipple grazed mine, and he worked one hand between us, pushing down my briefs so fast my head spun. But it wasn't enough. I arched into his touch, desperate for more contact.

"What are you doing to me, Chris?" he whispered, his rough voice sending me spinning.

I laughed helplessly but didn't answer. I couldn't explain it either; all I knew was how much I needed him. I wrestled my hand away from him, and he hissed in annoyance but didn't fight me when I reached down to grasp his hip. I roamed his skin with my hands, exploring the lean musculature of his lower body. Despite the slightness of his build, his ass had enough to it to grip, and he grunted when I used my strength to pull him harder against me.

He traversed my skin with his mouth, licking and sucking at my jaw. A stinging bite scored the tender flesh of my earlobe before he moved on to my neck. I felt him shaking over me, his entire body trembling with need as he devoured my neck. My left hand buried in his hair, the strands wrapping around my fingertips like every part of him was ensnaring me, drawing me in. Dimly, somewhere in the chaos of my mind, I wondered if we were making another mistake, but I couldn't stop. I didn't want to. Elliot was everything I needed.

I cried out again when he raked his teeth over my pec and then closed them over my nipple, sharp and aching pain blooming there before slowly fading. He moved against me, the thrust of his hips inelegant despite his usual grace. So precise and reserved normally, the feeling of him losing control made me equally frantic. With a shift of our hips, our cocks nudged each other, and it made me groan.

He brushed his lips across my neck softly before he bit down again. It made my body arch, and I begged him for more, pleading, demanding the release that seemed just out of reach. Elliot panted against my neck, his breath noisy and hot against my skin, and I felt more sweat build between our bodies, slicking the sliding movements we made. My fingers dug into his ass cheek, and he bit back a growl that resonated through his chest. Roughly, he slid a hand between our bodies, and his sudden grip around my cock was shockingly tight. I bucked up into his hand, crying out, and felt him shudder against me.

I chased desperate desire toward the release I knew was coming, wanting it now, now, *now* and knowing I'd want it to go on endlessly once the release came.

The abrupt loosening of his hand made me grunt in irritation, and I tightened my hand in his hair briefly before I let go. Elliot sat up, spit in his palm, and quickly slicked both our cocks before settling back over me. My heart raced in my chest as he began to move again.

It was quick and dirty, and there wasn't enough lubrication to let our cocks slide easily but it felt too good to stop. I wanted to beg him to fuck me, to thrust and fill me with the length of his cock, but I couldn't wait that long. I could hardly formulate words so all I managed was a grunt of mingled pleasure and disappointment. The movement of his hips made me wild, the fluid roll sending my head spinning back to the night I'd spent in his bed. I remembered that rhythm, the maddening control he'd had over my body. I could almost feel the stretch of his cock in my hole and the way he'd teased me before with short shallow thrusts interspersed with deep, long ones so that I never knew what was coming next.

Now, he stretched a hand out to capture my wrists and pin them back against the pillow above my head. I was by no means helpless, yet the illusion of it was enough. All I could do was rock against him, his torso flexing as he thrust against me, our cocks—slick from the sweat and pre-come—sliding together with just enough friction

291

to make my head spin.

I threw my head back, calling out a wordless sound of need as he sped up, gracefulness falling away again in favor of increased friction and more stimulation. My thighs tightened, the inexorable urge building in my body as my balls drew up. Come surged out of me, spurting between our bellies. I was still coming when Elliot buried his head against my neck, joining me with a broken moan, shuddering and shivering over me.

Too soon for my taste, he straightened and sat back on his heels, his eyes dark in the dim room, fathomless and deep, scorching my skin with their intensity.

He splayed a hand on my torso, dragging his palm across my ribs before coming to rest against my sternum. When he went to pull back, I gripped his wrist. I wasn't ready for this to be over.

With a sigh, he leaned down, lips brushing my cheek in a surprisingly gentle caress before he claimed my mouth in a hard, needy kiss.

"What are we doing, Chris?" he whispered against my mouth.

I laughed helplessly and tangled my hand in his hair. "I don't know, but I meant what I said earlier. I want to see where it'll go."

"Okay. Stay then." He rubbed his cheek against mine in a gesture so tender it made my heart nearly burst.

The combination of the physical release and affection from Elliot made me lose the tight grip I had on my grief.

I grasped his hair and buried my face against his neck as tears began to trickle down my cheeks. I splayed my hand on his back, trying to stifle the wrenching sobs that didn't seem to want to stop.

Elliot stroked my shoulder. "What is it, Chris? Did I hurt you?" He carefully loosened the tight hold I had on him and sat back, as if he was afraid I might shatter if he made a wrong move.

I wondered if he was right.

"No," I choked out, not wanting him to think that for even a fraction of a second. "Work. I lost a patient. I'm sorry, I'm ..." A fresh wave of grief choked off the words I'd been about to say, and I rolled onto my side as sobs continued to wrack my body.

Elliot gathered me close and nothing had ever felt better than his strong, narrow arms around me. "It's okay," he murmured. He nestled his head against my shoulder, crooning in my ear, allowing me to get it all out.

"She was seventeen, Elliot, and she's dead. She had her whole fucking life ahead of her and now she's *gone*. She had this whole list of things she wanted to do. A bucket list that she made once she got sick. She barely scratched the surface of it, and she was so ... God. There was *nothing* I could do to make it easier for her."

"You tried. I'm sure you did."

"It wasn't enough. I was too late to do anything for her."

I cried for my family, damaged and falling apart. I cried for the guilt I'd been carrying and knowing I finally had someone to turn to. I cried because it was such a relief to get all the pain out, to drain the poison that had been festering inside and sickening me and all the relationships around me.

With my shoulders heaving with gut-wrenching sobs, I cried until I felt sick to my stomach, until there wasn't another tear left in me. I felt the sweep of Elliot's eyelashes against my skin, and I shivered as the tears finally slowed.

I shifted onto my back and lay there, spent and shaking. Elliot curled around me, dragging his fingertips across my sternum in soothing patterns, the pressure a reminder that I wasn't alone.

"Is your patient dying why you came here tonight?" he asked quietly

"Maybe? I don't know," I said honestly, wiping at my eyes. I'd grown up in a family that had never looked down on men crying and I worked in a field that strongly encouraged healthy expressions of grief, but even I was a little uncomfortable with the breakdown I'd just had. I'd never allowed myself to be that raw and vulnerable with anyone. Certainly not with Alec. He would have gotten up in disgust and left me to cry alone. "I had an awful day, and I didn't—I couldn't spend another night all alone in an empty bed." Elliot turned his head and briefly pressed his lips against my shoulder as his arm tightened against my chest.

My heart beat too fast and I was sure he could feel the heavy thump there. Words tumbled from my lips, ill-advised, reckless, but true. "I needed *you*. No one else."

The words hung in the air for so long that I started to pull away, afraid I'd crossed a line somehow. Elliot's arms tightened into a band around my chest, pinning me in place. His voice was thick. "I'm glad. No one … no one's ever needed me that way before."

"Elliot ..." I said on a whisper, my heart breaking at the thought.

"No, it's true." His lips brushed my skin, featherlight and the words just as fragile. In the dark, our interaction felt different. More open. Or maybe it felt different tonight because *I'd* come to him. "They want me, they use me for what I can give them, but they don't need *me*."

"I do." He didn't fight me when I pulled away that time, and when I flipped over onto my other side so we faced each other, he settled his arm around me again. Even in the sickly yellow glow coming through the windows, he was beautiful. The light showed every plane and angle—the high, sharp cheekbones, the dark, slashing brow, the sensual curve of his lips. I reached for him, my hand trembling, and he didn't pull back when I traced his cheekbone with my fingertips. My tone was soft. "I meant what I said earlier. I don't want to fight this anymore, Elliot."

"Fight what, exactly?" His voice was equally hushed.

"Whatever it is I feel for you." I feathered my fingers down over his chin, to his throat, and then to his chest, ending with my palm pressed over his heart. A deep shudder ran through his whole body.

"You shouldn't want me. I'm fucked up, Chris." He flipped onto his back and stared up at the ceiling.

I let out a semi-hysterical gasp of laughter and pressed the heels of my hands against my eyes. After all we'd done together, after the way this had all begun, did he really think I was any different?

"You're not the only one," I muttered.

"So, we should be fucked up together?"

I lowered my hands from my face and turned to look at him. "Isn't that better than doing it alone?" I asked. But he didn't answer.

Without Elliot's body heat, I shivered, and my skin tightened with goosebumps. The wet remains of our mingled come on my belly felt cold and unpleasant. I reached for my discarded shirt and wiped my stomach clean. When I turned back to Elliot, he hadn't moved a muscle.

We lay there for several long minutes, the only sound our uneven breathing, Elliot's lighter and more ragged than mine.

"Are you sure you aren't going to regret this later?" Elliot asked, so quietly I had to strain to hear him.

"No." I was sure of that.

"Because I can't …"

"I know."

I wanted to reach out for him and pull him into my arms, but I hesitated because I wasn't sure if he would welcome it. A residual twinge of guilt descended on me as I remembered everything that had led us to this point.

I'm sorry, Cal. But unlike the last time Elliot and I had fucked, the guilt wasn't crippling. More sad and pensive and too fleeting to last.

It felt right lying beside Elliot.

I reached out to him again, despite my fear that he'd push me away, and brushed my fingertips across his hip. "I don't regret it now, and I won't tomorrow or next week," I said decisively. "I may not know what we're doing or if there's any way in hell we can figure out a way to make this work, but I came here for a reason."

He turned into my touch, and I felt nothing but relief at the slide of his skin against mine. "I'm glad you did."

When I closed the distance between us, he let out a groan. Although it was quiet, I could feel it throughout my body. I covered his body with mine and felt him tremble as the kiss grew deeper.

With my kiss, I told him how much I needed him. I told him he was the only man who had ever made me feel this way. I told him that he scared me as much as he excited me, that I wanted him beyond every sense of logic and reason.

I let the kiss speak to him in ways I could never verbalize and hoped—desperately—that I'd made the right choice.

I fell asleep with Elliot in my arms and a sense of peace I hadn't felt in a very long time.

I awoke a while later, face down on the bed, one arm under the pillow. I couldn't remember the last time I'd felt so relaxed and content. As always, I'd kicked the sheets down in my sleep. It left most of my back and the top curve of my ass bare. I felt too lazy to move, despite the cool air and Elliot's gaze on me.

I didn't have to open my eyes to know he was watching me, and the quiet scratch of his pencil was surprisingly familiar and comforting.

It wasn't until the pencil stopped and the room grew silent that I stirred, the sheets rustling as I flipped over on my back.

Elliot closed the sketchbook and looked at me as I stretched. He watched me impassively as I got out of bed, tugged on briefs, and walked over to him, crossing the short distance between the sleeping area and the kitchen in the open loft. Unlike the last time I'd been in his bed, his gaze held no hostility. He looked relaxed, the pout of his lips more pronounced than usual.

"Morning."

"Morning, Elliot," I murmured, liking the feel of his name on my lips.

I leaned in, my hand coming to rest on his hip. I kissed him chastely since I hadn't brushed my teeth this morning—much less the night before—but even the gentle brush of his lips sent a little jolt of pleasure through me. He slid a hand under the elastic at the back of the briefs I wore, and the contrast between the chill of his skin and the warmth of mine sent a jolt through my body.

"How long have you been up?" I asked.

"An hour or so," he said, leaning back against the kitchen counter as I straightened. He was still inscrutable.

"Sorry I slept in so long."

"It's not that late." He shrugged. "I told you, my schedule's fucked. You probably needed the extra rest though."

"I did," I admitted. I stepped forward and gave him a searching look. "How do you feel?"

He raised an eyebrow at me again and shrugged. He was shirtless, in nothing but a pair of low-slung pajama pants, and with his elbows resting on the counter, it showed off his lean musculature. "Shouldn't I be asking you that?"

"I'm fine. And I meant it when I said I'd have no regrets this morning." I stepped even closer, so I stood between his thighs. "Do you?"

Elliot shrugged again. His furrowed brow and the intent way he scrutinized my face sent a ripple of unease through me. "Did you change your mind about what we discussed last night?"

He chewed at his lip and glanced away. "Maybe. I don't know."

"Why?" My chest tightened at the thought.

"This is crazy, Chris."

"Maybe," I admitted, echoing his earlier words. "But fighting how much I want you seems crazy too. I tried it and it doesn't work. Why not give it a chance?"

"What is *it*?" he asked. "I don't know what you want. I don't even know what *I* want."

"I'm not sure I know either." I leaned in again, pushing his hair behind his ear so I could look him in the eye. "But I'd like to figure it out."

I looked at him for a long time, taking in the worried, solemn gaze of his.

"I want you to pose for me."

I frowned at him. "That wasn't quite what I meant."

"I know, but I really want that."

I gave him a hesitant glance. "Okay. I used to pose for Cal sometimes, but that was different. I'm not sure what to do for a drawing. I know you were sketching me earlier, but I'm not sure I really know what to do when I'm not half-asleep."

"I'll teach you how to pose." His tone was dismissive.

"Okay. What about … all the rest of it? Tell me what you want, Elliot."

"I want you to come here when you need me." His gaze softened and he reached out to brush his knuckles across my jaw.

"I can do that," I promised. I could easily picture coming to Elliot's loft after a rough day and falling asleep in his bed. In his arms. Despite the months of hostility and struggle between us, he felt like a safe haven now. "What else?"

"I don't want to be your dirty little secret."

There was no malice in his tone. In fact, it was very matter-of-fact, but I recoiled anyway. "Elliot, I would never—"

"Never *what*? Tell me, are you going to leave here today and tell your parents about me?" he asked, his tone turning harsh and biting. "Are you going to tell Dave we're seeing each other?" I flinched, and he laughed hollowly. "That's what I thought."

"Elliot ... I ... it's complicated."

He straightened abruptly and I pulled back. "Do you know your brother used the *exact same phrase* on me when I asked him to be open about his feelings for me?" he snarled. "You Allen boys are real pieces of work."

I staggered back, sinking down onto the bed when my knees gave out on me. "I'm sorry. Fuck ... I ..."

The anger seemed to leach out of Elliot, and he let out a heavy sigh. "I'm sorry too. I shouldn't have compared you to Cal. That was a low blow."

I smiled bitterly. "It was true though, right? He said that?"

He nodded.

My sigh was as heavy as his. "So, what do we do, Elliot?"

"Walk away and try to forget we were every crazy enough to think we could make something work?"

His words made me flinch. "Could you? Because I can't. I know I can't." I let out a quiet, bitter laugh. "If being with me hurts too much, if it reminds you of Cal too much, then fine, I'll walk away. But I won't forget you."

A myriad of expressions flickered across his face, too fast for me to catalogue all of them. He pushed off the counter and walked forward to stand in front of me. The bed was low and it put my mouth at the level of his hips, but there was nothing sexual about it when I reached out and curled my hands around the back of his thighs. I looked up at him beseechingly. "I don't want to walk away from you anymore."

"I don't want you to walk away either," he admitted, his hand coming up to rest on my hair. "I'm just ... I'm fucking scared, Chris."

"Elliot." My voice broke on his name, and I leaned my forehead against his hip, seeking comfort from him. He gently stroked my hair, and I shuddered.

I needed him. Everyone saw me as tough and as having my life in order. Cal thought I had it all together, but in truth, I was a wreck. I knew I couldn't rely on someone else to hold me together, but being with Elliot felt like the only thing that made sense. And despite the connection to my brother, he was the only one who made me feel like I might be able to figure out who I was without Cal in my life.
I lifted my head and looked up at him again, pleading for him to understand. "I'm scared too, but please don't give up now, Elliot," I said brokenly. "I don't know what I'll tell my parents or Dave. But give me a little time, and I *will* figure it out. I swear. Please, let's just try."

He nodded solemnly and slid a hand through my hair again. "Okay," he said softly. "We can try." He gave me a sad, tender smile. "And maybe you're right. Maybe it's crazy to expect anyone else to understand something we don't get ourselves."

I gently pushed him back so I could stand and look him in the eye.

"I don't ever want to treat you like a dirty secret, Elliot. I swear I won't." I wound my arms around his narrow body and pulled him close.

His nod was short and reluctant. "I'll give it a little time while we figure out what we're doing and how to tell them."

"Thank you." I pressed a kiss to his lips, promising him, and myself, that I'd do my best. Because Elliot deserved a lot more than he'd been given, and I refused to be the person who let him down this time.

Chapter Twenty-One

By the time I stopped kissing Elliot and looked at the clock, I was running late. I give him a final peck goodbye, ran home to shower and change, and barely made it to work on time.

I popped my head into Ed's office when I arrived, and he gestured for me to come in. He was on the phone.

I took a seat in one of the chairs by his desk and stared out the window. It was a beautiful, sunny day. The world was in full bloom with the recent combination of rain and sunshine, and the hospital's campus was nicely landscaped. Clusters of plants tucked under flowering trees gave it a picturesque air.

The nice weather had barely registered in my haste this morning, but maybe after I got out of work, I'd go out and do something. Enjoy myself. Knowing Elliot was in my life made the whole world a little brighter.

"Well, you're looking better today, Chris."

I looked away from the window and smiled at Ed. "I am better. I'm glad I took your advice."

"What did you do?"

My mind flashed back to Elliot pinning me to the mattress, and I had to clear my throat and shift a little in my chair. "Went to a friend's house."

Ed raised an eyebrow at me. "From the mark above your collar, I'd guess he's a little more than a *friend*."

I tugged at my collar, my fingers brushing the tender spot. "Err, yes."

"I'm glad you have someone to turn to."

"If you could keep that between us for now, I'd appreciate it." Ed raised an eyebrow at me in question, and I hastily added, "I don't want to get my mom's hopes up for anything until I'm sure that it's going to work out."

Ed nodded, but the lines on his face deepened as he frowned. "To be honest, I haven't seen Christopher or Sarah in a while. I've been trying to reach out, but they haven't seemed interested in seeing me."

"I'm not surprised. They've been struggling as much as I have." I wanted to tell him about my dad's drinking, but I wasn't sure how to broach the subject. Or if it was even appropriate.

"Of course. That's perfectly understandable. I've just been a bit concerned. Your father is one of my oldest friends, and I ..."

"I know. I'll suggest he reach out to you the next time I see them."

"Thank you, Chris."

I straightened and brought the topic around to work. "How did it go with Mrs. Benson?"

"Quite well, actually. She seems to be coping better." Ed rifled through a few files on his desk and pulled one out. He scanned the pages inside. "This is all in her electronic chart as well, so you can review it later, but I just wanted to discuss the highlights with you."

"Of course."

"You know how concerned she's been about what will happen to her adult, special needs son. Her daughter has been caring for him during her illness, but it's not a permanent situation. It appears her other son and his wife have arranged for him to move in with them soon, however."

"That must be a relief."

"Yes."

"Maybe I'll try to stop by a little later after my rounds today."

"That sounds like an excellent plan."

Ed and I finished our discussion, and I went to my office to prepare for my rounds. Later that day, as I passed by Hazel's old room, I felt a pang of sadness. She was a patient I would remember for a long time. When I returned to my office, I wrote a letter to her family, expressing my sincere sorrow for their loss and acknowledging what a wonderful young woman she'd been.

That evening at home, as I threw together a quick stir fry, my mind turned to Elliot. I hadn't heard from him all day, and I wondered if I should make the first move.

After I sat on the couch with my dinner and turned on a hockey game, I sent him a message. *How was your day?*

He responded a few minutes later. *Not bad. Mostly sketched.*

What are you working on? There was silence for a while, and then a picture popped up. It was a charcoal drawing of a woman with strange shapes and pictures floating over her head as if he'd captured her thoughts on the canvas. It spoke to her tortured mental state and evoked strong reactions. It was a powerful piece.

That's incredible. Do you have any shows coming up?

Not for a few months.

After several minutes, I realized my dinner was getting cold, so I ate as I continued to text him, asking him questions about his shows and how he planned them. He was uncharacteristically chatty, and with a jolt, I realized it was by far the most we'd ever texted. Hell, except for those rare moments at Cal's apartment, we'd shared very little about ourselves. Was I completely nuts for wanting to build a relationship with him?

Did we really have anything to base it on?

But I remembered the way he'd held me, let me grieve, anchored me. I had to believe it had meant something.

During a lull in conversation, I thanked him for the night before.

What about it?

Being there for me.

Glad I could be.

You didn't change your mind today, did you? I asked.

About?

Us.

No.

Good.

Were you worried?

A little, I admitted.

My phone was silent again for a while. *That's fair. I've been hot and cold.*

Neither of us knows what the hell we're doing.

No shit.

I've been thinking about how to tell my family.

Come to any conclusions?

Not yet. I'll keep thinking about it.

That's all I can ask.

But was it? Shouldn't Elliot expect more than something as basic as the guy he was seeing telling people about their relationship? But he'd probably never been given more than that. And that realization made my heart ache.

We spent the rest of the evening texting about relatively inconsequential things, but when I couldn't stop yawning, I finally sent him a message telling him I needed to get some sleep.

Wait. Do you have plans after work tomorrow?

Nope.

Want to do something?

I smiled down at my phone. Elliot was asking me on a date. *Yes. What did you have in mind?*

Hadn't gotten that far. Thoughts?

I pondered the options before a thought occurred to me. Elliot might be testing to see if I wanted to go out in public with him. And in this situation, who could blame him?

Maybe we could spend an hour or two at the Portland Art Museum, then grab dinner at my favorite Italian place. My phone lay silent for a while, and I felt compelled to clarify. *You've probably been to the PAM a billion times, so we can do something else if you want.*

No, came the prompt response. *No, that sounds nice actually.*

Meet you at your place after work? I don't know the exact time, but I can text you when I'm about to leave the hospital.

Sounds good. See you then.

By the time I arrived at Elliot's place, I felt keyed up and antsy. I wasn't sure if it was nerves or what, but I couldn't remember the last time I'd felt like a date mattered so much.

My palms were a little clammy when I knocked on Elliot's door. He answered it almost immediately. "Hey."

"Hi."

We stared at each other, the silence stretching and becoming awkward. I leaned in to kiss him just as he turned away, and I lurched into his apartment.

"Shit." Elliot reached for me, sliding a hand along my back to steady me. "Sorry."

"This is weird," I admitted. We stood close together, chests almost brushing. He hadn't dropped his hand. "Why is it weird?"

"Because we're making this up as we go along?"

"Yeah, that," I agreed. "Can we start over?"

Elliot's lips twitched with what looked like amusement. "Sure?"

"Hi," I repeated. I leaned in and brushed my lips against his. "How was your day?"

He kissed me again, quick and hard, before he drew back. "Good. Got a lot done."

"Show me?"

"Sure." Elliot closed the door behind me, and I followed him into the studio space. Several new pieces were tacked up on the walls, and I saw the piece he'd shown me last night on the easel. More details had been filled in and the image seemed to leap off the canvas.

"I didn't interrupt your work, did I?"

He hummed thoughtfully. "Yes and no. I wrapped up for the day when you texted me."

"Is that going to be a problem?" He raised an eyebrow at me in question. "My schedule being a lot more rigid when yours is all over the place? I don't want to disrupt your artistic process or whatever."

"Oh. There may be times I'm in a mad rush to finish something and I need to keep working. If you're flexible about that ..." He shrugged.

"Yeah, I can do that."

"Then we're good. It wouldn't kill me to have some more structure. Working fourteen, sixteen hour stretches, then sleeping for half a day probably isn't ideal."

"From a medical perspective, no, definitely not." I stepped closer to the easel. "I like this, by the way."

"Yeah?"

"It's very powerful."

"Thanks." Elliot ducked his head, looking uncharacteristically shy.

"Should we head out now?"

"Yeah, probably."

"Am I dressed okay? I wasn't sure what the restaurant we were going to was like." Elliot was dressed in skinny gray jeans and a black T-shirt.

"It's casual." I looked down at my own khakis and dark blue button-down shirt. I'd taken off my tie, loosened the collar, and rolled up my sleeves, but I still looked over-dressed. And very un-hip. "I'm just wearing what I had on at work."

"I kinda like it. I'm assuming you wear a tie usually?"

"Yeah."

"Leave it on sometime."

I grinned at him and stepped closer. "Yeah?"

"Yeah." He gave me a sly smile in return. "Word of warning. You might not want to wear light-colored clothes here. They get dirty."

I glanced around, not sure of what he meant. The place looked immaculate. "Dirty?"

"Charcoal."

"Ahh, okay. Is that why you wear all black and gray?" I'd sort of assumed that it was just Elliot's taste or something.

He chuckled. "It gets fucking *everywhere* no matter how careful I am.

Got sick of worrying about it so I stopped buying anything that wouldn't hide it."

"Décor too?" I gestured around the rather bleak apartment, and he nodded.

"It made sense. Why fight the inevitable?"

"Isn't there that sticky spray stuff you can use to keep it from smearing?" I vaguely remembered that from my middle school art class days. I'd had no artistic talent whatsoever.

"Sure. Doesn't help when I'm working though," he explained. "Well, there's technically workable fixative. It's not great. I don't use anything until the piece is done. While I'm working, I get charcoal on my hands, and I wipe that on my jeans, then I sit on the couch and ..."

"Charcoal dust everywhere," I finished. "Duly noted; no light clothing here."

"Sorry."

"Hey, if you're adjusting your schedule a little, I can adjust my wardrobe. No big deal."

His answering smile looked vaguely puzzled but appreciative.

"Are you read to head out then?" I asked.

"Sure. One sec." He gathered up his phone, wallet, and keys from the kitchen counter. "What's the weather like? I haven't been out all day."

"Nice, but it'll probably get cooler later."

"K." He strode to the closet beside the door and pulled out a leather jacket. He looked good in it. It was expensive and well cared for, not the thrift-store mid-90's grunge look he normally sported.

"Do you want to drive or should I?" I asked as we stepped out of his building.

"You know where we're going for dinner. I don't."

"Okay."

"Museum or dinner first?" I asked.

"Museum," he answered. "Unless you're starving."

"No, I'm good." I'd wolfed down a protein bar on my way to Elliot's just in case.

We talked about Portland and its various points of interest on the drive to the museum.

"I've got this," he said when we approached the ticket counter. "I'm a member."

"So this was a totally lame date then?" I asked as we entered the museum. "You must come here all the time."

"Not as often as I'd like. And rarely with someone."

I briefly thought about Cal and museums. He'd been temperamentally unsuited to them growing up, and that hadn't really improved over the years. Science and hands-on museums were more his speed. He loved the creative process of making art but always complained that staring at art hanging on a wall was boring.

"Well, good," I said when I realized I'd been silent for too long. "I haven't been here in years."

"What would you like to see?" Elliot asked.

I considered it. "Well, we'll only be here for a couple hours. Why don't you show me your favorite things?"

He raised his eyebrows. "Are you sure?"

"Of course. Why not?"

"Most people like to see their own favorites, not someone else's."

"I want to get to know you," I argued. "Besides, it's been so long since I've been here I'm not even sure if my favorites are even on display anymore. How about this? You show me what you like, and if we pass something I like along the way, we'll stop?"

"Okay."

"And we can always come back some other time," I pointed out as Elliot turned toward the modern and contemporary art.

"You like planning the future, don't you?" Elliot asked.

"Yeah. I suppose so. It's ... comforting for me to know what to expect."

"And when life throws you something you don't expect?" he asked.

I shrugged. "Then I'm a fucking mess."

He gave me a sad little smile. "Aren't we all?"

Without hesitating, I reached out for him. His steps faltered, but he allowed me to clasp his hand. "This okay?" I asked quietly.

"Yes." His voice sounded a little rough, but I felt gentle pressure against my palm. "Perfect."

We wandered hand-in-hand for a few minutes. Elliot clearly had a destination in mind, but he walked slowly enough for me to look at the art we were passing.

Eventually, he stopped in front of a moderately sized painting that, to my untrained eye, looked like something by Picasso.

"This."

I paused in front of it and surveyed it. A quick glance at the information placard told me it was by someone named Maude Kerns and painted in 1950. It was titled *Interlocking Life and Death*.

"Tell me what you like about it."

"Are you shrinking me?" Elliot sounded wary, and I shook my head immediately.

"No. God, no. I like to keep work away from my personal life as much as possible. Even if I did bring it home with me the other night, I guess."

"That's different. You had a bad day and needed me." His matter of fact tone made me happy. "The same way I might need you to do if I had a shitty gallery exhibition or something."

"True."

"It's not the same as you …" He seemed to be struggling with his words.

"With me using my professional training to get the advantage in our … interactions." I'd almost used the word relationship, but I wasn't sure how Elliot felt about that. We'd agreed to see each other, but we hadn't really discussed the word relationship or exclusivity or anything like it.

"Right, exactly."

"I'll be honest. I'm not sure I can always separate it," I admitted. "I'll try. But I can't really know for sure when I'm using it. I mean, I was always the guy people came to when they needed to unload about something. Even growing up. Is that what makes me a good psychiatrist? Is it my training? I don't know. I don't know how to tell the difference at this point."

"I get that." Elliot chewed at his lip for a minute. "Just don't … don't try to diagnose me or whatever."

I smiled at him, a little perplexed by his reaction. "Elliot, I wouldn't do that. When I'm out with you, I'm here as Chris. Not Doctor Allen. And besides, I don't see patients in an office the way most people typically think of a psychiatrist. I'm often dealing with people who are diagnosed with a severe illness or are in the end stages of their life. I'm there to help them cope and find ways to support the dying process. Some might have previous mental health diagnoses, and I can help manage those, but I'm rarely diagnosing people for the first time. And I'm certainly not in that mode when I'm out with someone."

Elliot looked strangely relieved, and I wondered how to tactfully ask him the question that had been swimming in my brain for the past few minutes. "Is there a reason you're so uncomfortable with that idea?"

He raised an eyebrow, and I let out of a self-conscious laugh, realizing how shrink-like that sounded. "Okay, never mind. Ignore that question. It didn't come out right."

He stood and stared at the painting for a minute. "No, I'll answer. At least partially. I had a shitty childhood. I don't want to get into it now, but I will tell you about it eventually."

"That's fine," I assured him.

"It made me very distrustful of authority figures in general and people in the mental health field specifically."

"Okay." I cleared my throat when it was obvious he wasn't going to continue. "I respect that."

"Thanks." He shot me a fleeting smile.

"Let me rephrase my earlier question. Tell me what you like about this piece as an *artist*. So I can learn more about the piece and what interests you about it."

The tense set of his shoulders relaxed. "Okay. I can do that."

I relaxed too.

Elliot talked. He talked more than I'd ever heard before while I just listened and nodded and asked a few relevant questions.

I liked watching Elliot at the museum. I spent as much time staring at him as I did the art pieces, but he was rather fascinating to me. He was generally so enigmatic, but I discovered the little micro-expressions that constantly flashed across his face as he studied the pieces of art. Curiosity, confusion, understanding, joy … tinges of sorrow. Elliot seemed so cool and calm, like a placid body of water, unruffled by the winds around him. But there were tiny waves, bright flashes of things rising to the surface. I didn't think it was my professional training that found that intriguing.

I was pretty sure I just found Elliot one of the most complex and compelling people I'd encountered in a long time. And I wanted to learn more about him.

"I'm starting to get hungry," Elliot said after a while. "Ready to head out?"

"Sure." I fell into step beside him. "This was fun though."

"It was."

"Well, let me know when you want to come here again. Or wherever. I like all kinds of museums and galleries and cultural events." At least, when I was there with someone who wasn't desperate to show off. Despite our fraught past, the few hours Elliot and I had spent together today had been more enjoyable than any of the events Alec and I had ever been to.

"Me too." He shot me a look out of the corner of his eye as we exited the building. "What are your thoughts on foreign and indie films?"

"They're great. Do you like them?"

"Depends on the film. Some of them are pretentious, but I like checking out the film fests. Sometimes, half the fun is making fun of the pretentious ones."

I chuckled. I wasn't used to Elliot's occasional sly sense of humor. "That sounds fun. Let me know when you want to go sometime."

Chapter Twenty-Two

"So, how'd you find this place?" Elliot asked after the waitress seated us at a tiny table in the back corner of the Italian restaurant.

"I discovered it when I was a student at Oregon Health and Science University," I explained. "I lived within walking distance and I used to come here with friends. It was pretty cheap, and they give you enough food to feed an army. I could take the leftovers home and eat for a week."

"It's nice." He looked around. "Nothing fancy. Good food, locally owned."

We exchanged a smile that warmed me to my toes. "This was fun," I said. "I haven't been on a date this good in a really long time."

"God, I can't remember the last time I went on *any* kind of date," he said.

I refrained from asking if he and Cal had really dated or just "hung out". I suspected the latter. "I haven't dated at all since my last relationship ended. It's been over a year."

He looked at me in surprise. "Oh?"

"He cheated on me. After that, I just needed some time by myself. I didn't trust anyone enough to get involved with them. But it's been lonely and made me very isolated," I admitted. "I mean, I don't have that many close friends to begin with. But dating isn't really the answer to that anyway, I don't think. Or maybe I'm just really bad at it."

He huffed out a laugh as he shrugged out of his leather jacket. "You're not the only one."

"Who is isolated or bad at dating?"

"Both." He toyed with the ends of his hair. "Come on, I work from home. In a city like Portland, I don't have to go out to buy food. I can have it all delivered. Hell, I can have art supplies show up at my door. If I didn't force myself to go out, I'd be a hermit."

Once again, I tried to picture him with my brother and wondered how on earth they'd made it work as well as they had. "Yeah, I suppose at least I'm interacting with people all day at the hospital."

"Exactly. I considered teaching a class just to get out of the house." He cracked a smile. "I sound ancient, don't I?"

"A little bit. But I—" The sight of the approaching waitress cut me short. "Sorry, I haven't given you a chance to look at a menu. Do you want another minute?"

"No. You order for me."

I looked at him in surprise, and he shrugged.

"You know what's good here, and I eat everything."

"Okay." I placed our order, and when the waitress left, I looked over at him. "Hope that's okay."

"Sounds great."

He asked me about my day at work, and while there was a lot I couldn't tell him, I told him what I could. The conversation I'd had with the janitor about the hospital needing a better recycling program, Sherri bringing in chocolate cherry brownies, and the annual, if adorable, nuisance of ducks nesting outside of the building.

"The ducklings hatched recently," I explained. "They do this every year. The mother duck builds her nest in a totally inconvenient place in a flowerbed near the main drop-off area; it has to get roped off so they don't get disturbed, and once the mom starts taking the babies out, security carefully boxes up mom and all the little fluffy ones and takes them down to the river and releases them safely."

Elliot shook his head, a small smile playing at the corners of his lips. "That's sweet."

"It really is. I think one of the local papers covered it one year."

"Slow news story that day?" Elliot asked.

"Probably." I laughed. "I'll have to ask Dave about that."

A shadow crossed Elliot's face. "That's going to be tough, isn't it?"

"What will be?"

"Telling him about ..." He gestured between us. "This."

"Yeah, probably," I admitted. "I really doubt he'll be thrilled. I'd like to think we're good enough friends that he'll support me however. Especially when he realizes ..." I trailed off, not sure how to word my feelings for Elliot in a way that wouldn't scare him off. "I mean, once I tell him it's more than just hooking up."

"Hopefully." Elliot didn't look convinced.

"We'll take it one step at a time," I promised, reaching out to him. "I'm not sure what the next step is, but I'll figure it out."

"It's okay," he said softly as he took my hand. "This is a good first one."

I felt a pang at how grateful he seemed to be for such a little bit of public acknowledgement and affection. I saw the waitress arriving with food and our soft drinks, so I held on until she was right up next to the table before I lightly squeezed and let go.

"Here you are, gentlemen. The plate the breadsticks are on is very hot so be extremely careful." She set it on the table between us, and I breathed deep, enjoying the scent of garlic and basil. After the waitress set down our drinks and left, I smiled at Elliot.

"These are their world-famous *pane con formaggio*. Well, maybe Portland-famous," I corrected myself.

"I've never heard of this place, so it can't be that famous."

But when he took a bite of the garlic and cheese-covered bread, he let out a small groan. "Oh, nothing should taste this good."

I grinned. "I think it has something to do with the volume of cheese, but I try not to think about it too much. And I hit the gym twice as hard after."

Elliot's gaze flicked across me in an appreciative glance. "Your dedication to the gym is clear. One of these days you *will* pose for me."

"I'll feel ridiculous, but sure. I always keep my promises."

"Glad to hear it."

"What about you?"

"I pose for myself all the time." I laughed and he continued. "No, I'm serious. I did a whole series of self-portraits. Some of them are hanging in the Holloway Gallery as we speak."

"I know. I saw them," I said. "And they're extraordinary. But I meant what do you do to work out?"

"Oh. I hate the gym, and I'm a smoker, so running is not fun." I tried not to wince but the knowing look he sent me indicated that he had noticed. "I do yoga."

"Oh. Huh. I can see that."

"What do you mean?"

"You have that look. Lean but really strong."

He looked self-conscious. "I believe the word you're going for is scrawny."

"Not at all." I leaned forward. "I think you look great. And I work out a lot, but lately, it's mostly been stress relief, you know?"

"Sure." His tone indicated he probably didn't find working out a stress reliever.

"How did you get into yoga?"

"One of my roommates at the Art Institute was into it, and I let her drag me along. I liked it, so I kept up with it."

"Do you take classes?"

He shook his head. "I haven't in a long time. I just stream videos on my laptop."

"Maybe you should."

"Take classes? Why?"

"Well, you said you wanted to get out of the house more," I pointed out and then wondered if I'd overstepped. I often tried to solve people's problems without asking if they wanted me to. "I mean, only if you want to, of course. It was just a thought."

"No. It's not a bad idea," Elliot said slowly. "I hadn't considered it. I'm not great at meeting new people."

"Yeah, me neither."

"Cal was—never mind. I shouldn't bring him up so much."

"I don't know. It's a weird situation for us both. But I wonder if not talking about him will just make it worse. Maybe we should just talk about him and acknowledge it's going to be awkward for a while. He was a big part of both of our lives; we can't just ignore that."

He flashed me one of his small, rare smiles. "You're good at having the difficult conversations."

"It's my job," I admitted. "Like I said, some of it's going to leak into my everyday life."

"I get that. I don't mind that part of it. But it reminds me how bad I am at it." A shadow darkened his face. "For a lot of reasons."

I was tempted to ask him to continue, but as much as we needed to have these difficult conversations, this wasn't the time or the place. "Anyway, yeah, Cal was your classic extrovert. And really handy to have around when you needed an introduction to new people."

"I don't get it." He sounded baffled. "How did he just strike up conversations with total strangers?"

"No idea," I said with a laugh. "I can do it when I have to for work, but I hate it."

The conversation was interrupted by the arrival of the waitress with our meals, and we moved on to different topics as we ate. I even managed to make Elliot laugh a few times, which brought me a strange sense of pride. He was so reserved, and it pleased me so much to see him let go of that and relax. He polished off most of his meal, then sat back with a contented sigh.

"That was good. I'm *stuffed*."

"No room for tiramisu?" I teased.

He groaned. "No. Maybe? Can we take it back to my place and have it later?"

There was no way I could refuse his hopeful plea. "Yeah, of course."

A few hours later, Elliot set a small plastic container on my still-sweaty chest and I yelped. "That's cold."

"Hold still. I don't want to spill it."

"Then why are you eating dessert on my chest?" I grumbled, but secretly, I loved this. I loved the closeness and the banter. We'd come back to his place and fallen into bed almost immediately. Full stomachs had necessitated trading slow, teasing blowjobs instead of rough, athletic sex, but I had no complaints. The sense of satisfaction that filled me was intense.

"You're the closest thing I have to a table," Elliot said as he cracked open the container.

I was totally on board with a post-sex snack of tiramisu, but I wasn't sure how I felt about being a table. *At least, I'm not the plate.* Then I'd be both cold and sticky. Mascarpone cheese and chest hair didn't seem like a pleasant combination.

Elliot scooped up a bite and put it in his mouth. He closed his eyes for a moment, then let out an appreciative hum. "Mmm. That's good."

"I told you," I said smugly.

He licked the spoon before he dug in for another bite. This time he held it up to my lips. "Hope you're not a germaphobe or something from working in the hospital," he said, sounding apprehensive.

"No, not at all," I assured him. I took the dessert from the spoon, and once I'd eaten it, I smiled at him. "Besides, I just swallowed your cock until you came down my throat. I'm hardly concerned with us swapping a little spit."

Elliot coughed. "I had no idea you had such a dirty mouth, Chris."

"Pun intended?"

"No." He took another bite. "I meant your filthy language."

"Are you *complaining*?"

"No." He returned the spoon to the container and came up with another scoop. I opened my mouth for it, but it went straight in his.

"Hey!" I protested. "That was my turn. No hogging it."

"Who said we're taking turns? I was nice and shared a few bites with you."

I sputtered. "I bought it for us to share."

"Next time, buy two." He grinned cheekily, and I felt my heart race. Naked, happy, relaxed Elliot was deadly. I wasn't sure my heart could take it. He scooped up another portion of tiramisu with his spoon. But instead of directing it to his mouth like the last two bites, it hovered in front of my lips. I didn't particularly want any more—I had just been teasing him—but I'd be an asshole to argue after all the fuss I'd put up.

"Thanks," I said after he removed the spoon with minimal clanking against my teeth.

"So," Elliot held the empty spoon up in the air and gestured with it. "You have a filthy mouth and you don't share desserts well. What else am I going to learn about you tonight, Chris?"

I loved hearing him say my name for some reason I couldn't quite pinpoint. Or maybe just didn't want to. "I don't know. What do you want to learn?"

"Biggest fear?"

"Like horror movie-type phobia or actual, deep-rooted fears?"

"Both."

"Spiders, I guess. Not all of them, just the weird translucent ones. Legs should not be *see-through,* especially when there're so many of them. You?"

"I wasn't afraid of spiders before now, but I'm starting to be," he said drily. "The other?"

I looked away. "Losing everyone I care about and being the last one left," I said softly.

Elliot was silent, and when I turned back to him, I could see the stricken expression on his face. "Oh, Chris, I'm sorry. I ..."

"You didn't know. I brought it up." I shrugged and cleared my throat. "Never mind. What about you?"

"Bears."

"Really?" I looked at him in surprise. "Bears freak you out?"

"I watched this documentary as a kid," he said, sounding a little defensive. "Do you know how big a grizzly's paw is? Massive. They can take off your head with one swipe. It's scary shit."

"Mmhmm," I said skeptically. But it didn't escape my notice that Elliot quickly steered the conversation in another direction.

By the time we polished off the last of the tiramisu, he still hadn't answered the question about what his deep-rooted fear was.

And I wondered if maybe it wasn't too far from my own.

When my alarm went off the next morning, I cursed under my breath, shut it off, and reached out to Elliot. The bed beside me was empty. The sound of pencil on paper clued me in to where he was. I squinted at the far side of the room and spotted him in front of the easel.

I dragged myself out of bed, slipped on my underwear, and walked over to Elliot. He'd started a new piece and it was too early to tell exactly what it was. He jerked in surprise when I slid a hand around his waist, but he quickly relaxed against me.

"Morning." My voice sounded raspy from sleep. "How long have you been up?"

"Couple hours."

I glanced at the time on the clock across the room. I hadn't originally planned to stay the night, so I didn't have a change of clothes or toiletries with me. Which meant I'd have to go home before I went to work.

In order to get home and arrive at work on time, I would need to leave in ten minutes. If I got in the shower with Elliot, it would take a lot longer. *Fuck it. When is the last time you let yourself just enjoy being with someone? It'll be fine if you're a few minutes late. Just skip your morning coffee break.*

"Want to take a shower with me?" I pressed a kiss against Elliot's temple.

"Sure."

"I understand if you need to keep working." He shook his head and set down the charcoal pencil.

He turned in my arms and smiled at me. "No, a break would be good."

"Okay." I brushed my lips across his. "I'll have to make it kinda quick though."

He nodded and tugged me toward the bathroom.

Although the room was basic, the shower was plenty roomy for two.

"You can borrow whatever you need." Elliot waved toward the shower. "Let me replace the blade on the razor first. I think it's too dull for the stubble you have."

"You're probably right." Ruefully, I rubbed my fingers across the heavy, dark growth. Elliot's face still looked smooth, and there was hardly even a shadow along his jaw. "Let me guess, you shave every three days?"

"Give or take." Elliot's smile was so brilliant it was disarming. "Jealous?"

"You have no idea. It's such a pain."

Elliot trailed his fingertips down my chest, and I followed the touch with my gaze. He stopped in the middle of my chest and toyed with the hair there. "I don't know. I like this."

I didn't have a lot, mostly just a patch between my pecs and enough at my groin that I had to keep trimmed regularly.

He followed the trail of hair down with his fingertips, but I grabbed his hand before he could reach my cock. "I don't have *that* much time," I murmured.

His lower lip protruded a little, but he pulled his hand away. "Fine."

I smiled at Elliot's faint pout. That was a new look for him.

"Get in. I'll get you a new blade."

"Thanks."

The water heated quickly, and Elliot joined me after I'd stepped in. He set the razor on the ledge, then handed me a bottle. "Shampoo?"

"Please." I caught a glimpse of the scent name on the bottle as he handed it to me. "Bergamot. Why do I recognize that?"

Elliot looked at me blankly and shrugged. "I dunno. I got it because it smelled nice." I stepped away so he could get under the stream of water.

When I squeezed a little of the shampoo into my palm, a familiar scent hit me. "Earl Grey tea has bergamot in it!" I chuckled quietly.

"Yeah." Elliot gave me an odd look. "I like the smell."

"No, you don't understand. This whole time I thought you smelled like Earl Grey tea, and I couldn't figure out how much of it you must drink."

Elliot chuckled. "I sip pots of it while I sketch but not so much it's coming out of my pores."

"I wondered if you bathed in the stuff. But it turns out you just shower in it," I teased.

Elliot slicked his hair back and gave me a faintly amused look. "You're much weirder than I realized, Chris."

His words made me smile. And after months of somber or fraught interactions, this new, lighter mood between us was a relief.

We both showered quickly, and Elliot got out before I finished shaving. I finished in the shower and toweled dry. I dressed, then styled my hair with Elliot's gel. I glanced at my watch as I buckled it on my wrist. I'd be cutting it close, but I had no regrets.

The scent of coffee greeted me as I left the bathroom. Elliot sat on the counter in pajama pants, drinking from a ceramic mug. A travel mug sat beside him.

He pointed to it. "That's for you. Coffee."

I leaned in and kissed his bare shoulder as I reached for the mug. "I thought you hated coffee," I murmured.

"I do. It smells nice but it tastes vile. Bought it for you yesterday when I was at the store. I figured you'd wind up staying over."

It touched me that Elliot had thought of me. "You bought coffee and made it just because I'd like it?"

Elliot shrugged and pushed his hair behind his ear. "I figured you'd want some. And I hoped maybe you'd be here in the mornings before work sometimes."

"Thank you," I said softly.

"Sure." Elliot brushed off my comment like the gesture meant nothing, but I couldn't remember Alec ever having done anything so thoughtful. "I picked up the French press too. I had to google how to make it, so I hope it's okay."

Ignoring the coffee, I gently coaxed Elliot to face me. "*Thank you. I mean it.*"

The corner of his mouth turned up like he was amused by my intensity. "You're welcome. Have a good day."

"You too." I gave him a quick kiss and grabbed the coffee. "Talk to you later."

As I turned to go, I caught a glimpse of what was on Elliot's sketchpad. It was me in the shower, laughing.

I smiled all the way to work.

Chapter Twenty-Three

The days lengthened and grew warmer as Elliot and I tentatively explored this new relationship. It should have been awkward, but those months we had spent cleaning out Cal's apartment had forged a surprisingly solid base for us to build on.

We fell into an easy rhythm, spending most evenings and weekends together. I'd often arrive at his place after the gym and find him humming quietly under his breath as he stirred something on the stove. He'd been shy about it the first time, as if he expected me to scoff at the effort. Instead, I tangled my hand in his hair and kissed him deeply.

We hardly spent any time at my place. Elliot's loft felt more welcoming to both of us, and it allowed him to have his pencils and charcoal on hand when inspiration struck.

I took over his kitchen on the weekends and prepped lunches for both of us so he'd have something to eat while he sketched. He cooked us dinner most nights. I watched his lean frame slowly fill out until the worrying thinness of his wrists was gone and the sharp angles of his face softened a fraction.

My dress shirts and ties began to mingle with his T-shirts and jeans. I kept a razor in his shower and there was always coffee ready for me in the mornings. His work hours smoothed out and became less erratic, and I noticed the anger that had lurked under the surface of my skin seemed to dissipate. I went to the gym still, but boxing lost its appeal now that I wasn't trying to battle my way out of my grief.

I felt a renewed sense of purpose at work. Breaking free of the heavy shadow of grief allowed me to set it aside when I counseled patients, and the necessary objectivity returned. I still thought of Cal, often, and waves of sadness would sweep over me when I did. But the hole in my heart was beginning to mend.

The only guilt I felt was that I hadn't told my parents about my relationship with Elliot yet. My mother knew I was seeing someone, but I told her it was too soon to share anything about it. The truth. But not the entire truth. I also felt guilty for not seeing them as often as I had been, but when it came to choosing between relaxed evenings in with Elliot and dinners at their house fraught with tension, it was an easy choice.

The snarky reserve Elliot had shown me before began to slowly melt until a warm, caring man tentatively emerged. He was still wary sometimes, like a skittish animal, but together, we seemed to find a balance we'd struggled with alone.

And before I could blink, a month had passed and it was mid-April.

One afternoon, we lay on the couch facing each other, our legs tangled together. We'd gone out for brunch together, and now, Elliot sketched while I read a psychiatric journal on my tablet. There was nothing exciting about the situation at all, but it was exactly the kind of thing I'd missed from my previous relationships, and my chest warmed at the easy closeness.

I glanced up and saw him staring at me with narrowed eyes. It was his sketching face. "Are you drawing me *again*?" He'd done hundreds of sketches of me already. It was a little disconcerting.

"Yes." He glanced down, and his pencil flew across the paper again.

"I don't understand it."

"Do you *mind?*"

Elliot and I were still getting to know each other, and we occasionally stumbled into an awkward moment as we navigated this new relationship. "No," I said, truthfully. "It's a little weird on my end, but I don't *mind*. I like being able to sit here with you and just do our own things."

He flashed me a rare, brilliant smile. "Me too. I like that you don't always have to be off *doing* something."

No doubt he was referring to Cal's obsessive need to be constantly on the move. Elliot and I had settled into a comfortable introvert routine. We'd gone out to dinner and to a concert in the park last weekend, which had been fun, but I enjoyed the lazy Saturday morning as much.

"My mom used to call me an old man. When I was about nine or ten. I'd read the newspaper while other kids watched Saturday morning cartoons or played outside."

Elliot smiled faintly as he continued to sketch. "I can see that."

"You never talk about your childhood," I commented. Elliot hadn't mentioned a single thing from when he was growing up. He talked about art school, but nothing seemed to exist from before he started at the Portland Art Institute. But despite his promise to tell me about it at some point, he hadn't broached the subject yet. I knew I should probably leave it alone, but my curiosity got the better of me.

Elliot sighed. "Yeah, well, there's a reason for that."

"Yeah, you hinted at that. Is it that bad?" I asked softly.

His lower lip disappeared between his teeth for a second before he set aside the sketch pad and pencil, then looked me in the eye.

"It was bad." His brow furrowed. "Promise me something?"
"Sure."

"I know I asked you this before, but I really mean it this time. Don't shrink me when we talk about this. I know it's probably hard, but just listen as the guy I'm dating, please."

"I promise I won't shrink you. I just want to know more about you," I said softly.

I rubbed my socked foot against his thigh in reassurance, and he smiled down at it. He took a few deep breaths before he began. "I grew up in Washington. Tacoma. Never knew my dad. He was out of my life by my first birthday, and all I have left of him is my middle name." He dipped his hand into his pocket and brought out a lighter. Not a good sign.

"What is it?"

"Michael." He fiddled with the lighter, stroking across the strike wheel with his thumb like he wanted to light it.

Elliot Michael Rawlings. I rolled the words over in my head. It had a nice ring to it. "What about your mom?" I asked.

Elliot snorted. "My mom was a hot mess."

"What do you mean?"

"She was a junkie. Diagnosed bipolar, but she was on and off the meds constantly, and she used the drugs and booze to self-medicate."

"That's pretty common," I said softly.

"Yeah, I know. I *get* it, I just … Anyway, she'd clean up for a little while and then go right back to it. She was good for a couple of years, starting when I was about seven. She cleaned up enough to meet George—my stepfather—and hold it together for a little while. Long enough to make me think it might last." He looked away, and my heart ached at the pain in his eyes. "She got pregnant and George went through the roof. He'd had some kind of illness or something as a kid that left him sterile so he figured out real quick that she was cheating on him. It all went to hell after that." Elliot flipped the lighter back and forth in his hands, the movements growing more and more agitated.

"What happened?" I was almost afraid to ask.

"He threatened to toss us both out on the street. She fell apart. Started using again. Nearly overdosed. Lost the baby. Which was probably just as well because if she'd given birth to a drug-addicted baby, CSP would have been all over it. I was thirteen, so if they'd realized the way she was treating me, I would have been stuck in foster care until I was eighteen."

"Is it possible that would have been better?" I offered, but he shook his head.

"Don't think so. Most of the foster kids I'd met were pretty fucked up, and it was a dirt-poor area. Not saying there weren't good foster parents out there, but I think most of them needed those checks. They did the bare minimum. And that's the ones who didn't beat the shit out of the kids or abuse them in other ways."

I nodded. That was, unfortunately, the case sometimes. Whether or not it was as prevalent as Elliot believed, I wasn't sure. "So, what happened after she miscarried?"

"George let us stay, but she was high half the time after that. He didn't give a shit about me, and I pretty much just kept to myself. I was sixteen when he found out I was gay, and he threw me out." His tone was flat, as if he were describing the plot of a movie instead of his life, but the lighter kept arcing higher and higher as he tossed it back and forth

.

I felt an ache in my throat. "Oh, God, Elliot. That's awful. What did you do to survive?"

He shrugged and caught the lighter, gripping it so hard in one hand his knuckles turned white. "I worked as a bus boy and dishwasher for cash under the table. I couch surfed and bummed rides. And when I'd saved enough, I bought a shitty car and slept in that when I had to. Friends let me shower at their places, and I just coasted until I was done with high school. A teacher convinced me to apply to the Art Institute in Portland, and when I got accepted, she hooked me up with a scholarship. After I moved here, I did some street sketching and panhandling. Plus whatever odd jobs I could to make ends meet."

My heart ached, imagining it. I'd grown up in a house with so much love. My family was struggling now, but I'd never experienced anything like Elliot had. It broke my heart to imagine him as a teenager, alone, fending for himself. I could picture him, rail-thin and awkward. No wonder he was so reserved. No wonder he didn't open up easily. No wonder he didn't seem to trust anyone. I remembered Cal's letter, and that even he hadn't known the full story about Elliot's past. It humbled me that Elliot had shared it with me.

I reached out and took Elliot's hand. He wouldn't meet my gaze, but he let me tug him toward me. The lighter disappeared into his pocket before he settled into my arms, his back against my chest. I pressed my lips to the soft strands of his dark hair and held him close. "I'm sorry you had to live like that."

He shrugged, but his body was still tense. "I survived."

I rubbed soothing circles into the tight muscles of his shoulders until they gradually turned pliable under my touch. "You deserved better."

His gulp was audible. "Maybe, but what can I do about it now?"

I closed my eyes. I didn't have an answer for him, but all I wanted to do was take his pain away.

"My family was pretty much perfect," I admitted. "At least by comparison. We had plenty of money, my parents loved us, Cal and I got along really well. When they found out I was gay, Mom joined PFLAG, and they all went with me to my first pride parade." The reminder of what I'd lost hit me square in the chest. "And now that they're falling apart, I feel so guilty I can't do anything to fix it."

343

"It's not your job, Chris." Elliot craned his neck to look at me. "Why can't you believe that?"

I shrugged. "Growing up, the more reckless Cal was, the more I felt like I had to be the responsible one. I was always following behind Cal and trying to soften the blow after he fucked up. I'd apologize to the neighbor whose flowers Cal accidentally trampled when a stunt went wrong. I'd glue together the lamp he broke before my mom spotted it. Over the years, we just fell into these roles," I admitted.

"Did you want to do that? Or did your parents just expect it?"

"Both, probably." My parents were great, but that didn't mean they were perfect. They'd made mistakes too.

"So what, now you have to fix Cal being gone? Clean up the mess he left?"

"Basically." I swallowed past the lump in my throat. "It's hard to sit here and do nothing. I want to help them deal with it. It's my *career*, Elliot. That's what I'm trained to do. Why can't I do that for my family?"

"It's not that easy when you're right in the middle of it."

"I know. I still feel like I should be trying."

He rubbed my thigh and the touch took away a little of the ache in my chest. I let out a sigh, and he carefully dislodged my grip and turned over, kneeling between my thighs. I reached up and pushed his hair behind his ear so I could see his face better.

"I want to help, Chris," he said softly. "I know I can't, but I want to make it stop hurting for you."

I smiled sadly. I wanted to do the same for him, but I was equally helpless to make that happen. I wanted to thank him and tell him how much that meant, but I didn't have any words to respond.

"Maybe just being here together is enough."

It was certainly more than I'd had in a long, long time.

The following evening, I went to my place. I'd gone to the gym, and Elliot was going to a new yoga class, so it had made more sense for me to spend the night at my place. I needed to water my neglected houseplants anyway. But the bed seemed large and empty with no one to share it with. I had just crawled into bed when he texted me he was home. I called him instead.

"How was class?" I asked.

"Good. Mellow," he said. "It's a slow flow class. Meditation at the end. I liked it."

"Do you think you'll go back?"

"Yes."

"Did you meet anyone there?"

"Wasn't looking." He sounded bewildered. "It's not like I'm on the market unless I missed something when we discussed the idea of monogamy?"

I laughed when I realized what he'd thought I'd meant. "Friends, Elliot. Did you meet anyone you might like to be friends with?" We'd talked more about how isolated we both were, although clearly he was doing better than me when it came to fixing that.

"Oh." He chuckled. "Dunno. Most of them are college students."

"You're only twenty-four. You're not that much older."

He groaned. "I feel older. At least thirty-four. They all seem …"

"Immature?"

"Carefree."

"That's a good thing, right?"

"It's weird. I can't relate." He sounded a little wistful.

"I know. Have you always dated older men?" I rarely thought about our age difference, but occasionally it came up.

"A few guys in art school were my age … No. Wait. They were older. Returning students. One was a grad student. Always a little older, I guess."

"I was just curious. Anyway, tell me more about yoga."

"The instructor seemed decent. Her name's Laura. She just got back from hiking the Pacific Coastal Trail."

"Cal and I did a leg of that."

"You did?"

"Yeah. We usually took a trip together during my breaks from school. So, a couple times a year, we'd go off somewhere. One time was the Pacific Coastal Trail. Anyway, sorry. I didn't mean to interrupt. You could ask the instructor if she wanted to grab coffee sometime."

"Are you trying to set me up with her or what?"

I flushed. "No. Sorry. I'll stop badgering."

"You're trying to help. I appreciate it."

"I don't mean to be pushy."

"It's fine." Elliot sounded amused rather than annoyed. "Maybe I will ask her next week. It's awkward though. I'll have to figure out a way to work you into the conversation first, so she doesn't think I'm asking her on a date."

"Do you have a lot of straight women thinking that?"

"It's happened before. Especially when I'm trying to get models for my work. Some of them think there's a quid pro quo, and it gets uncomfortable."

"That's disturbing."

"Yes." Elliot's tone was fervent. "The first time, she had my pants unzipped before I could open my mouth to tell her I absolutely wasn't looking for that."

"That's shitty. I mean, mostly that she believed it was expected."

"She couldn't look me in the eye for the rest of the modeling session. Thought she'd never come back, but she did. We worked together for a while." Elliot cleared his throat. "How was your day?"

"Uneventful. Meetings, seeing patients. Answering emails."

"Uneventful is good when you work for a hospital, right?"

"Yeah, definitely. You never want to have to evacuate patients because someone put something they shouldn't have in the staff lounge microwave and lit it on fire."

"That's happened?"

"Twice. Once during my residency when I worked an ER rotation, and once since I've been with the hospice department."

"Shit."

"Hospital staff members are human too. And particularly stressed, tired, and distracted humans."

"That seems crazy to me," Elliot said. "They make people work insane hours and expect them to make life-saving decisions with a clear head."

"Agreed." We sat in silence for a few heartbeats.

"I had an idea today." Elliot's voice was deceptively casual.

"Yeah? What's that?"

"You should move in." For a moment, I couldn't do anything. I couldn't formulate a thought or a response. There was just my heart beating way too fast in my chest and the sound of Elliot's breathing.

"Move in?"

"You don't seem to like your place. We never go there. Why not move in? There's plenty of space for you here."

"You're going to have to give me some time to think about that."

"Do you not want to?" Elliot's tone sounded clipped, and I wondered if my response had hurt him.

"I just didn't know you wanted me to. It hadn't occurred to me."

"Forget it. I shouldn't have—"

"Wait, Elliot!" I protested. "Come on! Give me a minute to wrap my head around this. I'm not saying I'm opposed to the idea, but I'm not the kind of guy who leaps before I think something through."

"I know you're not. I'm sorry."

And yet, I'd thought things through with Alec. I'd been sure he was a good choice. And look how that had turned out? But I couldn't really compare the two. They were very different people, and Elliot had been nothing but supportive of me. We meshed in every way that counted. He'd been there for me in ways Alec never had. And there was an underlying sense of respect for who I was and what our relationship meant that Alec had never given me. Elliot was a good man.

"I just need to be sure I'm making the right choice," I explained. "For both of us. I mean, don't get me wrong; it does make a lot of sense. It would save on bills for both of us, and it would be a lot less running around for me." I warmed to the idea. Careful, measured consideration had led to an unhappy relationship. Being with Elliot at all was a leap, yet I'd never been happier. Maybe moving in with him just required me to trust him to catch me when I leapt again.

"Those are all good things, right?"

"Yes." It occurred to me that I'd been focusing more on the practical aspects and ignored all the personal and emotional ones. "I do like the idea of waking up next to you every morning. Coming home to you at the end of every day."

"You do?" Elliot's voice softened a little. Funny, I'd never pegged him for much of a romantic, but maybe he was. Maybe he was just afraid to ask for it.

"I like the idea of that a lot," I said. It would take a little effort to break my lease or find someone to sublet, but that wasn't too much of a barrier. Elliot's place was a little farther from the hospital, but if I no longer had to drive to my place, that would more than even out. A thought occurred to me. "Shit. We can't. Not yet. Not until my family knows about you. And Dave."

Elliot was silent for so long I opened my mouth to ask him if he was still there. He spoke before I could get the words out. "When is *that* going to be? When are you planning to tell them?"

"I'll tell my parents this week, okay?" I blurted out. "I promise. I'll go on Sunday and tell them. And then we'll figure out how to tell Dave. Once everyone knows, yes, I'll move in with you."

"Okay." But Elliot didn't sound okay. He sounded remote and distant. Like when I'd first met him.

"Trust me, please," I pleaded, afraid I'd made a huge misstep. What if he pushed me away? I knew Elliot had a strong instinct to protect himself, and I'd sworn I'd never be the one to hurt him.

There was silence on the other end for several more painfully long moments. "Okay. You tell your parents this week, and we'll go from there," he finally said.

"I want to move in with you, Elliot," I assured him. "Look at it this way. It'll help motivate me to figure out how to tell everyone."

"Okay."

"I care about you, Elliot," I said softly. "And I want to be with you."

"I know you do."

But I knew I'd just chipped away at the fragile trust we were beginning to build. And I was afraid that if I made another mistake, I'd shatter it completely.

Chapter Twenty-Four

I arrived at my parents' house for Sunday dinner, nervous but ready and determined to tell them the truth about Elliot.

But the first flutters of nerves turned into full-blown anxiety as soon as I stepped through the door. I realized it had been weeks since I'd seen them, and they looked worse, not better. My mother was thin and pale in her gray cashmere sweater as she greeted me with a hug. The sweater was the open-fronted, draped sort, and she wrapped it around herself tightly as she stepped back, like it was all that was holding her together. My father's eyes were red-rimmed, and he clutched a glass of Scotch. But he didn't seem drunk at least. Not yet anyway. I couldn't stall any longer. I needed to do this *now* before I chickened out.

"Mom? Dad?" I said hoarsely as soon as the door closed behind me. "I have something I need to tell you."

"What is it, C.J.?" My mother's mouth tightened and small lines formed around it. Oh, God, clearly she was bracing herself for the worst.

"It's good news ... The guy I've been seeing ... it's getting more serious with him," I blurted out.

They both blinked at me before my mother's face lightened with a smile. It transformed her tired face. "Oh, that's wonderful. I am so happy for you, sweetheart."

"Thanks, Mom."

"That's wonderful news, Chris," my father murmured, and he sounded so sincere and like his old self that I felt a sharp ache in my chest. I had missed that.

My mother's gaze was searching. "How did you meet him?"

"Uhh, well, that's the funny part." I laughed, but it sounded tight and strained sounding. "Um, he knew Cal. He was at the funeral, and he knew Dave and Cooper and John." Why couldn't I seem to just come out with it?

"Oh, well that's nice. Has he been a good person for you to lean on since then?"

"Yeah." I shrugged. "I mean, it's kinda complicated, but we're getting there."

"Complicated?" Her brow furrowed in confusion. "Why is that, sweetheart?"

The timer going off in the kitchen prevented me from saying anything further.

"Hold that thought," my mom said. "Once we sit down to eat, you can tell us all about him."

As I walked to the dining room to set the table, I tried to psych myself up to tell them more about Elliot at dinner. As I set plates and glasses out, my thoughts turned briefly to the time I'd told my father about wanting to go into psychiatry. I hoped we wouldn't have a repeat of that dinner. Our family had been solid then, but it was resting on shaky foundation now. And I didn't have Cal as a buffer anymore.

Cal's empty chair still sent a stab of pain through me, but it had dulled a little.

"How are you doing?" I asked after we sat down and served ourselves. I knew I was being a coward by focusing on them and not continuing our earlier conversation.

My mother smiled tightly. "I'm okay. I've been volunteering a lot at the clinic downtown. Your father's been letting Dr. Weiss take on more responsibilities at the office."

"Are you thinking about retiring soon?" I asked, surprised. My parents had talked about retiring while they were still relatively young and healthy, then doing some traveling along with medical volunteer work, but I didn't expect it to be this soon.

"No." He shook his head but didn't elaborate. I looked at my mother to see if she would, but she wouldn't meet my gaze. Ahh, the drinking. If I had to guess, many days he was in no shape to practice medicine. I felt a pang of guilt that I hadn't done more to help.

"Dad?" I said softly. "Do you think it's maybe time you talk to someone about what's going on? Maybe get some help? You seem to be drinking a lot and—"

"I'm managing it fine!" He crossed his arms over his chest. "I don't know why you and your mother need to nag me about this constantly, but I'm just under a lot of stress right now, and it takes the edge off. That's all. I have it under control!"

"Do you? Because it doesn't seem like it to me. If Mom and I are bringing it up, it's because we're worried as hell. Ed's been asking about you too. He says you won't return his calls. Why don't you reach out to him at least? He helped last time and ..."

My father rose to his feet unsteadily, and the chair behind him tipped and clattered loudly against the wooden floors. "Why don't you all deal with your own lives and leave me to mine?"

He strode from the room, but he had to steady himself on the doorframe as he passed into the hallway. I stood, staring after him, my chest aching with worry.

"Just give me a minute," my mom said, her voice thin and shaky. I could see her struggling to keep herself together as she fled the room too. I heard my father's study door slam in the distance and the quick sounds of my mother jogging up the stairs. I was left alone in the dining room, the barely touched dinner cooling on the table as I wondered what the hell to do next. I dropped my head into my hands, a wave of despair washing over me. I hadn't even told them the truth about Elliot and Cal and Elliot and me, and things had gone to hell. I could only imagine what would have happened if I had.

I waited a long while for either of them to return while I poked at my food. I had no appetite, but I didn't want the carefully prepared lasagna and salad to go to waste. When it was clear that neither of them was coming back, I cleared the table, packed up the leftovers, and cleaned the kitchen. I was fully aware it was a feeble attempt at controlling the chaos around me, and ultimately, completely ineffective. The turmoil coursing through me didn't lessen even a fraction.

I stood in the kitchen after everything was done, wondering if I should try to talk to either of them before I left. My father was clearly a lost cause. He'd been drunk an hour ago when he stormed off, and I had no doubt he'd continued to drink heavily since. I'd be lucky if he was coherent, much less conscious. But maybe I could at least tell my mother about Elliot. Maybe that would be enough.

I was torn. It seemed unfair of me to dump this all on her when she was clearly so fragile. And yet, I owed it to Elliot. He deserved to be acknowledged. He was counting on me, and I couldn't let him down. I had made a promise to him that I didn't want to break. I took a deep breath and walked up the stairs, feeling like I was walking to the executioner's chair. At best, it would be a tough conversation. At worst ...

I expected to find my mother in the small sitting room at the top of the stairs, but it was empty, and so was my parents' bedroom. Cal's room, then. But the door to it was closed except for a crack when I reached the landing on the third floor. I could hear my mother pacing and the soft rise and fall of her voice. I wondered who she was talking to. Maybe her sister Eva.

I waited for a few minutes, hoping the conversation would wrap up. I wasn't trying to eavesdrop, but snippets of the conversations filtered through the door and into my ears as I stood there.

"I can't stand this anymore. It's like living with a ghost. He's drinking constantly now." She fell silent. "I know. I should. I just can't bring myself to break up this family even further."

My stomach dipped and swooped as the words registered. Was she thinking about leaving my father? I could hardly blame her, but the idea made my heart ache. They'd been together for forty-some years. I'd be losing what little family I had left. No matter how old I was, it wasn't easy to hear. Cal's death had brought about fears I had about being completely and utterly alone in the future when our parents died. This was another sort of loss.

Her voice dropped a little, turning softer and more intimate. "I don't know what I'd do without you, Paul. You've been my rock."

Paul? Who the hell is Paul? Jesus, is my mother having an affair? How could she? But even as I thought that, I wasn't sure I could blame her. How could I? My father was distant and cold these days, and they clearly didn't have much of a marriage anymore. The car that hit Cal had done more than kill him. It had shattered our entire family. And I'd begun to doubt we'd ever recover.

I crept down the stairs and let myself out of the house as quietly as I could, although I was sure neither of them had noticed anything. And maybe that was the worst feeling of all. The close-knit loving family I'd always had clearly didn't exist anymore, and I'd have to find my way alone.

My throat felt thick as I backed my car out of the driveway and headed for Elliot's place.

After I told him I'd let him down, I might not even have him to rely on.

"**Y**ou didn't do it, did you?" Elliot asked softly when I arrived at his loft, clutching leftovers and feeling like the world had rocked under me. Clearly, he could read the distress on my face.

I shook my head as I pushed the door shut behind me and walked into the kitchen, my legs heavy like lead. "Tonight was a mess. My father's slid into full-blown alcoholism, and the best I can tell, my mother's having an affair."

His mouth opened in surprise. "What?"

"I don't know." I set the bag on the counter and braced myself against it. I barely had the energy to stand. "I told them I was dating someone and that it was getting serious, but that's as far as I got." I struggled to remember how it had all gone down. It seemed like a blur already. "We sat down to dinner, and I had every intention of telling them who you were, but my father was drunk and he stormed off when I confronted him about it, and then my mother disappeared, and … I stayed for a while, hoping I could at least talk to her, but she didn't come back. And I overheard her talking to some guy named Paul. I don't know. I don't even know what I heard, but it sounded like …" I couldn't even say the words aloud.

Elliot cupped my cheek in his hand. "I'm sorry, Chris."

"What are you sorry for? I'm the one letting you down. I didn't tell them about who you are or your history with Cal," I admitted, miserable and guilty. "God, Elliot. I'm so sorry. I wanted to. I swear."

He rubbed his thumb against my cheek, and I heard the rasp of my whiskers against his skin. "It's okay. You did more than I expected."

"Is it that you have that low of an opinion of me or of everyone?" I asked. My words came out more biting than I intended.

His gaze turned sad. "Everyone."

His words made my heart ache, and I wrapped my arms around his hips, pulling him against me. I craved his touch. I needed it to anchor me. I had no idea what I'd do if he gave up on me. "I hate that."

"Do you blame me?" He rested his palms against my chest. They were warm, even through my clothing, and I wanted to pull him even closer until there was no separation between us at all.

"No. But I still hate that life has dealt you so many shitty cards that you assume the worst." I laughed mirthlessly when I thought about the conversation I'd had with my mother months ago about being pessimistic. Elliot outdid me in every way.

Of course, he did. He'd had a rough life from the get-go, and it hadn't gotten much easier. Sure, now he was financially stable and in a job he loved—which was nothing to sneer at—but he accomplished them without any support from his family. His turbulent relationship with my brother had ended with death, and I wasn't stepping up to the plate like I'd promised him I would.

Cal had pretended to the world—and his family—that Elliot hadn't existed. That he hadn't been anything special. And I'd just done the same.

He deserved better.

"Look, Elliot," I said firmly, "I want you to know I'm not going to leave you wondering where you stand any longer than I have to. I *will* tell my family as soon as I figure out the right time. I mean it."

"I know you do." He smiled, but it didn't quite reach his eyes. I buried my head in the crook of his neck.

"I was afraid you were going to leave me too," I muttered against the collar of his shirt, breathing in the comforting familiarity of his bergamot and vanilla scent. I'd lost my brother. My parents. Dave and I were struggling. I couldn't bear to lose Elliot too.

"I'm not going anywhere." He gripped me tighter. So tight my ribs began to ache. I welcomed it.

We had sex that night, and it was slow and desperate. My hands hardly left Elliot's skin as we moved together, and his kisses were deep and needy. I felt close to him, and yet I couldn't shake the sense that I'd driven a wedge between us that would be nearly impossible to remove.

It wasn't until I was drifting off to sleep that night in his bed that it occurred to me that he hadn't said he knew I would tell my family. Only that he knew I meant what I said.

Fuck that, I thought savagely, as I settled onto my side and wrapped an arm around Elliot. *I will be better for him. I have to. He needs me to. He's been let down by enough people in his life. I won't do it to him too*, I promised myself. And yet I was terrified that I would fail him. And myself.

With a sick, swooping feeling in my stomach, I remembered this coming weekend was Cal's gallery show. Time was running out.

Chapter Twenty-Five

Elliot paced in front of the gallery as I approached. I was surprised he didn't have a lit cigarette in his hand although he was fidgeting with his lighter.

"Hey." He paused in his pacing to give me a quick hug and brush his lips across mine. "You made it."

Work had run long and traffic had been a nightmare, but I'd arrived with a little time to spare. "I wouldn't miss this." I reached for his hand, but his fingers slid through mine without stopping and he resumed pacing. "You look great, by the way."

Elliot wore all black: nicely tailored trousers and a fitted black T-shirt with a supple black leather blazer over top. His hair was neatly pulled back, and he looked utterly gorgeous. I wanted to forget the show, go back to his loft, and peel him out of his clothes. He glanced down at himself as if he'd forgotten what he was wearing. "Thanks. My agent picked it out."

"It suits you. Also, I had no idea you had an agent."

He shrugged. "Sam is great. I'd show up in ripped jeans and boots, but she keeps me appropriately dressed for events. I'm wearing what she picked out for my last show."

I laughed and self-consciously smoothed down my silver-flecked tie, carefully selected to coordinate with my charcoal suit. "Is this too much?"

Elliot seemed to notice my clothes for the first time. A small smile played on his lips as he shook his head. "I want to get you half out of that suit and sketch you that way. Half-buttoned up, half-debauched."

I grinned. By now, I was used to Elliot looking at me like a moving work of art. "You can draw me however you want." Whether or not we'd be able to keep our hands off each other while he did it was debatable. I'd taken several pieces of clothing to the dry cleaner's with conspicuously placed dusty black handprints.

Elliot grinned back, but I could still see the tension coursing through his body.

"Should we go inside?" I asked.

"Give me a minute. Need to burn off some energy before I combust."

"I'm surprised you're not smoking," I said, only half-joking.

He cleared his throat. "Quit a few days ago. Patches." He patted his upper arm.

"Really?"

"You hate it. I *know* it's bad for me," he muttered. "Should have quit a long time ago."

"I never would have asked you to quit smoking for me."

"I know." He fiddled with his ponytail like he wanted to rip the elastic out and hide his face, but he dropped his hand instead. "That's why I did it. Besides, you gave me a reason to take better care of myself."

"I ... That means a lot, Elliot." He gave me a fleeting smile. I reached for him, pulling him tight against me so I could kiss his temple. *I'm sorry I haven't done more for you.* I'd hardly heard a word from my parents all week other than a brief, strained call with my mother where she'd assured me they'd be at the gallery tonight. There had been no opportunity to tell them about Elliot. When I'd told him, he'd nodded, his expression resigned, as if he'd expected it. It broke my heart.

He was going to have to spend the evening pretending like we were nothing more than acquaintances. I was doing exactly what Cal had done. No, worse because I damn well knew better. "I'm sorry," I murmured.

His smile was quick and weary. "I know."

"C.J.?" The sound of my mother's voice made me turn to see my parents standing a few feet away. I froze and felt Elliot pull away from me. "Elliot?"

My mother looked between us and a brief look of understanding flickered in her eyes before a half-smile lit her tired face. "Are you two seeing each other?"

"Yes," I croaked.

"I wondered," she murmured. "There was something about the way you two interacted at that first meeting here at the gallery. I sensed a connection. And last weekend when you talked about things getting serious with someone, I thought it might be Elliot."

I looked my parents over. They were both well dressed, although the dark circles under my mother's eyes seemed to have grown worse, and my father's suit hung off his shoulders. For the first time, I noticed he'd lost weight, and his face was beginning to look puffy.

"I'm sorry I didn't tell you last weekend," I said. "I meant to."

"Well, I'm very happy for you both." My mother hugged me, then pulled a startled-looking Elliot into a hug before he could stop her. "C.J. has said how much you've helped him since Cal's death."

Elliot shot me a look out of the corner of his eye as he patted her shoulder. "I've tried."

My father hugged me too, although there was a distinct coolness to it. He clearly hadn't forgiven me for what I'd said the other day.

"Shall we go in the gallery?" my mother suggested.

"I'd like to speak to Chris for a minute before we head in," Elliot said. His voice sounded strained.

"Of course. We'll see you inside."

After they disappeared into the gallery, I turned to face Elliot. "I'm so sorry. I know that wasn't how we'd planned to do it, but maybe it's for the best. At least, it's out in the open now."

Elliot closed his eyes for a second. "You've had so many opportunities to tell them, and yet you only did it when you had no other choice. When your hand was forced. Do you know how that makes me feel?"

The disappointment in his tone ripped through me. "I'm so sorry."

"Then tell them about the rest!" Elliot's voice rose, and I took a half step back.

"What? About your relationship with Cal?"

"Yes. All of it. No more secrets, Chris. No more lies. I'm tired of it."

"Now? This isn't the time or place."

"It's never the time or place though, is it?" he snapped. "There's always another excuse. Another reason to delay it. I can't keep doing it. I *won't* keep doing it."

"Just give me another day," I pleaded. "Tomorrow, we can go to my parents' house and sit down with them. I'll tell them everything. But not tonight. Tonight is about Cal and his legacy. We don't want to tarnish that."

Elliot drew back. "His family knowing he was bi and dating me would tarnish his legacy?"

"No! I didn't mean it like that." I shook my head. "It's just going to be a tough enough night as it is. Throwing in the news that Cal was hiding things will just make it worse."

"Please, Chris." Elliot reached out to me, his voice going soft again. "We're almost there. Just take one more step and we can move forward with no secrets."

"I can't," I said thickly. "Please don't ask me to."

The look Elliot gave me was filled with so much hurt it felt like my chest would cave in. I reached out to him, but he shook me off and walked into the gallery. I stood on the sidewalk staring after him for several long moments, feeling sick.

The sight inside the gallery took my breath away. Elliot had overseen the hanging of Cal's work, but this was the first glimpse I'd gotten. Massive canvases covered the walls, and I stood, awe-struck, as I took it all in.

"This is incredible," I whispered. Cal's work was even more stunning than I'd imagined. The snapshots had been gorgeous and so had the proofs on his laptop, but this, in larger-than-life size and displayed to the best advantage, was astounding. He had been so damn talented.

There was raw beauty in the intertwined bodies on the canvases. Love and passion mingled, and even the most erotic of the photos showed a tenderness that was staggering. "You did an incredible job," I said quietly.

Elliot shook his head. "It was Cal. All I did was put together what he created." On the outside, he appeared cool and unruffled, but there was a raspiness to his voice that betrayed how hard he was struggling.

I suddenly realized how emotional this night must be for him. This was work he'd done with Cal when they were dating. This was what they'd fallen in love over.

It sent a pang through me. God, I'd fucked this up. Tonight should have been an open and honest celebration of Cal's work, and instead, it was shrouded in secrecy and lies. I'd hurt Elliot when he was feeling especially vulnerable.

You Allen boys are real pieces of work, I remembered Elliot snarling at me in one of his rare, angry outbursts. We really were.

I would talk to my parents after the show and tell them the truth, I decided. It was the least I could do.

Elliot and I made a slow circuit of the room, enjoying Cal's work despite the lingering tension between us.

We were about halfway around when I spotted several portraits of Cal on one wall. It also held a placard containing information about his life—and death. The largest photo was the one I'd seen on his wall after the funeral. The one of him standing on the beach with his surfboard at sunset.

"How did they get that photo?"

Elliot gave me a perplexed look. "I was the photographer, Chris."

The thought had never occurred to me, but of course, it made sense. It was personal and serious. A side of Cal few beyond Elliot had ever seen of him. I should have known Elliot was the one behind the camera.

"We went to Port Orford," he said. "Out to Battle Rock beach. The big swells are usually blocked by Nellies Point, but that day, there were perfect conditions. Cal was out for hours. I've never seen him happier."

"Do you surf?"

Elliot shook his head. "I spent the day sketching and taking photos."

I nodded toward the photo we'd just been discussing. "You said he was happy, but he looks so solemn there."

A shadow crossed Elliot's face. "He was trying to figure out how he felt about me. We'd ... been intimate by that point, but he was conflicted."

I had no idea what to say to that. "It's a gorgeous photo. You're a great photographer in your own right."

"I was never passionate about it the way Cal was."

I nodded. I would have been a good pediatrician, but that didn't mean it was the right career for me.

I studied the photo again, wishing I could have been there for my brother at that time. Would things have been different if he'd been able to tell me what he was struggling with? The idea sent a funny lurch through my stomach. What if I'd helped Cal be a better boyfriend to Elliot? What if that had made the difference for them? What if their relationship had been more solid when Cal had died? It might have changed everything. I might never have gotten involved with Elliot at all. The thought made my chest grow tight.

I glanced over at him. He looked grave right now too, a little sad. "I'm sorry, I ..."

"Elliot, Chris, it's great to see you both." Joy beamed at us as she approached. "What do you think?"

"It's stunning," I said honestly, although I wished she'd just go away. "It's a wonderful legacy for my brother."

"I'm so pleased." She squeezed my upper arm, then pointed to a long table set up across the room where white-shirted waitstaff were assembling food. "Food and drinks will be available over there. I just have a couple questions to run by you both before we get started."

After we'd answered Joy's questions, she disappeared to finish the last-minute details. Elliot wandered away as my parents approached.

"I am so glad you suggested this," my mother said, hugging me. "Truly. Cal's work should be seen. It's beautiful."

"I'm glad you think so."

"You did well," my father said. His tone was distant, but the praise was nice at least. We made small talk for a few minutes, but he quickly excused himself. "Excuse me. It looks like the bar is open."

He made a beeline for the opposite side of the room. I blew out a heavy sigh and made a mental note to talk to Ed about some kind of intervention once this was all over. I was planning to stick to soda and lime tonight. I couldn't remember the last time I'd touched alcohol, and I wasn't sure if I ever would again.

"Is Elliot around?" my mother asked. Her smile was tight and strained. I couldn't imagine what a toll Dad's drinking was taking on her. I scanned the crowd and spotted him talking with a man in glasses.

"Over there."

"I'm so glad you had him to help put this together," she said. "He seems like a very good man."

"I am too," I said absently, as I watched him push a stray strand of hair off his cheek. I wanted so badly to start this night over. Re-do it. "And he is."

"People are beginning to arrive," Peter Holloway said. I nodded and tore my gaze away from Elliot. I turned to face the gallery owner.

Peter reached out a hand to me, and I automatically shook it. "Good to see you, Chris. As we discussed last week, you'll be standing in for Cal tonight. Typically, the artist would help play host, but given the circumstances ..." He cleared his throat delicately. "Do you have any questions for me?"

"None that I can think of."

"Then I'll start by introducing you to some people. You can give your speech in about half an hour."

"Sounds good."

When Peter had approached Elliot and me about which of us would host the evening, Elliot had shrugged. "It's not my place. It'll bring up a lot of questions we don't want to answer tonight."

It was an awkward situation at best. My parents knew about our relationship now, but Dave and Cal's friends didn't. Dave knew about Cal's relationship with Elliot, but not about Elliot and me. What a mess my brother and I had made of things.

If Elliot and I had been completely out as a couple, it would have been easier. He could have stayed by my side tonight, and we could have hosted it together.

Peter had looked between us. "Am I right in assuming you two are involved?"

Elliot went very still beside me.

"We are," I'd said, hoping that tiny sliver of acknowledgement would tide him over until I could tell everyone the truth later tonight. "Given Elliot's previous relationship with Cal, however, we're not advertising that right now," I explained. He already knew about Cal and Elliot.

"Understood. Your secret is safe with me," he assured us.

Secret. I *loathed* that word now. I was so damn sick of being weighed down by it.

"Then, Chris, if you come with me now, we'll get started. After your speech, I'll have you mingle with some of the potential buyers."

I stepped into the role of host easily enough. I'd been to plenty of hospital fundraisers and events, and the years dating Alec had given me even more practice. It wasn't something I enjoyed, but I mingled with the well-heeled crowd and talked up my brother's work competently enough.

Periodically, I craned my neck, searching for glimpses of my parents. They seemed to be doing all right. I could see Elliot in the crowd as well, talking to strangers, looking completely relaxed and at ease. But I wondered if it was all a show.

"Do you know what made your brother choose this subject?" a critic wearing thick, black-rimmed glasses asked me.

"To be honest, I don't," I admitted. "My brother was a bit secretive about this recent work of his. He has a number of friends who are LGBTQ, and he's always been supportive of me, so I assume that was part of it."

He nodded as if that made perfect sense. "It's quite a collection of work for someone just getting started. Very reminiscent of Mapplethorpe—without the more controversial edge, of course. I would have been curious to see how your brother's work progressed with time."

"So would I." My throat felt a little thick.

A touch of compassion flickered over the man's jowly face. "Of course. Well, it's quite a legacy."

Legacy. There was that word again. We all seemed obsessed with it. Myself included.

The man drifted on, and I took the opportunity to scan the room again. I saw Dave talking to Cooper and John and looking handsome in his dark blue suit. I approached a little hesitantly. I'd hardly spoken to Dave lately, and he had seemed quite resistant to the idea of this show to begin with. Now, he shook my hand rather than hug me, and I felt a stab of disappointment. It wasn't going to be easy to win him over when it came to Elliot and me. But it had to be done. And soon.

"Damn," Cooper said after we'd all made small talk for a minute. "I had no idea Cal was into this. The same sex stuff."

John looked around. "He's good though. Like *really* good. I'm not that into staring at the dudes together, but the women?" He whistled lowly. "Hot stuff."

I caught Dave's eye roll, and we exchanged a small, shared smile.

"I'm glad you could all make it," I said sincerely. "I know Cal would have appreciated it."

"Why do you think he didn't tell us about what he was working on?" Cooper asked with a frown.

I sighed. That was the million-dollar question, wasn't it? "I wish I could answer that."

The clinking of something against a glass prevented me from continuing.

When I glanced up, Peter Holloway stood at the front of the room. I weaved my way through the crowd as he spoke. "Thank you for coming this evening. Calvin James Allen was one of the most promising photographers I've seen in a long time. Last year, when Elliot Rawlings—another talented artist here at the Holloway Gallery—brought Cal's work to my attention, I was astounded by his skill and moved by the subject matter he addressed. I saw an incredibly talented artist, but he wasn't yet ready to share his art with the world.

"After he died in a tragic accident this January, his loved ones approached me. I jumped at the opportunity to curate this show in his memory. Without further ado, I'd like to introduce Cal's brother, Dr. Christopher Allen."

I stepped forward until I stood beside Peter and raised my voice. "Thank you all for coming tonight. When Peter asked me to say a few words about my brother and his art, I was at a loss. It seemed impossible to sum up a man who was larger than life to so many of us. I struggled with how to express how truly talented he was. I didn't know how to memorialize him. How to truly honor the kind of man he was. Someone who explored the world around him with a zeal unmatched by anyone else I've ever met. Someone who cared deeply for the people in his life and tried to take his good fortune and use it to help others. In the end, I realized Cal's work would speak for itself." I gestured to the room around us. "These photos of gay and lesbian couples, of the broad spectrum of the LGBTQ community, say everything. And I am thrilled to announce that all the proceeds from the sale of his work will go toward two causes Cal believed strongly in. A scholarship fund has been established in his name to bring art to underprivileged youth in neighborhoods where arts programs often get drastically cut. And the second beneficiary is the LGBTQ center here in Portland. The center provides safe spaces, community building, and empowerment for LGBTQ people in the Portland Metro and Southwest Washington areas."

Appreciative murmurs rose from the crowd.

I watched Elliot's face as I gave my speech and caught a glimpse of sadness. Once again, Elliot had been left out of the important role he'd played in Cal's life. He was a footnote, and I knew how deep that must cut. How could that wound ever heal if the injuries didn't stop? He was right, I should have come clean long before now. At least, it would have given him his rightful place in Cal's life. And mine.

"Although all of us who knew and loved my brother"—my gaze swept across Elliot—"were devastated by his death, I am confident that his memory will live on through his work. That it will go on to help others in need will be the best tribute to his life we could hope to achieve. Thank you for coming here tonight to support him and his work."

The crowd clapped loudly, and before I could blink, I was surrounded by people wishing to speak to me. Peter stayed nearby, introducing me to potential buyers but not letting me linger too long when the conversations got too repetitive or off-topic.

When there was a lull in the conversations, Elliot appeared at my elbow.

"Have you eaten?" he murmured. He held a small plate in his hand, loaded with savory bites of food. It looked wonderful, and my stomach growled with anticipation as I took it from him.

"I haven't. Thank you." I caught myself as I started to lean in to give him a quick kiss in thanks, and Elliot's face tightened when I halted, remembering all of the people who didn't know about us yet. Shit.

I picked up a mini vegetable tart and smiled at him. "This looks great."

"I figured you hadn't had anything since lunch."

"You're always looking out for me," I said lightly. "It's a nice change of pace."

He nodded in acknowledgement but didn't say anything else as my parents approached.

"Everything is wonderful, Elliot. You did a beautiful job bringing Cal's work to life," my mother said with a warm smile. As I ate, I found myself watching them interact more than I did listening to them speak.

She seemed more vivacious and relaxed than she had in a long time, and their easy interactions pleased me.

"I haven't had a chance to look at all of the work here," I heard her say. "Shall we all walk around for a little bit and talk while we do?"

"Sure." Her warmth seemed to relax Elliot a little too. He appeared less tense. I was glad. I hoped that seeing him like this would ease the blow of the news I was about to tell my parents when this night was over. If they liked him, that would make it easier, right?

My dad and I fell into step behind Elliot and my mom as we made a slow trek around the room. He didn't say much and neither did I.

When we reached the far wall, I inspected the work there. I hadn't seen any of it up close yet. My gaze lingered on one. Two sets of hands caressed a rounded stomach. The pregnant woman leaned against a partner who had a hint of an Adam's apple and full breasts. Cal had captured the nuances of the complex relationship beautifully, and the love between the couple and their unborn child was palpable.

I glanced at Elliot, wondering if he wanted children someday. I hadn't asked. It had always been so important to me, yet I'd never considered if that was the kind of future he pictured for himself. There was still so much we didn't know about each other.

Out of the corner of my eye, I saw my mother step back abruptly, and her hand flew to her mouth. "C.J.?" she said hoarsely.

I stepped closer to her. "What is it, Mom?" My gazed flicked over the art on the wall she'd been starting at. It was of two men in profile. Nude and intertwined. The more muscular one had his head buried against the throat of the leaner, lankier one. It was titled *Hidden Love*.

She looked straight at Elliot. "That's a very intimate shot of you and my son."

"That's not me," I protested as the blood drained from Elliot's face.

"I know it's not you," my mother said quietly but very seriously. "It's Cal."

"What?" I glanced at the photo again. I'd looked at it a dozen times in a smaller format. "How can you tell?" His face was totally hidden.

She pointed a trembling finger at the small of the man's back. "That birthmark."

My gaze traveled to it, and I felt a jolt of recognition. There it was, a small cluster of freckles that resembled a slightly lopsided constellation of stars. It was unique, yet something I'd seen dozens of times. Of course, my mother would recognize it. And with the photo blown up in large scale with the perfect lighting, I could make out the distinctive tangle of Elliot's dark hair in the background and the side of his cheek, although the rest of his face was in shadow.

My brain frantically scrambled for a plausible explanation to give her, tumbling and whirling with ideas for how to steer her away from the truth.

Of all the possible scenarios I'd considered for tonight, Cal's secrets coming out *this* way had never occurred to me. Elliot or I accidentally slipping up and giving something about his relationship with Cal? Yes. But not this.

I turned to face my parents. They were staring at Elliot, and he was staring at me. My parents looked more bewildered than anything. But Elliot ... he just looked resigned. He'd expected this to happen.

"Is someone going to explain what's going on?" my mother asked hoarsely. "I suppose Cal could have just posed as a model, but I don't believe that kind of emotion can be faked. This certainly looks to me like Cal and Elliot were quite intimately involved. Am I wrong?"

I opened my mouth, but no sound came out.

"You're not wrong," Elliot said. The stoic resignation on his face worried me.

She gestured around the room at all the photographs on display. "So, this subject matter wasn't just an artistic choice? Cal was ..."

"Cal was bisexual," Elliot finished for her. "When that photo was taken, we were in a relationship. He was just coming to terms with his sexuality, but he wasn't ready to come out to any of you. Chris didn't find out until Cal's funeral."

I heard a strangled gasp beside me from my father. My mother's gaze was pained as she looked at me. "You knew this whole time and you never told us."

"Mom ... I ... I didn't want to hurt you more."
"You think finding out this way doesn't hurt?" She wiped at her eyes. I hadn't even realized she was crying.

"I'm sorry. I made a mistake," I said, anguished. "I should have told you before now, I know that. I've been trying to tell you about Cal for months, and I could never find the right time. I didn't know that picture was of Cal and Elliot. I swear."

She shook her head. "But why did you all hide it from me? I don't understand."

"I don't know." Now, every excuse I had seemed flimsy and self-serving. Why hadn't I just told them from the beginning? I could have avoided all of this.

"I'm sorry, Mrs. Allen." Elliot sounded remorseful, and I realized he was blaming himself.

I felt a wave of regret and anguish wash over me. I had let him down by making him keep these secrets. And now he had to deal with the fallout in the worst way possible.

"It's not your fault, Elliot," I said wearily. The events of the day were finally beginning to hit me, and I suddenly felt drained. "None of this is Elliot's fault at all. He wanted to tell you. I was the one who couldn't seem to make myself do it. And now this is where we are ..."

I looked over at Elliot. He looked tortured and uncomfortable. "I'm sorry, Elliot."

I wanted to reach out and touch him. Reassure him. But I felt frozen.

"I know." Elliot nodded once, like he was confirming something to himself. "But I can't do this anymore, Chris," he said quietly, and I felt something in my heart break because I knew what he was about to say. "I can't. I need you to know I didn't mean for this to happen tonight. I chose that photo because I wanted a final link to Cal. Acknowledgement of what we'd been to each other, even though no one would ever know it was the two of us in the photo. I never imagined anyone would recognize Cal."

"I don't blame you," I whispered. "Not for a second."

"This has to end, Chris." The pain in Elliot's eyes made me ache. "I was your brother's secret. I can't be yours anymore. I can't do this again."

He turned to walk away and only then was I able to reach out and grab his sleeve. "Wait, Elliot. Just give me a second to *think*."

He shook off my grasp. "I've given you as much time as I can."

And then, he disappeared into the crowd before I could stop him. It was only then I noticed the people around us watching curiously. *Fuck*.

This was all going to shit, and I had no idea how to stop it. I started to go after Elliot, but I could hear the sound of my mother crying, and I was torn. I needed to stay and clean up the mess that was my family. I had hurt them too, and I needed to make that right.

When I turned to face them again, my mother gave me an anguished, bewildered look. "Sweetheart … please explain this all to me? Elliot is the man you've been seeing but he was also Cal's boyfriend?"

I closed my eyes for a moment, as if it would block out the truth of what was happening in front of me. But I knew it would never work. I had to face the consequences of my decisions. "Look, Mom, I told you things were complicated," I whispered. "But, yes, Elliot and I have been seeing each other for a while. That's why I didn't know how to tell you about Elliot last week. Not with his history with Cal …"

She let out a strangled sounding laugh. "Yes, I see why now."

"This family's a fucking mess," my father muttered, his words slurring a little. I glanced over at him. His face was red, and he had the ever-present glass of booze clutched in his hand. I wondered how drunk he was. And I suddenly felt disgusted with him.

"You're drunk, Christopher," my mother hissed. "You don't have much of a place to talk."

"And you're such a paragon of virtue?" he sneered at her. "I know all about you and Paul."

She staggered back, her face going pale. "What?" Jesus, it was all pouring out now. Every bit of ugliness under the surface was coming to the light, and I could do nothing to stop it.

"Paul Burns, right? That's the name of the man you've been having an affair with."

"I've never even met him in person!" she protested. "He's a *friend.*"

"Fine, maybe you haven't slept with him yet, but it's just a matter of time. What was it you texted him the other night? 'I'm so lonely. I just wish you were here to hold me?' Did I get that right?"

She burst into tears. "I *am* lonely. No one has been honest with me. I lost my son, and I miss my husband! I try to go to you and you shut me down. You drown yourself in your drinks, and it's like I'm living with a ghost."

"At least, I didn't turn to someone outside my marriage," he shouted. I could see even more people around us staring. *So much for Cal's legacy.*

"I *wanted* to turn to you. Our son was gone and all I wanted was my husband. You may have been physically there, but the minute we buried Cal, you checked out," she said spitefully. "I begged you to go to a support group with me, but you refused. Maybe I did turn to Paul for emotional support, but it was only because you weren't there for me anymore."

"Fine, go to him them," he sneered. "What do I care? Go screw half of Portland, if you really want."

"I don't want to! I want my husband back. I want you to stop drinking and deal with the fact that we lost our son," she shouted.

She clenched her hands into fists, practically shaking. I wanted to reach out to her and comfort her, but what if she rejected me? I couldn't stomach it.

She turned to look at me, and it was so filled with disappointment I felt like I'd be sick. "I want this family to finally be honest with each other." The words echoed in the otherwise silent room, and when they stopped reverberating, you could have heard a pin drop.

For a long time, we all stared at each other. With a soft sob, my mother turned and fled for the door, the only sound the staccato noise of her shoes on the concrete floor of the gallery as the silent crowd parted to let her through. My father stared after her with a stunned expression on his face. As the doors closed behind her, a hushed babble of voices rose in the air. My father shrugged a little, drained his drink, and set it on a nearby table.

"Looks like I'm getting a cab." A part of me wanted to stop him as he walked toward the door, stumbling a little. My family was fractured. Possibly beyond repair. And I was tired of trying to pick up the pieces. Tired of the lies. I was just plain *tired*.

All I wanted was Elliot.

I glanced over to my right, and the blood drained from my face as I saw a man glaring at me. I knew that face, but I had never seen it so twisted before. The angry scowl made him almost unrecognizable.

Dave strode toward me, and I met him halfway. God, could this night get any worse? Clearly, he'd heard the whole thing. Or at least enough of it.

"You're fucking him, aren't you, Chris?" he asked, his voice filled with disbelief and anger. I continued to stare at him, mute against his accusations. "You *asshole*. That's fucking low, and you know it."

"Don't do this here, Dave," I said tightly. He was absolutely the last person I wanted to deal with right now.

"When were you going to tell me about you and Elliot? I thought you were my friend." He put both hands on my chest to shove me, and I stumbled back, barely managing to stay upright

"I've been *trying*. But please don't do this, Dave," I pleaded. "Not here. Not now. This is supposed to be about Cal. We've already made a mess of things, but let's celebrate Cal's accomplishments tonight, and we can talk tomorrow."

He scowled at me. "Don't fucking give me that. You don't get to use Cal's memory to hide all your dirty little secrets."

"God damn it, Dave. You're angry with me. Fine. Maybe I'm a horrible person for not telling you about my relationship with Elliot, but for God's sake, what do you think this is going to accomplish?"

Dave merely glared at me. I could see the hurt lurking in his eyes, and I knew he wasn't thinking rationally anymore. He was just grieving and angry and lashing out at everyone.

"I didn't mean for it to happen!" I protested. "We got close when we were going through Cal's things and ..."

"I knew it," he shouted. "You goddamn fucking asshole. How could you do that to your brother?"

"He's fucking dead," I shouted back. "And you're as much of an atheist as he was, so I don't believe for a minute you think he's looking down at us from somewhere and judging! No matter how much all of us want Cal back, he's *gone*, Dave. Yeah, it's shitty, and I've beat myself up enough times about it already. I don't need it from you too."

"Oh, boo hoo! You're upset because you feel guilty? You fucking should!"

Rage simmered under the surface. "I never meant for it to happen. Elliot and I got drunk and turned to each other after Cal's funeral, and I've been beating myself up ever since. But he's also turned out to be the only person who understood what I was going through!"

"You *motherfucking cocksucker*." He let out a furious bellow as he lunged toward me. "You've been up on your high horse about Cal and me not being honest with you, and this whole time, you were screwing Elliot? Since the *funeral*? You fucking hypocrite."

My head snapped back when his fist connected with my jaw. Pain bloomed there, my head swimming from the impact. I staggered back, found my footing, and then charged, the pent-up stress and frustration boiling over in me. My shoulder caught Dave's chest, and we both went down.

As we grappled with each other, I heard a button on my shirt rip off and go pinging across the room. I grunted from a sharp pain in my sternum as his elbow slammed into my chest, and it knocked the wind out of me. It reminded me of wrestling when we were kids, but this was more than friendly grappling, and I knew we could do irreparable damage.

I wanted to damage him; I wanted to return the blow he'd given me and then some. I wanted to unleash all the anger and frustration that had been building up inside me, but I couldn't. "But I'm not just fucking him, Dave," I shouted as I fought to subdue him. I shoved him back against the floor. Hard.

"You *bastard*. That was for *Cal*," he snarled, still angry, but I pinned him down, my hands on his upper arms keeping him in place. "At least, someone should be loyal to his memory! His brother and his boyfriend clearly aren't!"

"Shut the fuck up. I need you to *listen* to me. Do you think I wanted this? I don't. I never planned it. But I love him. I ..." Now that he was no longer swinging at me, the aggression and rage were dissipating. "I love Elliot."

Dave went still beneath me, staring up at me in shock. I was a little shocked too.

"You have every right to be angry with me, Dave," I admitted, panting as the last of the anger leached out of me. "But you can't possibly hate me more than I hated myself when I realized I had feelings for Elliot. And now that I've hurt him ..." My throat closed up before I could finish. I ached with the knowledge that I'd hurt Elliot so badly I had no idea if I'd ever actually have the opportunity to tell him how I felt.

I stood, bracing myself for Dave to come flying at me again, but he just lay there panting, his face twisted into a scowl. "I fucked up, no question about it, but I really need you to be my friend right now. Talk to me when you can do that."

Suddenly, there were two men standing beside us, Peter Holloway and someone else I didn't recognize. Peter looked agitated as he raked a hand through his hair. The other man spoke. "Dr. Allen, would you like us to escort this man out?"

I weighed my options and nodded tersely. "I think you'd better."

And then Cooper and John were there. "We've got him," Cooper said grimly. They grabbed his arms and dragged Dave to his feet. I was sure they were none too happy with me either, but I appreciated them dealing with Dave.

"You've gotta be fucking kidding me!" Dave yelled as they manhandled him out of the gallery. "You've taken *everything* from Cal! His work. His boyfriend. You're despicable."

Dave's words were still ringing through the otherwise silent room as the door closed behind him, and I dropped my chin to my chest.

He was right. I was.

Chapter Twenty-Six

I straightened my disheveled clothing and left the gallery with my jaw aching and a sick feeling in the pit of my stomach. The night had been a disaster. Cal's show had been ruined, my family had shattered, my friendship with Dave was in ruins, but worst of all, Elliot had given up on me. I heard Peter Holloway calling after me as I strode to my car, but I waved him off. I couldn't deal with any more of the fallout right now.

I could only hope that tonight's debacle wouldn't have a negative impact on Elliot's future there. If it did, I'd never forgive myself.

It was a cool, rainy night, and I shivered as I walked to my car, belatedly realizing I'd left my overcoat in the gallery. I wasn't going back for it now.

Once in my car, the adrenaline began to wear off. I leaned my head against the headrest, struggling to take a few deep breaths. I wanted to go straight to Elliot, but I was shaking too hard to drive. I reached for my phone instead. Miraculously, the device itself was in one piece, but the glass screen protector had cracked in the fight. I couldn't manage the coordination required to peel it off, so I squinted through the spider web of cracks.

My immediate instinct was to call my parents, but it was Elliot's number I pulled up instead. In the past, I had made everyone but him my priority, and it was time I fixed that. There was no making any of this right until I talked to him.

The phone rang and rang, but it went to voicemail when he didn't pick up. I didn't leave a message. I took a few more steadying breaths and took stock of myself. I still felt shaky, but not so bad I couldn't drive.

I mostly felt numb as I navigated the rainy streets of Portland and across the Broadway Bridge that spanned the Willamette River.

Twenty minutes later, I knocked on Elliot's door. While I waited, a wave of fatigue washed over me, and I braced my hand against the wall. I closed my eyes briefly, trying to gather my thoughts and figure out what to tell Elliot. Just when I began to doubt he'd answer the door at all, it opened. I lifted my head to look at him.

He stared at me impassively. He looked as remote and wintry as he had the first morning I woke up in his bed. But it softened when he saw my face.

"Ouch." He gently ghosted his fingertips over the raw area on my jaw. It hurt, but I craved that touch. "That looks painful."

"It's not that bad," I muttered. "Can I come in?"

Elliot hesitated a second before he stepped back and allowed me in. "It looks like hell, Chris. It's definitely beginning to bruise."

I grimaced. "Great. Work is going to be fun on Monday."

"Tomorrow or Sunday will be the worst. It should begin to fade after that." I didn't like the cool dispassionate notes in his voice.

"Do I want to know why you know what bruising patterns look like?"

"No," he said shortly. I flinched. I could only assume his mother had been beaten, although for all I knew, Elliot had been too. I wasn't sure I wanted to find out, but I promised myself I'd delve deeper into that at some point. If he'd let me.

I worked my lower jaw back and forth. "I can't say I feel *good*, but I'll survive." I probed at my teeth with my tongue. "I don't think any teeth got knocked loose. Any chance you have frozen peas?"

"No. I'll get you an ice pack though."

"Can I ask why you have one?" He was such a minimalist, I was surprised he owned one.

"Cal," was his clipped reply as he turned away.

His one-word answer was enough. "Ahh. That makes sense."

"I assume you want to talk," Elliot said. I settled on the couch.

"Yes."

"And it won't make any difference if I tell you I don't want to." He brought over the ice pack wrapped it in a dishtowel.

I hissed as I settled it against my face, but as the cool gradually seeped through the towel and numbed my face, I began to appreciate it.

Thanks, Cal.

"If you don't want me to be here, ask me to go," I said quietly. "We're not going to get anywhere if you won't talk to me. But *I* definitely don't want to leave things the way they ended earlier."

Elliot didn't reply, but he did sit beside me with a weary-sounding sigh. I knew the feeling. I wanted to pull him into my arms and feel his heart beat against mine until we fell asleep. But mostly, I wanted to erase this night and start over.

"So, who punched you?" Elliot asked after a brief silence.

I shifted the ice pack a little so I could see Elliot better. "Dave."

"Makes sense."

"He's pretty pissed."

"Yeah, well." Elliot spread his hands.

"I know. I deserved it." My throat felt tight. "You should have stayed. My parents fought, and then Dave punched me. It was a hell of a show after you left."

"Are you blaming me for telling them the truth?" he asked tightly.

"What? No. God, Elliot, I don't blame you for *any* of this. It's me. It's all me. *I* fucked up. I set this all in motion, and now I've got to deal with the consequences."

He stood and began to pace. "I knew this was going to happen. Should have trusted my instincts. Should never have gotten involved with Cal in the first place." I hated the bitter note in his voice.

Does he regret everything then? Including being with me? I regretted a lot, but no part of me regretted getting close to Elliot.

No matter what happened after tonight, I'd hoard the memories of being with him. The touch of his fingers on my cheek and the words he'd whispered to me. Falling asleep in his arms. Being completely and utterly content for the first time in my life.

He was the most genuine person I'd ever known.

How could I ever regret that?

"I wish I knew what to say," I admitted. "I feel like no apology is ever going to be enough. How do I begin to make this right?"

He shot me a look I couldn't interpret before he walked over to the counter. He had his back to me, and I could see him fumbling with something. It wasn't until I heard the click-hiss of the lighter that I realized what he was doing.

When he turned back to face me, I could see a lit cigarette between his lips. "There is no fixing this, Chris," he muttered around it. I wanted to remind him he'd quit smoking, but this definitely wasn't the time to bring it up.

"Don't say that." My throat tightened again. "Please don't say that."

He shrugged. "It's true."

"It doesn't have to be!"

"This whole time, you put everyone else first. I came last. I can't do that." *Again* lay unspoken between us. I'd done the exact same thing

Cal had. I was just the last of a long string of people who'd let him down.

"I know." I looked down at my hands. *You have great hands. Artistically speaking.* I remembered him drawing them and wondered where the sketch was. "And I have to fix that. But tonight, I came here. I didn't go after Dave. I didn't go to my parents. I came *here.* For you."

"Too little too late, Chris."

My throat closed for a second, and I struggled to breathe through it. And I wondered would he throw away all the sketches he'd done of me? Would I see them in a gallery someday? Or would he pull them out occasionally, years down the road, and think bitterly of the Allen brothers and their lies?

"Too late *ever?*" I finally choked out.

"I don't know. I can't pick up where we left off." He gave me a solemn look. "Forget fixing shit with me. You need to learn to put yourself first. You're never going to be happy unless you do."

"You want me to be more selfish? I thought I'd already been *too* selfish."

"It's not the same. But until you know what the difference is, I can't be in a relationship with you."

I sat in my car outside of Elliot's apartment for a long time. I had no idea where to go or what to do. Everything had spiraled out of control.

Elliot had let me in. Trusted me. And I'd abused that trust.

I wanted to walk back up the stairs and pound on Elliot's door and *beg* for his forgiveness. The quiet click of the door behind me had felt so final. My throat felt raw with suppressed tears. What had he meant about needing to be more selfish? He was right that I had no idea what the difference was. His words didn't make any sense to me at all.

I glanced at the clock. It was late now. I should go to my apartment and try to sleep, but what was the point? If I closed my eyes, all I'd be able to see was his anguish. I'd hear his husky voice. I'd relieve every single mistake I'd made in the past five months.

Where could I go to make it stop?

Maybe instead of running away from it, I needed to sit with it a while. Find somewhere to go and think. But my apartment had no appeal. It wasn't home. The stark loft where Elliot lived was the closest thing I'd felt to home in a long time. Not because of how it looked or what it contained, but because of who was in it. *Elliot* was the only home I'd known. And I was no longer welcome there.

I started the car. There had to be somewhere I could go.

I drove aimlessly for a long time, searching for something. *Anything.*

Eventually, as I wove through the familiar streets of the Alameda suburb, the warm glow of a home drew me in like a proverbial beacon. I turned in the drive before I could second guess myself.

The large brick home belonged to Ed Washburn. I sat in front of his house for a while, wondering if I had the strength to reach out to him. I was terrified that once he learned the truth, he'd turn his back on me too.

Once I was outside of my car, it took me an equally long amount of time to work up the courage to knock on the door.

"Chris?" Ed looked perplexed as he squinted at me. Belatedly, it occurred to me what time of night it probably was. Ed looked neat and tidy in slacks and a button-down with the sleeves rolled up, so at least, it didn't appear I'd gotten him out of bed. "What on earth are you doing here? Have you been in a *fight?*"

"It's a very, very long story." A slightly unhinged laugh escaped me. "I don't want to interrupt your night but …"

"But nothing." He stepped back, ushering me into his home. "You know you're welcome here any time. What's going on?"

"I'm struggling right now," I admitted. "We both know it, and I'm not going to try to pretend otherwise. If you have the time …"

"You should know by now that I always have time for you, Chris," he said softly. "Come unburden yourself.

"Thank you." I hung my damp and tattered suit jacket on the rack by the door.

"Can I get you something? An ice pack, maybe?" He gave my jaw a pointed glance.

"No, I used one already."

"A drink then?"

Definitely not alcohol. My thoughts were grim. "Tea, maybe? If you have it. Coffee will make me too jittery."

"Of course. Go have a seat in the library, and I'll be in shortly."

Numbly, I walked to the room at the back of his home. The library was just as I remembered it. A cozy, traditional room, stuffed to the brim with books like any old library should be. It was Ed's retreat from the world. It felt like a safe haven to me right now.

I settled into a comfortable, leather armchair. A low fire burned in the fireplace, and I stared into it, hypnotized by the flickering flames. I was half-dozing by the time Ed walked in. I straightened in the chair, every inch of my body aching with weariness.

He set a tray on a small table between us, then took a seat in the matching chair.

"I'm sorry I couldn't be at the gallery tonight. If I hadn't already committed to the fundraising event ..." He shook his head. "You know I would have liked to see Cal's work."

"I know. It's just as well you missed it, anyway." I rubbed my hands over my face. "It was a mess."

"Tell me what's going on," he prompted as I poured tea from the pot into the two mugs.

It smelled fresh and sweet. Green tea, maybe. At least, it wasn't Earl Grey.

I handed him his mug, then settled back into a chair with a sigh, clutching my own. "I don't even know where to start."

"Start wherever you're comfortable."

"Thanks." My stomach churned with anxiety while I wrestled with what to say, and the scent of the tea filled the air. It was too hot to drink, but I cradled it anyway, appreciating the warmth and familiarity of the smooth ceramic decorated with the PMC logo.

I took a deep breath and blew it out. "Ed ... I ... there's something about Cal that I learned at his funeral."

He frowned and leaned in toward me. "What is it, Chris? You know you can tell me anything."

"I found out Cal had been dating a man," I blurted out.

Ed's eyebrows rose in surprise. "Your brother was bisexual?"

"Apparently. I had no idea."

"How did you learn this?"

I laughed hollowly. "After the funeral, I met the guy Cal had been dating, and he told me the truth."

Ed winced. "Your dissociative state that day is even more understandable."

I shrugged. "I'm not sure if the news caused it, or the fact that everything already felt unreal and that just tipped me over the edge, but I've been struggling since."

"Struggling how?"

Is there any aspect of my life I'm not struggling with? I bleakly wondered. "Questioning the relationship I had with my brother. Wondering where I went wrong that he didn't think he could talk to me about what he was going through. Feeling like I failed him. And that's just the beginning of it." Ed nodded but didn't speak, allowing me to continue. "I didn't know how to deal with the fact that I had this huge secret about Cal that no one else knew about. I didn't know if I should tell my parents or not." Now that the floodgates had been opened, the words came pouring out of me. "I didn't know if I was hurt because Cal was dead or I was pissed that he made me question my whole fucking life. I don't know who I am anymore. I've just been this cheap imitation of my brother and—"

"Chris." Ed's calm tone stopped my outpouring of words. "I want you to take a deep breath."

I realized I was shaking hard enough that the mug in my hand was in danger of spilling its contents onto my lap. I set it back on the tray and did as he suggested.

"Inhale through your mouth for four counts. Hold for seven. Exhale for eight," he continued. I followed his instructions, and after repeating it three more times, I felt my body relax a fraction and my heart rate slow. The technique was familiar to me. It was the slow, rhythmic breathing I often advised my patients to use. The irony was not lost on me, but I appreciated that Ed had snapped me out of the spiral of anxiety I'd been in.

"Okay. Better?"

I nodded, my throat too thick to speak.

"I want you to take things slowly, okay? Pay attention to your anxiety levels as we continue."

"Yeah, okay," I croaked.

"Now, I certainly understand why this caused so much turmoil for you." His careful, deliberate tone was soothing, and although I'd used the technique on my own patients countless times, it didn't diminish its effectiveness.

"It's just ... the information about Cal completely upended everything I knew about my brother."

"Why was your brother's sexual identity so important to you?"

I considered his question for a moment. "It's not ... it's not really his sexual identity that mattered," I said slowly. "It's that he'd hid it from us. I couldn't stop thinking about my parents, and I wondered how in the hell I could tell them about this when they were already hurting so badly.

"There's more too. I ..." I had to take a few slow, deep breaths before I could continue. "I slept with Elliot the night of Cal's funeral. I got drunk out of my mind, and I hooked up with him. I felt so ashamed but ..."

"Who is Elliot?"

I wet my lips. "Cal's boyfriend."

Ed had perfected his expression of calm understanding, but even he couldn't hide the fleeting look of shock. "I see."

"I know."

"Have you continued this relationship with Elliot?"

"It's ... complicated."

"Can you please elaborate on that?"

"Well, one of Elliot's other revelations was that Cal had an apartment none of us knew about. He was living there when he wasn't at Elliot's or my parents'." I filled Ed in about Cal's place and his passion for homoerotic photography. "He had this whole secret life we didn't know about. And Elliot helped me make sense of it all. We cleaned out the apartment and organized Cal's photos. It's weird, but we became ... friends."

"Why is that so weird?"

I shrugged. "Because of how it started, I guess. He couldn't stand me. He resented all of us for making Cal feel like he had to stay closeted."

Ed frowned at me. "Cal made that choice himself. You can't be held responsible for his decision."

"I know." I rubbed the back of my neck. "Or at least, I know that intellectually. And I think Elliot and I made peace about that."

"Have you and Elliot continued the sexual relationship?"

I shrugged. "We didn't for a long time. It was only after Hazel—" I couldn't continue.

"Elliot was the friend you turned to?"

"Yes." I stared out the window, watching headlights sweep across the backyard. A neighbor coming home. The windows were speckled, and I realized it had started raining again. "But it wasn't …"

"Wasn't what, Chris?"

"It wasn't about the sex. Elliot was the only person who understood what I struggled with."

"Both of you have been carrying a large secret for a while. It's understandable that you would feel a connection to him because of it."

"But what if—" I shook my head. "What if that wasn't the only reason? What if … what if we're good for each other?"

"Is that so impossible?"

"I don't know. It felt crazy. And then I often wondered if—if I only felt that way because I missed Cal. What if I was using Elliot to hold onto my brother?"

"Were you?"

"I don't think so. I wanted to believe I wasn't, but I had doubts sometimes. And sometimes, I worried that Elliot was confusing me with Cal."

"Perhaps he did, at least initially." Ed hummed thoughtfully as he seemed to consider the idea. "I suppose, on the surface, there are quite a few similarities between you and your brother. Physically, you're more alike than you are different. But temperament?"

I laughed mirthlessly. "We couldn't be more different. I know there's no comparison there."

"Why does that sound like you're putting yourself down?"

I shrugged. "Everyone knows I'm nowhere near as adventurous as Cal. Hell, I'm not even as nice a person. I don't know I would have stopped for that woman who had a flat tire. I'm sure Cal never thought twice about it."

Of course, it had gotten him killed.

"I know you, Chris, you're a kind, loyal friend and—"

"Am I?" I cut him off. "I slept with my brother's boyfriend the night of his fucking funeral. That's neither kind nor loyal."

"In hindsight, it may have been a poor decision. But we don't always think clearly when we're in the midst of grief. You know that."

I looked up at the ceiling. "Sure, but it doesn't exactly reassure me that I'm not as much of an asshole as I think I am."

"Chris, your brother is dead. You have to let go of your fears about hurting him. I know you want to be loyal to his memory, but I can't believe your brother would begrudge you happiness."

I wanted to believe Ed, but all I could hear was Dave's voice ringing in my ears. It felt like my conscience speaking my fears aloud.

"So, you and Elliot began seeing each other after Hazel's death. What happened after that?"

I told him about how good it was at first. And then the growing friction between us. About Elliot needing me to come clean to my family. About my father's drinking and my mother's affair. About the huge disaster at Cal's show tonight that ended with Elliot walking off and Dave punching me. Then going to Elliot and being rejected. "I've lost everyone and everything, and I don't even know who I am anymore." My tone was anguished.

"To be frank, I think Elliot has a point, Chris. What is it you want? You need to figure that out before you do anything else. I'm not saying you'll be able to fix things with Elliot. It sounds like he has some of his own demons to wrestle with. But you expressed unhappiness with the current direction your life is heading. I think perhaps it's time you consider what you want for your future. I'm not suggesting you ignore the impact your decision could have on your family and those around you, but ignoring your own wants and needs isn't the solution either. At times, you must put yourself first."

"Elliot said that to me tonight," I said slowly. "But I didn't quite understand it."

"Chris, you've spent your whole life taking care of Cal. Taking care of your family. Taking care of your patients. Have you taken care of yourself?"

"I've tried." I'd worked out regularly, eaten healthfully, and yet, I knew that wasn't what Ed meant. Or it was only a part of it anyway. "I really don't know who I am anymore," I repeated.

I'd dated shitty men like Alec in the hopes of building the future I'd dreamed of. But they'd been hollow imitations of what I needed. Men who'd said the right thing but never followed through. Men who'd told me one thing and done the other. I'd let their needs supersede mine and wondered why I was miserable. And then I'd just … stopped. Turned off that part of myself and thrown myself into work.

Cal had been out living life, and I'd been … stagnant. My brother had been far from perfect. He and I had both made decisions that had hurt the people around us. But at least, he'd had the courage to really live.

I'd been going through the motions. Dead inside.

I wanted to *live*.

But knowing that wasn't enough.

I knew how I wanted to feel, but I had no idea how to make it happen.

"I don't have a clue what it is I want anymore," I said softly. "Other than for things to make sense again."

"Take some time to think. You don't have to have all the answers today or tomorrow."

But I wanted them so badly. I exhaled heavily. "I will."

"Good."

"Being with Elliot was probably the most reckless thing I've ever done," I admitted. "But it—it felt so right."

Ed leaned forward again. "Chris, I want you to consider taking an extended leave from work."

"What?"

"I know how passionate you are about what we do, but you're in no shape to take care of yourself, much less your patients right now. I strongly recommend taking some time for yourself to get your life back on track."

And now I've lost my career, I thought with a sense of resigned numbness. It seemed fitting. He was giving me a chance to do it voluntarily, but I knew if I didn't go through with it, he'd likely force my hand.

But Ed had a point. I was a mess.

And our patients had to come first.

"You will be welcome to come back as soon as you're feeling up to it, you know that. I just want to make sure you're in a healthy place before you do."

"I don't know," I repeated, but my protests were weakening.

Ed frowned. "Chris, if you were me, what would you say?"

"That I need to put myself first."

"And if you were a patient, what would you say?"

"That I need to put myself first."

He gave me a pointed look. "And are you an effective doctor when you're feeling this way?"

I shook my head.

His palm was warm as he clasped my forearm and squeezed. "I'm just trying to look out for you."

"I know you are, and I appreciate it."

"You don't have to make a decision about that tonight, but I want you to think about getting some professional help too."

I nodded. My mind was whirling with everything that had happened in the last few hours.

"Now, what would you say if I offered to make up the bed in the guest room for you?"

Tears pricked my eyes. I was so damn grateful for Ed. The idea of going back to my lonely apartment was intolerable. "I'd say I appreciate it."

A faint smile broke through the worry on Ed's face. "That's what I hoped to hear. You'll be okay, son. It's just going to take some time."

I stood with a weary groan. "Thank you."

"You go on upstairs, and I'll be there shortly with extra blankets and a toothbrush."

I slowly walked toward the door, but halfway there, I turned back. "Can I ask you for one thing, Ed?"

"Of course. What is it?"

"Will you check on my parents tomorrow?" I cleared my throat. "I know I need to deal with my shit right now, but I need to know someone is looking out for them in the meantime. They're in a bad place."

Ed's smile was a touch sad. "I will. I'd already planned to."

"Thank you," I repeated.

Elliot, Ed, they were both right. I needed to focus on myself now. My priorities needed to shift. But that didn't mean I could easily forget about my family. It simply wasn't in me.

That I was sure of.

Chapter Twenty-Seven

I tumbled onto the comfortable mattress in Ed's guest room and slept like the dead. Not because my mind was clear or I felt better, but because I simply had no energy left. Any reserves were gone. I slept without dreaming or even thoughts of Elliot.

But it worked.

In the morning, I woke up well rested. I lay in bed for a few minutes and stared up at the ceiling. I recognized that I couldn't rely on anyone for what I needed anymore. It was time I grew up and figured out who I was *without* my brother.

I didn't want to be Cal's pale imitation or his replacement with Elliot.

If Elliot and I had chance of a future—and I had no idea if we did— it needed to be because I wanted him. Not because we were both chasing my brother's ghost but because what was between us was too compelling to ignore.

I had to say goodbye to Cal and the hold he had over my life.

The thought didn't bring the crushing grief and fear I expected. Instead, it brought the quiet sense of purposefulness I'd been searching for.

"I love you, brother," I said aloud. "And I have got to figure out how to let you go."

I thanked Ed, declined his offer to make me breakfast, told him I'd be taking an extended amount of time off, and drove straight to my apartment. My phone was dead, so I plugged it in while I packed. I had no missed calls or messages.

So I put what I'd need in a suitcase, filled a cooler with food, grabbed Cal's keys, old guitar, and surfboard, then went straight to my parents' house.

My mother's car was gone. My father's was there; although I searched the house, it was empty. A part of me half-expected to find him passed out—or dead—in his study or on the floor in a pool of his own vomit somewhere. My footsteps echoed off the wooden floorboards as I walked through every room. But the house was pristine. Like neither of them had been home last night at all.

I stood in the entryway to my childhood home, wrestling with the instinct to do *something*. I wanted to tear Portland apart searching for my parents. The desperate need to *help* rose to the surface, but I pushed it away. It wasn't my place to fix things for them anymore. Maybe it never had been.

They'd never explicitly asked me to be the fixer in the family. No one had deliberately told me I was the only one who could hold things together, and yet, in so many more subtle and unspoken ways, that was exactly what had happened. What I'd become.

My parents' choices—along with my own—had helped create the roles all four of us had fallen into. I didn't blame them. They'd been flawed and imperfect, but they'd done the best they could. Looking back, I could see how every interaction we'd had as a family over the years had shaped where we were now though. And if I wanted to move forward, I had to break free of that role. I had to do better. The first step was acknowledging that they were adults. If they came to me for help, of course I'd give it to them. But unless they *asked* me to, it was time I stepped back.

I'd begun to understand what Elliot had meant about needing to be more selfish. I couldn't hold everyone together by sheer force of will. And was I really helping anyone if I tried? We all needed to fall apart. To break. And, hopefully, to rebuild ourselves. It was time I allowed it to happen.

I sat at the dining room table and wrote out a letter to my parents. I apologized for what I'd done, for all the secrets and lies, and for my share of the responsibility in where we were now. And acknowledged that the rest of it was in their hands. I ended with letting them know I was taking some time to deal with my grief, and I hoped they would do the same.

I loaded Cal's Mustang with my belongings, drove through Portland, merged onto the I-5, and headed south.

To La Jolla.

It was the last place my brother and I had visited together, and it was time to lay Cal to rest.

Snippets of memory flashed in front of my eyes as I drove. I remembered Cal in the driver's seat, relaxed and carefree. Laughing. Always laughing. I missed his laughter the most.

I remembered him singing along to some awful playlist he'd put together of every song he could find that had a reference to California. Now, I found it on my phone and began to play it, only to realize that I hated it. I'd hated it then. The songs were terrible and yet I'd saved it.

"I'm still doing it, aren't I?" I muttered to myself.

It was like I had no idea how to exist without my brother. This trip was about following the path Cal and I had taken before. I wanted to honor those memories, but this time, I needed to do it my own way. I needed to do that with everything in my life. Hold onto what worked for me and do away with the rest.

I had to find what made me happy. Not Cal. Not my parents. Not even Elliot.

I had a career I loved. I was healthy and—luck willing—had a long life ahead of me. I hoped Elliot could be a part of that future. But there was still so much I didn't know about myself and about what other things I needed to create a meaningful life for myself.

"Thanks for the tunes, Cal, but no more Beach Boys and Katy Perry for me." With a swipe of my finger, I closed the music app.

I didn't delete the playlist—the last thing I wanted to do was erase Cal from my life—but what I needed to do going forward was make conscious choices for myself that would lead me toward the future I wanted.

I rolled the window down and let the wind be my soundtrack.

I stopped when I needed to. I ate when my body told me to. And I missed my brother the whole time. I sat with his memory, and I heard his laughter until I laughed too, and I felt like my heart would burst with it. The sadness, the love, the anger, the joy, all wrapped up together into an enormous flood of emotions.

Had I let myself grieve before? Or had I been trying so hard to manage it that I'd never let myself experience it at all? I'd tried to hold everyone together, yet I'd let the pieces of myself scatter until I wasn't sure I could find them again.

I'd found solace in Elliot. And I still believed that he was the best thing that had ever come into my life. He'd helped me so much, but I could see now that the timing had been all wrong.

I'd been too broken for anyone else to make me whole again.

I knew Elliot's strength had helped me get to this point, however, and I hoped—so desperately—that my journey forward wouldn't be solitary. I wanted my family and Ed, and hopefully Dave, to be a part of my life.

More than anything, I wanted Elliot by my side. I just had to do a little work on my own before I was ready to be the man he deserved.

I was nowhere near as fatigued as I should have been when I approached the hilly, seaside community near San Diego. I'd driven all day and through the night. The red sun was just beginning to peek through the gray morning clouds as I cruised through the city and came to a spot overlooking the Pacific. Surrounded on three sides by the sea, La Jolla was a mix of rocky coastline and sandy beaches that stretched for seven miles, and it rightly deserved its nickname of the jewel by the sea.

Based on memory alone, I navigated to my favorite spot: La Jolla Cove.

My eyes felt gritty and my bones creaked as I swung open the door of the Mustang. I was sore and stiff as I stepped out of the car, but I felt energized too. Like I'd broken free of something that had been trapping me for a long time.

It was a five-minute walk from the parking area to the cove itself, and it felt good to stretch my legs. I paused at the top of the bluffs, drinking in the sight in front of me. Even in the dim, early morning light, the view of the ocean was stunning. I closed my eyes and pulled the salty air in deep for a few breaths. The wind whipped at my hair and fluttered the hem of my jacket.

I slowly walked down the steps to the sandy beach below. It was a narrow strip even at low tide and the tide looked quite high now, although I wasn't sure if it was coming in or out. At this hour, the beach was deserted. A lone photographer stood a distance away on the rocky cliffs, facing out toward the ocean. He made me think about Cal and Elliot and new beginnings.

With a jolt, I remembered why I'd come here the last time. Cal had brought me to help me get over the breakup with Alec. Funny, I hadn't thought about that until now.

Cal hadn't asked me where I'd wanted to go; he'd *told* me where we were going. And I hadn't argued. I'd loved the trip though. Loved the drive down the Pacific Coast and the little beach cottage we'd rented and the fresh seafood we'd eaten. I'd loved the snorkeling and the sea turtles and the nights sitting out under the stars, sipping beer and talking.

I'd loved his bad jokes and his terrible taste in music, and the fact that he hadn't let me stay home and mope.

I'd loved my brother.

But he'd been selfish sometimes.

He'd lived his life recklessly. Carelessly. With little thought for the future and even less concern about how his decisions impacted someone else. His secrets had ultimately hurt everyone in our lives. His best friend. Our parents. Elliot. Cal had meant well, but he'd made mistakes, and I finally understood how both of those things could be true.

He was imperfect and wonderful all at once.

I didn't want to be Cal anymore. Or even C.J.

I wanted to start fresh.

And as the wind tugged at my clothes and I breathed in the clean, salty air, I knew I'd come to the right place to let go of the past and figure out what came next.

"Hear of any turtles being spotted lately?" I asked a vendor at the open-air market. I'd hunted down a place to stay, but I had some time to kill before I could check in.

"Sea turtles? Can't say that I have." He handed my change back
A man nearby spoke up. "I have. Jim said he spotted some
yesterday, in fact. If you want to catch them, you'll have to make it
quick. They usually only stay a few days unless they find something
particularly tasty to munch on."

"Guess I better get out there soon then," I said. "Thanks for the
tip." I raised the fish taco in thanks. It was a strange choice for
breakfast, but I'd enjoyed them immensely the last time I'd been
here. I wandered away, thinking about my plans for the day.

I'd brought my snorkeling gear, but I didn't want to go with a tour,
and I wasn't sure it was the smartest thing to go out alone when I
hadn't slept in more than twenty-four hours. The water of the cove
was colder than most beaches in the area, and the swells that came
in off the open ocean were strong. Even with lifeguards on duty, I
didn't think it was worth it. I wanted to take some risks, not kill
myself. But I'd get out first thing tomorrow and hope like hell that I
didn't miss the turtles. For Hazel.

I spent the afternoon getting settled into the inn. I'd been lucky to
snag one of their small guest houses. I'd paid through the nose for
it, but it had an ocean view, and I was looking forward to some
peace and quiet.

After I napped and showered, I walked to a nearby restaurant for
dinner. I watched the people at the tables around me while I ate.
Watching the families and couples interact made me miss the people
in my life. I'd never gone on vacation totally alone before. The
closest I'd come was work conferences, and those had been so
structured and filled with social events I hadn't had time to think
about being by myself. Now, it was strange not having someone to
share all the experiences with, but it was good too. I didn't have to

consider anyone else. I could do what I wanted, when I wanted. Looking back, had I ever experienced that before? Almost every decision I'd made had been through the lens of how it would impact my future career, my family, or my partner. But here I was, over a thousand miles away, and in the past twenty-four hours, every decision I'd made had been about *me*.

Surprisingly, I felt less lonely than I had in years.

The morning dawned bright and clear, and after breakfast, I headed straight for La Jolla Cove again.

As I wrestled my wetsuit on, I thought of the photo of Cal at the beach near Port Orford. The one Elliot had taken, and I stilled. Even if I worked through all my baggage and Elliot forgave me, would we ever reach a point where my brother's ghost didn't haunt us? There would always be memories popping up to surprise us. It wouldn't be easy. But was it worth it?

"Do you need some help with that, man?"

A good-looking guy with sun-streaked blond hair smiled at me, and I realized I was standing in the middle of the changing area with the wetsuit half on.

"No, I think I've got it," I said as I rolled my shoulders back and dipped my hand into the sleeve. "Thanks though."

"Sure." A tiny flash of heat filled his eyes as he turned away. It made me smile. Cal had always teased me about stuff like that. Half of the time, I was oblivious to guys hitting on me. They'd hit on him too, and I'd retaliated by teasing him that he had a knack for making people's gaydar go on the fritz.

But I guess I'd been a little off base with that joke. I really had been far too black and white about people's sexualities. Dave, my brother ... they were gray through and through. And that was okay. Why had I been so convinced that my opinion on it mattered at all?

The tide was receding as I waded into the cove, my fins slapping on the packed sand. The lifeguard nodded at me, and I waved. The sky was heart-stoppingly blue, and the clouds that lazily drifted by were few and far between. Even with the heavy neoprene suit, the water was cold, but Cal and I had snorkeled closer to Portland where the Pacific temps were even icier. My wetsuit was rated for the chilly water, and I knew once I began swimming, I'd be fine.

I spat on my mask and rubbed the spit in. As gross as it was, it was the surest way to prevent the mask from fogging. I could suddenly hear Elliot's voice, *Hope you're not a germaphobe or something from working in the hospital.*

No, Elliot, I'm not, I thought as I settled it onto my face, missing his skin against mine.

The sunshine and clear waters revealed the bright colors of the La Jolla shore. Golden sands made way for reefs as I swam away from the shoreline. The blues and greens of the water were so vivid they made my eyes hurt as I slowly acclimated to breathing through the snorkel again. It had been a while.

Small flashes of silver alerted me to the presence of fish, and I followed the school for a minute. I swam parallel to the shore until I was in the most sheltered area of the cove, protected by a rocky outcropping. The farther in I went, the more sea life appeared. I catalogued it all in my head, wishing I could tell Hazel about it. I could picture her face lighting up, her eyes sparkling with excitement as I described the sea stars and anemones and the brightly colored fish. I could almost hear her voice saying, *I am* so *jealous.*

I thought sorrowfully of all she had missed out on in the past and all she would miss out on in the future. I made a promise to myself that I wouldn't waste the time I'd been given. Cal was gone and so was Hazel. I couldn't live for them. But I could wring out every joyous moment from the life I had.

I snorkeled peacefully for a while—popping my head up periodically to be sure I hadn't lost my orientation—glad I'd gotten out early enough to avoid most of the tours. When my legs began to cramp a little from the weight of the fins, I rolled onto my back. No matter how much I worked my legs at the gym, swimming with the fins on made me discover several rarely-used muscles that now screamed in protest. I lifted the mask and floated for a little while, staring up at the sky and the seabirds whirling overhead. I hadn't seen a glimpse of a sea turtle yet, and I was disappointed. I'd been desperately hoping to see one. This didn't have to be my last day out here though. I certainly wasn't moving to La Jolla or anything, but I was in no hurry to return to Portland yet either.

The sea turtles weren't a permanent fixture in the area, but there might be time to see them again. I just had to be patient.

I flipped onto my stomach, settled my mask into my face, cleared my snorkel, and began to leisurely make my way through the rocky outcroppings and back to the shore. About halfway there, a large shadow appeared on the reef below me. I could see a huge body and the shape of flippers. I held my breath as I slowly turned my head. I was prepared for it to be a sea lion, swimming close, but the large curved shell and small head were unmistakable.

Thank you, I thought with a rush of relief, but I wasn't sure if I was thanking the turtle or the universe. I held still for a long time as it slowly swam around me. Occasionally, it dipped down to munch on eelgrass.

I shadowed the turtle for a while, trying not to crowd it. Several more of its kind swam a few yards away, but this was by far the largest. At least as big as the ones I'd seen here before, if not bigger. I wondered if it was one Cal and I had swum with before. The idea made me smile. *Wish you'd been here to see it again, brother.* But it was a brief, bittersweet feeling that rippled over me instead of a heavy wave of grief.

In the distance, a group of kayaks approached. I knew it was probably one of the tour groups, and their noise would make the sea turtles retreat to quieter waters. Not wanting to disturb the one near me, I let my hand float through the water between us. Near, but not quite touching. For a minute, we swam parallel, and then it dipped down, skimming by me close enough that my fingers trailed across its olive-green shell. With a flick of its fins, it was gone.

Thank you. I know someone who would have liked to have met you. If any justice existed in the universe, there *was* something after death. Maybe somewhere, some day, Hazel would get her wish.

Chapter Twenty-Eight

A week slipped by before I knew it as I hiked in the Torrey Pines Natural Reserve and kayaked to the sea cliffs. I explored nearby museums and listened to music on the gloomier days. It always surprised people that southern California was ever overcast and cool, but late spring and early summer could be remarkably similar to Portland.

I skipped the beer festival and golf—things Cal would have loved—and some days, I stayed closer to the inn when I needed the quiet time to think. I poked my head into art galleries and purchased a few small pieces that appealed to me, but none of them held the power Elliot's work did. I spent nearly every pleasant evening sitting on the small deck outside my guest house, watching the sun slip below the horizon while I played the guitar. Day by day, it grew a little easier.

I was solitary but not lonely, even though the only contact I had with anyone from home was an occasional message from Ed and photos I sent to Elliot.

Thoughts of him surfaced frequently. I missed him. Not with the clawing desperation I'd felt before, like I'd been using him to fill the hole within me, but because there were so many experiences I was eager to share. So I took pictures of things I saw and sent them to him. A sunset. Birds' tracks in the wet sand. Scattered shells washed up on the shore. My guitar. Little things.

No response came. I wondered if Elliot stared at them, missing me too. Or maybe he deleted them, annoyed that I wouldn't leave him alone. But he hadn't blocked me, and I held on to that. Not like a lifeline but like a faint thread that could lead me back to him when I was ready.

I missed his soft laughter and the quiet light in his eyes. I missed the way he listened to me—really listened—and the touch of his skin. I missed the way he took in the world around him. I missed him sketching me and seeing myself through his eyes. I missed more about him than I could ever put into words. But I'd found joy in the world around me again.

One overcast morning, I grabbed my wetsuit and Cal's surfboard. I felt a flutter of nerves as I walked along the sands of La Jolla Shores Beach and continued farther to Black's Beach. The Shores had reliable steady swells. Black's Beach had better beach breaks and was less predictable. I welcomed the challenge. I was ready for it.

When I reached the spot, I climbed onto the board and paddled out over the waves racing toward the shore.

Watch out for me, Cal. I aimed the board, then carefully shifted into a crouch. I closed my eyes briefly, tuning in to the surge of the ocean under me until I could feel its rhythm in my bones. I stood on shaky legs, my muscles burning with the exertion. It had been too long. But I embraced it, pushing myself to lean in as the wave crested. I laughed, loudly and freely as it surged and broke, and the stomach churning, swooping feeling of flying swept over me.

I *loved* this.

Not because Cal had, not because I was trying to *be* him, but because it made me light and free. The rush of helplessness in the face of the powerful waves didn't make me feel small or insignificant. Instead, I felt alive.

For another week, I slept and I surfed and I played guitar until I felt something in my chest break loose. The tight ball of grief and loss melted away in the bright sunshine and clear waters. And in its place was a quiet stillness that left me breathless.

When it was completely gone, I realized how long I'd been carrying all of that with me. Far longer than the almost six months it had been since Cal's death.

Longer than when I'd found Alec fucking someone else. Longer even than when I'd met him. I didn't know when it had begun growing. Maybe it had been there since I was child. Since my father's drinking began. When I grew up too fast. When I took on the role of looking out for my family. When I learned to put myself last so everyone else could be happy.

That night, I took my guitar and walked down to the beach. I felt like my time there was drawing to a close. I'd come to get away. To discover myself again. And I felt like I'd done that. I'd said goodbye to Hazel. There were just two things left: laying Cal to rest and deciding what came next for me.

It was well after sunset, and the beach was nearly empty. The few people who were there paid me no mind as I spread a towel out on a strip of dry sand. I was still close enough to hear the roar of the surf and see the white-topped waves in the moonlight.

I set the guitar next to me and stared out over the water at the stars that twinkled through the clouds and haze of light pollution. As I sat there, the faint glimmer of connection I'd felt to Cal strengthened and grew.

"There you are, brother," I whispered. I remembered searching for this feeling at the cemetery where he was buried. Maybe not being able to feel him at the cemetery hadn't been so much lack of faith as lack of connection.

Here in one of our favorite places, I could finally *feel* Cal again. If I pretended hard enough, I could believe he was sitting beside me. I spoke aloud like he was.

"I wish I could talk to you, Cal. I need your help. That letter you wrote me … it made a lot of things more confusing, not less. So thanks for that. Asshole." I laughed softly. But it wasn't filled with bitterness anymore. "I don't know what to do about Elliot. God, Cal, I know why you were in love with him. He's … he's incredible. But I've spent months feeling completely fucked up about him. About my relationship with him, about my relationship with you. I don't know if what happened at the gallery was a sign I'm supposed to fix my shit and fight for Elliot or if I'm supposed to walk away. I loved you so fucking much, brother, but you left a hell of a mess behind." The familiar thickness in my throat returned. "This time I'm not here to clean it up. I'm here to figure out what to do about my messes. This time, I need you to help *me*."

I closed my eyes and breathed deep. "Please, Cal, show me what to do. It sounds crazy, but I need a sign. Something. *Anything.*"

The waves continued to pound against the shore, and I heard the cry of a lone sea bird.

I'd lost my brother. Hazel. My parents. My friends. And Elliot.

All my worst fears had come true.

I had no one left.

And yet, I was still alive. It had hurt. God, it hurt like hell, but I had survived it.

I still felt a little lost, yes, but I could see the gleam of brightness in the distance. Leading me back to Portland. Back to my life there. Back to Elliot.

"Can you forgive me, Cal?" I asked the empty air. "Or am I just fooling myself? Am I trying to rationalize this? I don't know anymore. Help me," I pleaded.

"So you've been poaching my boyfriend, huh?" Cal's voice rang out, as clear as if he were truly there. I could hear the laughter in his voice, and it held no malice. My heart burned with the joy of hearing him again. "Why him, Chris?"

"I don't know. I never meant for it to happen."

"You're not usually the reckless one, brother."

"Somebody's gotta pick up the slack now that you're gone," I joked.

"True, true. Well, don't fuck it up with Elliot. I did enough of that."

"I think I already did. But I want to fix it."

"So fix it. You're good at that."

"Not as good as I thought," I admitted. "I have a lot to learn still."

"If anyone can do it, it's you."

"Shouldn't you be jealous and angry with me?"

"I'm dead, brother. What is there to be angry or jealous about? It's all just petty bullshit. You know that."

"I never wanted to hurt you."

"The dead don't hurt either."

"You loved Elliot," I argued.

"I did. And he loved me. But I fucked up a lot, and our time was coming to an end. Whether or not that car hit me, we were nearly over. You know that's true. I told you in my letter."

"You did. But for the longest time, this felt wrong. Like I was holding on to him just to hold on to your memory. And by the time I was sure there was more, I'd dug myself in so deep with the lies I didn't know how to get out."

"You did make a mess of things."

"Hey," I protested. "That wasn't all me. I was buried under a metric ton of your shit."

"Sorry about that."

"You should be. Asshole."

"That's it, brother. Keep fighting. I don't want to hear this woe is me shit anymore. You fight for yourself. If you love Elliot, you fight for him."

"I do love him. I haven't told him that yet."

"It seems to me like that's a good place to start. But what do I know?"

"You're okay with it then?"

"You really need to hear me say it, don't you?"

"I guess I do." A lump rose in my throat.

"If you need my permission, you've got it, C.J. But do you know what question you haven't asked yourself?"

"No. What?"

"Will you make Elliot happy?"

I thought for a moment, then finally admitted the truth that had been floating in my head for a while. "I desperately want to try."

"Then go for it, man. But be good to him. He deserves it."

And then Cal's voice was gone, like a light suddenly winking out. I sat there, stunned. It had seemed so real. But what was *real*, anyway? It had seemed tangible enough to me, but whether it was a desperate hallucination brought on by how badly I needed his approval or something else, it didn't matter. It had worked. I'd gotten what I needed.

The internal struggle was gone, replaced by a quiet peace that settled over me like a heavy blanket, warming my wind-cooled skin.

I brushed away the particles of sand clinging to my hands, then reached for the guitar.

I strummed it for a long time, feeling the music deep within me. I wasn't great. I probably never would be. But it brought me joy. And that was enough. And when my mind was quiet and my heart was light, I set the guitar aside, pulled out my phone, and brought up Elliot's number. I didn't hesitate to hit dial. The phone stopped ringing, and it was nearly silent except for the sound of Elliot's light, soft breathing, barely discernable over the crash of the waves.

But I knew he was there.

I put it on speakerphone and rested it on my knee. "I'm sorry," I said as I picked up the guitar again. "I'm sorry I hurt you, Elliot. I don't want you to say anything. There's nothing you need to say. You were right. I made a lot of mistakes. I lived in my brother's shadow. I hurt you. There's nothing I can say to undo that.

"Whether you're willing to forgive me or not, I'll do better in the future. I'll be better. For me. Because I deserve it. I don't want to live with secrets or lies. I don't want to be half-alive anymore. I deserve better."

I began to strum the guitar softly. Ideas had been floating through my head for days, and I let them form and spoke them aloud. It wasn't a song exactly. I was no singer, but that was okay. I just needed Elliot to hear them. My voice was hushed at first. A little halting.

"I've tasted lightning.

An effervescent burn on my skin.

Your hands, your voice, *you*.

Moments, snippets, fragments of memory. So real they feel like dreams.

Gone, leaving raw nerves. Silvery white scars like ghosts in my chest.

Slipped through my fingers before I realized I needed to grasp.

Mistakes, regrets, what ifs.

Was it ever meant to be captured?

But I've tasted it, and I can never go back …"

My fingers stilled and I heard nothing but the crash of the waves for endless heartbeats. And then … hope.

"Chris?" Elliot's voice broke a little on my name. "Come home. Please, come home."

Chapter Twenty-Nine

I flew up the I-5 like the demons I'd left behind were chasing me, but the drive back to Portland felt interminable. Twice as long as the drive south.

After Elliot's plea for me to return, we'd said little else. I'd told him I was on my way, and his one-word response of "good" was enough. I hastily packed my things, checked out, and hit the road.

My skin prickled with anticipation as I imagined touching Elliot again. The miles disappeared, but the need to be with him only grew.

I pulled into the parking lot next to his building and was out of the car as I fast as I could get the door open. I barely took the time to lock it before I bolted for the entrance. My hands were shaking when I knocked on his door, but he opened it almost immediately.

My gaze drank him in for just a few split seconds before I had him in my arms. I kissed him with a ferocity I'd never felt before, chasing the sweet vanilla tea scent of his mouth with my tongue.

We said nothing. There would be time to talk later. Time for apologies and plans and healing the hurts. But for now, there was only reconnection. His hands said everything as they splayed on my back, pulling me tighter against his body. I told him I'd missed him as I pushed him up against the door of his apartment. It was perfect and right and not enough.

I peeled off his black T-shirt to taste his skin. He slid his hands under my shirt and dug his blunt nails into my shoulders when I bit down. The sound he made set my body on fire. Against my thigh, his cock was hard through his jeans, and I pulled back just far enough to rub my palm against it. I needed to feel it in me, and I dropped to my knees, desperate to taste him. My hands were trembling as I struggled with the zipper of his jeans and pushed them down his narrow thighs.

I pressed my cheek to his leg for a moment and rubbed, enjoying the coarse rasp of my stubble against his much-softer leg hair. When I took his cock in my mouth, he let out a low, broken moan. He settled his hands on my hair, and as I began to move, he used them to guide me. The scent of his body made my head swim, and I felt half-delirious at the energy that zinged between us. I moaned around his cock and felt his grip on my skull tighten. I worked him over, plunging my head down to engulf him, nearly choking myself before I backed off. Tension coursed through his body, and his ragged panting egged me on.

I wanted to taste him, feel him flowing down my throat. I needed a part of him inside of me so badly I couldn't think straight. But he stilled my movements with the pressure of his hands, and I pulled away. I looked up at him, frozen as our gazes met. His hair was a wild tangle of dark curls, and the sculpted lines of his cheekbones were softened by the contrast of his heavy-lidded gaze.

His eyes held so much love it made me gasp.

I stood then, pressing him against the door once more to kiss him deeply. His little growl of need spurred me into action. We stripped, trying to help each other and hindering our movements more in our haste to get naked. I had a flash of memory of the first time we'd done this, drunk and desperate. The frantic desperation now was the same, but everything else had changed.

And then we were on the bed, and there was only the heat of his skin and the connection between us. We rolled together, clutching at each other's skin in an attempt to get closer. His mouth was on my neck, licking and biting, and I grasped his hair hard enough to make him gasp. The low rumble in his chest in response made me do it again. The half-drugged look he shot me through his lashes made my cock pulse with need.

Elliot shoved me onto my back, and I ran my hands up the lean, sinewy muscles of his arms. Our legs tangled together, and the rough-soft slide of his leg hair against mine wasn't enough. I needed so much more. He moved fluidly over me. The flex of his abs against my erection made me gasp, and I gripped his ass to pull him closer as we kissed.

He slipped a hand between my parted thighs to cup my balls. My eyes rolled back in my head. My testicles felt heavy and swollen with a need to come. The graze of his finger a few inches below that made a shudder work its way down my spine. I gasped out a garbled sound of approval, too lost in the feeling to articulate words. It was apparently clear enough to Elliot, though, because the heat of his body disappeared from mine, and a minute later, I heard the sound of lube being opened.

He knelt beside my hip, and I arched into his touch, seeking out the slick probe of his finger. I expected him to prep me quickly, but he took his time, drawing out the pleasure until I ached and thrust back on his slippery fingers. The frantic desperation had become slower yet somehow more intense. With one hand on my chest, he pressed me back down on the bed and drove his fingers in deeper with the other. I moaned, low and deep in my throat, and saw the answering flicker of heat in his eyes.

His touch disappeared just long enough for him to roll on a condom, and he pushed me onto my side. I held my breath when his cock pushed against my entrance, insistent and unstoppable.

I closed my eyes as he gripped my hip and pushed forward. He didn't pause or retreat, just pushed with a steady, inexorable pressure. He would fill me because he had to. Because I didn't want to draw another breath without him inside me; my heart didn't want to beat without him completing me.

This was right, this was what I needed. The man inside me was what every molecule in my body cried out for. I *knew* him on a level far more visceral than any I'd ever felt before. I clenched my eyes more tightly closed, pushing back against him, urging him to move.

When he pulled back, I felt my chest tighten at the slow, dragging pleasure of his cock finally moving inside me.

His quiet moan in my ear was filled with so much helpless need it sent a shudder through my body.

I was wordless, incoherent, and all I could manage was a low sound in response. Elliot slid a palm up over my ribs until it settled against my sternum, pressing me back against him. I reached behind me, gripping his shoulder to brace myself as he fucked me deeply, deliberately wringing every last ounce of pleasure from me. I hardly recognized the desperate noises I made.

When I felt like I'd lose my mind and couldn't take another second of it, he slid his hand down to wrap around my hip, digging his fingers in so hard I knew they would leave bruises. I welcomed them.

The room was filled with the sound of his skin slapping against mine and the harsh pants of our breathing. It smelled of sweat and sex, and I shuddered at the onslaught of sensation. His thrusts grew erratic, and when he drove hard into me, my stomach and thighs tightened. I tipped over the edge with a sudden clench of my body around his cock.

I cried out, shock and pleasure mingling, spinning and tossing me. My balls drew up, come spattering my belly and painting the sheets beside me as I came. I collapsed onto my stomach, and Elliot covered my body with his, driving me into the mattress as he chased his own pleasure. A few strokes later, he came with a hoarse moan, sinking his teeth into the spot where my neck met my shoulder and sending a sharp jolt through me that rocked my body with aftershocks of pleasure. We panted harshly, both of us struggling to catch our breath.

The bruising hold on me softened and became a caress. His bite was now a kiss, his lips and tongue moving over the sensitive skin in apology. I reached up, cupping his head in the palm of my hand and rubbing. He gave me one final kiss on my shoulder before he carefully withdrew from my body.

I flipped onto my back, and a short while later, he settled on top of me, pinning me to the mattress again. I could still feel the frantic beat of his heart against mine as he looked down at me.

"I love you, Elliot," I whispered. They were the first words I'd said to him since I'd left California.

He stared down at me for a long moment, so long I'd begun to count the heartbeats, and then a slow smile lit his face, and he pressed his forehead against mine. "I love you too, Chris."

I couldn't stop touching Elliot as we walked to the shower. I needed that physical reminder that he was right there beside me.

"How was California?" he asked when we were standing in the hot water, as if I'd gone on a work trip or a vacation.

"Enlightening."

His smile was soft. "I can tell. You look freer." He skimmed a hand up my arm. "Tanner too."

"I discovered I really love surfing. Well, re-discovered."

"Good."

I washed my hair while Elliot scrubbed the lube and come from his skin. I had so many things to tell him, but I was too drained to put them into words. The long drive, emotional overload, and staggering orgasm had taken their toll. Elliot didn't speak aloud either, but his touch and words were a language I understood.

My eyes were drooping by the time Elliot turned off the water. He dried me and maneuvered me into bed. I landed on the mattress with a contented sigh and was out in seconds.

I awoke to the sound of the door closing and the soft pad of Elliot's steps approaching. The loft was dim except for what light filtered in through the skylights and from a small lamp on the far side of the room. The smell of food wafted toward my nose as Elliot approached. He clicked on another lamp beside the bed.

"How long did I sleep?" I asked, squinting at its brightness.

"A few hours."

He settled on the bed beside me, holding a bag of what looked like takeout. *Something Asian* based on the garlic and ginger teasing my nostrils. I leaned in to kiss him. "Hi."

The corner of his mouth turned up in a little smile. "Hi."

"Thanks for letting me sleep."

"You needed it." He set the bag between us and pulled out cartons of food. "I figured you'd be hungry when you woke up."

I trailed my fingertips across his skin. "Thank you."

I peeked into a container and spotted shrimp wrapped in rice paper. "Thai?"

"Vietnamese. I wanted Pho."

My stomach rumbled as I helped him unpack the food. When we had both eaten our fill, I leaned back against the headboard and looked at him.

He was stretched out on the bed near me. In a gray T-shirt and soft sleep pants, and his hair messily gathered back from his face, he looked relaxed. Content. I'd expected a lot of things would happen when I got back here. A small part of me had prepared myself for him being cool or standoffish. I'd feared he might be angry or want to punish me for hurting him. But that wasn't Elliot at all. Once he'd let down his guard with me, his standoffishness and anger had disappeared completely.

This soft, easy welcome didn't feel like a copout or avoidance, however. It felt like we were both tired from the struggle and were ready to come together again.

"Should we talk now?" Elliot asked softly.

I smiled faintly. "Isn't that my line?"

"Maybe it'll be mine too. More often anyway. I did a lot of thinking too while you were gone."

"About?"

"About us. My fucked up family and my relationships. The way I spent the entire time we were together waiting for you to disappoint me."

A wave of guilt washed over me. "And I did. I'm so sorry."

"I know." He reached out and took my hand, weaving our fingers together. "But maybe I should have helped you instead of waiting for you to fail."

Given the chaos of his formative years, it wasn't a surprise. We all were products of our environments. I certainly was. And yet, I believed—I had to believe—that we were more than that. I had to believe if we worked at it, we could move past it and learn from it. What was the point otherwise? This idea was what my life's work was about, and yet now, I understood it on a deeper level than I ever had before.

I looked him in the eye. "I listened to what you said. I apologized for lying to my family before I left, but I have no idea what's been going on with them since things blew up at the gallery. I made a conscious choice to distance myself from them a little. Give them some space to deal with their own shit."

"I was a little harsh." Elliot sounded apologetic.

"But not wrong. And I'll take the honesty any day." I stared at him. "So, I went to La Jolla for a couple of reasons."

"From your pictures, I figured out you were somewhere along the coast, but I didn't know where."

Oh, right. I'd never told him where I actually was. Just sent pictures with no explanation. It had made sense in my head at the time. "Did you mind? The pictures, I mean."

"It was good. I knew you were okay, but it gave me some space to think."

"This is probably a weird question given the fact we're in bed together now, but … you do want to continue this, right? Build a real relationship?"

He squeezed my fingers. "I do."

I hadn't really doubted it, but hearing the confirmation sent a pulse of relief over me that was so powerful it left me a little lightheaded. "So where do we go from here?" I asked.

"Tell me about your time in La Jolla."

"I loaded Cal's Mustang with everything I needed and drove straight down there," I began. "No concrete itinerary. Just a whim and a tank full of gas."

Elliot shifted until his head rested on my thigh, and I reached out with my free hand to pull the elastic from his hair. It tumbled over his face, and I brushed it away so I could look at his eyes. They were the color of the Pacific. Not the vibrant blue of the cove at midday, but the soft gray of early morning, stretching fathomlessly into the distance.

I sifted my fingers through his hair as I talked. I talked until I was hoarse. I told him I'd said goodbye to Cal and Hazel and the weight of my family's expectations. I told him about the sea turtle and the fish tacos and the little guest house by the ocean. I told him that someday I wanted to take him there so he could sketch and take photos while I surfed. I wanted to teach him to snorkel, and I wanted to stand with the vastness of the ocean under our feet as I held him close.

He looked up at me with such need in his eyes that I dipped my head and kissed him.

"How do you feel now?" he asked quietly as I drew back.

I smiled. "Free."

We spent two days like that. Two days talking and making love. Rough, sweet, tender movements blended into a blur of reconnection.

I'd been so wrapped up in Elliot at first I hadn't paid much attention to his loft, but I quickly noticed an entire wall of it was covered in portraits of me. They were staggering to look at. They covered the gamut of emotions—everything from sorrow to joy. Every pencil mark spoke of love and longing, and I didn't have to ask to know how deeply he'd missed me while I was gone. There were also sketches of the pictures I'd sent him, and I could see La Jolla through his eyes too. I loved them all.

Elliot opened up more about his past. About the chaos of his childhood and the fear and the loneliness as he fended for himself after he got kicked out of the house. He shared how out of place he'd felt in art school among the privileged kids who seemed to be living in a world far removed from his own. About throwing up before his first juried show and then again when he'd read the glowing write-up in the Portland Tribune. How disbelieving he'd been when he'd gotten the first big check from the gallery. How one day, he'd stood in this loft he suddenly owned with nothing but a sketchpad and a small bag of clothes, wondering when he'd wake up in his car, hungry and chilled from a day spent sketching on Portland's damp streets in the hopes of making a few bucks.

I held him closer every time his voice broke.

He described how it had felt to get the call from Dave, telling him the man he loved was dead, and how angry he'd felt seeing Cal's features in my face as he stared at me across Cal's grave. We grew silent after that.

"Do you have the sketchbook you were using in January?" I eventually asked. Something had been tickling at the edge of my brain for a while, a question I needed an answer to.

Elliot shot me an inquisitive look with a single, raised eyebrow, but when I didn't reply, he stood and walked over to his work area. He returned and handed a spiral bound book to me before he settled on the bed again. I flipped through the pages until I found the sketch I remembered. My name and phone number were written in the lower right-hand corner where I'd left them. The smudge on the man's lower back wasn't a smudge at all, but a speckled constellation of birthmarks.

I tilted it so Elliot could see the page. "That's Cal, isn't it?"

He nodded. It didn't matter, not really, but I'd been curious. "That morning, I thought it was me."

"You don't know what it was like to see this man stretched out in my bed. Knowing it was you and yet half-convinced when you lifted your head it would be Cal instead. I wanted it to be him."

"I know." My voice was a little raw. "Who did you fuck that night?"

He looked away. "Both of you, maybe. I wanted to punish *someone* for how I felt, but I wasn't sure who that was."

It was exactly what I'd expected, but it still left a sting.

Elliot continued, his voice very soft. "It was eerie sometimes, the way I'd see him in you. I'd look up and you'd be staring at me with Cal's eyes, or you'd talk, and I'd hear his voice. And then one day, he was gone. I wasn't searching for traces of him in you. I looked at you, and all I saw was … you."

The words were a balm, soothing the earlier sting. I flipped the sketchbook closed and set it aside. I had no desire to rip it out or destroy it. It was a part of Elliot's past, and that's where it would stay.

After that, I told him about my childhood memories of my father's drinking and how helpless and scared I'd felt at the time and for years after. I described Cal's zeal for life and how it had made me feel boring and insignificant. How'd I'd put my needs second to his because I was sure if I could be good and fix what was wrong, I could make up for my shortcomings. I told him I'd succeeded in school and forged a meaningful career in the hope it would somehow make up for being less exciting, less vibrant and compelling than Cal. We talked about the desperate desire I'd felt to hold everything together, and how the tighter I held on to things, the more they seemed to slip from my fingers.

I told him about Alec. How I'd poured all my hopes and desires for a family and a future into him and ignored the fact that he was nothing but a mirage. Less of a flesh and blood man than a cardboard cutout. I'd been so desperate to achieve my next goal I'd let myself get swept up in the lies and empty promises.

Cal came up in the conversation often, and for the first time, it wasn't strange and fraught with tension. It felt easy and right, like we were both reminiscing about an old friend. Our wounds were beginning to heal.

"Will you move in with me?" Elliot asked hours later when we were naked in bed. I could still taste him on my tongue, and my balls faintly ached from the toe-curling orgasm he'd given me.

"Yes." My answer was swift this time. We could wait, but what was the point? Life was short, and even if we did fail, I didn't think it would be because of some arbitrary timeline of what was appropriate or not.

So, we emptied Cal's car of my things, drove to my apartment, and packed the rest of my belongings. I took only what mattered. Another day, I'd deal with the practicalities of changing my address, selling the things I no longer wanted, and getting out of my lease. Today was about new beginnings.

Chapter Thirty

I spent the next day unpacking and getting settled at Elliot's. I placed a few houseplants near the expansive windows and bought a small shelf for my books.

I hung Cal's landscape photos and the few pieces I'd picked up in La Jolla. I tried to hang the surfboard on the wall too, but no matter what I used to secure it, it fell off. For a brief second, I swore I heard Cal's laugh, reminding me not to make a shrine or a memorial to him but to use what he'd given me. I dipped my head in acknowledgement. I'd take the board out to the Oregon coast soon. Elliot gave me a curious look at the gesture but didn't question it.

And I was moved in.

A large part of me was tempted to stay like that forever, cocooned in Elliot's loft and avoiding the rest of the world. But he needed to work without me distracting him, and I needed to repair the chaos of the rest of my life. Elliot couldn't be the only relationship I had.

So, the next morning I went to the hospital, dressed casually in jeans and a button-down. I wasn't there to work. Yet.

Sherri greeted me brightly as I passed her desk at the entrance to the hospice wing. "Hello, Dr. Allen."

"Morning, Sherri. How are you?"

She beamed. "I'm well. You look like your time off agreed with you. It's good to see you smiling again. We were all worried about you."

"It did," I said with a smile. I hadn't realized how noticeable my state of mind had been to everyone around me, but I suppose it made sense. The demons I'd been wrestling with had been overwhelming. "I'm feeling much better."

"I'm glad to see that," she said warmly.

"Is Ed in?"
"He was in his office the last time I knew."

"Thanks! Have a good day."

"You too."

The air in my office was a little stale after being closed for several weeks, and the fern by the window looked shriveled and nearly dead. I fetched water from the break room and gave it a drink, hoping it would come back to life with a little care and attention.

My gaze lingered on the framed photo of my family. I missed them all terribly, but it was such a relief to no longer feel like their happiness rested solely in my hands. I also made a mental note to bring in a new picture to add to the window ledge. A photo of Elliot and me together would be the perfect addition.

I moved on to Ed's office. He greeted me with a wide smile and warm hug.

"Welcome back. You look wonderful, son."

I squeezed him back. "I feel wonderful."

"Take a seat while I make some coffee, and we'll catch up."

I brought him up to date on everything that had happened over the past few weeks, and he nodded in approval when I described where Elliot and I were. "I wish you the best. I sincerely do. It sounds like he's a wonderful man."

"He is. I'm very grateful we met even if the circumstances were less than ideal."

"We don't get to choose these things, do we?"

"I guess not," I said with a smile. I still wasn't sure where I stood when it came to religion, but I had to admit enough unexplainable circumstances had happened to me lately that I couldn't deny that the universe had a much bigger hand in shaping my life than I'd given it credit for in the past.

I grew more serious. "How are my parents?" I'd put off asking the question. As much as I wanted to know, I was afraid of the answer.

"Struggling." Ed's happy expression sobered. "Your father is in rehab."

I shifted in my chair. "I'm honestly surprised he agreed to go."

"He's a proud man, but he finally hit rock bottom."

"Why wouldn't he go the first time? When I was a kid? Why tough it out without professional help?"

"Because he was ashamed. He was too proud to admit to anyone but me that he needed help. He thought as a medical professional he was better than that and he could handle it alone. Plus, he didn't want that stigma following him around. He was concerned about his reputation if anyone found out and that acknowledging his alcoholism would damage the practice."

"Yeah, I can see that." I sighed. "So what changed this time? He sure as hell didn't act like he had any intention of admitting he had a problem when he left the gallery."

"Well, I got a call from him shortly after you left my house. He'd spent the night on the streets of Portland—well, sleeping in a TriMet station anyway."

I stared at Ed, my mouth hanging open. My father sleeping in a train station? I couldn't fathom it.

Ed's smile was a grim acknowledgment of my reaction. "Exactly. Someone from the transit police woke him, mistaking him for a vagrant. Christopher discovered he'd been pickpocketed while he was passed out, and his phone and wallet were missing. Eventually, he was able to convince someone he wasn't homeless and he'd just had a bit of bad luck, so they allowed him to use a phone. He called me to come pick him up."

I could imagine my father's complete and utter horror and shame at being in that situation. Rock bottom indeed.

Ed continued. "When I picked him up, he asked me to drive him straight to rehab."

"Which one?" Ed rattled off a name of a well-respected place not far from here. "Well good, I hope he gets the help he needs," I said aloud.

"I do too. I think it's a good first step."

"And my mother?"

"She went to stay with her sister for a while. I believe a neighbor is looking after the house."

"Is there anything I can do in the meantime? Do I wait for them to contact me? Or should I call them?"

"I think you should reach out. Your father has limited access to a cell phone for this first portion of the program, but you can leave him a message. Let both him and your mother know you're back and that you want to talk. Give them time and space if they aren't ready yet."

"I can do that." I let out a relieved sigh. The news wasn't great, but on the whole, it was the best it could probably be under the circumstances. "Thank you for looking out for them while I was gone."

"Of course."

"I've found an Al-anon group to join." I wanted Ed to know that I was taking my own issues seriously as well.

"I'm pleased to hear that. It's clear you did a lot of work on yourself during this trip, but it can't hurt to have outside support."

"I agree."

"I know you don't need my approval about your relationship with your parents, but if it helps, I think you made the right choice. You dealt with what you needed to, and they will too. I have hope that, with time, these wounds will heal for all of you."

"I hope so too." I reached out and clasped his arm. "And while I might not need your approval, I still appreciate it. Leaving like that was a tough decision for me."

"I know it was."

"Now, what do I need to do to come back to work?"

"There's a considerable about of H.R. paperwork to fill out, I'm afraid. I, uh, took a few liberties when I submitted leave papers for you." I raised an eyebrow. "Well, you needed a break, and I didn't want to bother you with the details. You had more important things to deal with."

Ed forging my signature made me smile. He was one of the most principled men I had ever met so it was wildly out of character. It wasn't like I'd complain to H.R. about it, so his secret was safe with me. It hadn't even crossed my mind to worry about filling out the paperwork, but if Ed hadn't done that, the hospital would have had every right to censure me, leaving a blemish in my file. I could have withstood it, but I was grateful that I didn't have to. "Thank you."

"Let me grab the copies I made so you'll know exactly what you supposedly signed."

I left the hospital feeling like my life was slowly beginning to get back on track. I pictured coming home to Elliot and grinned.

No, my life was on a *new* track. A better one.

O ver the next few weeks, Elliot and I settled into living together with relative ease. I went back to work with a renewed passion I hadn't felt in years, and I started going to the gym again.

Jason was busy with a client when I arrived, but he came over after to say hello while I was lifting weights. "Hey, you're back."

"I'm back." I settled the bar onto the rack then waved off the guy who'd been spotting me. No point in making him wait around until I finished my conversation "Glad to be here too."

"Really? It looks like you've been on vacation or something. That's quite a tan."

"I went down to La Jolla for a bit," I explained as I stepped away from the equipment. "Actually, that reminds me I want to talk to you about something. I did some snorkeling and surfing there. It made me realize I have a couple areas I need to work on. Think you could help me with that?"

"Happy to!"

Jason helped me with a few new strengthening exercises and promised to get back to me about a few more the next time I came in. Before he went off to meet with a new client, I stopped him.

"Hey, would you want to grab a drink with me sometime?" I asked.

A look of surprise made me hastily try to clarify. "I'm not asking you out on a date or anything. I have a boyfriend I just moved in with. I just ... Look, my brother died in January, and I realized I've been kinda isolated for the last couple of years. You seem like a great guy, and I thought ..."

I half-expected Jason to reply with some obligatory and banal promise to get together sometime, but his expression turned serious. "Yeah, I heard about that. Cooper was friends with him, right?" I nodded. "I'm really sorry to hear about your brother. Honestly, I know where you're coming from myself. It's been hard to make friends since I moved to Portland last year. I'm *here* all the time, and I don't get out much to meet people. I don't really drink, but if you wanted to grab a coffee or do dinner or something, that'd be great."

Pleased by his candor, I struggled to figure out how to reply. "Honestly, I don't know why I suggested drinks. Habit, I guess. I've quit drinking recently. My dad's an alcoholic"—those words left my mouth with startling ease— "and it would be great to have someone to socialize with where drinking *isn't* the focus."

"I hear ya," Jason said with a sympathetic smile. "So, my schedule's a little weird, but I've got some time next Tuesday if you're free."

And just like that, I had plans with a new friend. It felt good.

In addition, I signed up for guitar lessons and started going to the support group meetings for the family members of alcoholics. Elliot decided to go to a therapist to deal with some of his family issues, and I felt like slowly but surely we were getting our lives together.

During that time, I called and left messages for my parents, Dave, John, and Cooper. Cooper was the first to return my call, and we met for lunch. It was a little awkward, but when I explained the situation and apologized, he held up his hands.

"Hey, I get it. That was a tough spot to be in, man. It totally blew my mind to know Cal was living a double life. I can only imagine what that was like for you. I can't be mad." Cooper shrugged and sat back in his chair, his biceps bulging under his short sleeve shirt as he put his hands behind his head. "And, I know you don't need my approval, but for what it's worth, I'm glad you and Elliot are happy together. Your brother wasn't the kind of guy who held grudges about petty shit. Even if he were alive right now, he'd get over it pretty quick. It's certainly not my place to pass judgement."

While Cooper was right—I didn't need his approval—it was nice to hear, nonetheless. And he was spot-on about Cal.

John was a little cooler toward me when we spoke on the phone, but he did say he felt like what happened between Elliot and me was our business. He did give me a warning, however. "I can't vouch for how Dave is going to respond. He was still livid the last time I spoke with him."

"I was afraid of that," I said with a sigh. I thanked John and hung up.

Dave ignored every phone call I made. Every text I sent. I even knocked on his apartment door one evening after work. His car was in his assigned spot, so I was quite confident he was home. But he didn't answer. I hadn't expected it to be easy to repair the damage, but I hadn't anticipated he'd completely cut me off from any opportunity to try.

Finally, in desperation, I decided to go to his office building. The Associated Press office was in downtown Portland, overlooking the river. Knowing Dave usually went into work a couple of hours before I did, I got up early in order to meet him there before I went in to the hospital.

"G'luck," Elliot murmured sleepily from his nest under the covers. I kissed his bare shoulder.

"Thanks. Love you."

"You too." He was out again before I left the apartment.

The sky was streaked with red and gold as I pulled into the parking lot.

I'd been there a handful of times to meet Dave, and I knew the security protocols were tight. Staff had to badge in at the security desk, and any time I'd met him, I'd had to check in with security and wait in the visitor lounge until he verified I could come up to the newsroom—or, more often—he met me in the lobby. Getting up to his office would be virtually impossible. I felt guilty enough about ambushing him at work. The last thing I wanted was to cause a scene in the lobby.

I parked and walked over to a bench near the entrance instead. I'd dressed particularly well that morning in the hope people would assume I was there for an interview. Ideally, no one would hassle me for loitering, but it was a gamble. I'd jokingly warned Elliot he might have to bail me out of jail.

The weather was pleasant at least, and I caught up on emails while I waited, but doubts dogged me as people began to arrive. Several shot me curious glances, but no one confronted me. *Should I even be here? Am I crossing a line?* I *was* practically stalking a man who'd made it clear he wanted nothing to do with me. Maybe my joke to Elliot had some truth to it. I'd just made up my mind to leave when I spotted Dave striding toward the building. He had his head down and he was on his phone, so he hadn't seen me yet. As he got closer, I could hear part of his conversation.

"… shouldn't have come over last night. It was a bad choice." He sighed. "Can you not do this? I can't deal with it right now." His voice sounded tense and strained. "I've got enough on my plate as it is and—Chris?" He scowled at me as we made eye contact. "No. I just ran into someone I know. We'll talk later if you want, but I'm not changing my mind."

Dave ended the call and shoved his phone in his pocket. "What the fuck are you doing here?" His glare and combative tone made it abundantly clear he wasn't thrilled to see me.

"I came to talk to you."

"If me not answering your calls and not opening the door when you showed up at my apartment wasn't clear enough, let me put it in plain English. I have no desire to talk to you."

"We were friends, Dave. *Good* friends. Or at least I thought we were. I understand why you're angry with me, but there must be some way we can work through this," I pleaded. "For Cal's sake, if not mine. You know how much he'd have hated to see us argue like this."

As suddenly as if someone had pulled a plug, I saw some of the fight go out of Dave. His shoulders slumped, and he gave me a single, weary nod. "That's a low blow pulling the Cal card, but you're right. Fine. We can talk. I'm not doing this here or now, however. I've got a meeting in twenty minutes."

"That's fine. I need to get to work myself."

Dave shook his head as if he couldn't quite believe he was doing this. "Seven tonight? My place?"

"Sounds great."

He held up a hand. "Don't get your hopes up. I've just agreed to talk."

"I know. But I appreciate that."

He walked toward his building without another word, and I headed to the hospital, relieved that my gamble had paid off. It wasn't forgiveness, but it was a start.

Dave looked worn out when he opened his apartment door that evening, and he certainly wasn't smiling, but considering the situation, I was probably lucky he didn't greet me with another punch.

"First of all, I want to say I'm sorry," I said as soon as we were seated in his living room. "I know you think I betrayed Cal, and I understand why you're upset about that."

"But?"

"But nothing." I leaned forward. "It guts me to know I've hurt you in any way. I care about you, and the last thing I wanted was to bring you more pain than you were already in."

He nodded, but he still looked so serious and somber he could have been carved out of marble. I continued, hoping something I said would finally get through to him. "I want you to be honest though. When you think about my brother, do you truly, honestly believe he'd be angry about this? Or feel betrayed? That wasn't *Cal.*"

After a beat of silence, Dave sighed heavily. "You're right. It wasn't him." It was a grudging acknowledgement, but it was something.

"If I remember right, one of his friends dated Allie after Cal ended things with her. Shaun, maybe?"

"Cooper," he said.

"So, do you really think he'd want you to be pissed on his behalf? Because I don't see it." I looked down at my hands. "Look, I don't know how to say this so I'm just going to blurt it out, but I had a weird experience on the beach in La Jolla that I can't explain. I would have sworn I had a conversation with my brother. And odds are I conjured up his voice because I was so desperate for his approval, but I would swear to you, my brother told me he wanted me to make Elliot happy."

Surprise and confusion crossed Dave's face. "You can't really believe you talked to Cal's ghost."

"No," I said honestly. "And I'm fully aware all of this sounds self-serving as hell. But I know I heard *something*, and I know what I *felt*.

I'm at peace with this, and I have to believe my brother is too. I love Elliot, and I'm not giving him up. Not for anyone."

"That's a hard line in the sand you've drawn."

"It is. But he's worth it. And you know I don't say that lightly, Dave." I looked him in the eye. "Look, I have lost so much in the past few years. My relationship and the future I'd planned fell apart. I lost most of the people I thought were my friends. I lost my only brother. My father is an alcoholic. His relationship with my mother is on the rocks. I don't want to lose you too. I'm just asking you to take some time and think about what I've said. You lost family; you know what it's like."

Dave shot me a pained glance before he dragged his hands across his face. "You don't make it easy on a guy, do you?"

I shrugged helplessly. "I'm not trying to hurt you. I just want to be happy."

"And Elliot makes you happy?"

"More than anything."

Dave stood and walked across the apartment, staring out the window. His shoulders were tense, and he was silent so long I began to wonder if he'd forgotten I was there. Finally, he turned and looked at me. I rose to my feet too, standing in front of him like I was waiting for him to pass judgement on me. And in a way, he was. The fate of our friendship hung in the balance.

"Okay," he said finally as he reached out to clasp my hand. "It's going to take me a little time, but if Elliot makes you happy, I'll figure out how to be okay with it. I do know Cal wouldn't want us to fight."

A huge wave of relief washed over me, and I tightened my grip before letting go. "Thank you."

"I'm not sure I'm going to want to hang out with you and Elliot any time soon though, just so you know."

"Take all the time you need. I'm just glad you were willing to talk."

Dave shot me a look of disbelief. "You make it hard for a guy to refuse."

"Just part of my charm."

For a second, I saw a glimmer of a smile on Dave's face. "You know who you sound like when you say that?"

"Yes, I do." I glanced at my watch. "I should get going though. I have a support group meeting tonight. Al-anon," I explained.

"Damn, that's crazy," Dave said as he walked with me to the door. "I never would have pegged your dad …"

"He was good at hiding it."

Dave's expression turned troubled. "I guess we're all better at that than we like to admit."

For a moment, we just stared at each other. With the weight of worry about our friendship beginning to lift, I noticed again how drained Dave looked. "Are you okay?" I asked tentatively. "You look exhausted."

"I am." But he didn't offer an explanation as to why.

"You seemed upset this morning when you were on the phone. Is something going on with Nadia or something?" I asked, grasping at straws. Based on the portion of the phone conversation I'd heard, relationship trouble seemed the most likely culprit. Although, I knew everything else that was going on couldn't possibly have helped.

"No, it's not Nadia. I haven't seen her in a while." He hesitated. "Look, I'm dealing with some personal stuff right now, and I probably came down on you way harder than I should have because of it. I am sorry about that."

"It's okay. I understand. Do you want to talk about it?" I offered. "I'm here to listen, if you want."

But he shook his head. "We're not there now, Chris. Maybe at some point, but …"

I nodded soberly. He was right. We had a long road ahead of us to repair our friendship. I hoped, with time, it would come.

I felt a flutter of nerves work through me when I saw my mother's name flash on my phone's screen. I had to take a deep breath before I accepted the call.

"Hello?"

THE GHOSTS BETWEEN US

"Chris?" she asked softly.

"Mom."

"I'm glad you answered."

"I'm glad you called."

"I just flew back from Eva's yesterday. I've been there since ..."

"Since the gallery?" I supplied. I'd been referring to that night that way since. It had such weight; the words had almost taken on a new meaning in my head.

"Yes." She cleared her throat. "I know we have a lot to talk about. Would you be willing to come see me at the house soon?"

I licked my lips, hating that she doubted I would. "Of course, Mom."

Over the next few days, I drove Elliot crazy fretting about it until, eventually, he grabbed me by the shoulders and stared me in the eye. "Chris, you have got to relax or you're going to have a heart attack before you even get there."

"Which of us is the doctor?" I asked with a weak smile.

He leveled me with a serious look. "You're going through all of these possible scenarios of what might happen, and it's stressing you out. Why worry about something that may never happen?"

"I know. But what if ..."

"What if you can't work through it with your mom? Then we'll deal with it together. You're not going to have to do this alone."

Elliot drew me closer, and I pressed my lips to his, so grateful for his love.

Chapter Thirty-One

My mother looked subdued when she answered the door, but she looked less strained than she had in months, like she'd weathered the worst of it and come out stronger.

I knew the feeling.

I hesitated, unsure if I should hug her or not. She looked equally uncertain, but sad too. I hated feeling like my own mother was a stranger, so I held out my arms. She hugged me tightly, her cheek pressed against my chest for a minute.

"I'm glad you came over," she said after she drew back.

"I'm glad too."

"Can I get you anything?"

"I've been drinking a lot of tea lately," I offered. Despite the hot June day, inside the house was pleasantly cool.

"How's Aunt Eva?" I asked while she boiled water.

"Good. She said to tell you hello."

For all my talk about family and wanting more of it, I hadn't done a great job keeping in contact with her or my cousins. I made a mental note to do better in the future.

I sat at the kitchen table. My mother and I continued to make small talk while she pulled down mugs and tea bags from the cupboard. I ran my palm across the table's wooden surface, remembering her making me hot cocoa on drizzly, dreary winter days. I'd eaten so many meals here. So many after school snacks. I'd done my homework and colored pictures countless times while my mom cooked. I'd played board games and cards with my dad and arm-wrestled Cal. I'd let him win until he was strong enough that I had to fight not to lose.

We sat silently for a few heartbeats. She wrapped her hands around her mug, her face growing serious. I straightened, focusing my attention on her. "Chris, I want to say how sorry I am about what happened at the gallery."

"I was the one who lied to you."

"None of us were honest with each other."

I went still as I digested that. "True."

"Fighting over who has a bigger share of the blame isn't going to fix the damage, so let's set that aside. The truth of the matter is your father and I have been struggling since Cal's death. And I'm afraid we put too much of the burden on you. The letter you wrote made me realize we've been doing it for years." I opened my mouth to protest, but she held up a hand. "Please, let me finish. This isn't easy.

462

"It wasn't intentional, but I know we expected too much from you growing up. Cal demanded our attention, so he got an unfair share of it. You've pushed yourself so hard to succeed and please us, and you have, yet in the past few years, you've seemed so unhappy."

"I was," I admitted.

"And then Cal's death ... it just ... took its toll on all of us. I could see you were struggling, but I was too and so was your father. It wasn't your job to hold us together."

"I went too far with it."

"You certainly took on much more responsibility for it than was fair. Your father and I could have done so much better by you." She looked anguished.

"I thought we weren't supposed to be fighting over who was to blame?"

"We're not." She pressed her hands to her cheeks. "But I'm afraid I can't help it. You were so young when your father first started drinking. And I was so overwhelmed. I had no idea what to do when this wonderful man I'd been married to suddenly turned into someone else. I had two children at the time, and Cal was more than a handful. But it's no excuse. No nine-year-old should be dealing with what you dealt with, and I'm sorry for that. I should have insisted your father get help sooner and that he go through a program."

"Do you think it'll work this time?"

"I don't know. I hope so. I still love him so much, but ..."

"I know you do."

"But I have no excuse for my affair with Paul," she said quietly. "It wasn't a physical one. I've never met the man in person. But emotionally ... I absolutely did. And I can't swear that I wouldn't have gone to him at some point. Things with your father were so bad ..." She shook her head. "But, again, that's no excuse."

"It's a reason," I said softly. The loneliness must have been unbearable.

"It's over now. I cut off all contact with Paul immediately after that night. And once I got back from Seattle, I set up an appointment with a therapist so I can deal with Cal's death and my feelings about your father's drinking."

"That's good."

She reached out and touched my hand. "And I want you to know I understand why you turned to Elliot when you were hurting."

"It's more than that though," I said slowly. "He's a part of my life now. I love him, and I want a future with him. We moved in together."

Surprise flashed across her face. I could understand it. Moving quickly in a relationship wasn't something I'd ever done in the past, and I'd always talked things like that through with my parents. Not because I'd been asking for their permission but because I'd valued and respected their opinion. A lot had changed.

"Oh." She looked like she was struggling to find words.

"I know it can't be easy learning about Elliot the way you did. Learning who he was to Cal and …" I was struggling too.

"None of this has been easy."

"No, it hasn't."

"I know you looked up to your father and your brother and me. And I feel like we all let you down."

I felt a lump in my throat. "You didn't let me down, Mom. I … I don't know. I think I had these idealized images of who we all were. Who this family was as a whole. And seeing that fall apart was hard. But it was important too. Or, at least, I hope it will lead to something positive once we get through it."

She looked pained. "I want to try, but I can't guarantee your father and I will be able to work through this. There is so much hurt and distrust on both sides, and it's going to take a very long time for us to deal with it."

"I know." It was painful to admit, but I knew there was a chance my parents' marriage wouldn't survive everything they'd been through.

Over the next few weeks, my mother and I spoke more. She updated me about how my father was doing. "He's struggling but he's getting there. I don't want you to get your hopes up, but we've agreed that after he's back home, we'll be seeing a marriage counselor."

"It's a good start," I said simply.

I told her what I could about Cal and where his head had been in the months before his death. I told her about Elliot too. About his art and his sense of humor, and about how supportive he'd been.

We were still strangely hesitant with each other, but conversation by conversation it grew a little easier.

But still, my father didn't call.

"Is he angry with me?" I asked her one afternoon as I strolled around the hospital grounds. I'd called my mother on my lunch break to ask the question that had been nagging at me for weeks.

"Oh, sweetheart. Is that what you believe? He's not angry with you, he's angry with himself. He's ashamed, and he's afraid you won't be able to forgive *him*."

"I don't want to push him. I know recovery is complicated and difficult, and I don't want to derail his progress, but *if* you think he's ready, would you tell him I'd really like to talk to him? I'll come to the facility in person if that would be better."

"Of course."

But it wasn't until his final week there that she told me he'd like to see me.

"Do you want me to come with you?" Elliot asked that morning. I hadn't slept well the night before, worrying about how it would go. Now, I nursed a cup of coffee that didn't seem to be doing a thing to help.

I managed a weak smile. "No, I don't think I need you to. But I appreciate it." He'd done so much for me already. "It'll be fine. *I'll be fine.*"

"Call if you need me."

"I will." I reached out and grabbed him, pulling him close, breathing in the softness of his scent to tide me over until I got back. "Thank you."

The lobby looked more like an upscale hotel than a rehab facility. But I had no doubt it had seen more than its share of heartache and struggle.

Including plenty belonging to the man standing in front of me. My father looked grayer and a good deal older than I remembered.

"Thank you for coming, Chris," he said gravely as we took a seat at a small table. He sounded stiff and formal, and I hated that.

"How've you been?"

"Better." He did look healthier. Less puffy and his gaze was clear. "You?"

"I'm making progress."

We were both silent for a long while. I studied my hands, remembering the sketch Elliot had done of them. I wanted to be back at home in the loft with him. Reading while he sketched me. Playing guitar. Hell, scrubbing the bathroom. Anything but this strange awkward tension with the man who'd raised me. I missed the ease we'd once had.

I missed my father.

"I had all these plans for what to say," he blurted out. "And now I can't think of any of them."

I glanced up. "It's okay. I'm not sure either."

"I guess first, I should say I'm sorry." His throat worked briefly. "I let you and your mother down when you needed me the most. Twice."

I couldn't deny that. But I also knew it wasn't so simple. "It's a disease. I know that."

"I'm a doctor. I thought I could heal myself." He looked sorrowful. "But I failed."

"You didn't fail, Dad. You ... well, you didn't have the right specialty. The right treatment." He gave me a ghost of a smile. "When you started having shoulder issues a few years ago, you didn't try to heal it yourself. You—you went to an orthopedist who had the tools and the training to diagnose and treat it. It's no reflection on you that you weren't able to handle this yourself."

"I suppose you're right," he said with a sigh. "But I still made the wrong choice."

"You did. But you made the right choice eventually. You're here now, right?"

"I hope it's enough."

"I can't really judge you anyway," I admitted. "I didn't get professional help either. I was so sure I could manage my grief, but I wasn't doing it well. I should have reached out to someone. Other than Elliot, I mean."

He nodded. "I like Elliot, you know? He seems ... steady."

High praise indeed from a man who disliked flightiness.

"We've moved in together."

His surprise was as clear as my mother's had been, but all he said was, "I'm happy for you."

"We're making real progress. *I'm* making real progress getting my life together again."

"I'm amazed by how well you're doing," he said.

"I'm through the other side of it," I said. "Not with everything, obviously. But that's why I went down to La Jolla. I needed that time to just grieve and deal with all of this. And now I'm finally better."

"Ed and your mom said you were doing well, and I can see it too."

"I'm trying. I've been going to Al-anon," I admitted. "It's helped."

A pained expression crossed his face but he nodded. "That's good. I'm sorry we didn't send you to talk to someone the first time."

"It probably would have been helpful. But it doesn't matter now. We can't undo the past."

"No, we can't. Much as I wish otherwise."

"This is helping you though?" I asked.

"It is. I feel stronger and more in control of myself than I have in a long time."

"Well, that's good."

"I've done a hell of a lot of soul searching."

I'd certainly done that too.

"One of my biggest regrets is that I put so much pressure on you and Cal when you were growing up. I was ashamed of my failures, and I wanted so desperately for you and Cal to do better. I believed I was a good father and that I encouraged you, but it was too much. Too many expectations." I nodded. "And the two of you reacted so differently to the pressure. Cal rebelled, but you buckled down and worked harder." He sighed. "I can't imagine how much courage it must have taken you to tell me you weren't going into pediatrics. You must have wanted it so badly."

"Badly enough I risked disappointing you."

"And I responded terribly." He looked down, knitting his fingers together. I reached out and rested my hand on his. "But you came around."

He looked up, a frown carving deep wrinkles into his forehead. "Eventually, yes. But it set the stage for where we ended up. I told my family that my expectations mattered more than them finding a path that made them happy. I made my sons feel like they couldn't come to me when they needed to," my father said. His voice grew rough. "I can't begin to tell you how sorry I am about that. And that I wasn't a better example to you both. I failed Cal and I failed you."

I stared, open-mouthed, as I struggled to process his words. "You didn't fail us, Dad."

"My son died believing I would be more concerned with carrying on our family legacy than him finding someone he loved. That is a failure I don't know how to forgive myself for." His eyes were dry but red-rimmed, and I felt an answering sting in my own.

"But you know Cal. Even if he'd told you about him and Elliot and that he wasn't sure he was going to have kids someday, and even if the two of you fought about it, you would have worked it out. You always did. Cal had a big heart. He didn't hold grudges."

"He didn't. But I shouldn't have expected my son to be the bigger man than me," he said sorrowfully. "And you. Why aren't you angry with me? You'd have every right to be for everything I've done."

"Do you want me to be?"

He shrugged, but the look in his eyes said yes. I could understand that. Anger was easy for someone to deal with when they knew they'd done something to hurt another. Anger was punishment for mistakes. Freeing a person from guilt. Allowing for forgiveness.

Funny, I'd been raised Catholic and I'd thought I'd left most of it behind, but clearly, remnants lingered. Everything was framed in terms of sin and forgiveness. Penitence.

But why wasn't I angry with my father? It would be justified. I'd been angry for months after Cal died, but it had dissipated now.

Maybe it would come back at some point. Or maybe I'd simply burned through it all and had no reserves left. Al-anon meetings had helped me find some insight into my feelings, but most importantly, I felt whole now. I didn't need anything else to fill what had been lacking.

Anger wouldn't make me happier. It wouldn't repair the broken relationships. All it would do was waste precious time.

"I *was* angry," I admitted. "Angry with you for abandoning Mom and me and Cal when Grandpa Allen died. For abandoning Mom and me once Cal was gone. We needed you, and you weren't there. But I'm not angry now. All I want is to have my family back."

He looked up at me. "I don't know that your mother wants me back."

"I know. And I know she hurt you too. That's for the two of you to deal with. I'm not asking you to stick together for my sake. I'm a grown man; I'll deal with it if you can't work through it. Look, Cal's gone. Our family will never be the same. But I'm building a life with Elliot, and I hope you and Mom will be a part of that even if we have to find a totally new way to be a family."

My father stood and I did too. He hugged me hard, his grip tight and his breath ragged and choked. "You're a good man, Chris," he

472

finally said. I held on to him. Onto the man who'd done so much to make me who I was now. Both good and bad.

"I learned from you," I said simply. He was a good man. Because whatever demons he wrestled with, whatever hurts he'd caused or whatever mistakes he'd made, he was still trying.

One evening about a month later, I looked up from my laptop. "My mom invited us over for lunch."

"Okay." Elliot shot me an apprehensive glance from the other side of the couch. "When?"

"Next Saturday, if we're free. We don't have to let her know right away if you need some time to think about it."

"It's fine. I don't think we have anything planned."

"But do you *want* to go? Are you ready for this?" It would be the first time Elliot met my parents with the full knowledge of everything that had happened.

"I think so." But he didn't look or sound convinced. I set my laptop on the floor beside me so I could focus on him.

"We don't have to do this yet," I said softly. "If you need more time, we'll take it. There's no rush."

"Are *you* ready?"

"As ready as I'll ever be. It's going to be awkward; there's no way around that. And the last thing I want to do is drag you into more horrible family drama. But my dad seems to be doing well with his recovery so far, and from what they both said, they're making progress with their relationship."

"That's good." Elliot nibbled at his lower lip a little, and I held out my arms. I wanted to reassure him, up close and personal. Elliot tossed the book he'd been reading onto the floor and crawled over me, carefully settling between my legs. I rubbed my palms up and down his back, feeling his tense muscles begin to unclench and soften.

"You're my priority, Elliot," I said quietly. "If it goes sideways, we leave. It's a simple as that."

"They're your family though. I know how much they mean to you." He looked troubled.

I pushed his hair off his face and tilted his head to look him in the eye. "You're my family now too. I love my parents. I want a relationship with them but not at your expense. You come first."

The quiet sound of relief Elliot let out was almost as satisfying as the kiss he gave me after.

To say we were all nervous and uncomfortable was an understatement. We'd been sitting in my parents' living room for half an hour making awkward small talk, and it was nothing short of excruciating.

After a brief lull in the conversation, my mother smoothed her hair behind her ears and sat up straight. "All right, if no one else will, I'm going to address the elephant in the room. And that's the very uncomfortable situation we put you in at the gallery, Elliot."

My father cleared his throat. "I'm sorry we found out about your relationship with Cal under such uncomfortable circumstances. That was a terrible position for you to be in. And I'm sorry for my behavior that night. I was in an awful place, but it's no excuse. I'm getting help now, and I intend to do better."

"I think that's admirable that you admitted you needed help," Elliot said quietly. "My mother was a drug addict, and I wish she'd been able to do that."

My father flinched. I think he still had a hard time coming to terms with the fact that he was an addict of any kind. But he smiled at Elliot anyway. "Thank you. That's kind of you. I hope you'll be around to see that it's not the kind of man I intend to be in the future. My behavior that night was reprehensible."

"Let's be honest. The past six months have been some of the worst of all our lives. It's not what any of us wanted, but ..." I squeezed Elliot's hand. "Some good has come of it."

My mother leaned forward. "Elliot, you have every right to say no, but I do have some questions. Can I ask you a little more about your relationship with Cal?"

He was silent, and I could see the turmoil on his face. "I'll answer what I can," he finally said. I reached out, needing to reassure him that I was here for him.

"Thank you," she said quietly.

"What would you like to know?" I trailed my fingertips across his back until he softened, relaxing into my touch.

"I guess I'd like to know why he felt he needed to hide his relationship with you from us. Chris has explained it some, but I'd appreciate your take on it as well."

"Oh." Elliot let out a huge sigh. "That's tough."

"You don't have to answer it if it's too painful," she said.

Elliot shook his head. "No, it's all right." He licked his lips. "When Cal and I met, we never intended to get involved of course. I sketched him, and ..."

I watched my parents as Elliot explained the situation with Cal and why he'd felt the need to hide the relationship. Her hand crept out toward my father, and he clasped it and squeezed. It was a small gesture, but it gave me hope for their relationship. Maybe it wasn't damaged beyond repair.

When Elliot was through, she sniffled and dabbed at her eyes with a tissue. Elliot sat back, nestling against the side of my body. My arm automatically went around him, and we laced our fingers together and settled them on his left thigh.

I cleared my throat. "Elliot ran across a letter Cal had written to me. It was hard to read but it cleared up some things. If you'd like to read it, you can. It might help."

"Maybe sometime in the future. I don't know that I can handle it right now."

"I understand." She was dealing with plenty right now.

After a moment, she seemed to pull herself together. "The expectations my husband and I had for Cal clearly are a huge part of why he didn't tell us about you. While I can't apologize to him, I can apologize to you. I'm sorry Cal believed we wouldn't welcome you into our family. We would have been surprised, and I can't promise we would have reacted as well as we should have. We love both our boys so much, and I feel terrible that we put so much pressure on Cal that he felt he had to hide who he was. I can promise you that we would have wanted to get to know you and that we would have been glad Cal found someone he was happy with. We would have accepted it. We would have accepted *you*."

"I believe that now. And I think Cal would have come around. Eventually. He just ..."

"Ran out of time," she finished.

"Yes." He sighed. "But I don't think Cal and I would have lasted. He was a wonderful person, but he ... he wasn't ready for the kind of relationship I wanted. I don't know that he ever would have been. At least, not with me."

She gave Elliot and me a searching look. "But you two are ... are solid?"

"Yes." Our answers overlapped each other, and a faint smile crossed her face at the response.

"I know this didn't start the way you wanted, but I am glad you … I'm glad you have each other."

"So am I," I said softly.

"I don't know how to say this, but … even though I would give everything I have to bring Cal back, I think you and Elliot are made for each other. I only wish there had been a better way. Some way I could have had all three of you alive and happy at once." She dabbed at her eyes again.

"Me too," Elliot said quietly.

We all wanted that.

"Well"—my mother stood and clasped her hands together, clearly trying to lighten the mood—"how about some lunch? Everything's nearly ready, Christopher is just going to throw some chicken skewers on the grill, but it shouldn't take long."

"That would be nice. Is there anything I can help with?" Elliot asked, standing as well.

"You could set the table," she suggested. "Chris can show you where everything is."

We had lunch on the deck. It didn't escape my notice that it was something different. Saturday lunch instead of Sunday dinner. Maybe my mom felt the need to start fresh with a new tradition. Or maybe she knew it would be too difficult for us to sit at the dining room table and see the empty chair.

Whatever it was, I was glad.

The shady deck felt comfortable despite the blazing summer sun. Outside, the laughter came a little more easily and so did the conversation. We talked about Portland and Elliot's art. My work. My parents selling the practice to Dr. Weiss. They hadn't settled on what their future plans would be, but it was nice to see them making decisions together.

Elliot and I talked about a music festival we'd gone to the weekend before and the plans we had to go to the coast in a few weeks. We were all looking to the future.

We'd never get to have those family dinners in the dining room with my parents, Cal, Elliot, and me. But we had this now. And it felt like a new beginning.

"Take care of Chris," I heard my mom say to Elliot as she hugged him goodbye later that evening. "He needs you more than he'll ever let on."

I smiled faintly to myself. It was true. I'd changed a lot in the past few months. I was in a much better place now. But the happiness Elliot brought into my life was something I never wanted to do without again.

"I'll be there for him," Elliot said. His tone was earnest as he hugged her back. He liked her, I could tell. He was slightly more reserved with my father as they shook hands a few minutes later. Whether it was because Elliot's past made him wary of people with addictions, I didn't know. But he'd come here today and allowed himself to be vulnerable for me.

I felt humbled by the depth of his love.

Chapter Thirty-Two

E lliot had assured me that my family drama hadn't ruined his relationship with the Holloway Gallery, but when he'd told me about a meeting he had scheduled there, I went with him. I wanted to give Peter Holloway an apology in person.

Peter waved it off. "What you have to understand, Chris, is that all publicity is good. Even bad publicity." He grinned at me.

"I've heard that," I admitted. "But I found it hard to believe."

"Cal's work sold like hotcakes. And the critics mentioned the brawl in their articles, of course, which brought in even more people. I'm not about to manufacture drama at shows, but I can't deny that it's had a positive impact on my business." His expression turned more serious. "I do hope you were able to resolve your, uh, differences with your friends and family however."

"We've been trying," I said with a sigh. "It's still a work in progress. For the most part, though, yes, it's getting better."

Elliot had told me recently that the mid-May timeslot at the gallery we'd used for Cal's show had originally been his own. His show had been rescheduled for the end of July. He'd assured me it was no big deal, but it made me appreciate him even more. He had done so much for all of us.

"I'm glad to see you two were able to mend things." Peter nodded toward Elliot, who was deep in conversation with Joy.

"So am I," I said. "He's an extraordinary person."

As we left the gallery, Elliot and I discussed what to do next. We finally decided to just wander for a while and explore Portland.

It was a gorgeous June day. The week had been warm enough to enjoy being outside, but not so warm it was uncomfortable. A light breeze moved the air, and I could think of no better way to spend the day with the man I loved.

We stopped by The Armory to see what upcoming stage shows they had available, then bought ice cream cones while we contemplated what to do next.

Powell's City Books was tempting, but the store covered an entire city block. We both loved books too much to easily tear ourselves away, and it was too nice a day to spend it all inside.

We wandered around Tanner Springs Park instead. It was a preserved wetland in the heart of the Pearl District. We strolled the curving paths, enjoying the pond and the public art as we talked. Dozens of families surrounded us, and it drove me to ask him a question I'd been wondering for a while.

"Do you want kids?"

"Yes." Elliot's answer was so prompt, I turned my head to look at him. He caught my glance and shrugged. "What? I do. I mean, I think there's some stuff from when I grew up that I still need to deal with before I make it happen, but yes, I want a family."

It was odd that, at times, Elliot came off as the slightly aloof, loner type, but in the end, he was a warm and caring man once you got to know him. The walls he'd put up had been there for good reasons, but they'd begun to come down. Could I picture him with a child? I could actually. I could see him being calm and patient with a melting down toddler or cranky teenager. His calm, steady nature would serve him well as a father. It wasn't a stretch to see him teaching a child how to draw or use a camera.

"You still want kids, don't you?" he asked.

"I do," I said quietly. "Not an only child though. I'd like them to have a sibling or two."

His smile was soft and full of understanding. "That would be nice."

An image flash into my mind of Elliot napping on his back on the couch with our child sleeping on his chest while I played with another nearby. It was a future I wanted to work toward.

It would take time. Elliot was right; it would be better for him to deal with his family issues first, and I had plenty of my own I needed to work through. But it was a nice thought that someday we could have that together. And this time, I knew I wasn't fooling myself about the kind of man I was with.

As the afternoon wore on, we debated if we should go out to eat or cook. "Let's make something at home," Elliot said. "I don't feel like waiting in line at some ridiculously trendy place that'll have food that's overpriced and undersized."

I hid a smile. He sounded a good deal older than his twenty-four years when he talked like that, but he had a fair point. "Sure, I'm fine with that. There's a market on the way back to where the car's parked. We can grab something there."

"Perfect."

While I debated between spaghetti and bucatini, I heard a familiar voice. "Gave up on the low-carb diet, huh?"

I glanced up from the display of pasta and saw a completely unwelcome face. "*Alec?*"

My ex-boyfriend gave me a toothy smile. "Why do you sound so surprised, Chris?"

"I just didn't expect to run into you here." I'd shopped there plenty of times when Alec and I had lived together in the area, but he'd been so far from my mind lately that I hadn't considered I might run into him today. I retorted, "And *you* were into the low-carb diet. I was trying to be more mindful of what I ate."

Alec smirked. "You have to admit it's working."

I looked him over. Yeah, Alec looked good. He'd clearly been working out more since we'd broken up. His medium brown hair was short but stylish, and the chiseled jaw and cleft chin set off the hipster glasses he wore. In designer jeans and a perfectly tailored shirt, he looked every inch the successful architect.

But everything that had sent my heart racing a few years ago left me cold now. Alec was a cheating asshole and no matter how good-looking the exterior, I had a difficult time believing he had anything redeeming inside.

He frowned at me when I didn't respond. "What are you doing in this part of town, Chris?"

"My boyfriend and I were in the area."

Alec raised an eyebrow, and I relished the look of shock on his face. "Boyfriend?"

"Is it so surprising that I'd be dating someone?"

"Well, no, I just ..." He cleared his throat. "Last I'd heard, you weren't seeing anyone."

Apparently, Alec had been keeping tabs on me.

"I took a break after our relationship ended. Funny, but I found it difficult to trust anyone for a while."

He flinched. "Uhh, yeah. I am sorry about that."

I shook my head in disgust. "You cheated on me, Alec, and all I get is a 'I'm sorry about that'? You're a real fucking piece of work." But I wasn't angry. More bemused and saddened by how shallow he really was.

Someone walked up behind me, and I smelled Elliot before I felt him slide his arm around my waist. I settled against him with a profound feeling of contentment.

"Everything okay, Chris?" Although his tone was cool and even, I could detect an undercurrent of worry. God, it felt nice to have someone worry about *me*. Alec certainly never had when we were together.

"It's fine. Just ran into an ex-boyfriend." I nodded toward Alec. "We were catching up."

Elliot reached out a hand. "You must be Dickface."

A laugh escaped me before I could stop it. Elliot's tone was so deadpan. Alec blinked at him but didn't return Elliot's offered greeting. I felt Elliot shrug before he dropped his hand and settled it on my hip. He squeezed once.

"Let me guess. That was Cal's nickname for me?" Alec sneered. He and Cal had never really gotten along, even before the cheating. Which should have told me something, I suppose, since Cal had gotten along with nearly everyone. "It sounds like him."

"It was, yeah," I admitted. God, I missed my brother. We would have laughed ourselves stupid about this.

"How is he?"

I doubted he cared. I felt a perverse urge to shock him, and right then, I couldn't be bothered to try to rise above my baser instincts. "Dead, actually," I replied in a flat tone.

"Seriously?" Alec gaped at me, his mouth opening and closing like a goldfish.

"Do you really think I would joke about my brother being dead?"

Remorse flickered across his face. "Oh, God, I'm sorry, Chris. I didn't know."

The pleasure I felt at shocking him faded quickly. "You wouldn't have. It happened this past January." I pressed my lips tightly together for a second to gather myself. I refused to show weakness in front of Alec. "It was a car accident."

"I'm sorry." For once, Alec sounded sincere. "Are you okay?"

"His fucking brother died. What do you think?" Elliot snarled.

The sneer returned to Alec's face as he looked Elliot up and down. "Quite the scrappy little protector you have, Chris. I never knew you to go for teenage street musicians."

Given Elliot's current outfit of skinny ripped jeans, a black T-shirt, and combat boots, I could see where Alec had gotten that impression, but I still bristled.

"Fuck you and your snobby attitude, Alec. Elliot's the best thing that's ever happened to me. He's a kind, caring person. An incredible boyfriend and a successful studio artist. And since I know success is the only thing you care about, he's represented by the Holloway Gallery. Is that impressive enough for you?"

I wasn't one for name-dropping, but I knew it would needle Alec to no end.

"Sorry, man." He laughed uneasily, and his gaze flicked to Elliot. "That *is* impressive."

Elliot gave him a dismissive glance. "What do I care what you think?"

I stifled a laugh. Now *that* was an insult designed to cut Alec to the quick. There was one more thing to clear up though. "And for the record, Elliot is twenty-four. I don't date *teenagers*. That's your thing, not mine."

The guy Alec had cheated on me with had been eighteen, nineteen tops. Some college guy he'd picked up at a bar. Thankfully, Alec had the good sense to look abashed. It was too little, too late, but it was something. He opened his mouth to respond, but I cut him off.

"Elliot and I have some shopping to do before we go home. I'd say it was good running into you, Alec, but I'd be lying." I turned before he could respond.

Elliot grabbed a package of spaghetti and tossed it in the basket. "Do you want stuff for a salad too?" He slung an arm across my shoulder and kissed my cheek. The unexpected, but welcome, public display of affection warmed me to my toes. The fact that Alec had likely seen it made it all the sweeter.

"Sounds great." I smiled at him. "Want to grab dessert too?"

He dropped his hand from my shoulders to the back pocket of my jeans. "I'm sure we can think of something else for after dinner." He slid his hand inside my pocket and squeezed my ass. It was wildly out of character for Elliot to be so in-your-face about anything, but right then, it made me grin.

Eat your heart out, Alec.

It wasn't until we were at Elliot's loft that the topic of Alec arose again. We were both sweaty after the walk, and we showered before we prepared dinner.

"So does Dickface live in the Pearl District or something?" Elliot opened a can of crushed tomatoes and poured them into a pan with the ground beef, onions, and garlic. I was impressed that he was making the sauce from scratch. For all his talk of not cooking much, he was quite good when he put his mind to it.

I shrugged as I scrubbed the cutting board. "Yeah. As far as I know. He works downtown, but I doubt he's moved out of the building where we lived together. It's not far from that market actually."

"Oh, I didn't realize you'd lived there with him."

"For almost a year, yeah."

"How long were you together?"

"Two ... two and a half years?" I thought back. "Yeah, about two and a half."

"It was serious then."

"My mom was starting to talk wedding planning, so yeah. It was getting there."

"Cal talked like she did that with anyone he dated."

I laughed softly. "Well, Cal dating anyone was cause for celebration in the Allen household. I'm basically a serial monogamist, so my mom was pretty used to me being with someone for a while. Cal not so much."

The smile Elliot tossed over his shoulder was wry.

"Going home with strange men from bars wasn't your usual?" Elliot asked.

I chuckled and washed the knife. "No, it wasn't. I didn't even do it in college."

"Me either. I never had that many serious relationships, but I had some long-term but fairly casual lovers. Guys from art school or whatever. We weren't in love, but we genuinely liked each other, you know?" He shrugged and stirred the sauce.

"Yeah, I get that," I said softly.

"My mom fucked around a lot. Brought home guys from the bar before she hooked up with George. I don't know for sure, but I'm pretty sure she fucked guys in exchange for drugs." I winced. "Call me crazy, but I pretty much tried to do the opposite of everything she did."

"Understandable." I dried my hands on the towel resting on the counter, then walked over to Elliot. I squeezed his biceps. "I know it can't be easy sharing this with me, but it means a lot," I said softly. He'd been doing it more and more lately. It seemed the therapy was helping. His therapist had also suggested a support group. He went periodically, but I doubted he'd need to continue to do both for much longer.

As he continued to stir the sauce, I felt the tension leak out of him until he relaxed against me. "It's easier to talk to you than to most people. I'm trying, but I still have a hard time in the support group."

"I know. I'm glad you can talk to me though. I'd say that it's my job, but you know I'm not trying to be your psychiatrist," I admitted. I pushed his hair off the back of his neck and bent to give him a kiss there. "I just want to know as much as possible about the man I'm in love with."

"I get that." He sighed softly, and his head drooped forward, his hand slowing as my lips continued to trace up his spine. "I just meant that you're good at listening. You don't judge. And, God, Chris, those eyes do me in."

I lifted my head. "My eyes?"

"You don't have a clue, do you?"

"Apparently not." I was mystified.

"You have these sad, soulful brown eyes, and when you turn them on me, there's nothing I wouldn't do. Even tell you my deepest, darkest secrets."

"Really?" I'd certainly never heard anyone describe me that way. "That's good to know. I promise to only use them for good, not evil." I kissed his neck again, and he chuckled.

"Kissing me like that might be evil," he muttered.

"Why is that?"

"Because I'm going to burn the sauce." He laughed softly, and I let him go.

But when I stepped back, he clicked off the burner and turned to face me. "I didn't say stop." He had one of his increasingly more common smiles on his face, and my heart sped up at the sight.

"Yeah?" I felt almost breathless.

"Your ex is a fucking idiot," he said softly. "How the hell did he think anyone else could compare to you?"

His words stunned me. Elliot's reserve had been understandable, but the more we opened up to each other, the more compelling he became to me. I'd spent so much of my life playing second-fiddle to everyone. No one had ever looked at me the way Elliot did.

It rendered me mute.

I reached for him, taking his hand and drawing him over to the bed. I captured his lips with mine and kissed him deeply, my hands roaming across his torso. We tumbled onto the bed, and I stripped off his clothing as fast as my eager hands could manage. The feelings inside me were too great to be contained, and I needed my hands and mouth to convey them.

Elliot let out a quiet groan when I sat up to strip out of my own clothes. After, he pulled me down to him and I kissed his mouth again, nibbling at his lower lip with my teeth. I didn't linger there long, and my mouth followed my hands down over his chest, biting and licking his small brown nipples.

His abs contracted as I kissed the slight hollow between his pecs and shivered as I moved lower, tonguing the soft trail of hair that led downward from his navel. I tasted his hips and bit, making him squirm under me.

"Chris," he whimpered, his hands going to my hair. He tugged at it, trying to guide my head to his cock, but I resisted. I dragged my teeth against the lightly furred ropey muscles of his thighs, enjoying the small sounds he made. I could smell the clean musky scent of his groin, tempting me to taste his cock, but I sat up and coaxed him to flip onto his stomach.

He made an annoyed sound but settled with his forehead against the pillow. He lifted his hips briefly before he reached down to adjust his cock, and I watched the play of his lean muscles. I leaned in and bit at his ass. He yelped, but it quickly turned into a laugh. I smiled at the sound and kissed the spot. I roamed my hands across his body and followed them with my mouth, teasing and tormenting him. I traversed up and down his spine, across his ass, and down the back of his thighs. He panted as I slipped a hand between them to fondle his balls. The soft needy sounds he let out made my cock leak.

I stretched out over him, propped up on my hands. "Turn over again."

Elliot flipped onto his back. He reached up for me, trying to draw me down over him, but I shook my head and gave him a hard, needy kiss.

I shifted backward. Elliot's cock was tight against his flat belly and shiny at the tip from pre-come. He had a gorgeous penis, long and lean like the rest of him. I sat back and took Elliot's cock in my mouth. He cried out, and I glanced up at his face. He threw his head back and he had an agonized look of pleasure on his face. I watched his reactions as I slid down his cock, taking him as far down as I could before moving back up.

He whimpered. Spurred on by the sounds he made, I sucked him, worshiped him, made love to his cock like I'd never have a chance to do it again. He dug his hands into the covers below us, his whole body strung tight. He bucked his hips, forcing himself deeper into my mouth. "I'm going to come," he cried and I gently let his cock go.

His chest heaved with exertion as he opened his eyes. They were dazed, and I smiled at the sight. He reached for me, his hand shaking. "Will you fuck me?" he asked softly.

I answered by reaching for the lube in the bedside table. My hands were shaking by the time I slid a slick finger inside Elliot. He was tight, and it took me a few minutes of gently fucking him before he could handle a second finger. He writhed under me, pre-come oozing from the tip of his cock.

"I'm good," he gasped. "I can't take any more."

I sat back long enough to slick my cock and then stretched out over Elliot. He drew his legs up, wrapping them around my back. When I finally eased inside his body, we were both trembling. He murmured my name, his eyes closed, and his face contorted into the most intense expression of pleasure I'd ever seen. In that instant, I would have killed for Elliot's talent. I wanted to etch the memory onto paper so the whole world could see how beautiful he was.

Since I couldn't, I began to move with slow, even strokes.

I shifted back just long enough to throw his legs over my shoulders.

He was so limber that when I bent forward again, his knees folded up near his ears. I leaned down and kissed him. He cried out against my mouth as the position allowed me to push deeper inside him.

"Too much?" I asked, but he shook his head.

"S'good," he slurred, and I braced my hands on the bed and fucked him slowly. He used his arms to urge me to move deeper and faster, and he cried out, over and over, tiny little whimpers of need that spurred me on.

Even at the slow pace, the heat between us built. It slicked my skin and dampened Elliot's hairline. His chest flushed and the color rose to his cheeks. His eyes were closed, and his head was thrown back in complete surrender.

"Can you come this way?" I murmured.

"Mmhmm. Close."

I shifted my hips, changing the angle of my thrusts, and he let out a strangled gasp. His hands bit into my biceps, and I focused my energy on making him come. When he did, it was my name he called out, and it sent a rush of pleasure through me.

My own orgasm took me by surprise, and I gasped and closed my eyes against the surge of white-hot pleasure shooting through me. I emptied into him with a few harsh shudders.

I collapsed onto the bed beside him, shaking with the intensity of my orgasm. Elliot was still wrapped around me, and for a few minutes, I couldn't even move. All I could do was pant against his neck. He rubbed his cheek against the top of my head like a cat seeking to be pet, and I tangled my free hand in his hair. Eventually, my breathing slowed, and his did too. He let out a little sound of contentment that worked its way into my chest and lodged there like it would never leave.

I finally, reluctantly, moved when I softened within him. He let out a small sound of protest but let me shift him onto his back again. He flinched when I withdrew.

"You okay?" I asked.

"'M good," he slurred.

I grinned at his loopiness all the way to the bathroom where I cleaned up. I returned to the bed with a warm, damp cloth. Elliot was sprawled diagonally on the bed. He was drenched in sweat, and all I could do was stare as it trickled down his chest and over his sleek abs.

"Holy shit," he muttered. "Can't remember the last time I came that hard."

I knelt on the bed next to him and carefully wiped the come from his skin. He tensed when I wiped the lube from his thighs and between, but he didn't stop me.

The vulnerability and openness touched me, and when I was done, I leaned in to kiss him. My heart felt very, very full. My emotions were so close to the surface it was almost too much to bear.

When I drew back, Elliot offered me a tentative smile as if he was overwhelmed too. For a long moment, we just stared at each other until the cooling cloth in my hand finally drew my attention, and I turned away to deal with it.

When I turned back, Elliot sat propped against the headboard as he rummaged in the drawer of the nightstand. He came up with an elastic and deftly tied his hair back. Damp curls clung to his temple and the back of his neck, and even though I'd just come, I wanted to touch him again.

I felt like I could never get enough of him.

"C'mere," he said quietly when he saw me watching him.

As I slid onto the bed beside him and drew him into my arms, I felt a profound sense of gratitude. Whether it was my brother or something else that had brought us together, I had never been more thankful to have found Elliot.

Epilogue

"**G**reat party, man." Cooper slapped me on the shoulder. I looked up from the platters I'd been loading up with freshly grilled meats and vegetables. "Cal would have loved the shit out of this."

I laughed. "He would have, wouldn't he?"

"He always was running late to stuff. I half expect him to stroll in any time and make a dramatic entrance."

"If he does, this is going to be one hell of a weird memorial service." It felt good to laugh and joke about Cal like this.

Cooper snorted as he began piling food on his plate. "We'd never hear the end of his second coming puns."

"Ugh, you aren't kidding." In the past few months, Cooper and I had developed a pretty solid friendship. I'd gotten to know Jason as well. John was cordial, if not particularly close. And Dave ... well ... we still needed to do some work. But we were both trying.

"I like Elliot, by the way." Cooper nodded toward him. He was a ways down the beach. A couple of Cal's friends had brought their kids, and Elliot was helping them build a sand castle. "He's quiet at first, but he has this great dry sense of humor once you get to know him."

"I'm pretty fond of him myself."

Cooper smiled. "We can all see that. You guys are great together."

"Thank you."

"Well, on that note, I'm going to go excuse myself. Allie's been single for a while, and I'm thinking maybe it's time we rekindle things. We broke up after college because I was an idiot, but I'd like to prove to her I've learned from my mistakes."

I chuckled. "If there's one thing I know about my brother, it's that he'd approve of you using his memorial as an opportunity to pick up women."

Cooper laughed loudly. "That, my man, is the God's honest truth. Wish me luck. I wouldn't want to let Cal down, so I better do this right."

"Good luck!" I called after his retreating form.

Still amused, I looked around and let out a sigh of contentment at the sight in front of me. We'd been planning this memorial for the better part of a month, and it had come together nicely.

Rockaway Beach was about two hours from Portland, but plenty of Cal's friends had made the trek. Some had rented beach houses for the entire weekend of Labor Day. Others had just driven in for the afternoon. We'd skipped a stuffy, formal celebration with waiters and catering and planned a day on the beach with potluck food. We'd light a bonfire this evening.

And while there certainly had been some tears today, there was plenty of joy too.

It was a celebration of life and family and everything Cal would have enjoyed most. If Cal was still lingering out there somewhere in some shape or form, he was probably pissed he was missing an epic party.

Though, we'd discreetly passed along the word that we preferred no one bring alcohol to today's celebration in deference to my father's recovery. Everyone had been very understanding.

From where I stood by the grill, if I looked left, I could see Ed and my Aunt Eva talking to my parents. It was good to see them out and looking relaxed. The emotional upheaval they'd been through had left scars, but today, they seemed happier and more at ease with each other than I'd seen in a long time.

Rehab had helped immensely, and the couples' counseling seemed to be doing the trick. They were healing. And most importantly, they were doing it together. I felt closer to them than I had in a long time.

Would it be enough? That I didn't know, but I had hope.

Elliot was still a little wary with my family, as if he expected the rug to be pulled out from under him at any point, but he was beginning to let down his guard with them too. He seemed to look forward to the times we all got together. A sketch of his was hanging in a prominent spot in my parents' living room, along with some of Cal's work. My mom had expressed an interest in taking an art class to

Elliot, and he'd lit up, making suggestions of where to go and what to try first. He was less comfortable with my father, but they were both trying.

We were all in this for the long haul, and I honestly believed that with a little more time, we'd all get there.

Farther down the beach, I could see John and some of Cal's other friends playing volleyball. To my right, Elliot was still working on the sand construction project.

Once I was sure the food was taken care of, I wandered to where Elliot was.

Elliot was engrossed in his work, so I was able to watch him for a little while unobserved. He was dressed in a pair of board shorts, and he was crouched down as he packed sand into a bucket. Despite the fact that he'd spent most of the afternoon hanging out with the kids at the party, I wasn't worried about him enjoying himself. Even from yards away, I could hear him laugh.

He was never as loud or outgoing as most of the people we knew. But the more he got to know them, the more his aloofness melted away. He was quiet, thoughtful, and very aware of the world around him. I liked the way he seemed to take it all in before he spoke up. I didn't mind that I was one of the very few who had really seen him let loose.

Under the lean, lanky frame beat the heart of a passionate man. And he was all mine.

He looked up as I drew close, grinning at me. "Look what we've built."

"I'm impressed." I really was. The kids had apparently followed his lead, and the large sand castle was both sturdily built and beautiful. It had multiple turrets and walls, plus a moat. There were even small pebbles pressed into the damp sand in decorative patterns.

"Do you need me?" he asked, standing. He brushed the sand off his hands.

"I always need you."

He smiled. "Have you eaten or did you just make everyone else food?"

"I ate," I said with a quiet laugh. "I promise. Did you?" I looked pointedly at the elaborate structure he'd been diligently working on. "Oh, shit." His gaze slid sideways toward the kids as if he'd belatedly realized he shouldn't swear in front of them. But they weren't paying us any attention.

"Forgot?"

"Yes."

"Come on." I took his hand and tugged him toward the food. We were halfway there when I felt Elliot's grip tighten and his whole body go stiff.

"Dave's here." I followed his line of sight to where Dave stood, surveying the people as if he were looking for someone.

"Let's go say hi."

Elliot shot me a wary glance, but he didn't argue.

"Hey. Glad you could make it, Dave," I greeted him. He looked fit and tan as always, but it was clear he still carried an emotional burden that he hadn't shaken.

"Hey, Chris. Elliot." He nodded at us both. "Sorry I didn't make it earlier. Work."

Truthfully, I'd wondered if he was planning to come at all. But just in case, I'd come prepared.

"That reminds me." I dug in the pocket of my board shorts. "Hold out your hand," I said. Dave gave me a faintly puzzled look.

"I have something for you," I explained. He did as I'd instructed, and I dropped something onto his palm with a quiet jingle.

"What's this?"

"If you want it, Cal's Mustang is yours," I said quietly. "Hell, it always was half yours anyway. You two did so much work on it. I can't count the number of times I saw you both tinkering with it."

A wistful smile crossed his face as he closed his fingers around the keys. "We had a lot of fun doing it too."

"Anyway, it seems right that you keep it. It's a great car, but I don't need it." I realized Elliot had melted away, and it was just Dave and me now.

"I ... thank you." Dave's voice seemed a little rough. "You didn't have to do that."

"I know Cal would want you to have it," I said simply. "We can take care of transferring the title another day."

"It means a lot to me."

"I know."

We stared at each other until something in Dave's gaze finally softened. "Thank you."

He stepped forward hesitantly, halting and unsure, but I held out my arms. He went into them with a little sound of relief, and I wondered if he'd been afraid I'd reject him. We'd been through our share of ugliness in the past eight months.

As we stood there in silence, I remembered the night of Cal's funeral. The attraction I'd felt for Dave was gone, and I had no desire to revisit it. But I hoped this meant we could repair the friendship.

"I miss him so much," he said. His voice was rough and a little broken. I hugged him tighter against my chest, trying to reassure him that it would be okay.

"I do too," I said quietly. That would never go away.

The bonfire behind us had burned down to coals. One by one, people had dispersed. Cooper, Allie, and John remained along with Ed, my Aunt Eva, my parents, Elliot, Dave, and myself.

A little of the frostiness between Dave and Elliot seemed to have thawed. I wasn't quite sure how to mend the lingering tension between us all, but I hoped what we were about to do would help. After all, we were all there for the same reason.

"Are you ready?" Elliot asked quietly. He pulled a lighter from his pocket. He didn't smoke anymore, but the lighter still traveled with him everywhere.

I nodded and took a deep breath as I carefully removed a fragile rice paper lantern from its box. We'd debated on what a fitting tribute to Cal would be, but with a little input from Allie on what was marine life friendly, we settled on releasing a single biodegradable lantern over the Pacific.

I handed it to my father, and he bowed his head over it briefly before passing it to my mother. The idea was that each of us would think of Cal while we did so. A memory of him. A wish for ourselves. Our thoughts would travel out into the vastness and be set free. It passed from person to person until it reached Elliot.

I caught a glimpse of a sad, wistfulness in his eyes, but when he handed the lantern to me, it faded, becoming the calm, steady look of love I was so familiar with. He was saying goodbye to Cal for the last time, but I had no doubts about Elliot's feelings for me.

He loved me. Deeply. Fully. Without reservation.

I closed my eyes for a moment as I thought again about my brother.

Cal still existed in the memories of all the people who had spent the afternoon and evening sitting around the bonfire and reminiscing.

Those people carried him with them as they ate and drank. Celebrated his life.

His heart beat in someone's body. His corneas helped two other people see. Other people lived fuller, happier lives because of his generosity.

His art hung on the walls of the people it spoke to. A scholarship in his name helped students discover art. Perhaps someday, they'd become artists like Cal and Elliot.

In a way, Cal sat with my parents and Elliot and me every time we were together. I'd heard Cal laugh when I took his board out to the beach yesterday and tripped over a piece of driftwood. But I didn't fall, and for a second, I would have sworn I felt a hand on my elbow, steadying me.

Cal's biggest legacy was the lives we would all lead. Rich, joyful lives with the knowledge that at any time it could be taken away.

With the whoosh-hiss of Elliot's lighter, the candle was lit and the lantern glowed warm and bright. I stepped forward, letting the waves lap at my bare feet. I gently lifted the lantern to the night sky.

I closed my eyes. *I love you, brother.*

I opened them again as the breeze tugged at the lantern. One by one, hands touched me: Elliot's, my mom's, my dad's, Dave's. The people who'd loved Cal most in the world. The people who loved me.

I opened my hands, letting go, and the wind caught it, lifting it high over the dark water below.

Cal was gone, but he lived on.

And we would live each day to the fullest.

Not for him. But for ourselves.

The End

Bio

Brigham Vaughn is on the adventure of a lifetime as a full-time author. She devours books at an alarming rate and hasn't let her short arms and long torso stop her from doing yoga. She makes a killer key lime pie, hates green peppers, and loves wine tasting tours. A collector of vintage Nancy Drew books and green glassware, she enjoys poking around in antique shops and refinishing thrift store furniture. An avid photographer, she dreams of traveling the world and she can't wait to discover everything else life has to offer her.

Her books range from short stories to novellas to novels. They explore gay, bisexual, lesbian, and polyamorous romance in contemporary settings.

Looking for more of Brigham's work?

Pride Publishing
(Totally Entwined Group)

---Standalone Short Stories---
The Soldier Next Door (Right Here Right Now Anthology)

---Tidal Series w/ K. Evan Coles (Novels)---
Wake
Calm

---Speakeasy Series w/ K. Evan Coles (Novels) ---
With a Twist
Extra Dirty
Behind the Stick (Summer 2019)

Two Peninsulas Press
(Independently Published)

---Standalone Short Stories---
Baby, It's Cold Inside
Geeks, Nerds, and Cuddles
Love in the Produce Aisle
Not So Suddenly
Sunburns and Sunsets
The French Toast Emergencies

---Standalone Novellas---
Between the Studs
Corked (Wine Tasting Series Re-release)
Doc Brodie and the Big, Purple, Cat Toy
Three Shots

**Off Topic Press
(Independently Published w/ K. Evan Coles)**

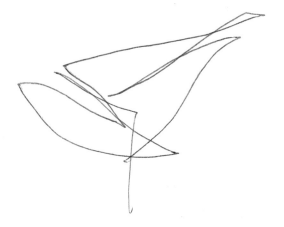

Made in the USA
Middletown, DE
14 June 2019